THE BROKEN LANCE

Best wishes

JESS STEVEN HUGHES

A HISTORICAL NOVEL

SUNBURY PRESS
Mechanicsburg, PA USA

Published by Sunbury Press, Inc.
Mechanicsburg, Pennsylvania

www.sunburypress.com

NOTE: This is a work of fiction. Names, characters, places and incidents are the product of the author's imagination or are used fictitiously, and any resemblance to actual persons, living or dead, business establishments, events or locales is entirely coincidental.

For information about special discounts for bulk purchases, please contact Sunbury Press Orders Dept. at (855) 338-8359 or orders@sunburypress.com.

To request one of our authors for speaking engagements or book signings, please contact Sunbury Press Publicity Dept. at publicity@sunburypress.com.

ISBN: 978-1-62006-719-2 (Trade Paperback)
ISBN: 978-1-62006-720-8 (Mobipocket)

Library of Congress Control Number: 2017941771

FIRST SUNBURY PRESS EDITION: July 2017

Product of the United States of America
0 1 1 2 3 5 8 13 21 34 55

Set in Bookman Old Style
Designed by Crystal Devine
Cover by Lawrence Knorr
Edited by Janice Rhayem

Continue the Enlightenment!

DRAMATIS PERSONAE
(IN ORDER OF APPEARANCE)

IN BRITANNIA

THE ROMANS

Marcellus Tiberius Reburrus – Cavalry Squadron Leader
Sextus Rufius – Cavalry Commander
Crispus – Cavalry Trooper
Obulco – Cavalry Trooper
Kimon – Cavalry Trooper
Albinus – Cavalry Trooper
* Aulus Plautius – General
Anicius Pedius Gallus, the Younger – Tribune
Corribilo – Cavalry Squadron Leader
Edecon – Cavalry Squadron Leader
Timoleon – Rufius's Greek Slave
Andubal – Cavalry Trooper
* Titus Flavius Vespasianus (Vespasian) – General
* Titus Flavius Sabinus – General - Vespasian's Older Brother
Mardonius – Cavalry Squadron Leader
Avaro – Cavalry Trooper
Indibil – Cavalry Trooper
Severus – Cavalry Trooper

THE BRITONS, ETC.

Llugar ap Nudd – Druid Priest
Cadwal – Scout/Warrior
Rix – Gallic Trader/Pimp
Kyar – German Slave Woman
Sigrid – German Slave Woman
Chulain – British Youth
Eleyne – British Princess
Karmune – Eleyne's handmaiden
Caratacus – British King
Mugain – Druid Priestess/Witch
Budar – Spaniard - Retired Centurion

IN ROME

Marcellus Tiberius Reburrus – Centurion
Eleyne – British Princess
Karmune – Eleyne's Handmaiden
Crispus – Junior Cavalry Officer
* Titus Flavius Sabinus – General/Senator
* Lucius Vitellius – Senator
* Narcissus – Greek Freedman/Imperial Secretary
* Claudius (Tiberius Claudius Nero Germanicus) – Emperor
* Pallas – Greek Freedman/Imperial Secretary
Anicius Cestius Gallus, the Elder – Senator
Publius Lucullus – Bandit
Priscilla – Jewish Woman
Alexias – Greek Slave/Steward
Aurelia Severa – Wife of Sabinus
Candra – Indian Slave
* Decrius Calpurnianus – Prefect of the Watch
Budar – Spaniard - Retired Centurion
Scrofa – King of the Beggars
Mico – Beggar
Casperius Niger – Optio of the Watch
Faenus Rufus – Centurion of the Watch
Nonius, Decimus, Fabius and Titius – Petty Criminals
Abroghast – Master Torturer
* Titus Statilius Taurus – Consul of Rome
Ulpius – Advocate/Lawyer

ROMAN EMPERORS – DATE OF REIGN

Tiberius Claudius Nero Germanicus – 41 - 54 AD (Claudius)
Lucius Domitius Ahenobarbus (Nero) – 54 - 68 AD
Servius Sulpicius Galba (Galba) – 68 - 69 AD
Marcus Salvius Otho (Otho) – 69 AD
Aulus Vitellius – 69 AD
Titus Flavius Vespasianus (Vespasian) – 69 - 79 AD
Titus Flavius Vespasianus (Titus) – 79 - 81 AD
Titus Flavius Domitianus (Domitian) – 81 - 96 AD

* Historical Character

CITIES AND GEOGRAPHICAL LOCATIONS

ANCIENT NAME	MODERN NAME
Britannia	Britain
Hispania	Spain
Gaul	France
Itius Portus	Calais, France
British Ocean	English Channel
Germania	Germany
Noviomagnus	Chichester, England
Alexandria	Alexandria, Egypt
Ostia	Rome's Seaport
River Rhenus	Rhine River
Moguntiacum	Mainz, Germany
Camulodunum	Colchester, England
Baetica Province	Southern Coast of Spain

PART I

BRITANNIA
44 AD

CHAPTER 1

EARLY FEBRUARY, 44 AD, THE BRITISH CHANNEL

"Secure the ship. Rig for storm," I heard the ship's master bellow over the wind.

The bearded Syrian glanced toward the swelling gray-green waves beyond the vessel's railing and black sky. He turned in our direction as the rest of the cavalry troop, sailors, and I ran along the deck of the old wide-beam merchant ship. As seamen covered hatches and struck sails, we troopers headed for the cages that held our horses amidships.

Roll after roll of thunder echoed across the ocean's turbulent surface. The rain sheeted down, nearly obscuring the ship's bow. From behind the stern, lightning flashed in a steely, wet light. Large rivulets of water washed along the creases in the timbered deck. Wave after wave smashed over the side of the aging vessel, causing it to rock and shudder.

Despite rain pelting our faces like sharp needles and soaking tunics and breeches, we fastened halters around the heads of the wide-eyed, terrified mounts, and tied them to ironwood belaying pins. We soothed the animals with reassuring words, stroked their heads, and patted their necks before lashing canvas covers over the cages' tops and sides to the deck with thick hawsers.

Our troop returned to the rat-infested hold. Creaking timbers echoed throughout the ship's dimly lit interior where the troopers were quartered and stored their gear. Four lanterns swung back and forth on rusty chains from the low crossbeams. The shadowy light danced from one end of the hold to the other. In the flickering light, the men's faces appeared as wraith-like ghostly images.

Shivering, teeth chattering, I cursed my lot in life. Soaked to the bone and freezing, we shook the water from our clothes. I dropped down beside my equipment, grabbed my bedroll, and removed the leather straps. We wrapped woolen blankets about our bodies letting the warmth enclose us.

I pulled mine tighter and thought back to the beginning of my journey.

At twenty-three, I had been sent to Britannia during the fourth year of the Emperor Claudius's rule. A lifetime ago. Our cavalry troop of thirty had left snowbound Germania, late in January, still in the clutches of winter. A week later we arrived on the frigid, windswept coast of Gaul, at the harbor of Portus Itius. Why we crossed then, I will never understand. The British Ocean, a channel really, is treacherous year-round, and in winter the worst. Storms and gales occur daily. I concluded that some Imperial bureaucrat in Rome, who knew nothing about winter seas, made the decision over the objections of Legate Titus Vespasian, commander of Legion Second Augusta in southern Britannia.

More than thirty of us had been crammed in the ship's hold that reeked with the bitter smell of pitch, bilge water, rancid olive oil, and spoiled pork. The horses, cheap cavalry nags, were kept amidships in heavy wooden cages. The *Poseidon's Eye,* an old deep-hulled merchantman, once had plied the Mediterranean between Alexandria and Ostia, carrying grain to Rome's seaport to make free bread for Rome's mindless mobs. Now it ferried us across the British Channel from Gaul to Britannia because there wasn't another vessel large enough to carry our contingent of men and horses.

Earlier that morning we had set sail. The sea was velvet smooth under a warm sun. From the coast of Gaul, I observed the chalk cliffs of Britannia in the distance, an unusual occurrence during winter months. Normally, they were enshrouded in fog and rain. A good omen. Although less than twenty-five miles away, it would be the next morning before we docked in the south of Britannia at the Port of Noviomagnus.

Now, we were below suffering from seasickness. The sounds of retching and the sickening smell of vomit filled the ship's hold. Other than experiencing a slight churning of the stomach, I kept from puking my guts. The angry sea tossed the ship like a cork. I was certain the old scow was going to break in half.

"Form a bucket brigade!"

The captain's order snapped me from my thoughts. Water sloshed around my sandaled boots.

"The ship's pumps can't handle this deluge," the captain said.

Our troop joined the ship's crew. A human chain sent slopping buckets topside and passing them back empty. Sweating, swearing, gasping for breath, without respite, we kept at it through the afternoon and on into the evening.

With the bucket brigade never pausing, the ship's master came below, his face contorted with worry. He wiped the water from his eyes with a grimy hand. Although he wore an oilskin coat, he was soaked. Dark and limp, his long hair dripped about his neck. He conferred with our troop commander the decurion, Sextus Rufius, beneath a swinging lantern at one end of the hold. When he finished speaking, the captain raised his head and the dancing light revealed resignation on his face. Laboriously, he climbed the ladder through the hatch returning to the storm-swept deck.

Sextus Rufius approached me and the other squadron sergeants where we stood a few paces from him and the ship's master. "We're taking on too much water," he shouted above the din of the gale raging topside. "But don't worry. The captain says we're not sinking, yet."

I studied the grizzled face of the oxen-chested decurion in the lantern's dim light. Each soldier had been issued two horses, but the ship only had room enough for one per rider. None of us had any idea when our spares, which should be coming from our old base in Germania, would arrive. As a *sesquiplicarius* in an auxiliary cavalry cohort of the Roman Army, I was the most junior sergeant in a troop of thirty men and horses. Each sergeant commanded a squadron of ten.

"Sir, what about the horses?" I asked. "How are we to get them off?"

"We'll herd them down the gangway as close to land as possible."

"What if we can't get them close enough?" another squadron leader asked. "I've heard the bottom is shallow and a long way out!"

A giant wave crashed on deck as Rufius opened his mouth. The old ship's beams groaned in protest. He looked upward and down again after a moment. "Then, by Melkart, we'll have to chance it. You three are responsible for getting the men and horses off safely. If we hit a shoal, pray that no one is injured. We can't afford to lose either men or beasts."

"The men will freeze to death as soon as they hit the water—it's as icy as the River Rhenus," the third sergeant said.

"Can't be helped," Rufius said. "They'll swim ashore all the quicker."

He paused, his charcoal eyes meeting mine. "The captain says ten or eleven miles—we can't make it."

A thunderous wave crashed on deck, followed by the howls of cursing men and whinnying horses.

I grabbed the low crossbeam to keep my balance.

"We'll be better off on shore even in this filthy weather," Rufius finished. "Gods know how much more this miserable tub can take."

We set about getting the men and ourselves ready. The troopers flung on their chain mail, iron helmets, buckled on long slashing swords, and woolen army cloaks around the shoulders of their blue tunics. They strapped shields, protected by leather covers, to their backs. Grabbing saddles, lances, and other equipment, we braced themselves for the inevitable shock of hitting the beach.

Above screaming winds, surf pounded as the ship approached the shore. Despite the storm's fury, the helmsman managed to turn the vessel shoreward. The tides were in our favor, and the ship moved rapidly toward the beach at a speed that would push us inland far as possible before breaking apart.

Waves cascaded over the deck as we waited by the open hatchway. Freezing water spewed through the exposed entry, drenching the poor devils standing too close.

The vessel struck a hidden shoal just below the surface. Grinding along the bottom, the ship jarred to a halt, throwing men, including myself, to the deck and scattering equipment.

My shoulder ached from the fall. I got up quickly and looked about. Crispus, my second-in-command, was on all fours shaking his head like a dog. "Still alive, I see," I said.

He stood and focused his black eyes on my outstretched, calloused hand. "I'll live if my skull ain't cracked. What about you?"

"Same with my shoulder," I answered while massaging it. "Check the others."

The rest of the squadron, including crooked-faced Obulco and the giant half-Greek Kimon, dragged themselves to their feet. Except for a few minor bruises, no one appeared seriously injured.

From above came loud scraping and sliding, as if one of the cages that held the horses had torn loose from its bindings. In terror, the mounts whinnied. Water gushed through an open hole in the side of the ship.

We were sinking.

The men grabbed their gear and rushed topside. Biting wind and chilling rain lashed through the night. It slammed my body like a sheet of ice as soon as I stepped upon the deck. I staggered, my shield pulled on the straps against my shoulders and neck nearly choking me. I almost dropped my saddle and bridle, before regaining my balance. I took a couple of deep breaths.

Rufius pulled himself to his full height and planted his boots squarely on the deck.

"Get those nags over the sides!" he barked. "Sergeants, move your men!"

Men rushed to cages lining the sea-swamped deck. Wide-eyed, whinnying, and jerking their heads from side to side, the terrified mounts attempted to break loose from halters tied to the thick, wooden bars. We flung open the doors and untied the horses, soothing them as best we could. I set down my lance and quickly placed the saddle on my mount, Argento, a silvery-gray Moorish gelding. After cinching him around the girth, I grabbed my weapon and moved the horse to the gangway. Crispus was the first over the side with his black gelding. His wiry body dipped beneath the churning waters. Seconds later he surfaced, coughing and sputtering. He grabbed his horse and pulled himself astride. "Take it easy with the nags!" he shouted into the wind. "The water's shallow and rocky as Hades!" A wave crashed over him. He sputtered then yelled, "Hang on for your lives!"

Although the troop had made many deep-river crossings in full gear, none of us had ever experienced the fury of a stormy sea. For the first time, I feared that some of us might drown.

I held tight on to my horse's reins when he tried to rear. A cracking groan shook the ship as the stern broke away and rolled over. A churning swell crushed it against a submerged reef. It splintered into countless pieces.

In the distance, the rolling white surf struck the black beach with a ferocity I had never seen before. Amid flashes of lightning, jagged silhouettes of wind-blown trees stood beyond the shoreline.

A thought raced through my mind. Would the enemy, savage Britons, be waiting for us on the beach? No. Roman forces occupied most of the Southern British coast, and even if the ship was blown off course, we would still land in friendly territory.

Above the beach, rising chalk cliffs towered like immutable monuments, defying the storm's onslaught. For a fleeting moment, standing amidst the confusion, I visualized the gods dancing on the inky clouds above, causing the thunder to explode in our ears. Lightning bolts flashed directly overhead, crooked luminous spears hurled by the mighty Jupiter at some invisible enemy.

Perhaps we were the enemy. Perhaps it wasn't Jupiter but a god of the Britons, angered by our intrusion upon his land. Yes, maybe their Taranis, the Thunderer, intended to destroy us.

Feverishly, the animals, men, and supplies were unloaded into the sea. Following Argento, I caught a high swell and slid down the ramp into the icy waters. The freezing cold sliced through my body like a Cretan arrow. I nearly succumbed to the numbing pain. For a split moment, a swell devoured me. Salt water rushed up my nose and down my throat.

Quickly, I surfaced, retching and throwing up water and foul-tasting bile. Coughing violently, I grabbed Argento's mane and pulled myself onto his back.

I had to get my men out of the frozen sea before they died of exposure. I cursed the god Neptune and his killer waters. The other squadron leaders and I herded the surviving men, troopers and sailors alike, and animals ashore. When we regrouped and tallied our losses, three of our men had drowned while eight out of twenty from the ship's crew had been lost. Five horses had to be destroyed because of broken legs. A tragic day indeed.

* * *

I could not sleep that first night. My clothing was soaked. Getting up, I futilely wrapped a woolen cloak around my shoulders and clamped on my icy helmet. I stepped outside of the ragged tent, which sheltered my squadron of men, not sure what I would do or where I would go. The gale had blown itself out, chased by a cold, piercing wind from the sea. I left the wretched little camp of a half dozen squalid tents pitched about fifty paces inland from the shoreline. Rufius had set a watch. Three shivering sentries, one from each of the three squadrons, patrolled the area. The horses had been strung to a guideline between a couple low bushes, but hobbled for good measure. A few men huddled around small fires—we found little drift wood. For want of a better reason, I decided to hike to the debris-strewn beach, and there I stood looking towards the *Poseidon's Eye* and beyond to Gaul. I strained to see the vessel, as the inky sea merged with the black sky—the foaming white caps erasing the horizon. There it was—the shattered remains of the ship's stern and a few splintered ribs from the hull. A dark blot suspended between heaven and Earth.

I don't know how long I stood watching and thinking—it seemed like forever. As I was about to return to the bivouac, I saw Crispus standing on the edge of the beach gazing in the same direction, staring blankly, lost in thought.

CHAPTER 2

With the ground too frozen to dig proper graves, we cremated the dead troopers in the gray dawn of the next morning. Using freshly cut tree limbs, which burned poorly, the incineration of the bodies on the funeral pyre was a slow and acrid ordeal.

Later, after a miserable breakfast of hardtack biscuits and vinegar water, the troop broke camp. The main food supplies and fodder were lost with the ship. The horses foraged on sparse grass above the beach line. Until we explored thoroughly, we dared not allow them to stray too far. Fortunately, we discovered a spring nearby to supply fresh water.

As the men from my squadron of ten hitched their mounts for the journey ahead, they were still in a dismal mood. Thick-lipped Albinus whined as he did about everything. "What are we doing in this gods forsaken hole? My guts are still empty."

"Aye, so are mine," Kimon, another complainer, added in a heavy Greek accent. "Why did they send us instead of the Germans and Thracians?"

A few other troopers, including Obulco the interrogator, muttered in agreement as they stood near their mounts. Crispus peeked across his horse in my direction but remained silent.

I straightened after cinching up my saddle glaring at the men. Silence. Then I stepped over to the half-Greek and Spanish giant, Kimon. I placed my hands on my hips and stared up into his pale-blue eyes. "Because we're Spaniards," I said, "the best horsemen in the army, that's why we're here. Our orders are to join infantry cohort, First Asturum, as a temporary detachment for reconnaissance duties. The rest of our cavalry cohort are expected to arrive in the spring."

Kimon's grumble came from deep in his throat. "Maybe so, but I'd rather be in Germania. At least we'd be in warm barracks and have full stomachs."

"So would I, but we're not. No telling when we'll return to Germania, if ever. Get used to it."

I turned to the other men. "That goes for the rest of you!"

* * *

As I returned to my horse Argento, I, too, wished that we were still with the Fourth Legion, at Moguntiacum on the upper Rhenus River. Then I could have returned home, in southern Hispania, near Gades, to be with my mother for a couple of months. About a week before we had left Germania, she sent news of my father's death, along with his ornate, gold belt buckle. It now belonged to me. Her letter said he died of heart failure. Although the old man had been stern, I held a deep affection for him. Because he had taught me so much, I truly mourned his passing. But it wasn't manly to display my grief. Instead, with Crispus's help, I got drunk. My request for leave was refused. Our troop was being transferred to Rome's newest and most remote outpost.

My mind returned to the task before us. I watched Crispus study the arrangement of his mount's breast plate. He wiped it once more with a doeskin cloth and glanced my way. "I thought the wind blowing down the Rhenus was like a fucking razor," he said, "but after crossing the channel, it's like a mild summer breeze."

"Aye, this is a land only the damn British and their gods could love," I said.

"When do we get to Iping?" Crispus asked. He stood near me holding onto the reins of his horse.

"Rufius says day after tomorrow," I answered. "We're due at Noviomagnus tonight."

"All right, quit your sniveling," Rufius growled as he approached the troop. "Mount up and wait for my command to move out. We'll be riding all day."

* * *

Journeying over soggy hills and through forests to Noviomagnus, on the southern coast, we received a sympathetic welcome from the garrison of Legion Second

Augusta on our arrival. I never saw a group of soldiers so grateful as ours for a chance to dry their clothing and equipment, receive a decent meal, and gain a good night's sleep.

The following day the troop headed northward along old native wooden trackways to Iping, the westernmost stronghold on the Roman frontier. A light snow fell late in the afternoon as we rode out of the forest of skeletal chestnut and birch trees, and onto an open plain. The base lay in the distance, across the meandering River Rother, and beyond a squalid village. It was little more than a fortified camp. A square, wooden palisade surrounded the home of First Asturum infantry cohort's nearly one thousand men.

After fording the shallow river, the troop crossed the wooden bridge over the defensive ditch surrounding the encampment. Hiding beneath the ditch's murky waters were hundreds of sharpened wooden stakes, called lilies, planted in the mud. Silently, they waited from any unsuspecting enemy to cross their path. A double guard lined the stockade wall. Shivering sentries, clothed in woolen cloaks, paced back and forth along the catwalks.

Beyond the fort lay the hilly lands of the renegade, King Caratacus, and warriors from the tribes of the Atrebates and Trinovantes. His own people, the Catuvellaunii, had betrayed him and pledged their allegiance to Rome.

I recalled that the First Asturum had been sent to Britannia with the Roman invasion force the year before. An army of forty thousand men, under the command of General Aulus Plautius, stormed ashore near Camulodunum in the southeast. I can only smile when I think of how relieved I was that my men and I had not been part of the initial invasion, especially when we learned about the Roman losses. The fierce resistance by the Britons had resulted in casualties heavier than anticipated. About three-thousand legionaries and auxiliaries had been killed or wounded. Fortunately, the Britons lost thousands more as the campaign swept from Camulodunum down to Noviomagnus. When the Emperor Claudius came to Britannia, he received the allegiance of eleven tribal kings, but not Caratacus. My question was, how long will they remain loyal? My experience in fighting the Germans was that you never turned your back on barbarians—at any time.

The acrid smell of smoke aroused me from my thoughts. From the back of my mount, I spotted a greenish-brown plume drifting above the stockade. From my experience in combat, I knew this was more than the usual camp fires. There had been a raid. Crispus and I turned toward one another. Both of us nodded as if coming to the same conclusion.

Rufius led us through the main gate, offset behind a timber barricade. Riding in columns of two, we slowly trotted up the muddy Praetorian Way. Plodding hooves slopped through the sucking ooze. Crispus and I rode side by side in the lead squadron of ten, behind Rufius who was accompanied by the signifer-standard bearer. The squeaking sounds of our leather saddles and jingling of brass pendants from the horses' breast straps echoed throughout the sullen camp like the sound of doom. My eyes followed the column of smoke coming from the far end of the camp. Laid out in grids of ten to twenty, the dark leather tents that housed the troops lined both sides of the roadway. Within each grid was an open center section with partially covered corrals for the horses and pack mules. At the far end of the post stood a large regulation log and barracks office, the headquarters of the cohort commander, the Tribune Gallus.

A centurion barked orders to a detail of soldiers as they picked up and shoved burnt remnants of wooden posts and canvas tents into an oxcart. Another dozen troopers used pickaxes to break up the frozen ground beneath the mud and shovel dirt onto the dying embers in the same area.

Part of the fortress wall and two adjacent tents still smoldered, and the hitching line for that troop's thirty horses stood alone. A third tent had been trampled. Four barbarian bodies trailed from the hitching rope to just outside the north wall gate. One was twisted grotesquely, a raised hand jutting up like a hawk talon. His corpse, clothed in a bloody tartan tunic and pants, was dusted lightly by the fine-powdered snow. Two soldiers stepped away from the detail and went over to the bodies. Pulling one down, they dragged the dead barbarian to the cart where they lifted and heaved him on top of the ashes.

"What happened here? Was this the work of Caratacus?" Sextus Rufius called to the centurion.

"Aye, the bloody bastards came over the wall just before dawn. Can't talk now." The centurion turned to the sweating, grim-faced men, who had stopped work when seeing our troop ride past them. "What are you lazy bastards staring at?" he barked. "Get back to work!"

We rode on.

The centurion had confirmed my thoughts about a raiding party attacking the stockade.

Crispus pointed with a jutting chin to four sentries on the north wall. "You figured it out, too?"

I viewed the sentries, their backs to the camp and staring toward the forest. The three sentries at the east wall gate seemed more concerned with dancing to keep warm. From the stables came an occasional whinny of a horse. Argento whinnied in reply. I patted him on the side of his neck.

"The way I see it," I answered, "the raiders came in just before dawn, after cutting the sentries' throats—two of them, judging from the size of the frozen clots of blood on the ground, where we entered the main gate, below the stockade wall."

"Then they dropped down," Crispus added, "opened the gate, let the raiding party slip into camp, cut a few more throats, and then made off with their mounts."

"Fortunately, they settled for a string of a dozen or so nags instead of going for the corral mounts," I concluded, not at all pleased with our theory. Sounds of shoveling dirt, hammers, and saws echoed near the sentries as partially burnt timbers along the fortress wall were being torn down and replaced.

"That's not all I don't like, Marcellus," Crispus remarked as he patted the mane of his mare's shaking head. "Even my horse knows something's wrong."

"Did you see the gate sentries?" I asked. "They're ghosts."

Crispus bared his teeth like an angry dog, turned, and spat. "This place reeks of death, raid or not." At that moment, two orderlies carried a blanket-covered body on a stretcher from the hospital tent to the rear. Rasping coughs and agonized groans came from within the canvas of death.

"I'd wager my quarterly pay," Crispus said, "that we lose half the troop to pneumonia by the end of winter."

I shook my head. "Gallus is mad," I said in a low voice. "He's built a tent camp in winter and a hospital next to the stable." Earlier, Rufius had informed me that the military tribune, Gallus, was commander of the cohort detachment.

"Anybody knows it's against regulations," Crispus said.

I nodded.

Ten infantrymen, led by their assistant centurion, the optio, slogged by us through the mud. The optio turned to us, a facetious smile curled on his big lips. "Welcome to our little bit of paradise!" He moved on.

"Then the rumors we heard in Noviomagnus are true," Crispus muttered.

"Gallus is a bloody thief—selling timber meant for building winter barracks," I said. "He's as corrupt as his father."

"But we just arrived. How do you know?"

"His father, Anicius Gallus the Elder, and mine were enemies."

"You've never mentioned him. Why?"

"No reason to air old grievances." I explained that old Gallus hated my father because he took him to court and won. Gallus the Elder had tried to cheat my father out of our prized race horses. He took the loss as a personal affront to his reputation. "But he got revenge," I added. "Old Gallus used his influence with Emperor Tiberius to refuse my father's admission to the Equestrian Order."

"I didn't realize your family was so rich."

"I've never said anything because the troops would resent it."

"But four hundred thousand sesterces ain't anything to ignore." That was the required income for qualification to the knighthood.

I shrugged.

Riding by the corral where extra mounts were quartered, a couple of troopers, probably on punishment detail, mucked out the acrid manure with wooden pitch forks, and into a small push cart.

I explained that my father's ambitions were squelched, but now that he was dead, I was expected to finish what he had begun.

"You mean—"

"My mother expects me to make every effort to advance to the Equestrian Order as a matter of family honor," I said. "I never expected this to happen. I was planning to be a cavalry officer like my father and our ancestors. But I honor my father's memory too much, and now I must try."

Crispus exhaled. "I don't envy you. Families have a way of fouling up a man's life."

"Whatever happens, Crispus, you're not to say a word about our conversation. No one is to know of my obligations—I'll make enough enemies along the way."

"You can count on me, old friend," he answered and looked about. "I don't see how the son-of-a-bitch expects the men to defend this shithole while they're freezing. He ought to be court-martialed."

"Like his father, young Gallus has nothing but contempt for provincials. As auxiliaries, we're at the bottom of the dung heap."

"Even so, by selling the wood that the men cut, and sticking the money in his tunic, Gallus is asking for mutiny."

* * *

The troop arrived, halted in front of headquarters, and dismounted. Rufius, the other sergeants, and I entered the cohort commander's office, illuminated by ten small olive oil lamps fashioned in the shape of gilded stallions. We came into the presence of the tribune and commanding officer, Anicius Gallus. Sitting on a folding chair, he shuffled through some parchments from behind a walnut table. To his back, imprinted upon an animal skin and stretched tightly between two poles, stood a map of the British tribal territories. To his left sat a young, dark-haired Greek slave feverishly copying reports. Four braziers warmed the room enough to turn the snow on our fur-lined sandals to slush and stung our eyes with smoke.

The young commander's slender face had a weathered handsomeness to it. His short, curled, blond hair accentuated a smooth forehead, light eyebrows, and a thin nose sat between small, dark-blue eyes. A small mouth drawn into a smirk marred an otherwise flawless face. He was of slight build and wore a gilded cuirass over a perfumed, white, and embroidered tunic trimmed in purple. Every finger of his manicured hands held a gold ring inlaid with jewels.

Barely acknowledging our presence, Gallus slowly raised his head and glared at Rufius. "It's about time you arrived."

"Sir, we were shipwrecked," Rufius answered. "It couldn't be helped."

"Yes, so I heard," he said. "Why didn't you come directly to camp?"

"Our losses were heavy. Men, horses—"

"That isn't my concern," the tribune snapped. "Your orders were to report directly to me, not the legion base in Noviomagnus. You could have been here in one day and out on patrol."

"But, Tribune, the men and animals were in terrible condition and exhausted and—"

Gallus cut him off with an icy stare. "That's enough, Decurion! We, too, lost men and horses because you failed to report promptly." He stood and glared into the veteran's bloodshot eyes. "I was told you were an exceptional scouting force, the best in the army. Indeed!" Gallus twisted his mouth into a sneer. "You stink like your nags, and your uniforms are filthy. Someone lied to General Vespasian, didn't they?"

"No, sir."

"For your sake, his informants better be right. We are the most critical outpost on the frontier. Our task is to gather information and keep General Vespasian informed on the movements of Caratacus. I will not fail him under any circumstances. Is that clear?" He glanced at our feet and scowled at the mud and slush we'd tracked in.

Rufius bit his lip and glowered at the tribune. But Gallus ignored his look of contempt. It was enough that he had tried to humiliate Rufius in front of his three squad leaders.

"Yes, sir," the decurion answered, in a slow and even voice.

"Good, I'm pleased that you see things my way," Gallus said crisply and sat down. "You know the penalty for those who don't. Your men are to be assigned to scouting duties, as of now. You will receive your orders shortly."

"In the meantime," he gestured to Rufius, "you can cremate those guards you allowed to be killed by your absence. All of you can leave except—" He studied me closely. "Except you. You're Marcellus Tiberius Reburrus of Gades, aren't you?"

"Yes, sir," I answered as Rufius and the other two sergeants departed.

"Of course, I sensed you were. Your name is on the roster of replacements. Stay here, I want a word with you."

CHAPTER 3

Gallus examined the documents on the table while I stood waiting. What did he want from me?

Gallus raised his head. "You are aware that my father hated yours?"

"I'd heard rumors, sir."

"It's not a rumor," he answered sharply. "Those horses rightfully belonged to us."

"I was too young to know any of the circumstances, sir."

Gallus sniffed. "I suppose that is true. We are about the same age, twenty-three. And how is your father?"

"Dead."

The young tribune remained silent, lost in thought. Then a sneer crossed his mouth. "For your sake, I'm sorry to hear about his death. But that leaves you free to follow in his footsteps, doesn't it?"

"My intention is to be a good soldier like my father, sir," I answered cautiously. Although we had only met, I suspected Gallus would attempt to make my life miserable.

"Come now, I think your intentions are much greater than that." He gestured, as if brushing aside the answer. "When the time is right, I have no doubt you will apply for admission to the Equestrian Order."

I wasn't about to reveal my plans. But I didn't understand his hostility. My father was gone, and his father was elderly, although still active in the Senate.

"My aim is to serve Rome," I said.

"Better as a knight than a common soldier," he retorted. "Don't you agree? You may speak Latin, and although your father became a town magistrate when he retired, you are not Roman in my eyes. You southern Spaniards have grown too powerful for your own good. Unlike the Asturians, you haven't learned your place. At least they have had the decency to keep their own foul tongue."

"But southern Hispania has been a Roman Province for more than two hundred fifty years."

"So has Greece, but they are no more Roman than you! Like my father, I will do everything in my power to block your admission to the Equestrians."

"But the dispute was between our fathers," I countered. "We were boys. Why should we be involved?"

"That's enough of your insolence, Spaniard!" His thin lips twisted into a snarl. He swept the documents from his desk onto the floor, startling his clerk nearby who left his chair to pick them up. "I agree with all *true* Romans that knighthood and the Senate belongs to Italian-born Romans. There are enough of your kind filtering our ranks. You have polluted the Senate."

"As a Roman citizen, I have the same rights as one born in Italy." My rage grew with each passing moment as I stared into his hate-filled eyes. But I held my tongue, fearing I would say too much.

Gallus rose halfway from his chair, leaned on both fists, and glared. "I don't argue with enlisted men about Roman rights," he rasped. "One more insubordinate word, and I will have you court-martialed! Is that clear?"

"Yes, sir."

"Good." He collapsed into his seat and in an instant appeared bored with the situation. He turned and glanced at the young clerk, who had returned to his chair and was reorganizing the spilled documents. Gallus's eyes quickly moving over his muscular frame. He flicked his hand in my direction. "You are dismissed."

* * *

During the following five weeks, our troop was ambushed three times. The attacks occurred when returning from patrol in the purple twilight. Tall, screaming savages sprang from the underbrush in the dark confines of pine and birch forests, only a couple miles from the garrison of Iping. Armed with iron-shod spears, axes, and longswords, they furiously hacked at men and beasts alike as if in blind rage. But their fighting was never coordinated and soon deteriorated into a series of isolated combats.

Despite our men's stiff resistance and superior combat skills, we lost five. Fortune smiled upon my squadron—I didn't lose a man.

After the last incident, the other two squadron leaders, Corribilo and Edecon, and I were convinced that the Britons' scouts assigned to our camp were spies. We decided that our suspicions should be brought to Rufius's attention. I was selected to represent the two senior sergeants, because, although I was a *sesquiplicarius,* a junior sergeant, I was on the best terms with the fifty-seven-year-old veteran.

The next morning right after breakfast I went to Rufius's tent before he left for his daily inspections of the troops and horses. He was as concerned about the condition of the horses as that of the troopers—and, well, he should be. Several of the animals had gone lame or died from colic, and we had received only half of our expected extra mounts.

I entered Rufius's quarters. There was a time, had I been given the chance, I would have killed him.

When I joined the army, five years before, and posted to Germania for cavalry training, Rufius was my drill master. They were the worst four months of my life. Every day, from dawn until dusk, the other forty recruits and I were on the dusty parade field drilling, running, and riding our mounts to his curses and vine cane thrashings.

Sextus Rufius was the decurion in charge of training. He broke the recruits as he would a horse, and then rebuilt them. Day after day, from every imaginable angle, we circled and charged fixed targets of wooden poles and stacks of hay, throwing javelins, and slashing our spatha longswords. As we charged and passed an assigned target, we learned to hold and hurl as many as four javelins accurately, including one over our shoulders. And gods help the recruit who missed. If we didn't get a vine cane thrown at our sides, he cursed our mothers for giving birth to something other than men.

He trained us to vault into the saddle fully armed from either side of a fast-moving horse, necessary should we fall off during battle. Every night I dropped into bed exhausted, bruised, aching, and slept like the dead.

Despite his constant humiliations and painful thrashings, I refused to show any sign of fear and incurred Rufius's wrath all the more. From the back of my horse, I could shoot an arrow into the sky and split it with another before it struck the ground. I was a skillful rider, an excellent sword and spearman, and he knew it.

One day Rufius summoned me to his office. Although he called me a fucking maggot, he also said I was one of the best troopers he had ever trained. But the decurion said I did too much thinking, which wasn't good for a soldier. If I wasn't careful, I would get myself court-martialed, sacked by the army, and bring disgrace on my family. He was concerned with the last point because my father had been his drill master and the best officer he'd ever served under.

He warned me never to say a word to anyone about our conversation or he would thrash me from Germania to the Pillars of Hercules. I promised.

Thereafter, despite his harshness, he wasn't nearly as tough on me as he had been in the beginning. Within a month after completing my basic training, Rufius was transferred to Cavalry Cohort First Hispanorum, and I was assigned to his troop of thirty. I had neither sought nor did I receive special favors from him, but the other men seemed to sense that I got along better with my ex-drill master than the rest of the unit. Word had leaked out that my father had been his drill master, which shouldn't have mattered, and fortunately, it didn't. I incurred no resentment from the men.

Timoleon, Rufius's Macedonian slave, was assisting with his uniform and equipment as I entered his quarters. I saluted, and he acknowledged with an inquiring nod. I spoke about our suspicions of the Britons. They were supposedly from the local Regni tribe, but they were taller and fairer than the natives I had observed.

"Marcellus," he said, poking his head through the tunic top, "I don't trust the bastards any more than you." He grimaced as he slowly sat down on a plain, wooden stool. The joints in his back must have been aching again, but he never complained. "The patrol was in places only we and the native scouts knew about."

"They're relaying the information of our movements to Caratacus," I said.

"Perhaps," Rufius mused, "but if headquarters' reports are correct, he's forty or fifty miles to the northwest in the territories of the Durotrigians. He would need someone whom he could trust nearby to maintain control."

"Any ideas?"

"I'd wager a gold piece that's where our trouble is coming from. Their temple priest, a blood-licking Druid, is behind the ambushes."

"Why is it against orders to attack the temples when they practice human sacrifice?"

"General Vespasian has other plans for the Druids. He'll get rid of them when it's to his advantage."

"But why does Gallus continue using the British scouts when we've lost so many men?"

"I expressed my concerns to Tribune Gallus," Rufius continued as Timoleon kneeled and shoved on his boots. "I said that I'd rather rely on my own men. But he insists his orders come from Legion Headquarters, and he won't disobey them." He shrugged. "Of course, what do you expect from a fucking Imperial hack? I've seen his kind before."

I nodded, knowing he was right.

"Be that as it may," Rufius continued, "next month Vespasian and Sabinus are coming to camp."

"Who is Sabinus, sir?"

"Vespasian's older brother, an Imperial inspector general, a decent sort I hear."

"That would be something different," I said cynically. "If he is, maybe he'll do something about improving living conditions here." The squadron had lost two men that week to pneumonia and eight since arriving in Iping. "Two of mine are down with fever." I thought of Crispus's bet about losing half to sickness before winter's end.

"One of Vespasian's retainers is a friend of mine," Rufius said. "He owes me a favor. I'm going to see if he can use his influence to get me a few minutes with the general. If he can, then I'll tell him about our miserable situation."

Timoleon laced Rufius's leather cords slowly and methodically, pulling each row of eyelets snug. "In the meantime," Rufius said, looking me directly in the eye, "you will continue scouting and not deviate from those orders."

"But, sir," I interrupted, "we're fighting men. Our mission is to make contact with the enemy, not to slink away like dogs—"

"That's enough, Sergeant!" he barked. "I'll treat you worse than a fucking dog if you disobey me. You better control that tongue of yours. You're bordering on insubordination." A moment passed before he continued in a more fatherly tone as he put on his belt. "Marcellus, I know how you feel. With the exception of you and me, none of the men are Roman citizens and are treated like horseshit. The command staff makes it plain enough."

I thought of how my father instilled in my brothers and me the pride and privilege of being Roman citizens.

"They'll call you Spaniard," he had said gravely, "for that's what Romans call the peoples of our land, but you are a Roman citizen, and no one can take that from you, not even Caesar."

My father had said he was fortunate to rise to the rank of decurion, the highest an alien could be promoted in the cavalry. He had been the first in our family to be awarded Roman citizenship upon retirement. This and his family fortune qualified him for a membership on the town council, and he eventually became a magistrate presiding over minor civil and criminal cases.

"But you, Son," he said with pride, "as a citizen, can rise higher." At the time, I thought he meant being promoted to the rank of military tribune. It had not occurred to me he was speaking of the Equestrian Order, the Knighthood.

Despite our Roman citizenship, mother instilled in us the traditions and heritage of the Turdetanian Tribe. She taught us the harsh-sounding language and worship of the god Melkart, to whom she was a high priestess. Unlike the Romans, who worship idols, Melkart is an invisible god. In generations past, he required human sacrifices. The coming of the Romans to Hispania brought an end to the hideous practice. In its place my people substituted the butchering of goats and bulls at the little hillside temple near our great farmstead, the *latifundia*.

Mother also taught us the gentle arts. Many nights I played the reedy twin-fluted *aulos* in the field, while keeping watch over our cattle. At harvest and weddings we danced the *Bastetana* to the strains of the twisted horned *tuba* and *aulos*. My family and I would hold hands with the other men, women, and children, forming a circle around the great bonfire. Weaving in and out, swaying back and forth, we sang songs of joy to the instruments' pulsating rhythms.

Unlike many women, Mother never followed the armies. She was too young, and Hispania too far away from the frontiers of Germania and the East, where the armies were garrisoned. She didn't meet and marry my father until he had retired from the army and returned to Baetica Province, the land of many Iberian tribes. The marriage was arranged, as most were. He was a wealthy landowner, forty-three and graying; she was a sixteen-year-old, auburn-haired beauty. He had money and property, her parents had none, but they possessed high tribal status and titles linking them to the line of Turdetanian kings—an ideal arrangement.

"It angers me," I said softly in a respectful tone to Rufius, "that the general staff takes the word of a lying, filthy barbarian over ours. I don't understand."

Timoleon handed Rufius his spatha, clutching the scabbard, after first cleaning off some invisible smudge from the longsword. Rufius glanced appreciatively, which seemed to please the slave.

"We're only Spaniards," Rufius said in a sardonic voice, "and not their stinking Legionaries, that's why. But they respect us. Remember, our ancestors fought the Romans for two hundred years, defeating army after army before they were subdued. Why do you think Julius Caesar recruited Spaniards exclusively for his personal legion, the Fighting Tenth?"

"I have no idea."

"Because we're the best. The Romans need us, and we're their eyes and ears. They'll find no better cavalrymen or infantrymen than us!" He stared at his weapon.

"That sword looks like it has seen much service," I said.

"Aye, that's true. It belonged to my great-grandfather. Like you, my family has a long tradition with the army. He rode with Julius Caesar against Pompey at Pharsalus." He took a deep breath and went on. "But so long as we are soldiers, we will do as ordered. Is that clear?"

I held my lips tightly together, controlled myself, and nodded. He dismissed me, I saluted and left his quarters.

But I was determined, more than ever, to prove that the British scouts could not be trusted.

CHAPTER 4

LATE MARCH, 44 AD

Weeks of drudgery rolled into the second month of continuous patrolling. Rains and muddy quagmires had replaced the severe cold. Drizzle turned into heavy rains, chilling and saturating us to the bone. Again, headquarters received word from the Regni that a small marauding force of Britons was cited on the move twenty miles to the west. I led my squadron of ten riders on the search. Our orders were to report their position to Gallus, but we were forbidden to engage the enemy in combat. So far, Caratacus and his demons had eluded us like ghosts.

The foul weather made patrolling extremely hazardous. Again, the rain turned trails into rivers of slimy ooze, treacherous to the footing and maneuvering of the horses. Under constant prodding they struggled through the muck. We hunkered within our protective, oil-based cloaks. But rain dripped off the edges of helmets, down the sides of necks and faces, and seeped into tunics underneath, soaking our exposed breeches, chilling us all.

Our patrol trekked along the rugged countryside, up and down green, rolling hills, dotted with overflowing streams and ponds, and by newly planted fields of wheat and barley.

A bleak village lay ahead, and the troops quieted. At our approach, the peasants scurried into wattle and daub-thatched roof huts, taking their goats and chickens with them. A shallow, muddy ditch served as a moat, and a rotting half-missing palisade surrounded the wretched little hovels, each with a soggy pile of manure by the door. Villagers peeked at us suspiciously through moving flaps of bark and animal skins.

"They see us no differently than the bandits who've robbed them before, do they?" Crispus asked as we rode by.

"Can you blame them? We're all the same in their eyes. At least this time their fears are groundless." We had standing orders to leave the peasants alone. This was a wise policy, because the army needed their cooperation.

"It's too small anyway to be a real village," Crispus continued, "probably only a big family and outside relatives live here." He spotted a woman's vacant face peeking from the door. "And by the looks of that one, in-breeding must be a favorite pastime."

The rain stopped. About a half hour after passing the village, I ordered a halt of the squadron at the edge of a large tree-lined pond where the thick underbrush concealed our presence. After posting a sentry, I ordered the troops to dismount. A loud sigh of relief came from the ranks as they stretched their legs and watered their animals. As usual, the men muttered among themselves, complaining about their lots in life.

Slowly and stiffly I got off Argento. I removed my iron helmet, with its bronze molding mimicking short, curling hair, and shook out my close, stringy locks. The rest did the same. We looked like a pack of drenched hounds shaking our coats.

I trudged a little ways from the rest along the calm water's edge, leading Argento behind me to where a giant tree sheltered the pond's bank with a canopy of outstretched limbs. The thick trunk provided sanctuary to a clump of snow from the heavy rains. A gentle breeze rippled by. I stood scanning the water, clearer than I expected. As Argento dipped his head and took a well-deserved drink, minnows and fingerlings darted about chasing one another past pebbles, dead leaves, and the submerged roots of stumps within the foot of the banks. The soft reflection of billowing white and gray clouds passed by on the pond's surface in shapes of bizarre animals from mythical legends.

As I stood, nearly mesmerized by the pond's beauty, Crispus's reflection slowly appeared on the water's surface as he approached from behind. Then I took a second look and saw the reflection of one whom I had not really faced in a long time—myself.

What mirrored back at me was not the smiling and haughty youth of eighteen, raised on a ranch. Instead, I saw an older-than-his-years, broad-shouldered, six-foot cavalry squad leader.

Crispus, who stepped to my side, was half a head shorter. His smooth, copper face belied the fact that he was six years older than me.

My yellow-flecked, brown eyes were lined with dark circles. A straight nose and a wind-chafed, olive face with high cheekbones and an angular chin and jaw stared at me. Crispus had black, deep-set eyes above a long aquiline nose. The lines at the edge of my lips seemed molded into a permanent frown. My reddish-brown hair did not conceal the lined forehead, or the slash of a scar left on my cheek from a German's sword. *Curse you Melkart, how you've aged me in only five years.*

"Hey, you Baetican bastard! This is no time to admire yourself." Crispus's deep resonance seemed to send ripples through the small inlet, blurring the images.

I grinned as I turned and gazed upon his stubbly face. "Why not, you Punic shit eater?" I'm better looking than the native mares who pass themselves off as women—come to think of it, better looking than you, too!" Crispus was from the Bastuli-Phoeni Tribe, an Iberian people who had intermarried with Phoenician colonists many centuries ago. Because of their Semitic features, the Bastuli were regarded more Punic than Iberian.

"The trouble with you, Marcellus," Crispus said, "is you're too damned picky about where you stick your spear. Why can't you be like the rest of us and get it where you can?" His cheerfulness could not mask the fatigue revealed by his drooping eyelids. Turning his back to me, he walked a couple of paces away unlacing his trousers. Spreading his feet, he urinated into a path of slushy snow, which steamed in protest.

"I like mine to take baths before I plow them," I answered, playing along with his game. "You never know what you could get, otherwise I might as well straddle a horse like you do."

"That's what you farm lads start with anyway, or is it goats?" he asked, and flashed a big, toothy grin. He shook himself and relaced his breeches slowly.

I gazed about the surrounding area. Except for Crispus, no one else stood nearby. I lowered my voice and told him of how the meeting the previous month with Rufius still ate at me.

When I finished, Crispus frowned and shook his head. "I was wondering why you were so quiet. It's not like you."

"It doesn't matter. I've got a plan that might work. We could be executed if it fails."

Crispus's mouth hardened as he looked over his shoulder towards the bushes. "Oh, *we* could be executed? Then, by Jupiter's balls, I don't want any part of it!"

"You don't have a choice. I'm thinking about the men we've lost on patrol. We've been fortunate that we haven't been attacked lately."

"May Castor and Pollux stay with us."

I hoped he had the favor of the gods of luck. "I know a Druid temple is somewhere up there." I nodded toward the scrubby, brush-covered hills, half hidden by lowering gray clouds that had snagged on them.

"Wait, you don't mean what I think you mean?" Crispus's eyes narrowed.

I raised my hand. "Hold on. We don't even know if it exists."

"What if it does? I don't like the look in your eyes."

"Don't kill a lion before you hunt it," I snapped. "And if it does exist, what's the harm in taking a look?"

"What if we run into a bloody Druid and his savages?"

"Hear me out!" I revealed my plan.

"You crazy bastard!" he whispered. "Is this some fucking scheme to advance yourself at our expense?"

"You know me better than that, Crispus. I'm thinking of the men."

Crispus kicked at the muddy embankment, spewing dirt into the pond. "Horse shit, it'll never work. No worry about being executed, the British will save our Roman lords the expense."

"It will work," I said, more calmly than I felt. "For once the rain will be our ally."

A moment later, small, icy raindrops bounced off our faces. "Your newfound ally is falling again," Crispus said. He took a deep breath, grabbed the hilt of his spatha, and in a slow and deliberate stride returned to his mount.

* * *

As the patrol continued, the woods gradually changed from scrub to a dense pine forest, carpeted with an underbrush of low-lying heather and bristly, yellow gorse. Black and brown rotting leaves piled thick on the trail, hid limbs and branches, and caused the horses to stumble. Tall, wet bushes jutted from the shadows and slapped the men about the face and body, annoying everyone with the smell of must and mildew. Tempers soon matched the climate.

"This place stinks like a hog pen," Albinus whined. "I haven't smelled anything this bad since I left the farm."

"If anyone knows the smell of hog pens, you do," drifted a reply from stubby-built Indibil. "Your nose is always up an officer's arse."

The men laughed, but I suppressed mine. "That's enough!" I said in a low, growling voice.

They continued to grumble, violating our standard orders. Enforced silence was mandatory while on reconnaissance patrols. I whirled Argento around, startling the men. They halted abruptly. I gave the surprised, weasel-eyed Albinus a withering look and glared at the rest. I yanked my spatha from the worn leather scabbard and pointed it in their direction.

"I'll slice off the fucking head of the next arsehole who says a word," I said in a hissing voice. "We're in enemy territory. I won't tolerate your insubordination. Is that clear?" They glanced at one another and a few looked at the muddy ground. Crispus, his anger apparently gone, winked in approval.

Still facing the men, I heard the muffled sound of hooves from behind me. The big-nosed point man, Andubal, who was scouting far ahead of us, rode slowly towards the squadron. He glanced over his shoulder and drew up alongside. "I've spotted savages."

"Where?" I slid my weapon back into the scabbard.

"They're in some sort of temple just ahead."

"How many?"

"Can't be sure, maybe a half dozen."

"Are they on foot or horseback?"

"They're mounted."

My heart jumped into my throat. Was this the rumored Druid temple? A feeling of dread seeped into my bones as tiny bumps formed on my arms and down my back. I knew the consequences if I carried out my plan. On the pain of death, we were ordered to leave the native temples alone, especially those bordering lands of the Regni and Durotrigians. King Verica of the Regni was supposedly a Roman ally, and King Unig was neutral. By leaving their temples unmolested, the Romans showed their supposed good faith and trust.

If my suspicions were correct, Verica was using the scouts as spies. I would expose his treachery and stop the raids and bloody ambushes at their source, saving more of our men from being killed. Then I remembered Crispus's remarks at the pond. If we succeeded, perhaps my daring would be recognized. It might be the first step on the road to the Equestrian Order. If we failed, then Gallus would have my head, a pleasure I'm sure he would relish. Either way, I was determined to stop the attacks against my troop.

I ordered the men to dismount, drop the horses to their knees, and maintain silence. The troopers stayed behind, quietly soothing the restless animals, as Crispus, Andubal, and I proceeded down the seldom-used path on foot.

A short distance later, Andubal motioned for us to halt. He continued looking about. A faint downwind breeze blew from the direction of the temple.

"How much farther?" I asked the point man.

"About three hundred paces."

We crept forward until we reached the edge of the clearance.

Less than a bow shot away, the temple sat surrounded by ancient, gnarled oak trees, sacred to the Druids. Hanging from many of the branches were gold bracelets and torc collars, brass quarter moons, stars, and other charms. It was common knowledge that worshippers had placed them there to appease the gods of planting and the harvest. The natives of Germania, where we had previously been posted, had similar customs.

A squared lattice archway formed a vined entrance to the sanctuary. On each side stood a long, narrow pole dug into the ground. Set into a niche within each post sat a bleached white, slack-jawed human skull, whose empty sockets gaped southward, forever blind.

An ancient earthwork consisting of a weed-covered mound and a shallow mud-filled ditch circled the temple. Nearby bubbled a small stream, sacred to the Druids. Only a narrow, wooden pathway crossed the moat, but it was large enough to support the weight of a horse and rider.

To the right of the temple, seven horses grazed next to a pillar. One mount looked familiar. Scattered among the animals, white temple geese arrogantly strutted, occasionally honking and nipping at the horses' shanks. Inside the multi-torch-lit edifice I easily discerned the figures of a half-dozen Britons, conversing as they milled about a dark-stained sacrificial altar. The tallest had grown a trimmed, white beard and wore a woolen, blue and green cloak with a hood. A large gold, half-moon disk, hanging by a chain, draped his chest, and he held a wooden staff in his right hand. He had to be a Druid priest. A younger, dark-bearded priest stood attentively near the sacrificial stone. The others were battle-dressed warriors wearing plain conical helmets.

A warrior stepped outside the temple.

We froze. Then quietly, we ducked behind the bushes before he spotted us.

He glanced around and momentarily peered in our direction before returning to the temple.

I recognized him. Even with little more than a dim, gray light filtering through the forest, I knew he was one of our scouts.

My suspicions were confirmed. He worked for the enemy. Druid priests hated Romans, and there was no doubt that the natives had orders from the priests to deceive and ambush our troops.

Now I could justify raiding the temple.

Did he see us? I prayed that he hadn't. I motioned to Crispus and Andubal, and we returned to the squadron.

A light rain began to fall. For a moment, I studied the gloomy faces of my troopers. “Load your slings and grab your swords,” I said with all the confidence I could muster. “Albinus, take the point, we’re going to catch a spy.”

CHAPTER 5

At breakneck speed, the squadron charged from the woods, screaming curses in breath fogged from the cold. The Britons, caught by surprise, without time to reach their horses, stood their ground. Even the two Druid priests attempted to defend themselves, pulling hidden swords from beneath their robes. The fight was furious but brief.

Albinus led the charge across the narrow bridge and into the sanctuary. I was close behind. Once across we encircled the barbarians. They threw themselves at us as if backed by an army. Albinus hacked a native's head and arm in a single blow, bathing himself and his charger in blood. Then he whirled left, stabbing another savage who had attempted to hamstring his mare.

I ran another through with my sword after he made a flying leap and lanced the left side of my face with his weapon. I didn't have time to think about the wound. A short javelin dart flew past my head and slammed into the chest of the younger priest. He screamed as his massive bulk toppled backwards across the sacrificial altar.

Crispus fended off a warrior's glancing blow with his shield and countered swiftly with a slice from his spatha splitting the enemy's head.

Out of the corner of my eye, I caught Indibil stabbing a shaggy warrior in the throat. Blood gushed from the wound as he stumbled, collapsed, and died. The native, who I had earlier recognized as one of our scouts, jumped bareback onto a horse and attempted to flee. I shouted at Andubal and Crispus.

Andubal, the point man, pulled a leather sling from within the satchel tied to his saddle and twirled it above his head. With a flick of his wrist, he hurled a small, lead ball from its pouch. At a speed faster than a Syrian's arrow, the ball flew toward the barbarian and careened off his helmet. The Celt galloped faster, jumping the ditch, with Crispus in pursuit. Crispus fired his sling, and the missile struck the savage in the small of the back. He yelped, flinging his sword away, and rolled off the rump of his mount. Landing hard, he tumbled facedown on the muddy earth, and for a moment lay motionless. Groaning loudly, he struggled to his knees. Crispus reined up and threw a noose of rope around the spy's neck. He tied the other end to the saddle pommel. Slowly, he worked the horse backwards until the noose tightened about the Briton's throat who suddenly came to life, desperately clutching the rope. Crispus stopped.

"Stand up, savage, or I'll wring your neck like a chicken!"

The barbarian seemed to understand, and with great effort, pulled himself to his feet. With another lunge on the rope to get his attention, Crispus cantered back to the temple grounds, the trotting native in tow.

By now, the priest had backed towards the covered altar. After glancing to his slain comrade, he dropped the sword and reached inside his robe.

"Albinus! Kimon!" I shouted. "Grab the priest!"

The Druid pulled a dagger and was about to plunge it into his own chest when Kimon knocked the weapon away. He and Albinus threw the Druid to the ground, and rolling him over, twisted his arms into hammer locks. They yanked him to his feet.

I dismounted and rushed forward, sword in hand. The Druid stood straight and tall, glaring defiantly as only those who face certain death can. "Unbelieving barbarians!" he spat in a guttural voice. "How dare you defile this sacred temple?"

"By the gods, the old boy speaks Latin," a surprised Crispus called as he removed the rope from the neck of the gasping scout. The Briton clutched his burned throat, but Crispus yanked his hands behind his back and bound them.

"We know the ways of many people, heathen," the Druid bellowed. "Yours and your Roman slave masters, too."

"Do you now?" I motioned for Kimon and Albinus to seize his flailing arms and force him to behave.

"I know all about your people," he crowed. "My spies are everywhere. Do you think us stupid?" His cruel, gray eyes glowered from beneath irregular eyebrows, as if trying to penetrate our souls. "You Spaniards are no more than cowering lackeys. The Romans treat you like pigs, but you keep coming back for more of their swill."

The Druid's words begged for a swift death, but I settled for backhanding him across the mouth. The blow settled him to his knees, and my guards released him. He sprawled on the compact, dirt floor longer than the blow deserved. The priest started to spit out another curse, but checked himself when he wiped blood from his crooked mouth. I realized that he was attempting to draw attention away from the matter at hand. We had a spy, and a better prize, in the priest.

"Bind him," I motioned to Kimon. The huge half-Greek and Spaniard seemed to take great pleasure in tying the priest's wrists behind his back, and as painfully tight as circulation would permit. The priest flinched, which was strange, for Druids were reputed to have great tolerance to pain. I ordered Indibil and six-fingered Severus to stand guard outside the temple while the rest of us surrounded the Druid and scout.

"What's your name, Priest?" I questioned.

"Llugar ap Nudd, Druid of the Council of Mona," he answered puffing out his chest.

The Isle of Mona, located off the west coast of Britannia, was reported to be the sacred isle of the Druids. Reports indicated that their council fully supported Caratacus in his raids against the Romans.

"Priest," I said, "you, too, are a mercenary. Only you expect rewards in the world of darkness, your hereafter, which may come soon." I nodded with a slight grin. Llugar ap Nudd seemed to appreciate the innuendo.

After Kimon finished tying Llugar, he checked the scout's bound hands, lashed tightly in front of him. Drawing the prisoner's elbows to the rear, Kimon locked them behind his back, shoving a short pole through them.

The scout mumbled something insulting to Kimon, who throttled him to the ground.

"What's that you said? The rope's too loose? Why, thank you." Kimon then placed a sandaled boot on his butt and pulled hard on the rope, provoking a satisfying cry of pain. "Well, they look the right shade of purple now. Let me know if they loosen up again."

I motioned for my *quaestionarius,* Obulco, who had been standing near Kimon. The torturer's toothless grin spread from ear-to-ear across a dark, grimy face. He had ways of inflicting pain that others considered too revolting. Obulco leapt over the prostrate barbarian and halted before me.

"We'll save most of the detailed questioning for the legionary torturers," I said, "but I need answers to important questions, now."

Obulco's oily face twisted into a violent scowl, which meant he was happy. His battle-scarred face was laced with jagged welts that twisted into a frown any attempt to grin. The more contorted the scowl, the happier he was, and this was the ugliest he had been in some time.

"Anything you says. When I finished, he'll tell you everything," he bragged. Obulco snorted, and with a dirty hand wiped away the thin film of mucous running from his oft-broken nose.

"Whatever you do, they're not to be killed," I whispered.

"Aye, how much time do I get?"

"As much as you need."

He exhaled heavily, his breath smelling of gamy meat and wine. "Good, it's better when I can do my work S-L-O-W-L-Y," he lisped, "so theys can appreciate my craft."

"Get moving!" I ordered.

I hate torture, it's a dirty business. To stop the pain and suffering, victims will tell what they believe their interrogators want to hear, though it be a lie. However, a liar will tell the truth because of the fear of the impending pain. Its necessity is unfortunate, especially when dealing with Druids, because of their defiance. But I was willing to do anything to save the lives of my men and those of the cohort. We had methods of confirming the validity of his information. Every cohort had a detachment of interrogators.

Obulco knelt behind the priest, forcing him to his knees. "You're smarts enough to hurts more if I tell you first," he hissed in the old man's ear. He placed the strap around the Druid's scalp. The priest tried shaking it loose, but Obulco shoved his knee into his back above the horizontal pole and grabbed and tightened the leather. He wrenched his head back forcing him to scream.

"Llugar ap Nudd," I said, "you can save yourself a lot of pain and grief if you simply answer my questions."

"Never! Never will I answer questions, Spanish SCUM!"

I nodded to Obulco, and he tightened the strap. The priest, face crimson, again screamed.

"Who is your master?"

"No one is my master! Only the gods!"

Again, Obulco applied the pressure, ever tightening the leather until the Druid cried out again.

"Where is Caratacus's main force concentrated?" I questioned in a low and even tone.

"Don't know!"

Obulco slowly turned the handle of the strap tighter around the priest's skull. His eyes bulged as another scream exploded from his lungs so piercing it could be heard throughout the forest.

"Llugar ap Nudd, where is his army? Speak up, or you will die!"

"Kill me!" he begged. "Kill me!"

"That's too easy. Your death will be long and painful, and your lackey," I emphasized glancing to the Briton scout, "will have to watch as your flesh is burned one bit at a time. You'll beg for a quicker death before we're through."

Obulco tore his clothing exposing the Druid's aging but sinewy body to the frigid air. I motioned to Kimon and Albinus to tie him onto the sacrificial altar. They shoved the fat, dead body of the younger priest onto the ground with a loud thud and tied Llugar ap Nudd with well-oiled leather straps on the altar. The scout was dragged before the Druid as Obulco unwrapped the cord and withdrew his prod from the glowing red coals he had placed earlier in the nearby hearth.

I bent my head and whispered to the scout. "Unless you and your friend confess, the priest will be scorched and slowly disemboweled."

The Briton closed his eyes and shook his shaggy, dark hair violently. Obulco slowly moved the glowing prod toward the priest's face.

"No! Don't!" the ruddy-complected native rasped in heavily accented Latin, "I'll talk, have mercy on him!" He gulped a couple of times attempting to raise his voice. The rope burn crossed his neck.

"Shut up, you fool," the priest hissed. "Tell them nothing!"

"No, Lord, I can't let them torture you," the scout said. "Your life is . . . is worth more than mine."

"Silence, dog, or I will excommunicate you. You know your soul will wander forever!"

The greasy torturer cuffed Llugar heavily with the back of his glove. Obulco grasped his testicles and waved a dagger dangerously close for the benefit of the scout. Noting the grimacing priest's closed eyes, and that the scout had turned his head, Obulco quickly jabbed the hot iron back into the fire and picked up a cold dagger. He jerked the sack hard enough to command the Druid's full attention, then laid the ice-cold blade broadside against the sack and made a harsh hissing sound. This brought the prized screech-of-terror with the damage of a hot blade. The priest fainted, and Obulco's face twisted like crumpled parchment.

"Stop! I don't care!" the scout begged. His wide, hazel eyes came to rest upon mine. "I've . . . I've seen a torturing of many, and if this was another I . . . I would not care," he said in broken Latin, a voice barely more than a whisper. He stopped and shook his head for a moment, as if feeling the pain of his own words. "But I cannot let a priest suffer. What . . . what do you want to know?"

"Why should I believe anything you say?"

"I tell . . . tell the truth so you'll spare his life. He is a priest, not a spy."

"Priests—spies—they're the same."

"Druids are special," he answered as if it were self-evident. "They're the lawgivers and . . . and wise men. No . . . no man is above them, not even kings. No harm must come to him." He hung his head, unwilling to look upon the face of the Druid, who slowly regained consciousness. Llugar ap Nudd raised his wavering head in an attempt to inspect the feared damage.

"Why are you in the temple?" I demanded.

"Passing information to . . . to my master," the scout said.

"Who is your master?"

"It's . . . it's . . ."

"Out with it!"

"Caratacus."

"Traitor!" the Druid screamed. "Thou art excommunicated, thy soul is damned forever!" Again, Obulco slapped him down.

The Celt stared at the old man, and his whole body shook. His face grew crimson, and tears welled in his eyes. "Have mercy on me," he pleaded. "I'm sorry, Lord, but . . . but I don't want to see you hurt anymore."

I found no pleasure in watching the old man suffer and was relieved that the scout willingly answered my questions. "I know that you've made a very difficult decision," I said, "and I respect you for wanting to save his life. I believe the gods will, too." At this point, I would have said anything to keep him answering my questions.

"My life is nothing if he dies. It don't matter if I don't see the gods."

"I'm sure the gods are more merciful than he would lead you to believe," I said. "We must proceed with the questioning. Where is Caratacus's army?" He attempted to speak but choked. I motioned to one of the men to give him water, then I repeated the question.

"The west, Maugh-Dun Castle," he replied in a resigned monotone. His large eyes, set far apart, stared blankly ahead.

"The capital of the Durotrigians? Their king is supposed to be neutral."

"King Unig has made an alliance with Lord Caratacus—he hates the Romans."

"When are they launching their offensive?"

"After Beltaine, what you . . . you call May." His eyes remained fixed on the fire.

"What day?"

"I . . . I don't know."

Obulco shot a hot iron to the base of his throat.

Even from where I stood I felt its piercing heat and metallic smell.

"You're closer than you know to a wanderin' spirit," the interrogator spat.

The scout's eyes widened as Obulco ripped open his trousers.

"And a wanderin' spirit without no balls is a sorry spirit indeed," Obulco said.

"I don't know! By . . . by Lugh, I swear I don't know."

"Let him be, he might be telling the truth, though I doubt it," I said with a sneer. "Is Verica in league with Caratacus?"

"Aye," he whimpered through quivering lips. "He secretly pledged his . . . his allegiance when he learned the Romans would not leave his lands."

It was common knowledge that Verica had persuaded the Emperor Claudius to invade Britannia and restore to him lands taken by Caratacus.

"What about his sons and daughters? Are they in league with Caratacus as well?" I prodded.

His face tightened before he nodded. "Aye, his sons, but I don't think his daughter."

"And why isn't she?"

"I . . . I don't know, that's what I hear, I swear it."

"What's her name?"

"Eleyne."

He seemed too eager to be excommunicated and answer my questions. He knew too much be a mere scout. His knowledge came from one who had access to the inner circle of the ruling class.

"What is your real name?"

"Alwynn," he answered, eyes downcast.

I nodded to Obulco, and he drifted his hot iron to the barbarian's testicles, singeing hairs.

The Celt screamed.

"What's your real name, you lying shithead?" I demanded. "You know too damned much."

His reddened eyes filled with terror as the hot prod lingered, scorching close to his scrotum. "Don't," he begged. "Cadwal, cousin of Caratacus."

My lower lip dropped in disbelief. "Why are you, a king's cousin, risking your head? You know it means certain death being caught as a spy."

"I know. My cousin says I'm not worthy of . . . of being his kin. My mother was his . . . his Uncle Epaticcos's concubine. He said I had to prove myself leading you into ambushes."

"Is it not the custom of the Celts to prove their bravery in a full-blown battle?"

"Aye, but I never took no heads like a real warrior. I've got to prove myself this way."

"You've had your last chance," I whispered. "No more." I pondered his revelations for a moment, and it occurred to me that for political reasons his life might be spared as a hostage. I knew from official reports that Caratacus had several half brothers and cousins, but no Roman had ever seen them. My prisoner could be lying about his identity. But if he were telling the truth, I was certain the Imperial Command would keep Cadwal incognito, until the right moment presented itself.

"If you're lying about who you are," I threatened, "I'll butcher the old man like a sacrificial bullock. Then I'll run you through your member." I pointed my spatha menacingly in that direction. "Do you understand?" Obulco's face grinned into another snarling and twisting mask.

"I swear it's . . . it's true. Don't kill him."

Obulco squeezed Cadwal's sack hard enough to provoke a whimper, then released it.

* * *

We returned to the camp in the pouring rain and darkness. I ordered the priest gagged and separated from Cadwal, lest he persuade him to be silent.

Passing through the main gate we brought the prisoners to Rufius's tent. I ordered the men to wait as I went inside. He sat at a small table, in the dim candlelight, writing reports. Next to the parchments was a small, earthen jug of wine and a gold cup with a lead base, his only concession to luxury in the field. In the shadows behind Rufius sat his big slave, Timoleon, cleaning his helmet. Rufius looked up as I entered, and the tension drained from his face.

"Where have you been? By the looks of that nasty wound on your face, I'd say you've been ambushed."

Obulco had cleaned and placed a smelly salve on the wound, but it still stung. I knew it needed stitches to properly close it.

"I can explain, sir."

"You'd better. And once you finish, get that wound taken care of before it festers. Now report."

"I've got something to show you." I turned and motioned through the opening, and four of my squadron, including Crispus and Obulco, shoved the two drenched Britons inside onto the planked floor in front of the decurion. Rufius's face flushed, but he said nothing until he motioned to the others to leave his quarters, except Crispus.

The old veteran's bloodshot eyes narrowed. "What in Melkart's name have you done? Your orders were no contact, no prisoners!" He carefully rose from the table as if in pain from aching joints, and came around for a closer examination of the prisoners. The old Druid stared defiantly, and the other one kept his eyes fixed on the floor. Rufius grabbed a handful of Cadwal's wet, matted hair and yanked his head up with a violent jerk. He recognized him as our scout. "Why is he shackled?"

"Our so-called scout is a dung-eating spy."

"A spy, is he?" he repeated, his tone changing.

"He claims to be Cadwal, Caratacus's cousin."

"Does he now?" Rufius smiled like a viper. "It's time I hear your report—it had better be good."

I related what had happened on patrol.

"You have the imagination of Homer," he said in a voice the mixture of amusement and suspicion. "If there is any basis to your tale, you might escape the axe. But by Jove's brass balls you better pray the generals believe it. It's your good fortune that they're in camp!"

CHAPTER 6

As we approached headquarters I spotted the mounts of Generals Sabinus and Vespasian and their entourage, protected by members of the emperor's palace troops. Nearby, other Praetorian guards huddled around a huge fire.

Tightly wrapped in crimson cloaks, two Praetorians guarded the entrance. They barred our way with thin-shank *pilums*. "The generals are in conference," the taller of the two sentries said. They pointed their javelins menacingly close to our chests. "They're not to be disturbed."

"You shall report that we have two prisoners," Rufius ordered in a stern voice. "One is a spy. His information is vital to the general's upcoming offensive. Do it now!"

A frown crossed the dog-like face of the taller guard. Obviously, an elite Praetorian resented taking orders from an officer of the auxiliary cavalry, even a superior officer. He exhaled and motioned us to wait as he stepped inside. A moment later he waved us through.

In the lamp-lit room stood ten officers surrounding the generals, who sat at a long table spread with a series of maps. Among them was Gallus. Outwardly, the tribune appeared indifferent, but he eyed our prisoners, as did the rest.

At thirty-nine, General Flavius Sabinus was Vespasian's older brother by five years. Nearly bald, his remaining hair was a thinning, sandy brown. Taller, but not as stocky as Vespasian, his round, smooth face and sparkling eyes, the color of mahogany, belied his reputation for persistence and patience. He had an impeccable reputation for honesty. But he was not above taking advantage of any weakness he perceived in an opponent. Nevertheless, he was respected by all, friend and foe alike.

The generals seemed puzzled by our presence but not angry—yet. We saluted. The prematurely bald and peasant-faced Vespasian, commander of the Second Augustan Legion, stared first at us, and then at our bound prisoners, who were forced to their knees. He scowled at the disheveled sight of Cadwal and the Druid. Sabinus appeared to be carefully studying the prisoners.

"Well, well, well, out of what hole did you find these crawling rats?" Vespasian asked.

"They were captured by Squad Leader Reburrus and his men, sir," Rufius answered.

"Can you tell us the meaning of this intrusion?" Sabinus inquired. "I see one prisoner is a Druid. Did you raid a temple?"

Rufius nodded to me.

"Yes, sir," I answered, looking directly into Sabinus's eyes. The muscles in my body tightened. I wasn't used to speaking to generals. "It was the one rumored to be in the hills to the west," I continued. "They're spies—they confessed."

"I confess nothing!" Llugar ap Nudd spat. Crispus grabbed his long, white hair and smashed his face to the floor. A trickle of blood oozed from his nose.

"They may well be spies," Vespasian replied, "but you disobeyed orders, and I will not tolerate disobedience."

Sabinus leaned over and whispered to Vespasian, who nodded. "Please, go on, tell us what happened." Sabinus's voice was as smooth as oil. "We would like to know more about your prisoners."

I related the events leading to their capture and summed up their questioning. I didn't mention that I wasn't going to tolerate the loss of additional men by entrusting their lives to lying, murderous barbarian scouts. When I finished, a low murmur swept the group.

"Great Jupiter Thunderer," Vespasian remarked, "you know that bat-fornicator Caratacus has eluded us for months."

"There is one detail I left out, sir. With your permission, I would like you to hear it from his lips." I nodded to Cadwal.

"Raise your head, man," Sabinus ordered in a gentle but firm voice.

No response.

"Do as I say."

Silence. General Sabinus glanced to me.

"He understands you well enough, sir," I said.

I motioned to Crispus, who pulled the barbarian's head by his long hair, forcing his skull back until he looked defiantly into the eyes of Sabinus, who stood above him.

"Tell the general who you really are," I ordered.

The barbarian eyed the Druid, who stared through him, and lowered his eyes.

I drew my spatha.

At the sight of the long blade, the fire in his eyes flickered out.

"My name is Cadwal," he stammered.

"Who is your cousin?"

"Caratacus."

"Louder," I said.

"CARATACUS!"

Another murmur came from the staff. Sabinus remained impassive while Vespasian smiled like a cat.

"My dear, Cadwal," Sabinus said dryly, "I was disappointed when your cousin did not pledge allegiance to Rome." A dark expression crossed his milk-fair face, "For your sake, I trust that you will make amends for his indiscretion by telling our interrogators everything we want to know. Otherwise, your cousin will be minus a devoted relative."

"If I hadn't been discovered, your sons would've had no father!" he blurted.

The staff officers gasped, and a stunned expression crossed the face of the generals. I placed the point of my spatha at the base of Cadwal's ruddy throat. Seeing my longsword, he offered his jugular.

"It won't be that easy, barbarian," I said.

His green-flecked eyes bulged as Crispus yanked the savage's scalp back by the ends of his stringy hair.

"Unless you want to be like your friend," I nodded towards the prostrate Druid, "and die a slow death after being nailed to a tree, you will explain yourself!"

"I was going to kill General Sabinus myself."

I jolted—his answer caught me totally off guard.

A loud murmur erupted from the officers standing about the table, including Gallus.

Vespasian glared at Cadwal.

Sabinus paled, his lips tightened.

"When?" I questioned. It would have been so easy to kill him, but that is what he wanted. I refused to give in to my urge to send him to the gods.

"Tomorrow," Cadwal answered.

"How?"

He hesitated, and Crispus's grip tightened. "When he left the camp," the Celt rasped.

"But then you would have died," Sabinus said, apparently having recovered from his initial surprise. "My guards would have killed you."

"No matter, my cousin would've been proud of me. I'd die a warrior's death."

Cadwal went on to reveal that he planned to murder Sabinus after approaching his guards and telling them that he had a very important message for Sabinus's ears only. Approaching the general, he would remove a message pouch from beneath his tunic. Inside was a hidden dagger. He meant to plunge it into Sabinus's throat before he could be stopped. He didn't hope to get away without being killed.

"Why me?" Sabinus asked.

"My cousin says you're dangerous. You could persuade others to betray their people like the eleven traitor kings!"

"We have treated the kings and their people decently," Sabinus said.

Cadwal spat. "They're slaves, not free like us!"

"You were free," Vespasian said in a snarling voice. "We're not finished with you yet. We have great things planned for you," he added with a grin. His raven-dark eyes glowed with pleasure.

"And we're not through with you," Cadwal threatened.

"Do something to dull his sharp tongue," Sabinus whispered loudly to his brother.

"There are questions still requiring answers, but that can be done at our leisure," Vespasian said. "Guards!"

Two entered the tent. "Take them away."

He nodded to a centurion. "I want a twenty-four-hour watch kept on these two. Bind them! At no time are they to be out of sight. I wouldn't want them to harm themselves. I will hold you personally responsible for their security."

The centurion saluted and left, along with the guards who had the prisoners in tow.

"Well done," Sabinus said, "you have more than vindicated yourselves, Sergeant. But consider yourself fortunate."

Then he paused for effect. "I like a man who has the courage to be daring, but take care that it does not cost your head. Had it turned out differently, you would have been executed. Nevertheless, I'll give you your due, Spaniard." Vespasian and the rest of the staff nodded.

Inwardly, relief rushed through my body, the muscles relaxing, but outwardly, I kept a sober face. I had not fully comprehended the ramifications of my deeds until Rufius, Crispus, and I stood before the generals. Thank the gods they were in camp. Had Sabinus and Vespasian not visited the garrison, Gallus would have punished me for disobedience, much to his delight, and taken all the credit for himself. Regardless, my squadron had halted one source of attacks on the troop making all the effort worthwhile.

Encountering the generals was an unexpected opportunity for recognition and a small step on the journey to the Equestrian Order. I imagined I had foreseen a mention of the incident in the weekly dispatch to legionary headquarters in Noviomagnus, possibly followed by a minor decoration.

As we were leaving headquarters, I heard Sabinus turn back to the business we had interrupted. "And now Tribune Gallus, about the horrendous conditions of this camp."

CHAPTER 7

The next morning Rufius and I reported to Gallus. As we hiked up the muddy main street of the camp, the grandly styled *Via Praetoria* to headquarters, a cavalry squadron noisily rode by us. Squeaking saddle leather, jingling brass pendants, and muffled sounds of hooves kicking up dirt clods filled our ears.

"Do you know why he wants to see us, sir?" I asked.

"I can guess. Can't you?"

"Because of yesterday, or last night?"

I expected he had more on his mind than the misconduct of my troops. Despite the lateness and foul weather, my men had gone to the tavern and brothel of Rix the Gaul in the village, got drunk and into a fight.

"If it were only the brawl in the village. Gallus is in an evil mood this morning, I hear. General Sabinus ordered him to rebuild the fort."

"Where did you hear that bit of good news?" I asked.

"From my friend, one of Vespasian's retainers."

"Thank the gods, he should have remedied this stinking mess months ago." I heard the scraping of shovels, turned, and spotted a detail of infantrymen, a short distance from us, digging shallow trenches, where tents stood just yesterday. I realized they were preparing foundations for the new barracks.

We walked a little further when Rufius motioned to halt. He looked back toward the building site and said in a lower voice, "They're too far away to hear us, but I'm not chancing it. There is more to the story. Besides ordering Gallus to rebuild the camp, he must pay for the construction out of his own pocket."

I snorted. "Serves the thief right. But he is sure to take his anger out on the troops."

"On us, more likely," Rufius answered. "The general gave him a nasty reprimand for the camp's condition. Then he rubbed Gallus's nose in the mud again."

"How?" We continued our walk down the street.

"He praised you all over again for taking the initiative and flushing out that nest of temple spies. Gallus was seething. Only Gallus's family's influence with the emperor saved him from being cashiered on the spot, according to Sabinus. If Sabinus had his way, Gallus would have been gone, family influence be damned."

Gallus wouldn't allow the general's compliments to pass without taking revenge. A shake slithered up my spine. I feared he was planning something vindictive. I had disobeyed his orders, and gotten away with it. In the process, he was made to look the fool. Worst of all, Gallus would view my deeds as another insult by my family to his.

We entered Gallus's office. A smoky brazier sat on an iron tripod in one corner giving off little warmth. His cold, blue eyes glared at us as from behind the table where he sat. The tribune's Greek clerk, as usual, was busy copying reports. But I caught the Greek's wry smile out of the corner of my eye. To Gallus's right stood a small, delicate, gold pitcher containing an amber-colored wine, probably an expensive Albanian. Close by sat a small ornately gilded drinking cup. He took a slow sip from it, swilled noisily, and then wiped his mouth with a silken cloth. He set the cup on the table and glared once more at me. "You can thank the gods that your prisoners were so valuable, Sergeant Reburrus. Otherwise, you wouldn't have seen dawn."

"Yes, sir," I replied, keeping a bland face, swallowing my contempt for him. The thought of killing Gallus crossed my mind, but his very real authority of life and death over me caused me to refrain from carrying out such a foolish act.

"When I issue orders, I demand they be obeyed. Do you understand?"

"Yes, sir, but the savages—"

"Silence! I'm not finished." Gallus took another noisy gulp of wine and belched. "It seems that you have found favor in the eyes of General Sabinus," he added sardonically. "For some reason I cannot fathom, he thinks you show promise. Personally, I find you insolent and disobedient. Of course, both of us know your true motive, don't we?"

Sextus Rufius gave me a puzzled look. I had never told him of my family obligation. He would have done everything in his authority to discourage me. Both of us had seen ambitious men who made reckless decisions in pursuit of glory. Had I not made the same mistake? This was never my intent, but the promise I made to my mother about becoming a member of the Equestrian Order was turning into a curse.

"From now on," Gallus continued, "he, or rather, *I* will be watching you. Now, listen very carefully," he spoke in a slower more deliberate tone, "if you deviate from future orders in any way, no matter how trivial, you will be immediately court-martialed. Is that clear?"

"Yes, sir."

"Very well." He turned to Rufius. "Decurion, you will be held responsible for his conduct."

"May I say something in his behalf, Tribune?" Rufius asked.

Gallus slightly turned his head in Rufius's direction and scowled. "What is it?"

"Despite his disobedience, Sergeant Reburrus found the secret temple. What was he supposed to do when he saw one of our scouts conversing with the enemy? He did what any good soldier would—kill or capture the enemy."

"It will not be done at my expense," Gallus replied. "It is outrageous enough to pay for the rebuilding of the garrison, but I will not be made a fool of in front of any general, especially Sabinus, no matter how valuable the captives may be."

Gallus delicately clasped the cup again with his manicured fingers and took another swallow of wine. "I am going to impress upon you once and for all the meaning of obeying my orders." For a moment, he studied me with hatred. "What is the penalty for soldiers who desert their posts in time of war?"

For a few seconds, I remained silent. What was his meaning? I had missed something and could not figure out his message. "Death by clubbing, stoning, or flogging, sir, the *Fustuarium*," I answered.

Gallus's mouth twisted into a cat-like smile. "So, you do remember. Yes, by soldiers of the offender's unit. Four nights ago, a sentry on picket duty from the second troop was discovered by the officer of the watch in the bushes plowing a native slut. He was court-martialed yesterday and found guilty. When you're dismissed, report to the decurion in charge of his troop at the parade field. You will participate in his execution."

My body tightened, and my face heated. Now, I understood the meaning of the command.

"You see, Sergeant, the whole camp knows you captured prisoners in disobedience of orders," Gallus lectured. "They don't know the reason, although I am sure they heard rumors, but they know you went unpunished. All they understand is that another man is going to die for his misdeed. I know there is no love lost between you southern Spaniards and the Asturians, but I am sure they are united in believing his breach of conduct was not as serious as yours. No, I cannot court-martial you, but I can make you an example and very unpopular with the rest of your fellow Spaniards." A sadistic grin revealing perfect, white teeth crossed his pale, narrow face.

Outwardly, I wanted to shake, it was all I could do to keep my body under control. I refused to give Gallus the pleasure of seeing my distress. Nearly every man in camp, outside of my own troop, would despise me. I had heard that Avaro, the trooper sentenced to death, had been arrested before my squadron was sent on patrol. He was quite popular in his unit. Now, his friends had been ordered to execute him. I could almost feel their hostility as I, who had escaped a similar death, would participate in clubbing their comrade to death.

Gallus raised a thin eyebrow and inquired in a mocking voice. "Is there something wrong?"

"No, sir."

"Good. Dismissed."

* * *

An hour later, all troops not on guard duty assembled on the parade field outside the fort to witness the execution. Nearly nine hundred men formed into an open square. The weather was cool as the sun peered over the horizon. Gallus stood in the center on a raised, wooden platform accompanied by the senior centurion of Infantry Cohort First Asturum and the senior decurion from the detachment of Cavalry Cohort Hispanorum Vettanom.

In the two months since our arrival, four more troops of thirty horsemen each had been transferred from Moguntiacum, our base in Germania, to Britannia. Except for the crimson plume worn crosswise on the centurion's helmet as opposed to the one worn front to back on the decurion's, the two officers wore similar uniforms of covered, chain-mailed tunics, breeches, and sandaled boots. However, the decurion was subordinate in authority and status to the centurion. Next to the officers stood the standard bearer-signifer, clothed in a ceremonial lion's robe, holding the cohort standard. Two staff trumpeters with long, circular instruments, the cornus, wrapped about their shoulders, stood on the same platform behind the standard bearer.

The senior centurion called the cohorts to attention. Gallus ordered the prisoner brought forward. From somewhere to the rear, ten guards escorted the captive to a position in front and below the commander. Hanging his head, he stood clad in a brown homespun cloak, his hands tied in back, outlined beneath the garment. Gallus nodded and the cornus blared a long, deep note followed quickly by a long, high one.

As the proclamation of execution was read by the senior centurion, Avaro looked skyward. Pink-tinted clouds drifted in pursuit of retreating purple skies. He appeared to be ignoring the edict and inhaled the crisp morning air, not out of fear, which he must have had, but perhaps in deep appreciation for his last glimpse of a bird in flight. Others before him had died miserably in rain and squalor . . . at least his death would not be one hastened by impatient men hating him for their temporary discomfort. It was a beautiful day to live, and to die.

When the centurion finished, the prisoner was prodded by lances to an area near a pile of hardwood clubs. The bearded senior officer turned to the senior decurion next to him. "Carry out the sentence."

The cavalry officer called the junior decurion of Hispanorum Vettanom's second troop forward. "Proceed with the execution," he commanded.

The junior officer saluted, did an about-face, and returned to his men. "Second Troop," he barked, "to your positions. Move!"

The officer did an about-turn. "Second Century," he barked, "to your positions. Move!"

The men left their places, in the formation next to ours, and quick-marched to where the prisoner stood. I fell in behind them. We marched to the pile of hardwood cudgels, each soldier taking one as he passed. Two parallel lines formed, through which the victim would have to pass. After grabbing an instrument of death, I sensed all eyes were on me rather than the prisoner.

Gallus and the other officers turned toward the killing ground to witness the event. He showed no emotion, but I'm certain he enjoyed my sense of guilt and humiliation.

I took my place at the far end of the line. The others glared at me, hatred in their eyes, in their twisted faces, and sneering mouths. They muttered among themselves. Standing next to me was Mardonius, a tall, curly haired squadron leader. "It ought to be you, not him, getting killed." He spat at my feet. "Avaro was one of my best men, you shit eater!"

I tensed and glanced at him. It was all I could do not to smash Mardonius with my club.

"Aye, he was a good lad," another trooper added behind me. "He don't deserve to die, not over a woman!"

"Shut your fucking mouths!" the pocked-face junior decurion roared. The guards brought Avaro forward. He was short but muscular, a tough one to bring down. They ripped off his cloak, and he stood naked with his hands tied behind his back. His grim face swung about, and he glance blankly at the nearby stretcher and grave diggers, who momentarily would carry him to an unmarked grave. After deserting his post, the condemned trooper wasn't entitled to the privilege of cremation. Probably knowing that we were the last faces he would ever see, Avaro stared at us one final time.

The senior officer raised his arm. "Carry out the sentence," he commanded, and dropped his hand. Again, the cornus sounded. The guards shoved the prisoner into the jaws of the gauntlet, and the flogging began. I don't know how he endured such a bashing, the sounds of wood on flesh echoing across the parade field. Silently, he endured the terrible pain as he stumbled, staggered, and spun forward with the fury of each crash to his body. Instant welts, raised from flat-sided blows, and deep gashes spurting blood covered his torso. Repeatedly he fell only to rise again, continuing on his tortuous passage down the line of death. His head and body became a mass of scarlet, bleeding welts. Blood gushed from his nose and mouth and streamed from his hair.

The men had been threatened with decimation. One out of every ten men in the squadron would be executed if they failed to carry out the sentence vigorously. They struck with all their might, crimson-streaked weapons thudding through the air, blood covering the faces and tunics of nearly every trooper.

Naturally, I would be blamed for Avaro's death no matter who struck the final blow. I was determined to put him out of his misery. It wouldn't take long. When he stumbled by, everyone seemed to know my intentions. The gauntlet of raised clubs lowered slowly, all eyes glaring at me as I lifted mine. Hatred itself seemed a living thing. As blood oozed down the side of his face, Avaro looked at me through puffed eyelids that seemed to plead for an end to his suffering. Curses and taunts drifted from the ranks of troopers. He dropped to his knees before me and bowed.

In that instant I turned and saw Gallus watching intently—he knew this would happen. For a fleeting second, he sucked the bottom of his lip as if in anticipation. I raised my club and with one swift smash to Avaro's temple, he fell to the muddied ground dead.

His broken body lay at my feet, fixed eyes staring thanks.

I dropped my weapon in an attempt to control my anger. It was Gallus whom I wanted to club—not this man. I wanted to sit down and weep. I wanted to vomit but swallowed it and stood erect, muscles tight, displaying a sober face.

As the senior centurion sauntered over and examined the body, my eyes locked with those of Gallus. The slightest hint of a smile upon his lips betrayed the stern, expressionless mask he wore and the mocking laughter in his eyes. Determining that the sentence of death had been carried out, the officer gestured to the litter bearers. He returned to the platform and notified Gallus.

When the cohort was dismissed, I handed the squadron over to Crispus for the rest of the day. He understood. I headed for the latrine and vomited. Afterwards, I trudged to the squadron tent and rooted out Crispus's jar of rot-gut wine.

I drank myself into oblivion.

But even as I drank, I knew my destiny and Gallus's were entwined, for the worst.

CHAPTER 8

EARLY APRIL, 44 AD

Within ten days of General Vespasian's order, the camp's reconstruction had been completed. Even Gallus seemed pleased. While the cavalry troops cut and faced logs, the infantry teams constructed the buildings. A new granary and hospital and ten long barracks, each divided into ten rooms quartering as many men, stood adjacent to new headquarters, the *Principia*. The timber walls around the camp were built higher and thicker. Double portals with guard chambers were added on each side of the fort, along with upper-story rooms looking out over the entrance.

However, the cavalry cohort troops constructed their own buildings—they required larger rooms. Unlike infantry, cavalrymen kept their tack where they slept. Saddles and harnesses took up space and could not be left in the elements to rot or be stolen. The quarters required four barracks blocks, housing two troops totaling sixty men, a final tally of two hundred and forty men and officers. Stables for an equal number of horses and one hundred and twenty spare mounts stood across the street.

On a piecemeal basis, over a period of two months, about half of Cavalry Cohort Hispanorum Vettonum had arrived from Germania.

One morning as I walked with him on his daily inspection of the stables, I asked Sextus Rufius when the rest would be transferred.

"They're staying in Germania." Rufius halted at the stall where hawk-faced Indibil was grooming his mare. The decurion pulled up the rear hoof of Indibil's horse. "I see this crack is healing nicely." He released the animal's foot.

"Yes, sir," Indibil said. "I used a coating of pine tar and linseed oil that Sergeant Reburrus recommended. If he hadn't spotted the break, my little Dama would have gone lame."

"Good man, Marcellus."

We continued walking through the stables. "Headquarters says we'll return to Germania at the end of the campaign season," Rufius said.

"Do you honestly believe the report?"

"No, my old bones say we're here, permanently." Rufius inspected the remaining stalls, and we returned to our mounts outside.

The decurion grabbed the front pommel of his saddle and pulled himself onto the gelding. "The men did a fine job building the stables and constructing a decent blacksmith shop."

"Aye, infantrymen don't have the same appreciation we have for horses."

* * *

During the afternoon, Gallus gave the new camp its final inspection and grudgingly allowed the men permission to go into the village.

"Here's money for the men's pleasures," I said to Crispus once the squadron had returned to the barracks. I handed him a small pouch of copper *asses*. The troopers knew I came from a wealthy family. My men were from good peasant stock, but to avoid resentment, I seldom spoke about the family fortune. On special occasions, such as building the barracks, I rewarded them for their hard work. Most of the money would be spent at Rix's tavern and brothel.

"Why don't you go?" Crispus asked.

"This is the men's treat."

"That's not the real reason."

"You know why. Rix is a stinking thief." I had been to his place once since arriving in Britannia. "I hate living a celibate life, but most of his women seemed diseased."

"You're too particular about your wenches."

"Horseshit, I liked the German women. Some were real beauties, and they took baths. Rix's are pigs. No, worse than pigs, flies die under their skirts."

Located on the outskirts of the village, Rix's camp sat across the river from the fort. The place was a motley collection of vermin-infested lean-tos, grimy hovels, tattered tents, clapboard shacks, and wagons. Like festering scabs, they lined the muddy path leading to the base. With their meager pay, the troops bought the displayed wares and trinkets at exorbitant prices. Rix's business, situated in the biggest dwelling, flourished. Only the wine was sold cheap. In turn, the men were freer to pay.

I knew Rix from Germania. He used the same tactic there.

Other buildings belonged to soothsayers, fake healers, fortune tellers, merchants, and other scum-suckers. For a percentage, Rix allowed them to ply their clandestine trades. On the edge of this grimy community, a number of huts housed native women who lived with some of the troops.

For the privilege of not being placed off-limits to the soldiers, Gallus extracted a twenty percent commission on all profits. Rix did not dare complain to General Vespasian. Soon after opening for trade, he had cheated a soldier by serving him a cheap Tarragonian wine after he paid for an expensive Samian. The trooper knew the difference, and Rix lost his left eye to the knob-hilt of a spatha. Upon recovery, Rix reported the incident to Vespasian in Noviomagnus. For his troubles, the general had Rix flogged out of camp. He threatened to crucify the Gaul if he ever complained again about being beaten or cheated by a soldier *he* had cheated. Rix got what he deserved. From what I had heard, the thief should have been blinded twice in each eye.

* * *

Not more than an hour passed before Crispus returned to the barracks. Except for myself, they were empty. I sat on my bunk, sipping hot gruel from a bronze cooking bowl.

Crispus stormed into the room. "That bastard Rix is cheating us again. This time he's gone too far!"

"What now?" I set the bowl on a small iron grate on the floor.

"He's doubled the price of his cheap wine. Worse, on his poxed whores!"

"That son-of-a-bitch!" I said wearily, as I stood up. "He's going to get their money anyway, why not let them get something for it?"

I grabbed my spatha and baldric, strapping them on. "We've been through this before, he never learns." I took my saddle from the high footboard and harness from a post on the wall.

"Let's go. I'll settle this right now."

* * *

The afternoon was cool but sunny as we rode the short distance to the village. The jingling of bronze pendants from the horses' harnesses and creaking of our leather saddles echoed across the narrow placid river to the edge of the settlement. "Why did Rix raise the prices this time?" I asked.

"That pox-brained Albinus shot off his mouth to every trader that you were paying for everything—price was no object—so Rix raised his prices."

Usually, Rix tried his cheating antics on paydays every three months. The next one was still another six weeks away.

"Wait until I get my hands on that dog-faced idiot," I said.

"Albinus or Rix?"

"Both!" I shouted so loud that it startled the horses. I lurched backwards in my saddle as Argento suddenly raised up on hind legs, his front hooves pawing the air. I gripped him tightly around the girth with my legs, leaned forward, said a few soothing words before he settled down. I noticed Crispus had a similar experience.

"That's not all," Crispus said once the horses were calm. "Rix says he's replaced his other women with prettier ones, and these are *guaranteed* to be clean and free of disease. So he has to recoup his expenses."

"Now they're pretty cows instead of ugly ones," I said in a sardonic voice.

"Almost. He claims he's serving better grades of wines, and that he's added Gallic beer and Syrian whiskey to his stock."

"All of it watered down!"

Crispus and I rode through the mire to Rix's place. A light breeze wafted in from the north carrying odors of the bivouac across the river. Here and there domestic pigs burrowed snouts into the mud, rooting out tidbits of garbage.

Outside Rix's tavern eight or nine cavalry mounts stood tied to the hitching rail, stoically waiting for their inebriated masters to return. They swatted blowflies with their stringy tails.

The front flaps of the noisy wine shop opened onto the street. Within the dim, lamp-lit place, troops occupied nearly all of the crude, wooden tables. Drinking and laughing, they played knucklebones, a game using four dice, or little brigands, using two dice and a pegboard. Three comely girls of Gallic or German origin served the tables, coaxing the obvious winners to buy their tables a round. They took more coins than the dice. Compared to the previous smelly and dirty females that Rix once employed, they were neat and orderly—the new expensive and guaranteed-clean types.

Crispus and I entered the tavern and looked about. At the table nearest to the entrance sat Albinus and Kimon across from one another playing knucklebones. Next to Kimon sat Andubal, who watched the game with interest.

"Gods! Venus again!" Albinus complained. "You bastard! You're wiping me out, Kimon!"

On the table three of the four scattered dice had turned up six. Albinus scooped up the dice, examining them quickly. He locked eyes with Kimon, and for a moment a fight seemed imminent. He flung the dice hard onto the table and cursed as only one rolled six, but held his tongue about cheating.

"Shut up, dog face, and pay me," slit-eyed Kimon demanded. "And you can quit eye-fucking them dice."

"That does it, I'm out." Albinus tossed the half-Greek a small, leather pouch of coins, his curses muffled by the clinking coppers.

At the far end of the room several troopers stood in line, including runny-nosed Obulco. Indibil and Severus also waited their turns with the daughters of joy. After drinking enough cheap wine, ten asses must have seemed a reasonable price for a wench. The usual price was three. A small dancing group of tambourine and drum players provided entertainment for the waiting customers. The women rotated from serving in the front of the shop to more profitable duties in the back. A sour old Gallic woman drooling from the mouth sat on a stool next to the access and collected the fees.

Despite the patch over his left eye, Rix saw us at once. He poured wine from a long-stemmed amphora behind the counter. The tall, sly, square-faced Gaul set the wine jug down and strode over to us. Barely acknowledging my presence, he greeted Crispus like a long-lost comrade. The old man embraced him, as claps of dust flew from the sleeves of his wine-stained tunic.

"Crispus, my friend, where have you been?" he lisped with a nasal drawl. Brown, rotting teeth peeked through a drooping, red mustache streaked with gray. "We've missed you."

"It's been no more than an hour, you thieving bastard. You robbed me and the men of every last copper."

Rix feigned a look of indignation, placing a hand on his chest. "My friend, you deeply wrong me. I'm only a poor businessman. After all, I have to make a living."

"Hades, you live like a king!" Crispus retorted. "At our expense."

Rix's breath reeked of garlic. "I would have given you credit, had you asked."

"At twenty-five percent interest? Not this man, you old thief! And by the gods, not my men either."

"But I'm only getting by." He seemed to ignore Crispus's threatening tone.

He turned to me. "Why, Sergeant, what a pleasant surprise. I've not seen you since you first arrived."

I studied Rix's leather face and guessed him to be about sixty, or eighty. "The quality of both your wine and women left a lot to be desired, Rix, so I did without. But that's not why I'm here."

I grabbed him by the throat and squeezed slowly.

"I'm sure you can guess." I glanced around.

Everyone stopped what they were doing.

Kimon, Albinus, and Andubal shoved away the table and stood behind Rix, keeping two of his henchmen at bay. Obulco, and other members of my squadron, moved instantly to where Crispus stood behind me, and I guessed he was keeping an eye on the rest of the crowd. Mardonius, who was at another table nearby, glared at me, not Rix.

I kept a firm grasp on Rix's throat. "You missed me so much that you wanted to keep all my money as a memento of the occasion, but what you really meant to do was honor my return by lowering your prices, didn't you?"

"But there are expenses," he squeaked.

"Lowering your prices beginning now, right?" I squeezed his throat tighter. "And that way I can hunt down the lying dog who said you are trying to cheat me—and kill him instead of you."

"But . . . but—"

I twisted my grip. His faced turned red, and he was near unconsciousness. "Give up, Rix."

"Please." His eyes pleaded.

I eased my grip slightly.

"You're dead, maggot."

"All right, five copper asses," he croaked.

"Bastard! That's robbery."

"Please, I can't go any lower, I swear. Gallus expects it." His earring tinkled.

I opened my hand and dropped him to the floor. "All right, it's still robbery, but it's better than ten."

"As I tried to tell you," Rix explained as if nothing had happened, "these women are of high quality. Why even one of them is the daughter of a German king, and she's clean."

"HORSESHIT! All of your women are princesses, or goddesses of one sort or another. Do you think I'm a fool?" I reached out to grab him again, but he evaded my attempt, raising his hands before him.

"No, I'm telling the truth, Sergeant."

Rix lied out of habit, even when the truth was in his best interest.

"I swear, it's true. Her father is Ataulf of the Chatti." He pulled back his hands

"Old Ataulf, the bandit king? We fought his outlaws for years. Why would he sell you any of his daughters?"

"Pay the five coppers for her services, and she'll tell you," he answered with a knowing grin. "I'll say this, she cost me many silver *dinarii*."

I looked about. "Which one is she?"

"That one." He pointed to a tall, statuesque girl whose auburn hair fell loosely halfway down her back. A green and red, plaid, woolen tunic covered her body well below the knees. The remaining part of her legs and feet were wrapped in wolf skins, for warmth against the cold that knifed through the drafty place. She poured cups of wine for the four cavalrymen sitting in the far corner of the room. One was the blond, scar-faced Mardonius, whose trooper I had killed in the *Fustuarium*. His beefy right hand reached around her as she bent her long-stemmed amphora jug, and he grabbed at her buttocks.

She yelped, almost dropping the vessel. Her expression quickly changed to anger, a frown crossed her full lips. She turned and poured the receptacle's contents on his head.

For a few seconds the thick-limbed sergeant sat stunned. Wine ran down his hair and dripped onto his tunic.

Crispus, the other troopers, and I howled.

Mardonius quickly recovered, brushing back his limp hair. "You fucking slut!" he yelled. "I'll cut your throat!" He yanked the dagger from the sheath hanging on his belt and leaped towards the girl. His friends grabbed and pulled him away just before he stabbed her.

An alarmed Rix rushed between the crowded tables to the drenched Mardonius. He slapped the girl, knocking her to the clapboard floor. He gestured wildly to her with his fists, as if worse punishment was to follow.

"A thousand pardons, good Sergeant," Rix apologized. "I'll see that the slut is severely punished."

"You better, or I'll slice the bitch yet," Mardonius threatened.

"Rest assured I will." He rubbed this throat and swallowed. "In the meantime, your next jug of wine is on me. I'll take care of the damage to your uniform."

The young woman lay on the floor, raising up partially on the elbows, not daring to move. Rix yanked her to her feet, placed her in a hammer lock, and shoved her to the back room. The thin canvas walls did not contain Rix's hateful yelling, in guttural German, his violent slaps, and her pitiful screams. I had seen prostitutes beaten before, but for some reason, punishing this one bothered me. There was something different about her. What it was I couldn't say, except that I didn't want her injured. Mardonius deserved what he got.

Crispus and I sat at a splintery table smelling of rancid wine. A plump, but pretty, blond wench brought earthen cups and a pitcher of water to cut the wine. She poured the dark-red rotgut, showing off ample breasts. "That young one will never learn," she whispered. "She thinks she's a princess."

We nodded, enjoying the view of her firm nipples beneath the thin, woolen top.

"What's her name?" I asked.

"Kyar," she answered.

"She has a lot of spirit," I said.

She narrowed her round, blue eyes. "Spirit? Such a temper could cost her life. Rix is a mean one. He beats us for everything," she replied in broken Latin, displaying a yellowish bruise on her forearm.

"What's your name?" Crispus asked, leering at her breasts.

She flashed a big smile. Her teeth were slightly crooked but still white. "Sigrid, what's yours?"

"Crispus, pretty lass."

"Will I see you later?"

"If you make it worth my while."

"Pay the price, and you won't be sorry." Sigrid winked and went on to the next table.

"She likes you," I said.

"Hades, she probably likes anybody with enough coppers."

I caught Albinus's attention and motioned him to our table. "I want to thank you for backing me with Rix."

"Anytime, Sergeant," he answered and stood before me with a puzzled look, arching a thin eyebrow.

I stared into his watery eyes as if peering to the back of his skull. "As a reward for your loyalty, I'm assigning you to cleaning up the squadron stable for one week, starting tomorrow."

His wide face paled. "What did I do?"

"Bragged about my wealth." I shook my head. "You know I've forbidden any mention of it."

"But it's not true." Albinus swallowed loudly.

I struck the table with the palm of my hand. Everyone stared in my direction. "Two weeks! Don't lie to me, we've known each other too long." I glared at the others and slowly they returned to their drinks and games. "You neither have the common sense of your good father," I continued, "nor that of your older brothers." Albinus's family owned a small vineyard near our *latifundia*. We traded them beef for a good grade of Baetican wine.

Albinus stared at Crispus but didn't say a word, no doubt fearing a third week of duty would be added.

"Not only will you clean each stall, without the assistance of the stable slave," I said, "but you'll be wearing full armor."

"Full armor! It'll get filthy!"

I jabbed a finger in his direction. "You will see that it doesn't. The stalls will be cleaned every morning before roll call. At ten minutes to a stall, you'll have more than ample time to clean them in two hours."

"Two hours!" he whined. "That means getting up before reveille."

"I'll inspect the stalls and your appearance every morning before you report for roll call. For each day you fail inspection, another day will be added to your detail. Is that clear?"

"Yes, Sergeant." He exhaled.

"Very well, dismissed."

Albinus trudged away and left the tavern.

"He's going to be shoveling shit for a long time," Crispus said.

"How did you guess?" We both laughed.

My mind drifted back to the young woman, Kyar. I hoped she hadn't been too badly injured by Rix.

CHAPTER 9

Kyar slowly stepped out of the back room. Red marks puffed on the left side of her face and her eyes watered. She trudged behind the counter, picked up another long-stemmed jug, and resumed her duties at the tables.

After she had waited on a few of the troops, Kyar turned and caught my eye. She strolled over and upon a closer look I noticed she was barely a woman, not more than fifteen. Her smooth complexion and high cheekbones were accentuated by a short, turned-up nose, forest-green eyes, and a small but pouting full mouth.

I grinned. "Do me a favor?"

"Why should I?" she snapped in heavy-accented Latin. "You're no better than the rest."

"You don't know me, but it doesn't matter. Just be careful. Don't do anything that would make Rix hurt you again."

"Why should you care about a slave?"

"I don't like to see anyone being mistreated, including slaves and animals."

She spat, "I'm not an animal, and I won't be treated like one." She splashed my cup and turned away. I shrugged, but followed her pleasing walk with my eyes. Definitely the body of a woman.

"How long has she been here?" I asked Crispus.

"About four months."

"Why didn't you tell me? I made an arse of myself with her."

"You're a grown lad. I figured you'd find out for yourself."

"Thanks, friend. Anyway, she's the one I want. I'll see if she has as much fire in bed."

"Unless she sticks a knife between your ribs first. As for me, I'll take Sigrid. Did you see the size of her jars?" he said, cupping his hands as if holding two large melons at chest level.

We lined up when the women rotated and awaited our turns. I did not have to wait for long. I paid the old Gallic woman, with a decaying smile, ten *asses*, double the going rate for more time with Kyar.

"Oh, you want princess," she said in broken Latin.

I nodded.

One at a time she inserted my two coins to the back of her jaw, found a tooth, and bit them. She grunted and flashed a rotten grin. Perhaps I was wasting my money, but something told me I wasn't.

The woman stood and motioned for me to follow. She turned and hobbled through a dusty animal-skin partition.

I stepped into a large cubicle, a room divided into sections by dirty, leather skins, little more than cribs. There was little privacy. The place reeked of stale sweat and urine, and through the thin partitions seeped the groans of amorous embrace, ruffling of blankets, and whispered conversations and giggles on both sides.

The Gallic woman grunted something I couldn't understand and motioned with her scaly hand. "There."

At the far end, a few feet beyond the other partitions, stood a much larger area, blocked off in goat skins hanging from floor to ceiling.

"Princess room," the woman rasped. "Make much money for Rix." She gave me a snaggle-toothed smile, brushed past me, and hobbled back to the front of the tavern.

As I entered Kyar's room, cockroaches raced up one of the bed-pallet's sides. I felt like complaining to Rix about his palatial pest house, then shrugged. He'd only claim the bugs were princesses or goddesses, too.

Despite the vermin, her attempt to keep the room clean was obvious. The compact dirt floor had been swept free of excess dust, and an empty chamber pot sat at the base of the pallet. A fresh bunch of yellow and white early spring flowers rested in a little terra-cotta vase on the squat table by the stained wall. Despite Rix's beating, Kyar had freshly scrubbed her face and neatly combed her hair into shiny locks, draping over her shoulders. About her was the perfumed scent of chamomile.

Kyar sat on the edge of the straw mattress brooding, staring into empty space. I gently tapped the pallet side with my boot and she slowly raised her head, and viewed me. "Oh, it's you," she said in a voice of indifference. "Humph, favor or not, I see you want me like the rest, don't you? Oh well, what's the difference, you paid for me, so I'm yours."

She pulled off her tunic revealing her full breasts, ample for her tender age, and a well-developed body. Her clothes had only accentuated her form. Shivering, she slid beneath the fur blankets.

* * *

"I'm not used to someone treating me so gently," she said later, as we lay together in the dimly lit room. "You're not like the others, they're animals."

"No reason to be rough. You're a woman like any other, slave or not."

"I'm a princess," she intoned, studying my face for signs of disbelief. "Humph, most men think I'm a piece of furniture, a footstool. But slaves have feelings, too. And I wasn't always a slave," she said bitterly. "My father is King of the Chatti. I will never forgive him for killing my mother and selling me to Rix." Her face turned crimson, she grimaced, and her eyes slowly clouded with tears. I pulled her head to my shoulder, caressed her softly, and ran my fingers through her perfumed, satin hair. I wondered how many times she had told that story to others. Was it true?

Kyar's weeping subsided. "You're so kind to me," she whispered. "I'm sorry I treated you the way I did."

"Pretend that it wasn't me," I soothed. "How long have you been with Rix?"

"About four months. He bought me two or three months before we came to Britannia."

"I've been to Rix's once since our troop arrived. Why didn't I see you then?"

"I must have been recovering from one of his beatings—sometimes its days before I heal."

"That stinking dog!" Didn't Rix realize he was destroying good property, a person of value? What a waste to keep injuring her.

"Please, don't say anymore," she whispered. "Someone might hear and tell him."

I nodded. Although her room was a few feet from the cribs, the whispers and amorous sounds of embrace seeped through the flimsy wall.

"Why did your father kill your mother?" I finally asked.

She gently stroked the bridge of my nose. Spent, I struggled to remain awake as she soothed my brow with gentle circles of her fingers.

"He accused her of sleeping with another man, which was a lie, she loved my father." Kyar seemed ill at ease discussing her tragic past.

Although she wouldn't tell me, I was familiar enough with Chatti customs to know what happened. Most likely, Kyar's mother was stripped naked before the family and flogged through the village stockade by her father. Afterwards, she was shoved into a wicker basket, dumped into a slimy bog, and died a humiliating death by drowning.

"Why would he sell you?" I asked.

"He wanted no reminder of my mother," she answered in a harsh whisper. "He said I resembled her too much."

"What happened?" I said sleepily.

"You don't care, it's all you can do to stay awake!"

Another round of giggling and whispers seeped through the wall.

I grabbed her finger. "Woman, stop putting me to sleep, and I'll listen to you all day."

She pressed her lips together and for a few seconds remained silent as if pondering her next words. "Rix's caravan camped next to my father's stockade the day after he murdered Mother. Father came to me and . . ." Her eyes grew cold, and she drew her blanket tight at her neck and paused. "He sold me. I never knew a man before . . ." She gasped. "Rix took me. Gods, I was butchered by a monster. My insides were torn apart." She paused and quietly sighed. "I was resigned to his raping me, and scared half to death, then he slapped me over and over and then . . ." She stopped, not saying anything for a moment. "I've hated him ever since, and every time he touches me—he knows it."

"Did you try running away?"

Kyar clenched her fist. "Of course, but he caught and beat me. I might have been killed."

"I don't see any marks."

"He can hurt you so the marks don't show. After all, he doesn't want to spoil the goods," she added in a scathing voice.

"That sounds like the old bastard."

Kyar snuggled closer to me. "I hope you return. I want to see you again."

I wondered how many others she had purred those same words to in the night. She sounded sincere enough, and I had to admit she was very good.

"Your time is almost up, so you have to leave, but come back, will you?" she pleaded. "You're so gentle with me, most men aren't."

"I will," I answered quietly and grinned. I put on my clothes and returned to the table where Crispus waited.

CHAPTER 10

Three days later news arrived that General Sabinus had marched to Noviomagnus with two cohorts, nearly one thousand legionaries. To ensure King Verica's loyalty, he took his daughter, Eleyne, as hostage. The following day raiders assaulted five Roman outposts, but inflicted little damage. The accusing finger was pointed at Bodvac, Eleyne's betrothed, who fled Noviomagnus the night she became a *guest* of the Romans.

"I've heard another rumor about moving out. Anything to it?" Crispus asked. He slid the brass scraping strigil across my shoulders, as we sat in the *tepidarium,* the warm room of the camp bath. Despite his ministrations, and taking a dip in the pool's tepid waters, I still felt the intense heat of the *caldarium,* the hot room, coursing through my body, where I had started by sweating off the dust of a long patrol.

"Nothing, but with the campaign season almost here, it's bound to be soon. Then we'll see if Verica will stay in his hill fortress."

Constructed of stone, the small bathhouse sat outside the fort above the river. Fires fed through two brick-enclosed stoke holes at the end of the building. Steam from the heated waters were forced through air channels running under the brick and tile floors and through the walls. Sunlight illuminated the vaulted room through four small, opaque glass windows at the base of the roof. At the far end a narrow hallway lead to the hot room—a light cloud of steam wafted down the passageway in our direction. I wiped the sweat from my brow and glanced towards the god-like bust of Emperor Claudius displayed on a marble pedestal in an alcove of the stone wall. I wondered if he was the fool rumors claimed him to be.

"Gods, we've got his daughter," Crispus said interrupting my thoughts, "that'll keep him tied down, especially after the raids."

"Maybe. But I think they're accusing the wrong man. My gut feeling tells me Verica's advisor, Togidubnus, is the one behind the attacks. He's using Bodvac to divert blame from himself." Known to be Romanized, Tiberius Claudius Togidubnus had ambitions to succeed Verica as the Roman puppet king of the Regni and Atrebates.

"You sound like a politician fixing the blame," Crispus said. He continued scraping down my back. "So what if it's a lackey or a hothead? We're soldiers. Let the generals figure it out."

"It's only a guess," I answered, "but I know this much about the Celts—once they give their word in public, they honor it. Think of Verica's sworn oath to the emperor. That's not to say he will, but I hear Togidubnus hasn't sworn an oath to anyone. He's using Bodvac and ingratiating himself to the Romans at the same time."

"Bodvac didn't give his either," Crispus grumbled. "Anyway, Verica's daughter's still the cause of the raids."

I twisted my head and saw Crispus out of the corner of my eye. "No, the Romans are, taking her hostage. The attacks give Vespasian the excuse he needs to launch another offensive against Caratacus."

"But Bodvac fled to the Durotrigians."

"And we know from Cadwal's confession they are allying themselves with Caratacus." I turned away and watched the steam drifting up as wispy bands of silvery and delicate pearl gray from the heated pool.

"All I can say is, we'd better be marching soon," Crispus said.

"And keep you away from Rix and his lovelies?" I mocked, then winced as he scratched my back sharply.

"You're no different. I saw how you took to that German wench, Kyar. She's a pretty one, but don't let your spear do your thinking."

"Who says I am?"

"By the look in your eyes when we left, your spear's the only brain you have," he said. "Hades, think of her as a good-tumble and nothing else, or you'll get in trouble."

"Like you said once before, I'm a grown lad. I can take care of myself."

He dropped the strigil on the bench, the metallic thud echoing through the small bathhouse. "Aye, but consider this. She'll smile sweetly as long you jingle your coppers, but short her one copper *as* and she'll claw your eyes out."

"Gods, you act as if I'm going to marry her."

Crispus stood and threw off his towel. He jumped into the warm pool and splashed me, then spat out a mouthful of water.

"I didn't say you were. But it wouldn't be the first time a man has fallen for a whore."

He bobbed his head again, which gave me a moment to suppress a flash of temper. "She's not one by choice. Any other objections?"

"Yes. She can't cook!" he retorted. "All she can do is—" His voice trailed off, and he grinned.

Emerging from the pool, Crispus retrieved his towel and dried off. "I know it's not her fault, but it's obvious some women don't mind. That doesn't bother me, it's Rix."

"What about that thief?"

"You know he's a treacherous bastard. He'll do anything to fuck up your intentions, if you have any. If nothing else, he'll raise the price if you buy her."

"My only intention is to enjoy her every chance I get."

"Just beware friend, anything can happen. Personally, I think any man's a fool who gets himself tied to any female. I like my freedom."

* * *

That evening I visited Kyar. Rix seated me at an empty table in a corner of the tavern. The place was ablaze with the light of foul-smelling candles and smoky olive-oil lamps. Kyar waited on the nearby tables. She spotted me, and a broad smile crossed her lips, but her expression quickly changed, her look sober. No doubt she didn't want her besotted customers to get the wrong idea.

She strolled by my table and, bending over, poured my cup. "You came back," she whispered in surprise. Her beautiful white teeth sparkled.

"I promised, didn't I?"

"But I didn't believe it. You know how soldiers are, making promises, but never keeping them."

"I suppose a lot don't." I'd been guilty myself.

"Where's your friend?"

"Crispus? He's on picket duty. Why?"

"Oh, nothing. Sigrid will be disappointed, though. She likes him."

At a table across from us, Sigrid giggled uproariously while being pawed by a drunken infantryman. Another soldier lay passed out next to his feet.

I shrugged. "His loss. Right now, I'm more interested in how Rix is treating you."

Kyar pursed her lips. "The same," she answered.

"You know you've got to stay out of his way."

"I know, but—"

"No arguments," I whispered. "If you don't start behaving yourself, he'll kill you. I won't let it happen, do you understand? You're too—" I paused, struggling for the right word. "Too nice," I added, immediately unhappy with the word.

"I'll try."

"Good, that's all I ask."

She moved on to the other tables, promising to return shortly.

I sat drinking and waiting for her, and watched fat, ugly cockroaches racing up the leather hided wall, disappearing behind the pole of the wooden frame that supported the tent. I scratched my cheek and wondered why I was so intrigued with Kyar. True, she was young and pretty, but there was a bit more than just her womanhood. I reached beneath my tunic and absently jingled the copper coins in my pouch hanging from the waist of my breeches—the ones Crispus assured me I'd need.

Kyar had been forced into prostitution or die. I didn't like the word whore, but it was true. In spite of her situation, she intruded on my thoughts several times while on patrol, taking my mind from my duties.

She reminded me of a beautiful lynx—hostile, suspicious, and lashing out when attacked or mistreated. Kyar literally had fire in her eyes. Yet she responded to kindness and tenderness, and after being in Rix's clutches for nearly five months, needed a lot of it. The degrading conditions of slavery bring out the worst in the best of people.

Kyar returned. "I'm going to my cubicle now. Hurry, get in line so you'll be with me first."

I paid the old Gallic woman triple the usual rate, allowing me three hours with Kyar. She led me to Kyar's room.

This time there wasn't any resignation in her voice. "Here, let me," Kyar said, helping me to pull off my tunic. Quickly, she unlaced the front of my blue, woolen trousers. As I dropped them, she squirmed out of her long, tartan tunic and slipped between the furs on her bed pallet.

I slid in beside her. I brought my hand to her face, and with the tip of my fingers stroked the line of her soft, curving jaw.

"No, Marcellus, I want you now, the caressing can wait."

Before, when I had given myself to Kyar, I thought I knew what love making was all about. But she gave herself like a woman seeing her man off to war, returning the passion tenfold. We became one, as if in communion with the gods. Our love making swirled in a maelstrom of ecstasy, rising to heights I never dreamed possible. In a sublime moment of rapture, we responded to one another's most subtle movements. Was this the magic promised by the muses, by Ovid and Sappho? A magic you never wanted to end?

I don't know how long we made love—I wanted it to last forever. Then in a final burst, we came together, our voices crying as one. Gradually, we melted away, spent, briefly drifting off to sleep.

* * *

Later, as I held Kyar in my arms, she told me about her life among the Chatti. She was amused to learn that I had fought her people and considered them bandits.

"You are no better than we, bandits indeed," she chided in a harsh whisper. "After all, you're the invaders. My father fought for what was rightfully his. The land belonged to our people before you Romans came."

"So you're a politician among your other talents," I teased. As always, sounds of passion from the other couples seemed to seep through the leather walls.

Playfully, she gave my cheek a soft slap. "That's not funny. He is my father, and was defending our homeland." She stroked my brow. "You know I might have seen you at a distance when my father fought you Romans."

"How do you mean?"

"The women followed the men to battle. We brought food and tended their wounds. We compared the gashes of men folk with warriors belonging to other women. We were so proud. My father and brothers had the most wounds—they were the bravest of all our fighters."

"You mean they didn't think about survival?"

"Dying is better than being captured, or fleeing like a coward. Before going into battle we reminded the men of what could happen to their wives and daughters if they were taken as slaves."

"What did you do?"

"We screamed warnings, and then bared our breasts. It was enough. You killed many of our men, but never captured us."

"But your father sold you."

"Yes," she answered slowly. "Yes, he did." Kyar bit her lip, and tears streamed from her eyes. For a moment, she wept. "My mother was innocent of my father's charges, but I'm not. No man will ever want me, not a whore."

I understood. The Germans considered any young woman who lost her virginity before reaching the age of marriage an outcast and a slut. "Maybe not a German—"

"No man," she retorted, "and I hate what I am, I hate it!"

"There are men who'd want you."

She made a sound of contempt. "Not good men. It doesn't matter, even if no man wants me, one of these days I'll be free."

"Maybe you will." Thoughts raced through my mind. It was too early to consider taking Kyar as a concubine. Months of campaigning loomed ahead of us, and no one knew how far the army would advance before constructing another permanent base. And what would my mother think about my taking a woman? After all, if I gained admission to the Equestrian Order, she would expect me to take a proper Iberian, or better yet, a Roman wife. And, as custom dictated, she would arrange the marriage. Because it was illegal, a slave wife would be out of the question. My father, had he been alive, would have understood my situation. Many knights kept mistresses. I could buy any woman I wanted, that was my right. As heir to the family fortune, Mother did not have the power to disinherit me. And no man can wait forever to keep a woman. Nonetheless, I preferred Mother's approval.

"Your mind is wandering again, Marcellus," Kyar said, gently tapping the bridge of my nose.

"Sorry, but when I'm with you I feel I'm in another world."

"Oh?" she pretended offense. "I didn't know I had such an effect on men."

"Of course you didn't," I grinned. And Zeus doesn't live on Mount Olympus either.

Another minute passed. "You have to go," Kyar said quietly. "Come back soon, will you?" She stroked my face tenderly. "You're too good to me."

I dressed, kissed Kyar, and departed. I passed Mardonius, waiting just outside, her next customer. I suddenly felt compelled to strike, although I settled for an accidental bumping. He cocked his right arm and balled his hand into a huge fist. For a moment, I thought he was going to throw a punch. I stared into his blue-gray eyes, daring him to make the next move.

"The line for goats and boys is around back," I snapped. "This line is for women." His eyes flashed. He mumbled something unintelligible, spat at my feet, and turned away entering Kyar's cubicle. I left hurriedly from Rix's.

CHAPTER 11

MID-APRIL, 44 AD

A couple of days after I had seen Kyar, Legion Headquarters received word of large movements of Durotrigian warriors raiding local farms, west of our outpost. At the instigation of Caratacus, they confiscated livestock and murdered every peasant—men, women, and children alike.

Early, the following morning, as an icy rain pounded in sheets against the camp's buildings, Gallus summoned every decurion and sergeants from the cavalry cohort to his office. He had received orders to flush out the enemy from every suspected area, including Druid temples. General Vespasian ordered all temples razed. After relaying his instructions, the tribune dismissed all the leaders but me, whom he ordered to stay behind.

"Had you waited a few more weeks, Sergeant Reburrus," he lectured me, as I stood at attention in his office, "you could have destroyed the Druid Temple in obedience to orders."

"Yes, sir," I answered, puzzled as to what his true reason was for ordering me to stand by. For a moment, Gallus scanned the half-dozen thinly stripped message tablets, made of alder wood, on his desk.

"Instead," he continued, "you suffered yourself the humiliation of executing a fellow soldier and hatred of the men."

Surprisingly, there had been little animosity vented toward me since Avaro's death. Why was Gallus reminding me of events still fresh in my mind? He had spoken little to me since the execution, partly due to the fact I avoided anything that would draw his attention.

"But we wouldn't have broken the spy ring and learned about Caratacus's movements," I reminded the tribune, "if I hadn't raided the temple."

With one swipe of the hand, he scattered the tablets onto the floor, the noise bringing his Greek clerk from the next room. Gallus waved him away. "Insolent as ever! How fortunate the generals were inspecting the camp." His cold eyes glared up at mine.

"I had no prior knowledge of their planned inspection, sir."

He raised his nearly invisible eyebrows. "Indeed, Castor and Pollux must favor you. The gods of good luck often protect fools."

The muscles in my body tightened. I gritted my teeth but managed to keep a straight face.

"I have written my father," he continued, "about your tricks."

"Tricks, sir?"

"The attack on the temple, Sergeant, what else? If General Sabinus has any plans for your future, which I doubt, my father shall see that Emperor Claudius squashes them. Don't waste your efforts on becoming a hero."

"I won't. In combat, good soldiers don't have time to think about heroics. We're too busy killing the enemy and trying to stay alive."

"See that you remain a good soldier," Gallus warned, "or you may *not* survive. Now, get out!"

I left his office barely containing my anger. Gallus didn't have enough strength to deal with me on his own. Now my father's old enemy was dragged into this absurd matter—all this for a knighthood. I couldn't understand how one equestrian made a difference to the Gallus family. Was this an example of the ruthless power his people used against anyone they considered a threat to their interests? Why had I been singled out? Did he embrace all his father's foes as family enemies? I could never be his rival. I had no aspirations for the Senate, nor the money, one million *sesterces,* required to qualify for that lofty position. I realized Gallus's cold heart pumped larger quantities of hatred and bigotry than blood.

* * *

I returned to my troop who were already saddled, waiting to go on patrol. The rain had stopped, the sky clearing, puffy, white clouds receding in the distance. Rufius gave me a questioning look. I was about to explain when he told me to mount up. "We'll discuss it later," he said.

The troop headed out of camp, and we rode westward, searching the last area where the marauders had been sighted.

About midafternoon the unit crossed the top of an oak-covered ridge. Below, in a narrow valley, lay the charred remains of a peasant's farmstead. We investigated the blackened ruins, smoke still wafting above the charred debris. I discovered the bodies of a husband, wife, and three small children who had been hacked to death. A black stream of ants crawled over the bodies, and flies buzzed about. I was sickened. What the barbarians hadn't burned, they took with them. Dozens of horse tracks and the hoof prints of cattle left a wide trail leading westward.

We searched the place further but found no survivors. After burying the victims, our horsemen set off after the killers, following the tracks most of the afternoon through fields and across numerous small streams. We gained on the outlaws as their trail of broken wine jugs grew fresher and wetter. Soon, the troop would clash with them. My chest tightened. A knot developed in my stomach. Perspiration ran down my face. I experienced the same feeling before every conflict—the fear of death, and how I would acquit myself in battle. Never had I acted in a cowardly manner, but I still prayed I wouldn't fail to do my duty.

As we approached the crest of a ridge covered by beech and yews, the point man Andubal galloped back from the top. Rufius signaled a halt and briefly conversed with him. The decurion beckoned for the sergeants. We dismounted and followed the commander through the bushes. The four of us spotted about forty or fifty enemy horsemen crossing the valley's half-moon shape floor below, herding a nearly equal number of horses and cows.

"Look at all that loot," Edecon said in a low voice, gesturing to the booty-laden spare mounts.

"They're an overconfident lot," I added. Bunched together, the barbarians deployed neither a rearguard nor forward scouts on their flanks, as they headed for the great forest of fir and pine trees at the other end of the small valley.

"Aye, but we've got to cut them off before they reach the woods and scatter," Rufius added. "Back to our mounts. Move out!"

* * *

The battle was over almost as quickly as it had begun. The few surviving bandits fled, swallowed by the forest. Our troop tended to the wounded and laid the dead over their horses, for return to camp and a decent cremation. Our troop of thirty lost six men including two of mine, Albinus and Severus. The Durotrigians lost more than forty, plus five wounded prisoners we executed.

Including those belonging to the raiders, we confiscated the cattle and over eighty horses. The stolen goods included a huge cache of full beer and wine jugs. I also hacked off the finger, containing a silver boar's head ring, from a savage I had slain. After pulling off the ring, I tossed the bloody appendage away.

Later, the patrol returned by way of the ruined farmstead. As we rode by, Corribilo spotted a boy, not more than ten years old, scavenging through the debris. The lad saw us and ran, but Corribilo quickly caught up to him on his mount. He lifted the youngster, who pummeled him with his little hands, off his feet and onto his horse. The sergeant pulled to a halt, grabbed the child's arms, and in his own language spoke to him in soothing words. Corribilo was our interpreter.

Riding back to us, Corribilo pulled up, the youth now calmer. "The dead people we found are the boy's family," Corribilo said. "He'd been up in the hills when the raiders attacked the farm, and hid in the bushes. Then he saw us and thought we were raiders, too."

"What's his name?" Rufius asked.

"Chulainn, sir," Corribilo answered. "He says he refuses to leave his home."

"He doesn't have a choice," Rufius said. "I'm not going to leave him to starve or to be butchered by another pack of savages."

"What are we going to do with him, sir?" I asked.

"There is a peasant's farm near our base," Rufius said as he looked back over his shoulder. "He seems to be one of the more prosperous ones, if there is such a thing in this land. We'll leave the boy with him."

Corribilo brought Chulainn along. When we reached the farm, Rufius persuaded the farmer into taking the boy. The decurion offered him three cows as payment, a fortune because these people seldom owned more than one or two. Chulainn pointed to a brown, spotted-faced cow, among the herd we had confiscated, and claimed it had belonged to his family. He asked the farmer to accept the animal as one of the three. Rufius nodded, satisfying the boy.

I approached Chulainn when the others returned to their horses and gave him the boar's head ring. I wasn't sure why I did, except I knew it to be valuable, and it was my way of partially compensating him for the loss of his family.

As we rode away, Chulainn waved farewell. We had drawn first blood in the spring offensive, and the men were anxious to return to camp with their tales of heroism.

"What did you give the lad?" Rufius asked as I rode by his side.

"Nothing significant, sir, a boar's ring," I had threatened the old farmer, perhaps too harshly, with an oath of what would happen if Chulainn *lost* the silver ring, or met a sudden death.

I wondered if I would ever see the lad again.

CHAPTER 12

MAY, 44 AD

During the first week of May, at morning roll call, Sextus Rufius notified the troop the spring offensive would be launched in two weeks against the Durotrigians. Breaking their pledge to remain neutral, they had allied themselves with Caratacus. The cohort had been ordered to join Legion Second Augusta during the second week in May, and preparations for the march would begin immediately.

Although pleased the cohort was included in the new campaign, I hated leaving Kyar behind. Rix sold his women on a regular basis. If she were bought by another slaver, I would never see her again. In the meantime, I was determined to visit her as often as possible.

That evening, I returned to the tavern and paid the old Gallic woman triple to spend additional time with Kyar.

As we lay together, after our love making, I told her about our unit's plan to leave on campaign.

She gasped. "What? So the rumors are true about the army leaving? I didn't want to believe them. I can't stand the thought of your leaving."

I pulled her closer to me, smelling her sweetly scented auburn hair. "Unfortunately, they are, but don't fret, I've made up my mind."

"About what?"

"I'm going to see Rix, and make an offer for you." I pulled on the blanket.

Kyar pushed herself away and looked me in the eyes. "You really mean it? You're going to buy me as your woman?"

"Of course, I am," I answered, puzzled by her question. "Don't you believe me?"

Kyar sighed. "I was hoping you would, but you know how soldiers are. They'll say anything to have their way with women."

"I'm not that kind," I countered. Gently, I took her in my arms and lightly kissed her naturally pouting lips. "I truly want you for my woman."

"Please, be careful, Marcellus." Even in the murky light of the cubicle, Kyar's dark-green eyes seemed to be pleading, and she clung to me as if something fearful would happen if she let go. "He'll rob you if you're too eager."

"The old thief will anyway. I know how to barter, I'll get the price down."

Rix's price for Kyar would be exorbitant. He knew I was from a rich family. By army standards, I carried a lot of money, but for the purchase of Kyar, I feared it wouldn't be enough. If Rix's final offer was too high, would he be willing to take a partial payment from me until I received the balance from home? Would he accept a token of security guaranteeing she would not *work* while I was on campaign? Naturally, she would have to remain with him, an idea I considered revolting, but this was an unusual situation. No one other than Gallus had the money I needed, and I wasn't about to ask him for a loan. Not wanting to alarm Kyar, I wouldn't say anything unless it reached that point.

"You'll still pay too much," Kyar said, pulling me out of my thoughts.

I studied her soft face, accented by high cheek bones and a small turned-up nose, and smiled. "You're worth it."

Our time was up, and after I got dressed, Kyar kissed me for luck.

"I'll return as soon as I make the deal," I promised.

Outside in the bar area, I approached Rix, who wore his usual wine-stained tunic and breeches, as he argued with a trooper over the price of a dancer. A few minutes later we entered his dingy, makeshift office and sat at an expensive sandalwood table covered with parchments, an inkwell, and stylus. I took a seat on a wooden stool across from him.

"You know she's my best woman," Rix said, after I offered to purchase Kyar. He narrowed his gray right eye, the left covered by a greasy patch. A mocking black-toothed grin crossed his blotchy square face.

"Is she?" I asked. "A *worthless slut* were the words you used a few seconds after the fight the evening I first saw her."

He pushed aside the documents with scarred fingers, the nails cracked and filthy, and folded his arms. "Nonetheless, she's in great demand. For all the problems she causes, she brings in a lot of money. If I decide to sell her, the price will be very high."

"From you, that's no surprise."

"This isn't a game, you know, it's business," he added in a voice of contempt, gesturing toward me.

I bit my tongue and controlled my eagerness. "How much?"

"Five thousand sesterces," he said.

I slapped the table, palm down, the sound carrying beyond the office confines. "Outrageous, three hundred! One hundred more than any whore is worth." Kyar was no whore in my eyes, but I dared not tell Rix, or his asking price would soar.

"And you're insulting. I'm a businessman," he answered in a snarling voice. "You know she's special. Besides, you're a rich soldier from an important family. However, for you, I'll let her go for forty-five hundred."

"Seven hundred."

"The guards, where are they when I'm being robbed?" he cried, gesturing his hands skyward in prayer. "Not a sesterce less than four thousand!"

The haggling went on for another half-hour. "I'll give you two thousand sesterces, and that's my final offer, it's all I have," I said.

"Sold," he snapped. He shook his head in mock defeat. "You drive a hard bargain, Sergeant, no wonder you're rich."

"And you made a huge profit. Remind me never to buy a horse from you."

"Likewise, my Spanish friend."

Now came the moment I was dreading. I barely had twelve hundred sesterces in the cohort bank, equivalent to more than eight year's pay, and a fortune to most soldiers.

I planned to hold back two hundred for emergencies. But would Rix agree to my proposition?

"Rix, there is one problem?" I said uneasily.

"Oh. What is it?" his lips twisted into a sneer.

"I can only pay half now, but I can give you the other one thousand in three months when it arrives from Hispania." I could get it in two, but there might be delays. I needed extra time.

Rix glared, studying me for a moment. "That wasn't part of the bargain, Sergeant," he said in a growling voice. "You tricked me into believing you had the money. That's not how I run a business. Unless you have the money agreed upon, the wench is not for sale!"

A sense of desperation welled within me. I had to remain calm and somehow convince Rix of my sincerity and, above all, that he was getting the better deal. I wasn't about to lose Kyar when I was so close to claiming her for my own.

"Consider this, Rix," I explained, "you'd get half of my money and this." I pulled from my money pouch a small but heavy gold belt buckle covered by a protective plaque. The center motif contained the hammered formed images of a dozen tiny warriors fighting lions on a granulated background, bordered on four sides by stylized palm leaves. I handed it to him.

Rix's eyes widened in awe as he rubbed his fingers over the palmettes. "Where did you get this little treasure?"

"It belonged to my father, which I carry in his memory. It's an ancient Turdetanian warrior's ceremonial belt buckle."

"You would give this to me for a woman?"

"I want it back, Rix. Consider it as security towards her upkeep, which I'll pay in addition to the balance of her purchase."

Rix seemed to ponder the proposal for a minute. I could almost see him praying to the gods for my death so he could keep my family heirloom. A trace of a smile appeared on his lips. "All right, I'm a fool, but I'll accept your absurd offer. Half now, and a quarter more by tomorrow! There will be an additional charge of twenty-five percent interest on the unpaid balance," he spouted. "After all, if a better offer came along after concluding the agreement, I couldn't sell her, I'm an honorable man." This from Rix the thief, in an indignant tone. He waved his hands with great animation. "And what if you're killed? Your cohort leaves within two weeks."

"If I die you'll still have my money and Kyar. Either way you gain."

An evil grin crossed his fetid mouth. "Aye, so I will. Pray that you survive."

Where could I get a quarter more? Impossible.

And then I knew where and hated the answer.

"Agreed," I snapped, before reconsidering the consequences and true cost of my plan.

"You'll have no more than three months to pay the balance," Rix continued, "otherwise she stays, and so does your deposit. If the money is lost or stolen en route, that's your problem, not mine—three months!"

A sense of relief rushed through my body, but almost as quickly, a queasy feeling churned my gut. "You'll get it," I answered.

I was about to turn away when something else crossed my mind. I stood and leaned across the table and glared into Rix's cruel eyes. "One other matter, you are to leave her alone," I warned. "Outside of waiting on tables and cleaning the bar area, she is not to work, you know what I mean? If I hear so much as one rumor that you've harmed Kyar, I'll cut your balls off and stuff them down your throat—understand?"

"I assure you nothing will happen," he answered soberly. "I value my life, not to mention money and what's between my legs, too highly to waste either on a whore, I mean, slave."

"Don't forget!"

* * *

As I rode Argento up the Via Praetoria, the fort's torch-lit main street and surrounding barracks were deserted. Except for the glum sentries patrolling the wall's catwalks and key buildings, most of the men were at Rix's. It was the third hour after dusk, and I started having second thoughts about approaching Gallus this late in the evening. Perhaps I should have waited until morning. But I couldn't stay away. I had to get an answer about the money now.

Approaching the Principia, the whitewashed headquarters building that doubled as Gallus's home, I noticed a glow filtering through the wooden archway at the entrance to the courtyard. After dismounting my bay, I asked the guard on duty if Gallus was in his office.

"Aye, Sergeant, he's working late." The bored sentry waved me through.

I tied my horse to the hitching post and passed through the cobblestoned courtyard and by the cohort chapel. Inside, raised on a wooden platform above the floor, the standards of six centuries from the infantry and four from the cavalry troops stood in a half-circle, around the life-size statue of Emperor Claudius. Dressed in the uniform of a general, the bust's youthful face was illuminated by an equal number of oil lamps.

At the nearby adjutant's office, Gallus's Greek clerk busily filed several documents in the cubbyholes of a wall cabinet containing hundreds of wax tablets. A smoky brazier and three olive oil lamps dimly illuminated the office. I rapped the wooden counter, jolting the slave out of his thoughts.

I told the servant to inform his master that I requested permission to see him.

A moment later, the Greek returned and nodded to Gallus's office door.

I stood at attention in the murky lamplight, while Gallus kept me waiting as he scanned and signed the parchments on his desk. A few minutes later he glanced up from the reports and inspected my appearance. "At least your uniform is still fit, Sergeant. Unlike you, I have responsibilities, and little time for drinking and whoring."

The words were difficult for me to mouth. Humiliated. Desperate. I hated asking a family enemy for a favor. No doubt he would enjoy my squirming.

"I came to you, sir," I answered, "because you're the only one who can help me."

Gallus dropped his reed pen into the pot of lampblack ink. He pursed his lips and nodded. "You're asking my help? You must be desperate."

"I need a loan."

The tribune raised his nearly invisible eyebrows. Slowly a smile, like a cat who has cornered a mouse, appeared on his thin lips. "Aren't you being presumptuous that a superior officer would loan a subordinate money?"

"You know my family is good for the cash, sir. I can repay you in about three months, when I receive the amount from home."

"True, you are rich enough. Should I consider your request, how much would you need?"

"Five hundred and fifty sesterces."

Pulling on his chin with a thumb and forefinger Gallus studied my face. "Why do you need the money?"

"I'm buying a woman, Kyar, from Rix." I wasn't about to ask him for the entire balance, although it meant she had to stay with Rix. No doubt I was making a mistake, but my pride wouldn't allow me to ask Gallus for any more than necessary to satisfy that camp-following pimp.

Gallus crinkled his nose in disgust. "I might have guessed this involved a whore."

I winced at his snide remark. I wanted to strike him but dared not. I could not even clinch my fists. I was still at attention. He would have seen them at my side and considered it an act of insubordination.

"I will give you credit for your taste," Gallus added in a more amiable voice. He dropped the hand from his chin and poured a cup of wine from a jug sitting on one side of the desk. "If the rumors I've heard are true, she's certainly an improvement over the women Rix has provided in the past." He took a noisy gulp.

His words jolted me. This wasn't the Gallus I knew. Why the sudden friendliness?

"All right," he said, "I will grant your loan. You can stand at ease." As I relaxed, Gallus called his clerk and whispered something in the Greek's ear, who nodded and left the office.

"What are the terms for repayment?" I asked, certain he would add an outrageous usury rate, like Rix.

"My loan is interest free."

For a few seconds, I stared at him. What was his motive?

"Why does that surprise you?" Gallus asked in a cordial voice, as if he had been offended by his best friend.

"Most lenders charge interest, sir," I answered as diplomatically as possible. "I wasn't expecting your terms to be so generous. After all, this is a business proposition."

The clerk reappeared and handed Gallus a small bulging, leather pouch, clinking with the familiar sound of coins.

Gallus handed me the sack as soon as the servant departed. "Of course," he added, "I may ask a favor from you in the future."

"What kind, sir?" Naturally, he wanted something in return, no doubt, far higher than any interest rate.

"An honorable one of course. Nothing, I'm sure you wouldn't hesitate to grant. I will tell you at the appropriate time."

Besides money, what else could Gallus want? His family was one of the richest in Rome. I had been on my best behavior since my humiliation at Avaro's execution. I was posted in the most remote and gods-forsaken province in the empire, considered by many as a form of punishment. However, in my desperation, I would have said anything not to lose Kyar.

"The favor is yours!" I told him.

* * *

Back in Kyar's cubicle, we sat on the bed-pallet. I explained that she had to stay with Rix until I received the rest of the money.

"Must I?" she groaned, clinging tightly to my shoulders. "I hate him!"

"You have to stay, only three more months."

"I'll die!"

"I hate it as much as you, but Hispania is far away." I motioned with my head toward the room's entrance. "It'll take that long for the money to arrive. The worst part is your purchase must be conducted as a business matter."

"Like a piece of property." Her naturally pouting lips turned into a frown.

"You're not to me," I answered, trying to reassure her, "but to the law, you are."

"How much did you pay?"

"Two thousand sesterces."

"Two thousand! By Great Tiu and Donar, he robbed you," she blurted, but, at the same time, seemed pleased, judging from the hug she gave me. "He bought me for eight hundred, and that's because I'm a princess."

"You're worth every copper."

"No, I'm not. But I would have died if you hadn't paid the price." Tears came to her eyes. "The idea of being with another man makes me sick. I don't know if I can do it any longer. I hate being a whore."

"You're not any longer."

A gasp erupted from deep in Kyar's throat. "No, Marcellus, you don't mean it."

"It's true, I gave Rix a personal item as a measure of security. He's promised you'll never be used again—by anyone."

"Are you sure? He's so evil. What if he forces me when you're gone?"

"He won't but you must behave. The time will pass quickly, you'll see. When I receive the money, you won't have to live like this. You'll be my woman and no one else's."

"Oh, to be your woman, I want it so much." I held her in my arms as we sat in silence. Kyar was soft and warm to the touch, and I ran my hand through her long, sweet hair. She sighed, tracing the line of a thin scar along my shoulders. "I'll watch my temper, but please hurry, get the money. I'm afraid of Rix—I'm afraid." She clung to me, not unlike a frightened child.

"He's been warned. He's a dead man should any harm come to you, but don't provoke him either."

"I know he wants you killed. He hopes you won't survive the campaign, and he can keep the money. I have been with Rix long enough to know he wants everything both ways."

I kissed her and grinned. "Rix's in for a disappointment, I'm coming back. But I'm not gone yet, we have a few more days."

We made love again before I reluctantly departed. As I said good-bye, Kyar pleaded with me to stay just a little longer. I dared not. We kissed again before I insisted I must go.

"I love you," she whispered. "Hurry back."

I forced myself to leave the room before better judgment gave way. I couldn't bring myself to say that I loved her, too.

From childhood I was taught a strict division exists between Roman citizens, freedmen, and slaves. I broke the prohibition by falling in love with a woman, who in the eyes of Rome was a slave and prostitute. In my eyes, she was still a princess, even if she was a so-called barbarian, and I planned to give Kyar freedom after an acceptable period of time elapsed.

* * *

Fearing that someone might intercept the letter, I wrote my mother that night in the old Turdetanian language, asking for money and explained the reason. I didn't mention that Kyar was a prostitute. Mother would have never understood, deeming it a hindrance in my future admission to the Equestrian Order. However, I knew of men who had been admitted with far greater omissions.

The next morning, I took aside the legion courier, transporting military dispatches to Hispania and Rome, and gave him my letter. I slipped him twenty pieces of silver for the risk involved carrying private letters against regulations. He said for that price he would break all the rules. I assured him if there was an answer to my letter, he would receive the same again for his troubles.

After concealing the folded parchment, he spurred his Gallic mount and bolted for the camp gate. Soon he was out of sight heading down the road to the harbor of Noviomagnus. As I hiked back to the barracks, I prayed to Melkart that I would receive the money in time to free Kyar from the clutches of Rix.

CHAPTER 13

The stables reeked of urine-soaked straw and steaming manure. As I passed the slave groom cleaning the stall, I spotted Crispus at the far end, bridling his mare for the afternoon drills. I checked the adjacent stalls, making certain no one was about.

"You're acting secretive, Marcellus," Crispus said. "What are you hiding?"

Earlier, I had explained to Crispus that upon discharge he would receive Roman citizenship and could marry any Roman female who would have him, a fact he knew well. I suggested he search for a rich widow who would leave a legacy, setting him up financially for life. The empire was full of legacy hunters.

"Remember our conversation this morning about marrying a Roman citizen?"

Crispus gently slipped the snaffle bit into the dappled gray's mouth and pulled the bridle over its ears. "What of it? May I be sacrificed to Melkart before marrying any poxed woman."

I cleared my throat. "I have a similar problem, but in reverse."

Crispus turned from his mount and scowled. "And I can guess who she is."

A horse at the far end of the stable whinnied. I listened for approaching footsteps, and, except for the sound of the slave's rake, there wasn't any movement. "Crispus, this is to remain between you and me. No one is to know, understand?"

"Don't I always keep my mouth shut?" He turned back to his horse.

I raised a palm and dropped it. "I bought Kyar."

"You didn't!" Crispus jerked too tightly on the throat latch, and the mount snorted and snapped its head from side to side.

"Quiet!" I warned, hearing shuffling footsteps coming our way. Obulco and Andubal entered the near end of the stable, carrying saddles and bridles, heading for their horses. Another minute passed while Crispus soothed his mare.

He locked eyes with me. "I should know better than offer a man advice on a horse or a woman. But since you're asking, don't do it! You're letting your spear do the thinking." He bared his teeth.

I shook my head. "No, I'm not. I've given this much thought. I want her, and she feels the same way. The trouble is, I only had half the money, and sent a letter home asking for the rest."

Crispus rebuckled the bridle's nose band. "That's worse! Rix will sell her as soon as we move out, long before you get your money."

Obulco, who had placed the saddle blanket on his mount, started over to join the conversation. Crispus barked, "Bugger off!"

"He's greedy," I continued, "but he's a coward and values his life more. Besides, I gave him my father's gold belt buckle for security. Kyar won't have to work any longer."

Crispus snorted as he tightened the saddle's cinch. "That's worth a fortune. He'll melt it down before we're gone a week and still get rid of her."

"He won't—he's dead if anything happens to Kyar or my buckle."

"How would we know? There's nothing to keep him from moving north and following one of the other legions. He has to wait and get permission to follow us. Remember, Vespasian hates Rix and threatened to crucify him if he was seen anywhere near the legion camp."

I rubbed his horse's silky-smooth nose, attempting to contain my irritation to his prodding questions. "The closest legion is Fourteenth Gemina in Camulodunum. They're launching their offensive on the same date as the Second Legion. Rumor has it they are marching to the northwest. Rix won't follow them."

"Why wouldn't he?" Crispus persisted. Finished with the saddle, he stooped and gave the hooves one final inspection.

I wiped my clammy hands on the side of my woolen breeches. Knowing how Crispus would react, I hadn't wanted to tell him the details. But he was my best friend, and I trusted him to hold his tongue. "Gallus won't allow it because he'd lose his percentage on the profits. His family's spies would track Rix down and arrange for a timely accident. And he knows about my agreement with Rix."

"That's not surprising."

"No, especially since I had to borrow part of the money from him." Reflectively, I reached for the money pouch tied beneath my tunic.

Crispus froze. Then he dropped the mare's hoof and spat on the straw-covered floor. "Are you mad? Why did you borrow from Gallus?" His black eyes bored through me as if I didn't exist.

I gripped the hilt of my sword and leaned against the stall railing. "I realize I'm knee deep in horse shit, but this is why." I explained the circumstances surrounding the loan.

"Now I know your brains are between your legs," Crispus said when I finished. "An interest-free loan means a hidden rope hanging from the other end, and Gallus is the hangman." For a split second, he gripped the front of his throat with a hand.

I gestured toward my chest. "I have to take the risk. He gets nothing if anything happens to Kyar. He'll see that no harm comes to her."

"For your sake, my friend, I pray you're right."

* * *

The following night I visited Kyar one more time before the cohort left on campaign. She sat on the edge of the bed-pallet, waiting as I entered her freshly cleaned cubicle. Earlier in the day, I sent word that I had received permission to see her. A smoky lamp burning rancid olive oil sat on a corner stool. Its shadowy light exaggerated the paleness of Kyar's complexion, as if all color had vanished since my last visit. She claimed she had suffered from a woman's sickness, but refused to say what kind. I suspected what it might be but held my tongue.

Kyar got to her feet and rushed to me, hungrily covering my face with kisses.

"I was so afraid you wouldn't come," she said. "I prayed they'd let you see me."

"Aye, Rufius is a good-hearted commander." I drew her into my arms. Her long, thick hair smelled of perfumed soap, sage, rosemary, and dried chamomile. I buried my face in it.

She wriggled from my embrace, and deftly slid from her lavender-scented tunic.

She placed her hands around my shoulders and pulled off my tunic. Quickly, she unlaced my trousers, and then we stood revealed to one another. I touched her cheek, slowly slid my fingers along her jawline and curved them across to beneath her lower lip. My calloused hand lingered on her mouth as she caressed my chest, the tip of her fingers circling the taut nipples. Then our hands moved together, cupping each other's face, lingering and drawing away, lingering and drawing away.

* * *

Awakening later, I turned over and snuggled next to Kyar as she lay with her back to me. She sighed, and a few minutes later I sensed she opened her eyes. I kissed her shoulders.

She turned and smiled. "Gods, tonight was beautiful."

I grinned. "You know I like making you happy."

"You've always loved me so well, Marcellus." For a moment, her mind seemed to drift. "It's different with you. Before you came along . . . all I knew were soldiers who took my body as a stallion would a mare—jabbing like passionless animals. Then they would leave and brag to their friends how good they were. But tonight . . . I never knew love could be like this." She paused again, as if thinking.

"It's hard to explain," she said slowly, "but you allowed me to open in a way I've never known before. You touched something deep inside me that I never knew existed."

I kissed her again and held her tightly in my arms.

"I'll always love you, Marcellus, even if I'm never more than your woman."

"But I love you, too," I blurted, puzzled by her last remark.

"I know," she answered, "I saw it in your eyes. I felt your struggle to admit it."

She had to know the truth. "I fought against my feelings because of a promise I made to my mother."

"What did you promise?" Her soft fingers caressed my shoulder.

"I must become a knight," I answered through tight lips.

She stopped and turned her head toward me. "I don't understand."

"I have to become a nobleman."

She sighed. "Then I can never be more than your concubine."

"I never said that." I shook my head and exhaled.

"You don't have to, I know."

I started to protest again when she put a finger to my lips.

"It's all right," she whispered. "I know you'll have to marry a highborn Spanish or Roman woman, and I accept what you must do. But I will still be yours. I'm the first woman you have truly loved, and no wife can ever take that from me."

"Regardless of what happens, Kyar, I do love you, and one day I will set you free."

"You have already given me my freedom, Marcellus. By law my body may be a slave, but my soul belongs to me. You've set it free."

We made love one lingering last time.

Afterwards, I was about to leave when Kyar, who had gotten up with me, held up her hand. I waited. She stooped and extended her fingers beneath the straw covered mattress. Slowly, she pulled out a thin, gold chain on which hung a broach. Straightening up, Kyar turned and stepped toward me. "Here, take a look." She handed over the amulet.

Upon closer inspection, I discovered the talisman was an engraved silver image of a mountain cat. "Where did you get this?"

She looked away for a second. "It belonged to my mother. She gave it to me before she was killed by my father."

I remember Kyar saying her mother had been accused of cheating on him. "I'm surprised your father didn't take this from you."

"He didn't know mother gave it to me," she answered through tightened lips. "I hid it from him and later from Rix."

I gave the charm back to her. "You better hide it somewhere safer than under your mattress."

Kyar nodded. "I wanted you to see it first." She glanced to the cubicle entrance and back to me. "If you see anyone else wearing this, you'll know I am dead."

I was about to protest when she placed a couple of fingers to my lips. "No, Marcellus, so long as I remain with Rix I will be in danger, we both know that—it can't be helped. Remember, I will never give up my amulet while I live."

I grabbed her fingers and kissed them and her soft lips. She was right, and it would be futile to protest, but I hoped she was wrong and the money I paid Rix would be enough to satisfy him. There was no more I could say or do. I hugged and kissed her once more and departed. Whatever the future held, I knew Kyar would be with me in spirit and love, and she would always be more than just my woman.

I prayed to Melkart to watch over both of us, and that I would return from campaign free of injury to Kyar's waiting arms.

CHAPTER 14

The following morning the infantry cohort and cavalry detachment departed Iping to join Legion Second Augusta. The camp would remain as a road station with a small police detail keeping order in the region.

Although the day was gray and misty, the infantry, loaded down with seventy-pound marching packs, soon worked up a sweat. We rode ahead of them along an ancient plank road, built by the Celtic Britons, which soon splintered into an overgrown trackway through forests of pine and cedar. Crispus and I trotted side by side just behind the mounts of our decurion, Sextus Rufius, and the standard bearer. The rest of the troop and squadron followed us.

"I still think you're a fool for buying her," Crispus said above the noise of our horses jangling pendants and squeaking leather saddles.

"That's for me to decide. Anyway, it's done."

Crispus exhaled and with one hand readjusted the shoulder straps that held his shield against the square of his back. At this stage of the march our troop was in no danger of attack from the enemy, about forty miles distant. "Look, I hope fortune smiles upon you two. But my gut feeling says otherwise."

"Are you convinced something will happen to her?" Argento farted, and I futilely attempted to wave away the foul odor.

"Rix holds the cast of Venus, if you know what I mean."

I nodded. "He holds the dice, but not for long. And there's no use worrying. He loves money above everything else, and the balance is yet to be paid."

"True enough," Crispus said. "I was thinking about the black snake crossing our path this morning when we were walking to the stable."

"A ridiculous superstition."

"Maybe so, but it's still a bad omen. A shame it wasn't a green one—they're good luck."

"Gallus wouldn't wait an extra day to begin a march if a black snake had slithered across the path in front of him, especially after this morning." At dawn, and witnessed by the troops, the tribune had taken the auspices at the Altar of Victory, and the sacrificial goat's liver was clear. The augur-priest declared the signs good for the march. "I'm sure if Gallus knew about our encounter, he'd pray for my death."

Crispus shrugged, and we rode in silence. I dreamed of when I would receive the balance of my money and claim Kyar as mine alone. I prayed that Crispus was wrong about the omen.

* * *

Our detachments, infantry cohort First Asturum, and cavalry cohort Hispanorum Vettonum, joined General Vespasian's Legion Second Augusta and supporting auxiliaries two days later. The campaign began with a vengeance. During the next three weeks, the army stormed and captured six fortified settlements. The largest, Hod Hill, fell in an hour after a heavy concentration of *ballista* fire of iron bolts from giant crossbows, on the chieftain's hut. Most of our twenty thousand men bypassed the battle without breaking stride. Like a great wave, the army quickly overran the fortress. We rolled further west closing in on Maugh-Dun Castle, the Durotrigian capital.

Eleyne, King Verica's daughter and Roman hostage, had been brought along on the march rather than left behind by Vespasian in Noviomagnus. I saw her for the first time when our troop was assigned to escort the baggage train's flank. I rode along one side of her wagon, a creaky mule drawn vehicle, where she sat with the driver and her servant. My breath caught in my throat at the first sight of her. Shapely and dark-haired, Eleyne was a little more than fifteen. She wore a flowing, red and yellow, tartan skirt, cinched at the waist with an embroidered golden belt and triskele buckle. I knew from experience that most Celts are fair in complexion, and apparently, her angular face had sunburned during the campaign march.

Unlike Iberian and Roman women, she refused to wear a protective hat.

Rufius had given us orders to keep a close watch on her and her heavyset maid, Karmune. They might attempt to escape with the help of Eleyne's betrothed, a rebel named Bodvac. Talk was, she had resisted attempts to be taken hostage. Aided by Karmune, she had kicked and punched her escorting Praetorians. Only with great restraint and threats of court-martial by General Sabinus did the guards keep from slaying the woman with their short swords.

Through the churning dust of a hundred wagons, the princess's sea-blue eyes continually scanned the dark woods surrounding the countryside. Was she looking for a means of escape or hoping for rescue by her people? Yet, as I observed, she seemed to make the best of her situation, causing no trouble.

The day before reaching Maugh-Dun Castle, on a hot midmorning, the baggage wagons slowly moved down a gentle embankment and across a newly built bridge over a swelling river. Shouting teamsters cracked whips over the backs of the mules urging them forward. Although master bridge builders, Roman engineers still had to contend with the gods of spring and the avenging river goddesses of the British. In spite of the cut logs being skillfully fastened, and stakes angled against the dark, rushing current that hissed and swirled, the spans near the embankment creaked and groaned with the crossing of each laden cart and wagon. Along the river's edge on both sides the cavalry provided a flanking guard.

On the far side, a decurion shouted orders to the teamsters from the back of his mount. "Get your wagons moving off the bridge, you fucking slugs! You're holding up the army!"

Eleyne rode on a large leather-covered, four-wheel affair overloaded with belongings and furniture, hauled by four straining mules. The driver, an old grizzled soldier and an experienced teamster, slowed as he approached the bridge. His ruddy face scanned the rushing waters before starting across. I halted at the river's edge a few feet from the wagon when I spotted the dray's left, front wheel wobbling slightly. As it began to creep over the dirt-covered planks, the four-wheel cart ahead dropped a large keg, banging as it struck the planks and kicking up large clods of dirt. It rolled back toward Eleyne's wagon, somehow missing the mule team's legs.

One wheel of Eleyne's wagon bumped over the barrel and slammed down, the cracking noise echoing on our side of the river. The axle snapped, flinging the driver into the churning river, his splash barely heard above the stream's loud din. The weight of his armor dragged him beneath the waters, pulling his body downstream. He never surfaced again. The girl was tossed from the rig into the swift-moving torrent beneath the bridge. Her maid, sitting in the back, was thrown free and landed with a thump on the dusty bridge, uninjured.

Shouting troops immediately converged on the banks of both sides of the river. Seconds later, I spotted Eleyne's bobbing head and shoulders as she emerged from under the bridge. She screamed as she grabbed one of the bridge stakes and struggled to hang on. The roaring waters ripped it from her grasp, hurtling her downstream. I tossed my shield and lance to Crispus.

"Take the squadron and follow me along the riverbank!" I barked. "I'm going after the princess!"

"You'll need help, I'm going with you!"

"No!" Riding into the rushing river was risky enough for one, let alone two. No sense in anyone else drowning. I prayed I would reach her in time.

I spurred Argento, but he balked and refused to budge. Although cavalry mounts are trained to swim with fully armored troopers, a raging river can terrify the best of horses. I squeezed his sides with my legs and spiked him once more. He bolted into the icy waters carrying me with him. A freezing shock raced through my body, numbing my hands and legs. For a split-second, I thought I would lose control and slip off my gelding. But I recovered my wits, held the reins tightly in my hands, and squeezed down on the horse's girth with my legs.

About the same time I pushed Argento forward, I saw Eleyne going under again, reappearing seconds later gasping and choking, as she struggled to swim with the current. She shouted for help again as she snagged a partially submerged tree limb and held fast. The branch snapped, and the hissing, foaming water carried her away.

Argento and I barely kept our heads above the swirling current's surface as it swept us downstream, out of sight of the pursuing squadron. I swallowed several mouthfuls of the river in the process, on which I choked but spat out. Gradually, I maneuvered him close enough and grabbed Eleyne's long, knotted braids. She yelped, and then had a coughing fit, spitting water. I battled to keep her head above the raging waters as she bobbed and dipped from side to side like a struggling fish on a hook.

"Ow!" she cried and sputtered.

"Don't fight me!" I shouted above the noise of the crashing torrent.

As we rounded a bend, the current pushed us close enough to the bank for Argento's hooves to catch hold of the gravel bottom. Seconds later we reached shallow water. Argento shook his mane, spraying us with icy droplets. The air hit my drenched clothing, chilling me to the bone. I released my grip on Eleyne's hair, and she fell to her knees, spat more water, and gasped. Soaked as a wet badger, she stood and attempted to catch her breath, choking up more fluid. She stumbled ashore, across the slippery, moss-covered rocks, shivering and belching.

Limp and scraggly, Eleyne's long, black hair, which had come undone, hung down her back like an old mop. At first glance, her small face reminded me of a fragile child. But then I noticed how the long, clinging tartan tunic snugly outlined her body of a well-developed woman. For the length of a heartbeat I stared, then I remembered my love for Kyar. Quickly, I reminded myself there were more serious matters at hand.

I dismounted and moved to her side. "Here, this will help."

Eleyne shook her head.

"Don't be foolish, you'll feel better." I gave her a couple of hard taps on the back between the shoulder blades, and she vomited more water.

"Better?" I questioned inanely once she stopped.

Her teeth chattered and she beat her arms. "Yes," she sputtered. "I-I-I think so. I-I-I'm freezing." Eleyne huffed and twisted one way then the other, stepped on her left foot than the right. "Y-y-you had no right t-t-to drag me like a c-c-common prisoner."

"If I hadn't you would have drowned—somebody had to rescue you." She violently coughed again, and I gave her another sharp tap.

Shivering, she wheeled around, grasping her elbows with her small, scratched, white hands and broken fingernails. "M-m-maybe you're right," she said. "I'm a-a-a good swimmer, b-b-but the water w-w-was so cold, I c-c-couldn't move."

"Aye, it's terrible. Here, you better hold onto me until you warm up."

"What?" Eleyne winced. Her lips pressed together, and she quickly looked about.

"Don't be afraid, my intentions are honorable, I mean you no harm. We're both freezing and it's a cold ride back. We need warmth—now." The river's swift current had dragged us far down stream. There was no telling how long before my squadron arrived.

"C-c-can't we build a f-f-fire?"

"There isn't any dry wood." I looked about and noticed the scattered driftwood along the shoreline molding and rotting, drenched from the high run-off. Freshly cut branches were too green to burn properly.

"V-v-very well," she said in a huff, "b-b-but only for a-a-a moment!"

I placed my hands on the shoulders of her sopping-wet tunic and drew her to my chest. The top of her delicate head came to below my shoulders.

"I suppose I'm not as good a swimmer as I thought," she said in crisp, slightly accented Latin, apparently feeling a little warmer. Her teeth no longer chattered, but she shivered again.

I attempted to draw attention away from her discomfort. "Where did you learn to speak such good Latin?"

"From a horrid little Greek." She added a disdainful grunt.

"When did you start?"

"About three years ago—the man was insane—he was never satisfied with my progress."

I had read reports that the princess was learning Greek and Latin from an excitable and demanding tutor, known as the Mad Midget of Megara.

Eleyne pushed herself away. "I'm all right now." One hand stayed on my chest a moment too long, and she blushed and backed away. Somehow, I wished she had kept it there longer. Why was I thinking this when I had Kyar waiting for my return?

"Time to ride back," I said.

"I suppose we must," Eleyne said, resigned. "After all, you have to do your duty," she added in a sarcastic tone. Quickly, she searched the woods reaching down to the shoreline, and then shrugged silently. As an afterthought, she asked, "Before we go, would you tell me your name?"

"Marcellus Tiberius Reburrus, my lady."

"We *Regni* are not so formal," she said. A faint smile formed on her bowed lips. "Call me Eleyne. I'm not used to Roman customs, yet. And I hope I never am!"

I smiled and leaped upon Argento. I reached down and gave her a hand-up to ride behind me. With Eleyne's arms clinging about my waist, I turned my gelding about, and we headed upstream toward the bridge.

"Regni women can ride as well as any man," Eleyne said a few minutes later as we rode along the edge of the river. Cautiously, Argento placed his hooves among the rocks choking the shoreline. The clattering noise echoed off the bank and carried on the breeze.

"Spanish women can do the same."

"There's something different about you," Eleyne said. "You're not Roman, are you?"

I partially turned my body around. "I am a Roman citizen, but I'm what the Romans call a Spaniard."

"Interesting. Had you not been so tall, I would have mistaken you for one of our hill people. You're nearly as dark. Where is this place you come from?"

I was about to explain when Crispus and the squadron charged from around the next bend in the river. Not far behind rode Sextus Rufius, General Sabinus, and his entourage. For an instant I regretted their arrival had been too timely.

Sabinus recognized me at once. "Well done, Sergeant Reburrus, I thank you for saving our honored guest." As the general and the others reined up before us, he shouted orders to someone in the retinue to bring blankets for Eleyne and me.

"Yes, sir," I answered, "I was fortunate to rescue her—that's one treacherous river." I wasn't accustomed to a general thanking me for anything. But at the same time, I swelled with pride.

"I had to act, sir," I continued. "The princess was in danger of being swept away—I wasn't about to see her drown."

"Nevertheless, you bravely risked your life," Sabinus complimented. "We fished the driver's body out of the river not far from here. Again, you have served Rome well."

Sabinus turned to Eleyne. "And how are you, my child?" he inquired in a concerned tone.

"Better, thanks to Marcel—to Sergeant Reburrus. I'm freezing, that's all."

"I assure you, not for long." He motioned to us to ride by his side. "Come along and explain the circumstances, Sergeant."

I rode between Rufius and him, Eleyne still clinging to my waist, distracting me. In a matter of minutes a couple of blankets were brought by one of Sabinus's scouts and handed to Eleyne and me. Gratefully, we wrapped ourselves about the shoulders. My soggy, woolen trousers and tunic, along with my hip-length armor, hung on me as if their weight had increased one-hundred fold. Eleyne started to shiver and moved closer to me, laying her head against my shoulder.

I don't know why, but for some reason I found myself attracted to this comely young woman. My mind should have been on Kyar, she was the one I loved. I forced Eleyne from my mind by turning to General Sabinus and filling him in on the details of the rescue.

By the time I finished my report, we arrived at the bridge. Eleyne's wagon, being swiftly repaired, was parked to one side along the bank. Her maid waddled toward us as fast as her bulky frame would carry her, crying, arms flying, and squealing something in the Regni tongue. Eleyne leaned over and reassured her in a comforting voice.

I helped Eleyne down. Now that her clothes were beginning to dry, she seemed to weigh no more than a feather.

She addressed me in a formal voice, which I believe was for the benefit of the officers, "Thank you, Sergeant. I'm grateful to you for saving my life. May the god Lugh and the goddess of this river smile upon you." She climbed into the wagon with her serving woman and rode across the bridge with a new driver at the reins.

Sabinus motioned to me, and we clasped the inside of one another's arm at the elbow in Roman fashion. "Rome does not forget her soldiers, Sergeant."

After releasing my grip, the general turned to Rufius. "You command a brave group of men, Decurion. You must be proud of them."

"I am, sir."

"Rome shall be duly notified in my next dispatch of Sergeant Reburrus's brave act," Sabinus continued.

Once Sabinus had ridden away, Rufius and the men congratulated me. As the ancient Turdetanian saying goes, this had been the second time the general and I had *crossed the path of the sun and the moon.* Were our destinies intended to be intertwined? I was beginning to wonder. Then I derided myself for such superstition. All the same, it was a portent of good fortune. A man of his power and station could help my efforts to become a knight.

But would fortune smile upon me?

CHAPTER 15

JUNE, 44 AD

Maugh-Dun Castle loomed ahead as our troop scouted three miles in front of the legionary forces late afternoon of the following day. Overpowering in size, the great monolith shimmering in the scorching heat crowned a long, narrow hill, surrounded by three deep, defensive ditches.

An hour later, the forward elements of the Second Augustan Legion arrived in the area, and soldiers started building a fortified camp. Even as construction of our legion base proceeded, on a rise opposite the enemy fortress, Spanish and German Batavian cavalry patrolled the woods and surrounding countryside, making certain no enemy reinforcements slipped through.

Later that afternoon, our cohort received word from Legion Headquarters that the hillfort population was concentrated at its east end. For reasons known only to the Durotrigians, they had abandoned the western side. Now, it was used as a cemetery. Still, the gate at that end could be used as an escape route.

Posted primarily along the fortresses eastern perimeter, the Durotrigian guards confidently watched us from behind high stone walls and wooden battlements, yelling challenges and obscenities. But Syrian archers, strung out along the top of the third outer ditch, still in range, kept them at bay. Just before dusk, after one Celt bared his butt to our ranks and took an arrow in the cheek, their taunts dwindled sharply.

After the troop had returned from a reconnaissance of the area and penned in the horses for the night, Rufius, now senior decurion of Cavalry Cohort Hispanorum Vettonum, gathered the men around him outside the corral. The squadron and the rest of the cohort had been billeted in a series of tents behind the *Praetorium,* Legion Headquarters, near the *Porta Decumana,* north entrance of the fortified camp.

"There's no telling if the Durotrigians received reinforcements before we arrived," Rufius told us. "At least no more of the buggers will be getting through. Is that right, lads?"

"Yes, sir!" the men responded as one.

"Couldn't they have hired mercenaries?" I asked. "They're considered wealthy." I turned my head in the direction of Maugh-Dun Castle and back to Rufius. "The fort is big enough to an army the size of a legion."

"That's General Vespasian's belief—they could have been reinforced," Rufius said. "In fact, legionary scouts spotted a couple hundred warriors sneaking into the fort before dawn on the westside. They said the leader fit the description of Caratacus."

"Cartatacus?" I said. "Are they sure?"

"As certain as they can be given the circumstances. The head man was taller than the rest of his warriors with big shoulders. He wore a bright red and gold cloak over chain mail and bright tartan breeches."

"He's known to wear flashy clothing," Crispus said. "It could be him."

"Last reports said he was north of the Tamesis River," I said.

Rufrius nodded. "We're bound to find out sooner or later if the scouts were right. So be alert."

"When the savages lose this battle, and they will, they'll use the west gate as an escape route," I explained.

"It'll be our job to keep a watch and then funnel them into the trap that's waiting for them." Rufius explained what was in store for the enemy.

I looked about seeing the troopers murmuring among themselves, some grinning, including Crispus.

Rufius twisted his head toward the main part of the camp past the Praetorium where hundreds of tents were set up in grids crisscrossed by three main avenues and several narrow pathways. The camp was a hive of activity. The whinnying of horses echoed from the nearby corral, cooking fire smoke wafted on the gentle breeze, soldiers bantered, centurions barked orders, and noise from chinking armor resonated as soldiers marched into camp from patrol. The decurion turned back and surveyed the sentries moving along the ramparts, peering outward, eyes searching the perimeter for enemy infiltrators. Rufius turned back to us and spat. "We'll see if the bloody ground pounders can wipe out those savages. It'd make our jobs easier. If not, then we'll slice up the escaping survivors."

"Storming the fort is the infantry's job anyway," I said. "No room for maneuvering horses."

"Ain't these Durotrigians supposed to be nothing more than iron makers and traders, sir?" Crispus asked Rufius. "Doesn't sound like they'd put up much of a fight."

Rufius shook his head. "Don't underestimate them, they'll slice your guts as easy as the next savage. They're warriors. If Caratacus is there, he'll cut their throats if they don't fight."

Crispus surveyed the fortress walls. "In other words, stay on guard and expect anything."

The decurion nodded. "Better chance of keeping your head."

Darkness fell, but all through the chilly night, batteries of *Onagers* catapulted weights and stones over the ramparts, while *Ballistas* hurled large bolted arrows and fireballs of oiled rags onto the thatch-roofed homes and shops within the fort, igniting dozens of huts. The hilltop was aglow with flames.

* * *

At first light, the army assembled into cohorts outside of the camp to the blare of the trumpeting circular cornus. In the presence of General Vespasian, the white-robed *haruspice* sacrificed a pure-white goat. The reader of entrails found the liver flawless and proclaimed a great victory for the general. After a brief harangue by Vespasian, in which he called the men "my brothers-in-arms," the army cheered and advanced on the fortress.

Using the forest as cover, Batavian and Spanish cavalry forces, including our unit, deployed along the northwestern end of the hill to cut off enemy escape. The hill sloped gently from the great hillfort into a plain, bordered on both sides by thick forests. The River Frome meandered in the distance. Deployed with Vespasian's legionaries and other auxiliaries, Infantry Cohort First Asturum participated in the main attack.

As our squadron perspired in the morning heat, we watched the assault from our mounts on a rise. I patted Argento on the side of his neck and shoulder calming him with soothing words. He was a little jumpy and kept swinging his head from side to side, occasionally snorting. I had ridden him in several campaigns in Germania and now, Britannia. No doubt he sensed the coming battle.

Several cohorts of Roman legionaries, followed by Gallic, Pannonian, and Spanish auxiliaries, moved toward the fortress's twin eastern portals. In unison, the troops marched up the snaking road between the three high defensive ditches, to the main gate. Locking shields tightly together to the front, the sides, and above their heads, the troops fell into the protective formation known as the turtle. Once they came into range, the barbarians found it nearly impossible to penetrate with their arrows, spears, leaden balls, and stones.

Covering the advancing troops, barrages of iron-tipped missiles, fired by crossbows known as scorpions from small mobile platforms, whisked skyward and fell like a deadly, black cloud of locusts upon the defenders.

On higher ground, Syrian sharpshooters sprayed a shower of arrows covering the infantry attack. Despite the hail of missiles cutting down dozens of defenders, the surviving Durotrigians hurled javelins and a murderous barrage of small, leaden balls and rocks down on the attackers as they attempted to smash through the thick, wooden gates.

Crispus sat on his mount to my right. "The only good thing about this position is that we have a view of the battle."

"That's the only advantage," I replied. "At least we won't get picked off like those poor bastards." Straining my eyes, I surveyed the top of the fortress wall. Then I saw him, I thought my heart would stop.

"Look, Crispus, it's Caratacus." I pointed to a warrior taller than the rest, wearing the clothing and helmet described earlier. He darted along the palisade wall ducking incoming arrows and missiles, his escorting retainers blocking them with protective shields. Handed to him by his men, he hurled several javelins down on our troops.

"That's him, all right, damn!" Crispus said. "Right in the thick of it."

We watched from a distance as our infantrymen reached the fortress

"For once I pity the Romans," Crispus said, "especially, with Caratacus on the wall, he'll kill his share of our troops."

"Too bad Gallus isn't commander of one of the infantry units, instead of ours," I said. "I wouldn't shed any tears if a stray enemy arrow downed him. Even better if Caratacus struck him down."

Crispus grinned, revealing his yellowed teeth. "Aye, you wouldn't have to repay your loan."

I chuckled. "The thought entered my mind."

"More than once, I'd wager." He shrugged. "You have to admit he has never shrunk from his duty."

I turned toward Crispus. A sneer crossed my lips. "Only because General Vespasian keeps breathing down his neck."

"Still, the whoreson has the luck of Castor and Pollux," Crispus said. "I've seen more than a few Briton javelins fly past his ears during this campaign."

"Aye," I answered grudgingly, "he's no coward, but then, he's no friend of the Iberians either."

We watched the legionaries battling their way up to the gates. Despite the continuous rain of missiles by the artillery, the Durotrigians resisted the Roman assault, relentlessly hurling rocks and javelins on the troops below. Caratacus continued to run back and forth among the enemy, hurling more spears. In the distance the sounds of battle cries reached our ears along with the gut-wrenching screams of the wounded struck down by the enemy.

Crispus spat, "Gods, I'd give anything to kill that bastard."

"We can't do anything right now," I said to Crispus. "Our job is to block the escape of any survivors. Still, I don't like it, sitting here while our comrades go to their deaths."

"They know what they're facing," Crispus said. "It's the risk every infantryman takes."

He was right. All we could do was sit and wait and grit our teeth until the infantry breached the gate. The legionaries might be fortunate enough to kill or even capture Caratacus.

"We'll get our chance yet," Crispus said, "you'll see."

The battle raged. Drifting columns of smoke obscured the castle. A minor victory brought war cries from the wall. After a desperate struggle, the legionaries breached the barricade. Behind them followed the Gauls, Pannonians from the central Danubus River Region. The roar of war cries came from inside, and the clash of metal on metal and agonized screams resounded on the breeze. Because of Maugh-Dun Castle's huge size, I wondered if our forces would capture the fortress without anyone escaping. I remembered an earlier conversation with Rufius and Crispus, *be ready for anything.*

Crispus pointed to the hillfort. "Look, the Britons are deserting the wall!"

"It's not over yet," I said. "This isn't Hod Hill, I'd wager they've got a whole army in there."

"And Caratacus, their leader," Crispus said.

After what seemed like hours, a loud rumble erupted from the direction of the western gate. Bursting through the entrance, a large host riding small Celtic horses and pony-drawn, wicker chariots, wheels rumbling over the chalky earth, hooves clattering loudly in the direction of the River Frome.

From the back of a sleek, gray mount, a tall, powerfully built warrior led the group, his chainmail dirty and bloody. His tarnished sunset hair streamed beneath an iron helmet topped with a silver eagle. Nearly one thousand riders followed in a cloud of swirling dust, armed women among them. I had heard said in times of crisis, Celtic women fought alongside their men.

Immediately, my shoulders tightened, and tiny bumps rippled up my back and arms. The sun's morning heat, which I had barely noticed, turned my mailed armor into a boiling cauldron. Perspiration poured down the side of my face and neck. I wiped sweaty hands on my breeches and shortened Argento's reins. Pulling the staked lance from the earth next to my mount, I gripped the weapon and turned to Crispus. "Now it's our turn."

Sextus Rufius raised his sword, and the signifer elevated the standard of the Roman eagle. "Get ready men, and remember your orders. On my command—now!" A trooper sounded the advance on his half-curled trumpet, the *lituus*. A war cry erupted from the men.

Rufius led the troop forward at a trot, changing to a canter, and then a gallop. The cavalry pursued, but deliberately holding back, nipped at the enemy stragglers' flanks, herding them blindly into the jaws of our trap.

The screaming enemy horde flowed within the narrowing terrain, funneling through the banks of a wooded tree line that stood between them and the river. Chariots hurtled downward toward the muddied banks like a flash flood, with no battle order, every man for himself.

At the last moment, the trumpeter sounded another call, and the cavalry of Batavians and Iberians veered away. The barbarians' momentum carried them forward. We halted at a vantage point on the upper grass plains sloping towards the river.

"Now, we'll see if the plan works," I said.

Two cohorts of auxiliary infantry, the Vascones from the Pyrenees, and another of Gauls, sprang from both sides of the narrow gauntlet and formed a human dam, fifty shields across and twenty deep. One thousand spears begged for a taste of blood.

Unable to slow the tidal wave, the Celtic horde's main body followed the leader like a snapping whip, impaling themselves with a roaring thud on the first Vascones' lines, followed by echoing screams of agony and dying from friend and foe alike.

Branches of the whip drew blood of their own, gouging deep into the ranks, nearly splitting the cohort like a parting sea. Because of their Roman discipline and training, the Vascones closed the breech as Gauls from the rear quickly filled the wounded lines and hooked the interlocking flanges of their shields to their comrades.

Nearly forty infantrymen died in those few seconds of violent turmoil. Like an undertow, the Celtic wave rushed into the gap. But a hail of javelins rained from the ranks into the turmoil of screaming horses, chariots, and maimed and dying warriors.

The great horde spun in confusion. Dust roiled everywhere. Clots of chariots and men spun off toward the black woods, only to be pinioned by spears. A few dozen Celtic footmen had survived the mass of pursuing cavalry, only to stand impotently cursing their own chariots for not giving them sanctuary.

Death plowed the field, severed clumps of human bodies disappearing beneath trodden hooves and Roman boots. The sick-sweet stench of blood, urine, and feces drifted on the wind. Death, a certainty before the barbarians, a certainty beside them. Through us was their only hope of survival—less than five hundred Spanish and Batavian cavalries!

Rufius motioned to the trumpeter, who sounded the charge.

The decimated Britons banded together in a frenzy.

We raced toward the enemy to the deafening sound of clattering hoofs and snorting horses. I readied my lance and set sight on a sweating, bare-chested, tattooed savage looming ahead. He came into range at the moment our line clashed with theirs. Bracing myself against the twin saddle horns, timing myself with Argento's rising and falling stride, I leaned forward and hurled the missile, striking him in the stomach. Blood gushed from his mouth as he doubled over and fell from his mount. I drew my sword and hacked through several Britons, the blade almost lodging in the last victim's spine before I pulled it free, nearly falling from my mount.

Straight ahead rode a fiery-eyed, flaxen-haired woman wielding a long, slashing sword. She screamed like a Fury from the underworld, and rushed towards me, swinging her bloodied weapon. Her screeching rose above the din of battle, and sent chills down my neck. Initially shoving back my weapon with a loud crash, I barely parried her blow to the side. Then with a downward thrust I stabbed her through the breast, hearing the sound of crunching as my weapon pushed back towards me. For all her shrieking, she died in shocked silence. It was the first time I had killed a woman, but I didn't have time to dwell on it.

"Look! Rufius is surrounded!" someone shouted.

Sextus Rufius wielded his gelding desperately, trying to defend himself against a dozen warriors. I slashed my way through more Celts and rushed to his aid. He received a blow to his shoulder by one attacker cutting through his protective chain mail. Another warrior hamstrung his black and white piebald, spilling him onto the ground. He rolled from his horse in agony. A savage was about to run him through, but I swung my weapon, nearly slicing him in half, his bones snapping and blood spattering on my mailed armor.

Rufius was wounded but alive. As I jumped from Argento, the decurion lurched to his feet. With renewed frenzy, we fought viciously back to back, gouging and downing more warriors. Bellowing like a madman, I hacked fiercely, slaying one wild man after another until my troops smashed through the circle of Celts. Argento rammed a warrior, reared and trampled his body, then crushed another's chest with a solid hind kick.

Suddenly, the battle was over—the enemy annihilated. Argento settled down and stood nearby, panting, mouth foaming, as I guarded Rufius. He sank to the ground, next to his dying horse. My commander had lost much blood from the wound high in his shoulder and from a dagger still buried in his thigh. There was little bleeding from the leg injury. If he lived, the blade could be safely withdrawn later by a *medicus*. I removed strips of linen dressings from a small, leather bag tied to my saddle. Kneeling, I pressed them against his shoulder wound. I prayed to the gods to let him live long enough for the surgeons to arrive. Tough but approachable and fair, he was too good an officer to lose.

"Did . . . did we get them?" he asked in a weak voice. "Did . . . they get away?"

"We killed most of them," I answered. "Only a few escaped." I glanced quickly at the battlefield strewn with the victims of Mars. For the length of a dozen heartbeats, I felt an impulse to charge into the smothered chaos and hack the wounded enemy.

"Good. Did . . . you get the . . . the bastard who . . . killed me?" he rasped slowly.

"You're not dying, sir," I said, attempting to comfort him. Blood seeped through the gauze staining my hands.

Andubal approached us, bloodstained sword in hand. Other troopers covered in blood, including Crispus, followed behind him. "He saved your life, sir," Andubal said. "I saw it all." He turned to me. "You'll get the *Corona*—"

"Shut up!" I exploded. "How can you think of medals? We're talking about a man's life." I was embarrassed by his remark, and Rufius could still die. For the first time, I noticed blood splattered all over my chain mail, breeches, and bare arms, hands sticky with the slime of death. My mouth was parched and arms and legs the weight of lead ingots, I could hardly move. "I did what any soldier would have done," I added wearily.

"Horseshit!" Crispus exclaimed. "You cut your way through those whoresons into the eye of the storm! Gods, we couldn't keep up with you. And the way you fought—Jupiter Thunderer—there was almost no one left for us to kill! Don't be so fucking modest. You saved his life!"

For how long?

"Enough, dammit!" I said. "He needs medical attention." I yelled to a nearby *medicus* checking a wounded trooper. He came over, examined, and ordered two men to help him place Rufius on a horse-drawn stretcher. Leading the mount by the reins, he rushed the decurion over the churned muck, between strewn bodies, to the field-dressing station. *Piss on their stinking medals. It won't bring back the men we lost, or Rufius, if he dies.* I grabbed the water bag from my saddle and took a long drink.

Crispus muttered, "That whoreson got away again."

"Caratacus?" I asked, splashing the cool water on my dirt-encrusted face and head.

"Aye, the same" he replied loudly, knowing the surge of battle-fever was still hot in his blood—like mine.

"I had a feeling the crafty bastard would escape, he's like a wolf."

"We could have captured him if the shit-smearing Batavians had done their job."

I wiped the excess water and sweat from my face with a tunic sleeve and corked my flask. "No point fretting about it. Besides, the Batavians fought well enough. It's not the first time that devil's been underestimated."

Crispus spat. "He fled across the river and disappeared into the forest. We'll never find him."

* * *

We rode into the fortress and found a smoldering village. Legionaries rounded up survivors and herded them into pens in the center of the fortress. The civilians would be sold as slaves, but the warriors would be impressed into auxiliary cohorts with other Britons and stationed on the Danubus River on the northeastern frontier of the empire. Other soldiers searched the remnants of blackened huts for survivors and booty. One detail dragged away the dead to be buried en masse in the cemetery at the fortress's west end. Another group loaded debris into carts and transported the rubbish to a designated dump outside the stronghold's walls. The rest were put to work establishing a camp inside the fortress.

The purple shadows of dusk crept through the rubbled castle when Sergeant Corribilo approached me. The squadron had finished grooming and feeding its horses and were pitching tents. I thought about Rufius and planned to visit him. Corribilo, now acting-decurion of the troop, returned from a meeting at Legion Headquarters. His naturally long face formed a big, toothy horse grin. "Good news about Rufius, the surgeon says he's going to live."

A sense of relief rushed through my mind and body. "Thank the gods. I shall sacrifice to Asclepius for his quick recovery. You won't find a better officer," I added.

Corribilo agreed.

"Any other news?" I asked.

"Well, it's still too early to be official, but chances are you'll receive the *Corona Civica*—congratulations." He extended his hand.

I don't know why, but an uncontrollable shudder raced down my spine. "What? You're joking."

"No, it's true, you saved his life."

We shook hands. I knew what he meant. The *Corona Civica* was the empire's highest award. I still felt embarrassed since I did what any other trooper should have done.

"Every soldier that's awarded the *Corona* has been promoted to decurion or centurion," Corribilo said. "That's a big jump. Think of the pay and the women it'll buy." He laughed, knowing it meant little to a man from a wealthy family who already had the woman he wanted.

I shrugged. "If I get it." Final approval had to come from the emperor. Perhaps Rufius would refuse to admit I had saved his life. He would have to personally decorate me, and denials were common. Officers hated admitting they had been saved by subordinates. "There are many others, including you," I continued, "that deserve to be rewarded, too."

"Rewarded? By the lucky twins, survival is good enough for me."

You're so right, my friend.

* * *

Eight days later the legion assembled on parade. Awards for valor were given by Vespasian and Sabinus, after Vespasian gave a long-winded speech on the bravery of Rome's finest troops in killing thousands of barbarians. Many were decorated, including Corribilo and me. He and I received two silver *armillae* arm bands for exceptional bravery. I would receive the *Corona Civica* at a later date, if I received it all.

In the presence of Gallus, Sabinus presented me with the silver armbands. He spoke in such a low voice only I heard what he said.

"So far, you have lived up to my expectations. Although I cannot make any promises, with the emperor's approval, an even greater award awaits you. You will go far if I have anything to say about it, and I do. Soon you will hear from me."

"Thank you, sir." A deep sense of pride overcame me despite my previous doubts and objections about awards.

* * *

The next morning Legion Second Augusta marched from Maugh-Dun Castle, heading westward into the hill country. The bloodletting would continue for another five months before the conquest of southwest Britannia was complete.

I hadn't received any messages from Kyar since we had left Iping. I prayed she was well.

I didn't know when I would next see her.

CHAPTER 16

AUGUST, 44 AD

Nearly six weeks had elapsed since the army departed Maugh-Dun Castle. Another fifteen hill fortresses were overrun before General Vespasian halted the advance at Isca, capital of the Dumnonii, far to the west.

Caratacus had vanished like a phantom in the night.

After Gallus's daily morning briefing of his cohort and troop officers and sergeants in the headquarters tent, he dismissed the group, but ordered me to stay behind.

Barely the first hour after dawn, the heat of summer pressed down on the legion camp like a breathless demon, all activity slowing to a crawl. Despite wearing a protective soft, woolen scarf, the top edge of the chain-mail armor chafed my neck.

"You realize," Gallus said, as he sat behind his portable table, "only three weeks remain before your loan is due?"

"Yes, sir, I'm aware." I stood at ease in the stifling cohort command tent. "I expect the money to arrive from home any day," I added.

"Repayment may not be necessary."

His remark piqued my curiosity. What devious thoughts were running through Gallus's mind? "I don't understand."

"If you are agreeable," Gallus continued, "I will propose an offer that will cancel your loan."

Immediately, I suspected the rope Crispus warned me about months ago when we departed Iping on campaign. Would Gallus now play hangman? Crispus was right, no loan is interest free. "What's your proposition?"

Gallus clasped his hands together on the table and cleared his throat. "Your family owns a parcel of land I want to buy. It includes the foothills and the coast road between your family home and the town of Abdera."

"That's prime grazing area," I answered. No doubt, he knew it was the best we possessed. "It includes our sacred ancestral grounds, where my father is buried, and the shrine to Melkart, maintained by my mother as high priestess."

The tribune nodded. "Of course, and I pledge to respect its sanctity for all time. You and your family will retain the right to visit your revered temple and burial grounds whenever you wish—that is only proper."

I carefully chose my words. "You are aware, sir, the river running through those properties drains into the rest of our lands, including my mother's home. What guarantees do I have you wouldn't cut off our water supply?"

"I would guarantee your water rights for the next three generations." Gallus gestured to the jar of lampblack ink and blank parchment laying on one side of the table. "Naturally, the agreement will be documented and witnessed before magistrates of your choosing. Am I not being reasonable?"

"So far, yes. What is the offer?"

He quoted a generous price of more than one million sesterces—a small fortune not to be taken lightly. I turned the price over in my head. Why was Gallus making such a lucrative offer? A sense of excitement and turmoil rolled through my being. I had to maintain control of my thoughts. Should I sell? There was nothing to keep Gallus from reneging on his agreement. Damming up the water supply, precious to the prosperity of the *latifundia*, meant drought and starvation. Magistrates were easily bribed to change their decisions, which would leave Gallus free to purchase the remaining land for a fraction of the cost. Filing suit in court required years of litigation and a financial drain on the family fortune in legal fees. We would lose everything before receiving a favorable judgment, if we received one at all. Regardless, the lands were sacred to the family. I could no more sell the property than kill my own mother.

"Your offer is most generous, sir, but I can't sell what has belonged to my family for generations."

Gallus flinched. He glared at me for what seemed a long time. “You realize,” he said slowly, “this is the favor I expected you to repay for my loan.”

Drops of perspiration ran down the side of Gallus’s sunburnt face and neck, disappearing beneath his white corselet tunic. The same flowed down the back of mine from inside of my helmet to within my clothing. The enclosed stifling tent reeked of its stale, salty smell.

He waited for my answer.

“Sir, had it been anything else I would comply. But not ancestral lands. It would be like cutting off my fighting arm.”

“Sometimes one must cut off a gangrenous part to survive.” He snorted. “I made you a generous offer, and won’t bicker over the terms.” He jabbed a finger toward me. “Since your word of honor is meaningless, I’ll find another way. One you won’t like. In the meantime, since you have broken your word, I shall amend mine. You will repay the loan with an additional interest charge of one hundred percent.”

“That’s outrageous, I never agreed to those terms.”

“They just changed,” Gallus answered coolly. “Be thankful they’re not worse.”

Heat rushed through my body and muscle tightened. Not daring to show my anger, I kept my face blank. He knew he had me in a bind. I dared not go to higher authorities to report the illegally high usury rates. It was my word, as an enlisted man and auxiliary, against a Roman officer. I had to pay the amount if I didn’t want Gallus making my life any more miserable then he had already.

“Very well, Tribune, I’ll pay the full amount, including your criminal interest rate.”

“It is not unreasonable, considering the gracious offer I made.” He smiled sadistically. “Is your slut still worth it?”

* * *

General Vespasian left a garrison of four auxiliary cohorts at Isca and wheeled the army northward to the hill country of the Dobunnii. The Second Legion advanced through a land of contrasts—low-lying, sun-bleached plains, high, jagged limestone cliffs, and forested, gray-stone hills mantled in a cloak of dark shadows, surrounding the River Severn. Its narrow tributaries ran into deep mountain caves, gouged away by eons of swift-flowing currents.

A realm of superstitions, witchcraft, and elfin legends lay before us. Local natives claimed lost souls wandered aimlessly, cursing all they touched. Soon, the more superstitious troops became infected by the foreboding tales. The deeper we advanced into Dobunnii territory, the more sacrifices and votive offerings the legionaries made to the gods. They feared evil spirits more than the enemy.

I believed little of what I had heard, but as a precaution, I, too, sacrificed to the local gods.

One humid morning our troop scouted the hilly, wooded area near the River Axe. Futilely, the sun attempted to burn away an overcast sky. As I baked in my chain mail and tunic, we rode several miles ahead of the advance column, following a deer trail up a broad ravine. Except for the soft clatter of hooves and snorts of horses, the land seemed eerily silent. In the distance stood a cluster of ash trees in a jagged half-circle, a natural site for the outdoor ceremonial rites of the Druids.

Ahead of us, down the path, hobbled a stooped old woman wearing a dirty cloak and hood over a dusty, white tunic that hung to the ankles. She supported herself with a wooden staff clutched in a gnarled left hand. Purple woad tattoos, the markings of a Druid, covered her emaciated face and hands. She stopped and raised her staff upon our approach.

"Beware soldiers of Caesar—beware!" she cried. She cackled and again cried her warning.

Corribilo, the acting troop commander, signaled a halt. The troopers looked about as if unnerved by her appearance and shrill warning. They grasped the hilts of their spathas and looked about.

"She's a witch," Andubal murmured uneasily.

Others nodded in agreement. Obulco, whose bravery in battle was unquestioned, stared at her in saucer-eyed silence.

"What's the meaning of this, old crone?" Corribilo demanded. "Step aside!"

"Take heed of my words, oh, lords of the world," she crowed in mockery, and dipped her head in an aged bow. "Beware of the evil spirits lurking in the hills and forest. They will curse and haunt those who do not appease them." She scanned the surrounding forest, drawing our searching eyes along with hers.

"Rubbish," I snarled, fearing more unease from my men if I didn't act. "Move aside, you old vulture."

She glared at me through eyes no more than slits and pointed a veiny finger. "You, young warrior," she hissed, "especially you, must beware."

She gave me the evil eye, and I immediately blessed myself, spat on my chest, and silently lipped the sounds, "*Papa-sima, papa-sima,*" to ward off her curse.

The witch jabbed her staff at the rest of the troop. "Beware, for the dead will haunt you. The spirits of the unburied and headless travel the land searching for peace and revenge!"

The old Druidess paused a moment and slowly nodded to me. "A few weeks ago a young woman died a hor-rrible death at the hands of another. There was much blood. Now her soul wanders these very woods." She stabbed a bony finger toward the grove. "And the river," she said, motioning in the direction of the River Axe, "seeking her lover. She will rest only when she is avenged." Her voice trailed away. "But there is more."

Again, she pointed a knotted finger at me, or so I thought. But the crooked finger curved unnaturally, and it could have been pointing at Corribilo. Seeing that I was not sufficiently intimidated, she brayed, "Yes, you! You must respect the gods and above all . . . ," she paused briefly, "beware of the god from the East."

"Which one?" I asked in jest. "There are hundreds."

"*You* will know when the time comes."

"What can we do to ward off the evil spirits?" a shaken Corribilo interrupted. He viewed me suspiciously, as if I were some possessed demon.

"Sacrifice to the forest gods, especially to the sacred ash and oaks, nothing else will save you."

"We have neither incense, nor goats with us," Corribilo protested.

She smiled, exposing her black teeth. "They will accept your tokens of coppers," she intoned with a humble bow of the head. "My name is Mugain, and I am the *Brig Bretach,* the Druidess of Judgment, and Priestess of the Woods. I shall gladly accept, on their behalf."

Obulco's coin bounced at her feet almost before her lisping had finished. Like the others, and not wanting to tempt the spirits, I threw her a sesterce.

Her watery eyes grew wide, and the crooked smile broadened at the sight of the coins. "Bless you," she cackled. "May the gods, whose names I dare not say, forever guide your paths with good fortune.

"But remember . . . ," she glared at me once again, "young man of Iberia, respect the gods and beware of the Eastern one. Your offering will not change anything." She picked up the copper piece and tossed it to me. "Do not come under his spell." The priestess retrieved the rest of the money and shuffled away in renewed vigor, disappearing among the oak trees.

"Why did the witch curse you, Sergeant?" Obulco asked.

I shook my head. "I have no idea. I don't know anything about an Eastern god." Why had Mugain chosen me?

With the exception of Crispus, the men avoided me for nearly a week. But a few times out of the corner of my eye I caught Crispus staring at me. No doubt he, too, wondered why the crone marked me. Did they believe that I was cursed? And what about the dead young woman? Was it Kyar?

No, it couldn't be.

I shrugged. This was no time to be intimidated by foolish superstitions.

CHAPTER 17

MID-AUGUST, 44 AD

The following day the army halted to regroup and wait for supplies near the meandering River Axe. A reinforced marching camp was established on a narrow plain rising into black, cavernous mountains called the Mendips.

One afternoon, a couple of days later after returning from patrol, I found my father's youngest brother, Budar, with his four German retainers, casually conversing with the slave grooms outside the corral. I halted my squad, turned and dismissed them, including Crispus.

I dropped off Argento, nodded to a slave to take his reins, and approached the old veteran. "Uncle!" I exclaimed with the enthusiasm of a boy. "What in the name of Melkart are you doing here?"

We embraced and clapped each other's shoulders.

"Ha! What do you think?" Budar roared. His gray-bearded face flashed a wrinkled smile. "Do I need an invitation to visit my favorite nephew?" He removed his white Turdetanian tribal hooded cap and wiped the perspiration from his scarred forehead. Solidly built, the crusty, retired centurion in his midfifties was as trim as the day he was discharged from the army four years earlier. The dusty white and scarlet-edged tunic, blue calf-length breeches, and muddy boots, made of tightly woven esparto grass, underscored his muscular build. An Iberian spatha, encased in a gilded sheath, hung from the leather baldric circling his right shoulder.

"When did you arrive?" I inquired.

He tugged at his beard and crinkled a matted eyebrow. "This morning with the supply convoy. We landed at Noviomagnus last week and hitched a ride."

I motioned with my head. "Once I've finished stabling Argento, let's talk in the wine shop, not here."

I warily eyed his shaggy-haired bodyguards, dressed in bear skins and wearing longswords. "Must they follow us?" I asked. "You're safe here."

"I'll send them to our quarters. I found a place at Mattan, the Sidonian's trading camp. He's not a bad character, for a thief."

Budar dismissed his bearded Germans from the Hermunduri Tribe in their own guttural tongue. Scowling, they viewed me suspiciously, although knowing our relationship, but seemed reluctant to leave. He gave them a sharper command, which sounded like a curse, and they finally departed. Shuffling away, they continued to glance over their shoulders.

"The trouble with Hermundurians," Budar said, "is once you've bought their loyalty, they're like puppies. They follow me everywhere, and are wary of anyone who gets close." He laughed, sounding like a horse. "Why, once they even tried cutting out the tongue of a trader who cheated me. He deserved it, but since I'm responsible for their conduct, I had to stop them."

After putting Argento away, we hiked to the makeshift wine shop of Mattan, the Sidonian. His tavern, a large, grubby goatskin tent, was situated in the Forum, an open area along the *Via Principia,* near the Praetorium, the only place in camp where traders were allowed to conduct business. Because of potential security problems, the wagons remained outside the camp. The day before, word came from another trader that Rix, with his motley band of followers and women, was expected any day. However, he would have to conduct his trade beyond the stockade walls. Vespasian's order to crucify the Gaul remained in full force should he set foot in camp. But there was enough business for both Rix and Mattan. I desperately missed Kyar and eagerly anticipated her arrival. I had not received word since we left Iping in the spring. Had Rix kept his promise about treating her well?

Two sides of the crowded shop were open to let in sunlight. We found an empty table near the back in the shadows. After gulping our first round of wine, Budar spat. "Gods, this tastes like horse piss!"

"Remember, a soldier can adapt to anything," I mocked.

"Aye, but I forgot how bad this swill tasted, worse than I remembered!" Although Budar cursed the wine, his expression seemed content. Veterans, especially centurions like Budar, were welcomed at a Roman camp. They could be temporarily pressed into service if the base faced imminent danger from attack. His dark eyes searched about. Seeing no one paying any attention to us, he reached beneath his dusty tunic. He pulled out a brown, leather pouch and placed the heavy bag of clinking coins firmly in my hand.

"Here's the money you wanted from your mother," he said in a low voice.

I stuffed the sack under my tunic, tying it to an inside waist band.

"She told me about your woman," Budar said. "I volunteered to bring the money because I'm the only one she trusts. Your wench better be worth the price. You paid too much."

I narrowed my eyes. "You didn't come all the way just as a favor."

Budar leaned slightly forward in a voice little more than a whisper, "To tell the truth, I'm supposed to see your woman and give final approval, for your mother's sake. She almost didn't give me the money."

"Why?"

The crusty veteran shook his head. "Because she feared the woman would get in the way of your promise."

"Then you know?"

"I'm the only one she's told."

For a few seconds I straightened my back, annoyed by my mother's doubts. "How would Kyar interfere with my becoming a knight?"

Budar's cold, ebony eyes stared at me. "She's got the half-baked idea that you'd eventually free and marry the wench. I convinced her you had enough horse sense not to do anything so stupid. Right?"

"Of course not, she's strictly a concubine." *Regardless, one day I will set her free.*

"Good man, I knew you wouldn't," he said, apparently relieved by my answer. "Don't tell her about our conversation, you're not supposed to know."

"I won't say a word."

"Your mother is a beautiful woman for her age, but vain. When she read that a *German* reminded you of her, she was flattered and furious at the same time—women, you can never figure them out."

My mother could still turn the heads of men at age forty-one. "She won't be disappointed."

The old veteran sat straighter and shrugged. "No matter, the journey was an excellent excuse to see you. After all, if my favorite nephew needs help, then, by Melkart, he'll get it.

"Your mother and I are very proud of you," Budar continued. "Not many troopers are promoted to sergeant in less than four years. And now this," he motioned to my silver armlets. He took a deep breath. "I only regret your father isn't alive to see what you've accomplished. He would be pleased."

Uncle Budar patted me on the shoulder. "Tell me about your wench. She must be a real beauty."

I grinned. "She is, Uncle."

Crispus showed up and sat at the next table with some other troopers. I gave him a nod.

"Who did you buy her from?" Budar asked, lowering his voice. "I know most of the dealers."

"Rix the Gaul."

His eyes narrowed, and a sneer crossed the corner of his chapped lips. "The one who traded along the Rhenus?"

I motioned with a hand. "The same."

"You'll never see her again," he said flatly.

Instantly, my muscles tightened. Heat rushed to my face. "What do you mean? I know he's a thief, but—"

"He's a cutthroat and a liar." He gestured towards me. "You've made a bad bargain."

"How can you be so certain?" I asked, my voice little more than a croak.

"The whoremonger and I go way back. I should've cut his mangy throat when I had a chance—damn!" He pounded his fist on the table, shaking the earthen cups. He waved off a slave, who thought he signaled a refill.

"That's not everything," I said, knowing he should hear the full story. "There's more."

"So it's worse than I suspected."

I glanced to Crispus, who shook his head as if to say, *I told you so.*

"I gave him father's ceremonial belt buckle for security," I said.

"My brother's treasure?" Budar roared. All eyes turned to us. But after the length of a half-dozen heartbeats the other patrons resumed their own conversations. "Why did you give it to him?" Budar asked in a milder tone.

I exhaled. "To guarantee Kyar wouldn't have to work."

Budar shook his head, gulped the rest of his wine, and wiped his mouth on a sleeve. "You're a fool if you thought he'd stop using her. The woman is working if she's with him, which I doubt. And worse, the buckle's gone. What other fool things have you done?"

"There's Gallus." I explained about the loan and his offer to buy part of the *latifundia*.

"At least you were smart enough to refuse him," Budar growled. "Your mother would have cursed you to the grave. And I'd have broken every bone in your body." He demonstrated with a gesture of his fists.

"Thanks for your comforting words."

"Not much I can do about Gallus—you'll have to repay him, no matter what happened to Kyar. But beware, if he's like his scheming father, he's not through with you yet."

Anger welled within, but I managed to keep my wits. "We've got to find Rix at once and see if she's still with him." I should have known better. Why had I trusted that thieving pimp?

"Leave it to me," Budar advised. "I come and go as I please. You can't, and I don't want you deserting your post."

I huffed. "I'm not stupid."

"Oh no?" Budar crinkled his nose and frowned. "You're hot-blooded enough to try. When you're young, your hard spear does all the thinking."

"I wouldn't desert no matter what happened."

He jabbed a finger toward me. "See that you don't!"

"Regardless of what you learn, I'll confront him. This is my problem, not yours."

"So tell me, how will you handle Rix?"

For a moment Uncle Budar studied my face. My mind was in a state of turmoil—I couldn't think of anything, hard as I tried.

"That's what I figured," he said, "run out and cut his throat."

"What would you do?" I responded defensively.

Toying with his cup, he eyed the table top for the space of a couple of heartbeats. He flicked a dead fly away with a snap of his middle finger.

"Carefully," he answered in a soft voice. "I leave tomorrow morning. When I find Rix, I'll see if he has your beauty. If not, I'll learn where she's gone."

"Don't tell him we're related."

"I won't. Gods, knowing him, he'll sell her to me, if she's still his property."

We did not chat long, because my mind drifted to Kyar. I worried about her fate, and the words of the witch, Mugain. We parted company for the night, and I returned to my tent. What Uncle Budar said about Rix churned around and around in my mind. Tossing and turning, I hardly slept. The following morning Budar and his fierce Germans left camp.

* * *

Three days later, my uncle returned. He entered the temporary stable, which we had built over the last two days, where I was grooming Argento. Rain poured off the high-pitched straw roof in heavy sheets. Grimly, he stared as water dripped from his oil-coated cloak. "I found Rix, and, regretfully, I was right." For a moment, only the sound of the downpour stood between us. "I'm . . . sorry."

"Kyar?" I asked. Numbed by his words, I managed to keep my voice and temper under control.

"He sold her."

I slammed the bristled horse brush against the wooden railing, bouncing it into the next stall. "That son-of-a-whore!" Every muscle in my body knotted. I didn't speak for several minutes. Looking down, I saw a jagged splinter had embedded deep into my palm from where I caught a stable post for support. I had to regain my composure, essential to deal with Rix and stay out of trouble.

"Who did he sell her to? Why?"

Budar cleared his throat. "He claims the owner, meaning you, was killed at Maugh-Dun Castle, and had paid only three quarters of her price. He had to recoup the rest of the money."

"Killed? That sounds like something he'd say. Who bought her?"

"The lying bastard said Chosroes of Parthia, who doesn't exist."

"When's that dirty thief coming here?"

"Only the gods know. Maybe he's bold enough to think you'll believe more of his lies. He's tricked you before."

Trying to calm myself, I pulled the splinter out of my hand, tossing it to the floor. Only a couple drops of blood oozed from the cut. I licked my palm and spat. A horse whinnied from a nearby stall. I shook my head. "Never again."

"Easy, lad. It's possible he really believed you're dead. Even that Gaul doesn't have the brass balls of Jupiter to come here knowing full well you're alive. Gallus would've somehow gotten the word to him."

"Obviously, he didn't."

"Still, I'd have wrung the truth out of Rix. Since you wanted to handle it your way, I kept my tongue."

I shook my head in acknowledgment. "How did you manage to get the information out of the thief? He knows you don't trust him."

Budar snorted. "The bugger never gives up playing new tricks—he keeps lying out of habit. I think he'd lie even if the truth was in his favor, which it isn't. He'd swindle his own ma. He treated me like a long-lost best friend. I said I heard Kyar was for sale and interested in buying her. After telling me she was gone, he tried selling me a wench named Sigrid."

"Sigrid, that's it!" I looked toward the stable entrance. "She'll know the truth. She's Kyar's best friend—we've got to find her."

"Maybe we can, for your sake."

"Rix . . . Sigrid. I must find where Kyar is."

"Wait until Rix arrives," he warned, "and then take along Crispus, you trust him. I fear you'll lose control, and do something you'll regret. I know he'll lie, and you'll wring his neck. You'd kill him without learning the truth of whether she's alive or dead. Or learn what he did with the money or your father's belt buckle. Then you'd be in real trouble."

"One way or another, I'll learn what happened." My muscles were tight as a bow string. I took several deep breaths as I struggled to get myself under control.

"If you'd explode and get it out of you, I wouldn't be as concerned. But you're too calm, and that bothers me."

CHAPTER 18

Five days later, Rix's caravan appeared outside the legion camp. Crispus and I rode out to confront him. It was midmorning when we entered his place, one of several dilapidated tents and lean-tos lining a muddy path. Except for the Gaul and one of his cronies guzzling wine at a planked bar table, the makeshift tavern was empty.

Squinting his eyes, Rix watched as we approached in the dimly lighted room. He gasped aloud, dropping his cup to the earthen floor, its sound a muffled thud. Stepping back, he blessed himself, crossing his arms in front of his chest. He bowed wide-eyed like one who had seen a ghost.

"Sergeant, this is unexpected," he said in a quivering voice. "I heard you were killed. But you live, praise the gods." He raised his hands, drew his head back, and looked skyward.

I reached the bar, leaned across, and stuck my face within inches of Rix's. His foul breath almost gagged me. "And you, dog, wasted no time in selling Kyar, you thieving bastard!"

"I assure you, had I known for one minute you were alive, she would be here today." He cringed.

It took all the discipline I could muster to refrain from strangling his dirty carcass.

"How did you find out?" he sputtered.

"I have my sources. Where is she?"

"I sold her to Chosroes, the slave dealer," he answered all too quickly.

Partially hidden by Rix's tunic, I saw the mountain-cat broach belonging to Kyar. He wore it on a gold chain, dangling from his chest. I remembered her words: *You'll know I'm dead if Rix has the amulet.*

The tremor of fear creeping through my body turned to anger. I ripped off the broach and grabbed the Gaul by the scruff of his neck. "You're a lying pig, where is she?" Rix's eyes bulged, his face purpled as my fingers squeezed his throat, pushing through his lumpy flesh. "Where is my father's buckle?"

Crispus threw his arms around my waist and pulled me away. "No, Marcellus, not now! We'll get him later!"

At the same time, Rix's henchman drew a dagger. "Put it away, you fool," Rix ordered in little more than a whisper, "do you want us killed?" The Gaul shoved the weapon back into his waistband.

Rix caught his breath and massaged his throat. "I told you the truth." His voice shook. "If you threaten me again, I'll go to Gallus—he'll know how to deal with you."

"You won't live long enough." I loosened myself from Crispus's grip.

"Easy, Marcellus, you're making this worse. Let's get out of here!"

Crispus was right. "You haven't seen the last of me, Rix!"

"Wait! Here's your money." Rix pulled a leather pouch from behind the bar and held it out to me. "I sold your buckle because I believed you dead, I swear it! This is all I have left. If you give me a little time, I'll get the rest."

I knocked his hand away, scattering the bag of sesterces across the floor, and stormed out of the place.

In my blinding fury toward the Gaul, I nearly missed the plump figure of Sigrid, partially hidden by an opening to a small tent, down the muddy path from the tavern. She pointed to the sun in the west, and motioned to the grove beyond the Gaul's camp.

* * *

Dusk fell before she could sneak away. After wading through the clump of oaks, she appeared in the clearing and ran to Crispus. She embraced and kissed him passionately, then drew back, tears clouding her eyes, and running down her rosy cheeks.

"What's wrong, Sigrid?" Crispus asked.

Shaking her head, she cupped her face with her hands.

"Sigrid, what happened to Kyar?" I asked. Her body shook, and she wouldn't look at me.

"Nothing, it's like whatever Rix told you." Crispus had told me earlier that Sigrid feared Rix, who no doubt had threatened her life. "I can't, it's too hard to say," she cried softly.

"Sigrid, tell Marcellus, please," Crispus said in a firm voice. "He has a right to know."

"It's so hard . . ."

"Sigrid, I don't know if Kyar ever told you," I said in a soothing tone, "but I was in the process of buying her. It's important that I learn the truth. Tell me, we'll protect you from Rix, I promise."

She peeked at Crispus through spreading fingers, and he nodded. Sigrid wiped away the tears, smearing her rouged face. "Kyar weren't sold to no one," her voice quivered. She trembled again. "Oh, Crispus, I can't say it, I can't!"

"Take your time, Sigrid," Crispus said in a soothing voice. He held her tight about the waist.

A few minutes passed before she regained her composure. "Kyar's dead!"

A numbing sensation swept through my body. "How?" I asked simply.

"Rix murdered her," she answered in a subdued tone, as if a heavy burden had been lifted from her mind.

Gradually, the numbness changed to rage—heat rushed through every pore in my body. But I had to keep my wits and learn the details. "I had known as soon as I saw Rix wearing her broach. How did it happen?"

"Kyar stole your buckle from Rix."

"Why did she steal it?"

"He had a buyer and was going to sell it. She knew it belonged to you and your father and was worth a fortune."

"How did Kyar steal it?"

"I don't think Rix had any idea at first. He searched our cubicles and found nothing. Maybe he thought she stole it, because you were buying her and she knew about it."

"Did Kyar take it?" I asked. My breath labored heavily as I grabbed the handle of my sword, gripping so tightly my knuckles turned white.

"Yes."

"Did she tell him?" I asked through clenched teeth.

"No, Kyar died before she confessed."

"Damn that rotten bastard!" I pulled my sword half way from its scabbard, determined to kill him.

"Easy, Marcellus," Crispus urged. He motioned for me to shove the weapon back in place.

I hesitated, glaring at him. Exhaling, I nodded and slid the spatha back into the leather covering. "How did she die?" I asked Sigrid.

She bit her lip and whispered, "He tried to beat the truth from her. He slapped, beat, and kicked her in the stomach. Over and over." Sigrid paused. "She bled to death. He didn't know she was with child." Sigrid clutched her abdomen. "Before you left with the army, Kyar was sick."

"For the love of the gods, if I had only known." I would have swallowed my pride and borrowed the entire amount from Gallus and freed her from Rix's clutches instead of leaving her with him. She could have joined the other camp followers as the army moved on campaign.

"But Rix made her work," Sigrid added, ripping me from my thoughts. "He didn't pay no attention to your warnings. When she refused, he slapped her a lot. Kyar got so afraid, she did what he said."

"That fucking whoreson," I muttered.

I remembered her coughing and drawn appearance as the cohort departed Iping—all of it coming back with Sigrid's words, including Rix's greedy approval at the time. Had the child been mine? Perhaps. But Kyar's child for certain, and I would have loved them both.

I barely breathed.

"When did she die?" I asked.

"About five weeks ago."

"Where is she buried?"

"She's not."

I froze, knowing the meaning of her words.

Sigrid's eyes pleaded with Crispus. "It's all right, Sigrid, tell him."

She drew a deep breath and then exhaled. "He threw her body into the river."

"The witch's story!" I gasped. "Kyar's the one in the witch's tale! Her soul will wander forever in this accursed land. She'll have no peace."

Crispus hushed Sigrid before she asked what I meant.

I saw a vision of Kyar's battered, bloated body, floating downstream or snagged beneath a submerged rock and fed on by the fish. I wanted to yell, but dared not because we were too close to Rix's encampment. Instead, I turned and leaned against a spindly tree. My body shook, eyes burned and welled with tears. "Now, I'll gut him for sure," I swore through bitter tears streaming down my face. "Kyar, what has he done to you?" I wept. A roar swirled between my ears like surf pounding the seashore. My head spun, and I grabbed the tree to keep from falling. Flashes of Kyar's soft face and small turned-up nose rushed across my mind. I could almost feel my hand running through her long, sweet hair after our love making.

Then I felt Sigrid slip to my side, touch my arm, and share my sorrow.

"Easy, man," Crispus said, "we'll take care of that fucking pimp." He placed a hand on my shoulder, but I turned away.

"Come on, Marcellus, I know how you feel, believe me, but now, we must leave. Sigrid will be in great danger if she doesn't return to Rix's camp."

I was silent. Sigrid stepped back to Crispus's side.

"Rix will kill her if he learns that she's seen us. Get your wits together. You'll have to save your grief for later, when you're alone."

Slowly, I straightened up and wiped my eyes in the darkness. "You're right, I don't want Sigrid killed."

Sigrid nodded. "Kyar was my friend. She loved you very much, and you had to know the truth."

Sigrid kissed Crispus, who held her briefly about the waist, and turned to leave.

"By the way," Sigrid said, "I have the buckle."

A chill went down my back. "What?" The pain of Kyar's death had erased all thought of the buckle from my mind. "How did you get it?"

"I will tell you when I bring it to you, later. I must go before Rix misses me."

"But where is it?" I asked.

"It's in Kyar's hiding place." Sigrid paused and her eyes met mine. "Kyar called for you before she—I can't!" She hiked away as fast as her plump body would carry her toward the poorly lit camp.

In falling rain, Crispus and I returned to the Legion camp in silence. Jumbled thoughts of Kyar rattled around in my head. Images of her ivory face, her lithe body, clothed and unclothed, our love making shot through my brain like racing chariots in the Great Circus, impossible to control, to slow down. A part of me died with Kyar, a wound from which my soul could never heal. Sounds of jagged clasps of thunder pounded my head, flashes of lightning hurled through my mind in which I glimpsed Kyar's ghostly image, the gray pallor of death. Her hand reached toward me. Then she was gone.

I shook my head as if that could remove the images and blasting sounds from my skull. Had our love been too intense? Deep inside I must have feared losing her. Is that why I risked paying Rix most of the outrageous price for her in advance? Now, she was gone. Most people viewed her as merely a slave, a piece of property, but she had been a live human being, and I loved her.

Never again would Rix murder anyone. I began plans for revenge.

CHAPTER 19

Back in our quarters, after stabling Argento, I dropped my saddle at the foot of the makeshift bed pallet. The tented barracks reeked of rancid saddle leather mixed with the sweet-sour odor of lathered horses.

Crispus produced a small earthen jug hidden beneath his bedding. "Have a drink," he said in a lighter mood. "You need it, and so do I."

"Aye, that's the truth."

I pulled a bronze cup from my saddlebag and sat down at the crude, wooden table. Crispus splashed it full of his favorite rotgut. Then he filled his a little fuller than mine. I gulped down the acidic-tasting stuff, barely noticing as it burned a passage down my throat.

Crispus refilled my cup. Initially, I refused his undiluted swill. I needed a clear head for planning my revenge. He said the wine would relax and allow me to think better.

"No, it won't," I said. "I—"

"What are comrades for? Would I bridle you wrong? And this stuff is diluted—tastes rotten, that's all."

The first cup had eased the tension. Another drink wouldn't matter. "All right, but only one more."

"Naturally. After all, you've got to think how you're going to deal with that fucking Gaul."

"Tomorrow, I'll tell Budar about Kyar's death. He'll know what to do. I don't feel like facing him tonight, knowing what he'll say." Crispus poured a third cup, which I drank rapidly.

I continued rambling about Budar and my plans to avenge Kyar, and Crispus kept pouring refills until I quit counting. The wine broke down the will restraining my tears and caused me to look away, burying my head in my arms on the table. Before long, I passed out.

* * *

Reveille sounded too soon. The cornus's brassy sound shot through my head like a thunder clap, bouncing from side to side. Sprawled on top of my pallet, I barely moved. My head felt like a roaring avalanche pounding the inside of my skull. Thank the gods those accursed trumpets only blew in the morning and for taps. Painfully getting to my feet, I staggered outside and headed for the latrine, oblivious to morning camp activity. Centurions shouted orders, legionaries marched along the path heading out to relieve the night watch on sentry duty. Others with axes in hand headed outside to the nearby forest to cut wood to shore up the stockade's defenses. Smoke from cooking fires drifted upward, disappearing in the gray morning sky.

Before I had gone too far, Crispus approached. "Thanks friend," I grumbled, "just what I needed, a drunk."

Crispus looked about. "I had a reason, Marcellus. I can't explain here, I'll tell you later."

"Now, dammit!" I winced. "Gods, my head!"

A soldier snickered as he walked by.

"All right, let's go to the stable. No one ought to be around yet."

Being close to feeding time, Argento was happy to see me. His soft mouth slimed my shoulder, staining my tunic. I grabbed a wooden pitchfork and threw him some fodder as Crispus and I conversed.

"Kyar is with the gods of her people," Crispus said in a low voice, "her soul is at peace."

"There's only one way that could happen," I said quietly, praying my throbbing headache would go away.

"The pimp is dead."

I dropped the pitchfork, a thud erupted as it hit the dirt floor. The only other sound in the stall came from Argento munching his hay. "How?"

"Budar."

"Why? Revenge was mine, not his."

"We didn't want you involved."

"What do you mean, *we*?" I eyed him suspiciously.

Crispus tapped his chest. "Me, Budar, Obulco, and the Germans—they helped, too."

"What is this, a conspiracy?" Argento raised his head as if on cue. His bulbous hickory eyes seemed to be studying me as strands of hay hung from the side of his mouth. Then he returned to his feed.

He stiffened and shook his head. "No friend. We saved your arse. In your state of mind, you would've left a trail wide enough for the whole legion to follow. Gallus would love to charge you with murder."

"What about you?"

He glanced around the stable. "Don't fret, we cloaked ourselves. Whether you know it or not, the entire squadron respects you."

I shrugged.

"No matter," Crispus continued, "Obulco gladly volunteered when I told him what I had in mind. Others would have, too, but I figured the fewer who knew about the plan, the better." He paused. "Everybody hated Rix. No one will miss his thieving carcass, except Gallus, and he'll investigate. So we made certain none of us were seen."

"What makes you think Gallus won't accuse me of being involved? Knowing him, he'll find a way."

"He won't," Crispus answered with a wink. "Kimon stayed with you most of the night. He'll truthfully answer you didn't go anywhere."

"I never saw him." I placed a hand to my still-throbbing head and rubbed my temple. A waste of time. I lowered my hand.

"He came in about the time you passed out. After helping me tuck you safely in your bunk, he kept an eye on you until I returned."

"How did you kill Rix?"

Crispus grabbed the hilt of the dagger strapped to the side of his waist. "We kidnapped him late last night."

My friend explained that he and the rest of the conspirators slipped over to Rix's wagon sometime after midnight. He and Obulco left camp by the south gate where the Asturians stood sentry duty. Earlier he learned the password, so they could return safely. Crispus bribed the Northerners not to report their movements. When the guards asked where he was going, he said to visit Mattan's women. They chuckled and waved him through the gate.

"Obulco and I joined Budar and the Germans at his quarters," Crispus related. "We rode to Rix's camp keeping downwind from the horses and mules."

He went on. They had approached the Gaul's quarters and dismounted, muffled the hooves of their horses with soft deer skins, and silently crept the remaining distance. No one was around. Budar posted two Germans at the entrance to guard against any surprise. Without making a sound, the rest entered.

"Obulco gagged Rix while Budar and I tied his hands and feet," Crispus said. "But the stinking pimp continued to struggle, until Budar put a dagger to his throat and threatened to run him through unless he stopped resisting." Crispus continued, saying that Rix gave up. They carried the Gaul to a horse, placed him face down across the saddle, and traveled about ten miles up the River Axe to where it entered a black cave, the freezing water running chest high on their mounts.

Inside, their torches revealed a wide, pebbled shore along the slow-swirling water's edge, but failed to illuminate the high ceiling. As the group spurred their animals up the bank onto dry land, they startled a swarm of bats that streamed out the cavern.

"Obulco was eager to torture Rix," Crispus said, "but Budar said to wait. He had his own way to handle Rix."

"Aye, he would," I said. "What torment did he devise for the butcher?"

"Your uncle ordered the Germans to tie Rix's arms and legs to four separate horses," Crispus said.

The mounts slowly stretched him in opposite directions until he screamed for mercy, the agonizing sounds echoing off the shadowy walls. Budar threatened to tear him apart unless he spilled the truth about Kyar. Rix refused. The horses continued stretching his limbs. The Gaul screamed louder, filling the cave with the wails of pain and horror. Budar warned he wouldn't halt unless Rix cooperated.

A horse whinnied at the far end of the stable interrupting Crispus's tale. We both turned in that direction. No one.

"Rix confessed, Marcellus," Crispus continued. "It happened just as Sigrid described, but worse."

"What could be worse?"

"After he had beaten and kicked her, Kyar miscarried and bled to death, right in front of Sigrid and Rix in her cubicle. They couldn't stop the bleeding." Crispus hesitated.

"Go on, don't stop now," I ordered, even as my mind reeled at the sickening revelation.

"After Kyar died, Rix forced Sigrid to wrap her blood-spattered body in a blanket and weight it down with large stones," Crispus continued.

Late that evening he and his cronies carried Kyar's body down to the river where they had camped for the night. Rix swore he couldn't remember its exact location. They led the horse, carrying her body out into the current, and released her corpse into its murky depths. Upon returning to camp, Rix threatened to kill Sigrid and the other slaves if they said anything.

"Then what did you do with him?" I asked.

Crispus snorted. A smile, one that seemed to be of satisfaction, crossed the lips of his narrow face. "Budar told Rix his soul would suffer Kyar's fate. He screamed for mercy." Crispus went on to describe that Rix offered Budar his entire fortune, but his uncle said he didn't deserve mercy and wouldn't touch his filthy money. He ran the murdering Gaul through the testicles with his sword. Rix howled. Crispus, Obulco, and the Germans untied him from the horses and dropped him roughly to the hard-packed ground. Tying stones to his mangy hide, they dragged him deeper into the cave's recesses. As Rix screamed for mercy, Obulco jammed a stinging centipede down his throat. They threw him into the deep-running stream, the splashing resounded through the cavern. He sank straight to the bottom.

"Rix has paid for Kyar's murder," Crispus concluded. "She's with the gods, and these accursed spirits will let her rest in peace." He placed a hand to his chest and blessed himself.

"For her sake, I hope they exist." A sense of relief flowed through my mind now that Rix was dead. Although she had been avenged by my family, I had been cheated out of vengeance that was rightfully mine. Was she truly at rest?

The doubts still lingered. Nothing seemed to matter. Everything appeared unreal. How could she be gone? Our love was too genuine to ever die. And I still had to repay Gallus.

* * *

About midmorning, Budar appeared at the stables just as I was saddling Argento for patrol. My headache was finally fading away.

"I heard about Rix, Uncle," I said. "Thanks for taking care of him."

He halted before me, and with a hand reached out and briefly touched my shoulder. "Aye. Now it's done, and I'm leaving."

"Good idea, Gallus is bound to become suspicious about his disappearance."

Budar scanned the area. "That's why I'm here. Crispus didn't tell you everything."

For a couple of heartbeats I studied his craggy face. "He said Rix was dead, that's enough. Kyar's dead. What more could there be?"

"It was Gallus who ordered Kyar's death."

At first, a sense of disbelief numbed my consciousness. The bridle I placed over Argento's head slipped off. I grabbed the leather straps, but he nearly choked on the snaffle bit as it wrenched free from his mouth into my hands. Slowly, my mind cleared, and I understood Gallus's part in Kyar's death. Rage surged to the forefront of my thoughts. The muscles in my chest and limbs tightened like the cords on a catapult. "The son-of-a-whore!"

"Careful, Nephew!" Budar warned. "Others not as sympathetic might hear."

I turned away, fighting back the hate in my soul, the urge to commit murder. Facing him once more, I asked, "Why? What was she to him?"

"Nothing, and that's the object. The whoremaster told me everything." Budar related it was Gallus who had a buyer for the buckle. The tribune learned Rix had received the buckle from me and knew its true value. He could sell it for enough money to buy my family's property without involving a loan from his father.

"Gallus made a deal with Rix," Budar added, "giving him twenty percent of the profits. Rix had no choice if he wanted to stay in business, but he'd still make a small fortune."

Budar continued. Gallus had learned the buckle was missing, and Kyar was the suspected thief. He ordered that she was to be tortured until she confessed, and then to kill her after revealing the hiding place. Unfortunately, Rix took it upon himself to viciously beat a confession out of Kyar before receiving his instructions. She died, telling him nothing."

A roar like a stormy sea breaking against the cliff rushed into my ears. My chest tightened, and I balled my fists at my side, but I kept my mouth shut while Budar spoke.

"Gallus was confident you couldn't touch him," Budar said, "because you'd need proof of his involvement. An Iberian's word against a senator's son is worthless in court, Roman citizen notwithstanding."

"That dirty shit eater." I wanted revenge, but dared not lift a hand against an officer. So long as I remained under Gallus's command, I had to pretend ignorance. But I swore one day to take vengeance.

"I hate telling you," Budar continued, "but you had to know. You must be strong, the family mustn't be disgraced."

I threw the jumbled bridle to the ground. "Always the damn family! What about me? What about Kyar?"

"Easy, Marcellus . . . Son," Budar said quietly, as he placed a hand on my shoulder. "Your loss is painful, I know, but don't try anything foolish. Killing Gallus would mean your execution and confiscation of the *latifundia*. Your mother would lose everything your father worked for. Remember, legally you're head of the family, not her. That isn't what you want. It won't bring Kyar back."

"I know . . . I know," I answered slowly, as my sanity returned.

"I figured you'd see the reasoning. The family fortune would have been washed out to sea, forever."

"Did Gallus know Kyar was pregnant?" I asked.

"It's doubtful. It wouldn't have mattered to him, but when Rix discovered she was, he got angry. He planned to resell Kyar, and knew her value would drop on the auction block. That's why he forced your woman to abort by kicking her, and you know the rest."

Budar eyed me for a few minutes before continuing. "Your body looks awfully tight, can I trust you not to do anything stupid?"

"Yes, Uncle." I exhaled. "I promise not to wring Gallus's fucking neck."

He touched my shoulder again. "Good man, there'll be another time and another way. Be patient, the stars aren't right for vengeance."

My uncle turned to leave but stopped. "I almost forgot, there's one other matter."

"What's left?"

"Sigrid, she gave me the buckle." Budar's eyes searched the stable, and then he pulled out the object from inside his tunic. "I'm returning it to your mother for safekeeping."

I started to object, but realized the wisdom of his decision. "Under the circumstances, it's for the best."

"Good thinking, Nephew, I agree."

"Where did Sigrid find Father's buckle?"

A thin smile crossed Budar's lips. He snorted. "In Kyar's monthly women's cloths. Rix didn't search there."

"What about Sigrid? Won't she be in danger?" I looked around—only horses in the adjacent stalls and the two of us.

"I doubt it. I went to Rix's place this morning, as if I knew nothing about last night. When his henchmen said he'd disappeared, naturally I faked ignorance and disbelief. I said I wanted to buy Sigrid. He'd offered her to me a few days before. They said I'd have to wait for his return."

"But he won't."

"Right, but she'll be safe—trust me." Budar exhaled. "Now, I'm leaving. Remember my warning, stay out of trouble."

CHAPTER 20

Later, after Budar departed, my squadron mounted up. I led a patrol into charcoal hills to the north, a hostile area not completely under Roman control. An hour had passed when the squadron came upon a grove of half-circled ash trees at the foot of a high gorge. Again, we stumbled upon a deserted place of worship used by the Druids. The nearby spring was dry and weed-filled. A few old and corroded votive ornaments remained on the brown, woody branches. Yet, in its presence, I sensed a feeling of peace—something I needed to experience, if only for a little while. I signaled for a halt and waved Crispus to my side.

"Budar told me about Gallus."

Crispus's face tightened, and he stared at his reins. "Sorry, Marcellus, but he made me promise."

I waved off the apology. "You're an arsehole for not telling me, but I understand."

Glancing about, I came to a decision. "Take over the patrol, Crispus, I'm staying here for a while."

His dark eyes narrowed. "Do you know what you're doing? You could be charged with desertion." He turned in the direction of grove. "This place is bewitched."

"By the condition of this grove I'd say the spirits left long ago."

He twisted in his saddle toward the other riders. Their eyes seemed to be searching about—for something evil? "What do I tell the men?"

"You don't," I snapped. Then in a milder voice I added, "Let them believe Mugain's witch curse caused me to stop and worship their gods."

"They might believe you, but I don't. What's your true reason for stopping here?"

"It's something I can't explain. I saw this grove and knew I had to stop. Don't ask why, because I don't have an answer."

Crispus shrugged. “I think it’s strange, but if anything happens to you, what do I tell Corribilo?”

“Simply tell him you were following orders, but nothing will happen.”

He frowned. “All right, but I say it’s madness. Where should we meet you later?”

“Here. Give me a couple of hours.”

“A couple of hours!” he exclaimed in a loud whisper. “In these hills? It’s too dangerous.” He studied the sky as thick, slate-colored clouds formed overhead and turned back toward me. “There’s a storm brewing.”

“Easy, Crispus, nothing is going to happen, I promise. Now go!”

He shook his head and turned his dappled gray mare away, but glanced back once again as if he were seeing me for the last time. He and the troopers headed up the nearby ravine.

I dismounted Argento, strapped my flat, oval shield beneath the saddle blanket, and tied him to the limb of a tree near the old spring. A longsword hung from my baldric, and I carried a lance in my hand as I trudged from tree to tree searching for what I know not. The clouds darkened, and a light drizzle began. The scar on my face itched as it always does when it rained. Lightning flashed in the distance.

Seconds later, a loud crack of thunder echoed above. The tapping sound of cold rain struck my helmet and ran down both sides of my face and neck, onto my shoulders and down my back. It soaked through my woolen uniform to the skin. I shuddered. Despite my growing misery, I soon found myself lost in thoughts of Kyar, but not for long.

Argento grew restless, nervously pawing the ground, swinging his head from side to side. I returned to the hazel tree and comforted him. In a futile attempt to stay dry, I wrapped the soaking cloak tightly around my shoulders. If Jupiter was kind, the storm would quickly pass.

More than likely the patrol would find shelter in one of the hill’s many caves until it ended. I rammed the iron-pointed butt of my lance into the clay mud and patted Argento’s black mane. I soothed the nervous dark bay with gentle words and considered leading him to cover of a large shrubbery wood. But memories of Kyar rushed into my mind like ocean waves breaking on the rocks. The wind whistled through surrounding trees as the thunder grew more intense.

Sharp blasts of frigid air raked the forest's naked limbs. And despite the claps of thunder, the wind's sound grew eerie and haunting. Was it my imagination? The longer the wind blew, the more it sounded like a woman's voice—*Kyar's.* Was I going mad? Had I truly fallen under the spell of the sorceress Mugain? I shook my head, somehow thinking I could erase the curse from my mind. The voice grew louder and clearer, echoing over and over again.

"Marcellus," the voice beckoned, a drawn-out echo. "Marcellus . . . us . . . us."

Vainly, I stared into the blinding rain, searching the radiant glow of lightning flashes. The voice rang out again, but nothing appeared except the towering, brush-covered limestone cliff across the trail. Again, I heard my name, this time in a haunting, near-whispering tone.

"Marcellus."

Another bolt of lightning seared the sky, and for an instant I saw an apparition—the outline of Kyar flitting towards me. I closed and opened my eyes. In my heart, I strained to believe Kyar was real.

Her hands beckoned me.

Darkness fell again. Seconds later, another flash, the phantom drew closer.

This is madness, I'm bewitched. But I had to learn if this ghost was real. Releasing my grip on Argento's mane, I cautiously moved in the direction of the shimmering image.

A thunderclap exploded.

Argento whinnied and violently snapped the scrubby limb he had been tied to and galloped into the darkness. *Damn!*

Alone. Thunder grew louder and closer with each lightning bolt. Magically, Kyar leapt nearer with each series of blinding flashes. When the image reappeared, she was at arm's length. The spirit placed the palms of her hands together and rested them against the side of her head. I understood the meaning. Still, I reached out, only to grab emptiness.

"KYAR, don't go!" I cried aloud. "KYAR, don't go!" In vain, I grabbed thin air. I clasped my face with both hands. *I'm going mad!* I shook my head attempting to suppress tears and grief.

The stories are true. The hills and forests are possessed by demons and witches. Have I not been cursed by one? Why else am I seeing Kyar, knowing she is dead?

I stood soaked in the windswept rain, chilled. I didn't care. Too numb and no longer wanting to contain my grief, I cried aloud, my curse lost in the roaring thunder. "Oh, gods! Why did you take her from me? Why did you take away my Kyar? Why?" I cried over and over, demanding an answer from the heavens until my voice grew hoarse.

I sank to the muddy earth, my head between my knees.

Something hard struck me on the back of the head. A searing pain shot through my body followed by unstoppable, overwhelming darkness.

* * *

I awoke to a clear, crisp night. Countless stars filled the sky above the skeletal trees. Then I recalled my vision of Kyar. Had I experienced a bad dream? A stinging pain shot through the left side of my head. I removed my dented helmet and touched the swelling lump with my fingers. The evening breeze soothed me. A large tree limb lay at my side, its broken end seared and blackened by lightning. No dream was this.

Struggling to my feet, I clamped my helmet back on my head, wrung out my rain-soaked cloak, and trudged toward camp. Hungry and freezing, I prayed to stay free of pneumonia, killer of many good soldiers. I found my lance, scorched, split in two, laying on the muddy ground. Picking up the two jagged pieces, obviously struck by lightning, I examined them. The blade on one section was in good shape, dirty but still sharp. The iron-pointed butt on the other piece remained intact as well. I thought about discarding them, but decided against it. There was enough left of the two segments that they could be remade into short but deadly stickers by an enterprising barbarian. I carried them with me as I hiked along the branch-strewn trail.

A brilliant moon bathed the woods in a pale-white glow. By its position overhead, I must have been unconscious for at least a couple of hours. If that were the case, where was the squadron? They should have returned to the grove.

Soft shadows seemed to hush the night sounds, and the soothing calmness of nature fell upon me. No doubt Argento found his way home—he was intelligent for a horse. How would I explain to Corribilo the loss of a patrol —a court-martial offense.

I hadn't gone far when I discovered Argento peacefully grazing in a nearby meadow. He tossed his head, nickered a greeting, and trotted to my side. The last being unusual for Argento. Usually, horses are more concerned with eating than paying attention to their masters.

I dropped the broken pieces of the lance and stroked the little barb's mane and patted his soft nose and cheek, speaking kind words. He nudged me and nibbled at the sleeve of my tunic before I gently pushed his head away. For some reason a feeling of relief and inner peace swelled within me. It was as if Argento's appearance was a reassuring sign from Kyar that everything was well.

I was neither a philosopher, nor a soothsayer. Soldiers aren't supposed to possess philosophical insights, but perhaps this was Kyar's way of saying farewell, not to be concerned for her afterlife. At that moment, a sense of inner peace flooded my soul. Although my grief lingered, I knew Kyar no longer wanted me to lament for her.

I picked up and tied the pieces of the lance at the back of my saddle. As I mounted Argento, I heard the sound of muffled hoof beats beyond the nearby trees. Barbarians? I cantered to the nearby clump of overgrown scrub brush for concealment. Peering through the scratchy vines, I recognized the patrol and rejoined them.

"Thank Father Jupiter, you're alive!" Crispus exclaimed. "I was afraid that accursed place had driven you mad or, even worse, the savages got you. By the look of you, something did happen." He eyed my saddle. "What's that—a broken lance?"

"I'm not injured, my friend." I winced from the stinging bump on my head. "As to the lance, it was struck by lightning—good thing I wasn't holding it. I didn't want to leave it for any savage to reuse."

Crispus nodded. "Aye, could make nasty little weapons."

"What about you?" I asked. "Where have you been?"

He motioned with his head toward the hills. "Held up by a flash flood in one of the canyons we rode through—this place is full of them. Happened about a half hour after we left you. The goddess *Fortuna* smiled on us, and we found a hill above a ravine, otherwise we'd be wondering souls."

I grinned and tapped his shoulder. "Let's go home."

My concern now was Gallus. He was certain to make inquiries into Rix's death.

Would he accuse me of murder?

CHAPTER 21

LATE AUGUST, 44 AD

Within a week, Gallus began inquiries into Rix's disappearance. Rumors spread that he suspected foul play and planned to request General Vespasian's permission to conduct an investigation. When commander of his own little garrison, Gallus was a powerful man. Now, he was but one of General Vespasian's many tribunes, subject to his authority. Gallus could no longer manipulate the lives of others without bringing his own conduct into question.

Early one morning, during the same period, Corribilo sent me to Legion Headquarters in his place to receive orders for our troop that day. His horse had gone lame, and not trusting the cavalry's incompetent veterinarian, he was treating the mount's leg himself.

I stood by a table, along with several other officers, while one of the general's indifferent Greek clerks searched for a copy of our unit's orders. Within seconds a loud argument erupted between Gallus and General Vespasian about Rix. The flimsy goatskin wall separating his corner office from the rest of the command tent was embarrassingly thin, and all but the lowest whispers could be overheard.

By the tone of Vespasian's voice, the general seemed to be suspicious of Gallus's motives and demanded to know why he was interested in the whereabouts of a thieving Gaul. Hiding the truth about his business connections, Gallus answered he had received unconfirmed reports that Rix was murdered by one of his soldiers.

"As cohort commander," Gallus said, "duty demands that I make inquiries. Therefore, I am requesting your permission, sir."

"Request denied, Tribune Gallus," the gravel-voiced Vespasian said.

"But, sir," Gallus pleaded, "I am obligated to investigate any allegations of murder by my troops."

"Didn't I make myself clear, Tribune? No soldier of mine will be accused of such an outrageous crime, especially if it involves that miserable Gaul. Rix is a cheat and a thief. If he's dead, which I doubt, he deserved his fate—it's long overdue."

"But still, murder!"

"What murder?" Vespasian answered in a snarling voice. "We both know it's not uncommon for a scummy vagabond to *disappear* when it's to his advantage. As far as I'm concerned, good riddance, I'll hear no more. Dismissed!"

Flush-faced, Gallus pushed the leather flap aside to Vespasian's office and shoved his way past us. Although he attempted to put on a sober face, he failed. He glared, stomped by me, and stormed out of headquarters.

I had no doubt that soldiers and camp followers alike guessed Rix's true fate—he had many enemies. Mattan, the Sidonian, absorbed his business. Although as dishonest as the Gaul, he kept his business dealings discreet and treated the women better.

About five days after his purchase, I received a secret message from Mattan. He explained that Uncle Budar had made a clandestine arrangement with him to buy Sigrid, in gratitude for disclosing Kyar's true fate and recovering the buckle. Freeing her, Budar gave Sigrid enough money for a small dowry and passage to Roman Germania. There, among the newly settled Roman colonists, she could find a husband who would ask no questions about her past.

By now, Uncle Budar and his Germans were safely aboard a merchantman sailing to Hispania.

* * *

A couple of weeks after Budar departed, Sextus Rufius returned to the troop. Although he recovered, the wounds had extracted their toll. Drawn and gaunt, his once craggy face was but a shadow of itself. Gone was the spark from his gleaming eyes. A bald spot surfaced through the back of his white hair, which a few short months before had been a mane of gray.

During the evening muster, Corribilo officially returned command of the troop to Rufius. Later, Rufius invited me to his quarters. His shaky hand poured two cups of wine from a jug on the table. He motioned to a stool nearby and offered me one of the bronze goblets. Taking a long drink, he exhaled and sat in meditative silence.

"I won't forget what you did for me at Maugh-Dun Castle, Marcellus," he remarked softly.

I started to protest. Stiffly, he waved off my objections. "Wait, I'm not finished."

I nodded.

"I know you'd have done the same for anyone," the decurion resumed. "Nevertheless, you saved my life, and I'm grateful—although sometimes I think you shouldn't have."

"But, sir, it was right thing to do. You're a good officer."

Rufius shrugged, smiling half-heartedly. "I must be growing old. I almost died from the wounds, and now I'm always tired. Maybe I'll retire once and for all."

I knew that ten years before, after twenty-five years of service, Rufius had been discharged and received Roman citizenship. He found farming was not the life for him and returned to the army as a veteran a few months later. The army was his true home. Even in death they would take care of him. His contributions, which all soldiers made to the burial fund, would guarantee him a decent funeral and a tombstone listing his deeds and praising his dedication to Rome.

"Alexandros said your wounds weren't serious," I said.

Rufius grimaced. "Lies. The quack nearly botched it. Why do you think my recovery took so damned long?" He paused and refilled his cup. "I had a lot of time to think. Too much." He gulped his drink and wiped his mouth. "Thinking is something no soldier should do—remember my warning when you were in training?"

"I didn't forget."

The decurion nodded. He stared through me as if I didn't exist. "You know you'll be awarded the *Corona Civica*?"

"I'm not a medal seeker." The award was the highest honor a soldier could receive in service to Rome. Usually, a promotion followed.

"Don't protest so much," Rufius advised. "You haven't received it yet. Remember, I have to admit you saved me." He paused, seeming to enjoy the implication, but finally, my silent gaze prompted him to continue. "If I were younger, I would deny everything. Now I'm older, and maybe a little wiser.

"This much I do know—to deny you the award would be vanity on my part. Just the same as this blood-drenching campaign is being waged to satisfy our emperor's vanity. He's got his triumph and title, *Britannicus, Conqueror of the Britons*. But the south wasn't enough, he wants the entire island."

He exhaled. "At fifty-seven, I'm getting sentimental. I've seen a lot of bloodshed—enough to be numbing—to make me indifferent. When you have too much time on your hands, you think."

"Even if you don't, it happens," I said.

"In your case, yes. You've always been a thinker, which led to your trouble with Gallus. If you're to survive," he raised his voice in warning and pointed his cup at me, "you've got to use your head. My instincts say you'll not spend all your life in the camps. Who knows? You may go to Rome. Either way, get rid of your Greek ideas of humanity, or you'll be crushed by your enemies. In this world, seek your own interests first."

His eyes held mine for a long moment. When he seemed satisfied that I took him seriously, he grunted, and a smile came to his chapped lips.

Rufius sat in silence, taking another long swill. I tried to digest his words. He was right. One day, I would go to Rome. The *Corona Civica* opened another door to the Equestrians. I had not sought the honor, but I would never allow any filthy barbarian to slay the man, who, next to my father, I held in deepest respect.

"Enough of this nonsense," Rufius said. "I sound like a harping female. The fact remains the emperor has approved your award, and word arrived today by courier."

I jolted, nearly dropping my cup. For a split-second I thought my heart jumped into my throat. Despite his reassurances, I believed the *Corona Civica* was out of reach. "You mean it's true?"

"Aye, have no fear, I'll be honored to announce to the whole legion you saved my life. If the rest of my fellow officers don't like it, they can piss up the River Rhenus!"

* * *

The following morning, I stood on parade before the entire camp, including Generals Vespasian and Sabinus, as Rufius proclaimed that he, as an officer and Roman citizen, was saved by a subordinate in battle. He placed a tightly woven oak leaf crown on my head and strung the *phillarae,* a medal of silver with gold inlay and embossed with a gold oak leaf, across my coat of chain mail. I regretted that Budar was not present to relate the details to Mother.

Although a great honor, I suddenly felt foolish. I wanted to lower my eyes as I stood before the army. But regulations required that I stand at rigid attention, lest I be considered insubordinate and disrespectful. I tightened the muscles in my body and stared straight ahead. As far as I was concerned, every soldier who fought at Maugh-Dun Castle and survived deserved the *Corona.* I dared not reveal my true thoughts, lest I injure Rufius's pride. His admission had been out of gratitude and, perhaps, affection.

Later, I reported to General Sabinus's quarters. Seated at his desk, the legate was signing a series of documents. Looking up as I saluted, his reddish-brown eyes sparkled, and a slight smile creased his lips. "At ease, Sergeant."

Sabinus laid the quill pen on the table and carefully pushed aside the parchments. I respectfully declined the cup of wine he offered me from a gold pitcher. He nodded his approval while taking a short sip. He leaned back in his chair. "Earlier, I promised you would go far," he said pleasantly. "I'm a man who keeps his word. I've been recalled to Rome. The emperor, in his infinite wisdom, has appointed me City Prefect."

The City Prefect was one of the most powerful positions an emperor can bestow upon a Roman who was not a member of the Imperial Household. The post gave Sabinus the authority of Chief Magistrate of Rome, Commander of the City Guard, and City Administrator. As a member of the Senate and former Consul of Rome, he was more than qualified.

"Congratulations, sir, a great honor for you," I said.

"Thank you," Sabinus replied. He paused. "There is more. You are coming to Rome as my retainer."

I stood speechless. Less than an hour before, I had received the *Corona Civica*, and now a new position with one of Rome's most highly regarded noblemen. I never dreamt of traveling to the heart of the empire so soon. "I'm honored, sir," I stammered. "I've never seen Rome."

"Haven't you?" he said with amusement. "There's no place like it on the face of the earth. Rome is like a woman. Sometimes you love her, and other times you hate her, but by the gods you'll never forget her. Then it's all set. Of course, you will be promoted to a legionary centurion, not an auxiliary. As a Roman citizen, that's where you rightfully belong."

The promotion capped the greatest day in my life, and it must have been apparent to Sabinus. He cricked an eyebrow. "Why did you join the auxiliaries instead of enlisting as a citizen legionary?"

"Family tradition, sir," I answered, snapping out of my dazed state. "My people have served in the auxiliary cavalry of Rome for nearly two hundred years."

Sabinus nodded. "Most impressive, and Rome appreciates such loyalty. Now, it's time for a change in tradition." He smiled again. "Consider yourself the first of many future generations who'll serve as officers in the legions of Rome."

"Yes, sir, why not?" I grinned. My thoughts spun. Rome! The world! What else was there?

"May I ask what my duties will be, sir?"

He pursed his mouth and nodded. "A fair question. First of all, I chose you because you are loyal and trustworthy—despite the Druid Temple incident. Like my duties, yours will vary."

He explained I would be his bodyguard and investigate situations he could not entrust to others. There was the possibility of receiving a temporary command in one of the City Guard's four cohorts. "One or two of the commanding tribunes have unsavory reputations," he explained, "and it is my intention to replace them."

"Whatever you have in mind, I'm ready for the task, sir."

"Excellent, I like your spirit." He went on to tell me as his retainer I would stay at his home, on call at all times, day and night. "At first glance, your duties may seem time consuming, but they aren't. You will see there are benefits in being my retainer."

As he paused, a terrible thought occurred to me. Crispus! He couldn't stay behind. Although Rufius had returned, Crispus would be at Gallus's mercy. Despite General Vespasian's denial for an investigation into Rix's disappearance, Gallus would continue his private inquiries. He knew Crispus and I were good friends. If he discovered the truth about Rix, he would concoct a plan to get rid of my friend.

Crispus had to join me in Rome. I needed someone in whom I could confide while living in that strange city. I didn't know if Sabinus would grant my request, but it was worth a try.

"Are there any further questions, *Centurion*?" Sabinus inquired.

"Sir, may I ask a favor?"

"If it is reasonable."

"As your retainer could I have my own assistant, an aide-de-camp?"

"That can be arranged. Whom do you have in mind?"

"Acting Sergeant Signatius Crispus, from my squadron, sir."

"Is there something special about him?"

"He's an excellent soldier who has a very sharp mind. He's a fast learner, and would render both of us invaluable assistance."

He creased his forehead as if pondering the request. A gust of wind rippled the side of the headquarters' goat-skinned tent and faded away. "Very well. I will give him the opportunity to prove his worth. Your favor is granted."

"Thank you, sir. You won't be disappointed." Then as afterthought, I inquired, "May I ask as to when we leave?"

"Tomorrow."

I blinked.

* * *

Dusk fell as Crispus and I strolled along the protective open ground running between the inside of the camp stockade wall and tents around the perimeter. Being seventy paces wide, enemy missiles hurled over the ramparts would fall harmlessly on the trampled earth.

"Well, old friend," Crispus said, "looks like this is the last time I'll be seeing you."

"Oh? Trying to get rid of me so soon?" We halted and faced each other.

Crispus cocked his head and scowled. "You said earlier you're going to Rome, aren't you?" He paused and exhaled. "Are you saying—?"

I raised my hand. "Hold on. Consider this . . ." I explained about my promotion and the request for his transfer to Rome along with mine.

When I had finished, Crispus searched the area and exhaled. "Gods, help us—you know we'll be sheep in a wolf's lair."

"I do."

"Tell me, what do you expect to gain by going to Rome? And what do you expect by taking me along?"

It was my turn to look about. "It's not a matter of gain, it's what we'll lose if we stay."

He grabbed the bone handle of his dagger. "Like what, our heads?"

"You're closer to the truth than you realize, Crispus."

Crispus shook his head. "How?"

"Gallus."

"What does he have to do with our leaving?"

"Think about it."

He did and spat. "I see what you mean. Rix."

"Exactly."

"Then it's settled," he said in a sullen voice, "like it or not."

"Don't look so glum, *Sergeant.* You're being promoted to the rank of *sesquiplicarius.* After all, you'll probably find

Rome to your liking. I hear the city is full of women on the prowl. That should make things a little easier."

"Somehow, I doubt it."

* * *

The next morning, after I had been to the stables to say good-bye to my faithful mount, Argento, and had turned him over to Corribilo, whose own horse had died of colic, I returned to my quarters. I now donned the new centurion's uniform issued by the quartermaster section. After wearing a blue uniform and chain mail of the cavalry for five years, the scarlet, woolen tunic and the segmented armor of the infantry seemed foreign to me. Carefully, I knotted my neck scarf beneath the armor vest and strung decorations across its front.

As I finished placing the new silver greaves on my shins, a runner brought word that I was to see Gallus immediately. Whatever the reason, I suspected the encounter wouldn't be pleasant. Grabbing my helmet, I stroked its transverse horsehair crest across the top, the insignia of centurion. I touched the twisted, hardwood, vine cane, symbol of my new rank. Then I made a few more minor adjustments and left for headquarters.

Gallus's quarters reeked of stale jasmine and smoky fumes rising from olive oil in his new bronze cat-shaped lamps. He sat at a portable desk dictating a letter to his Greek clerk, writing with a metal stylus on a wax tablet, enclosed by citrus wood. The tribune glanced at me, dictated for another moment, and then dismissed the slave.

"Congratulations on your promotion, Centurion." Gallus smirked. "And receiving the *Corona*, you have earned it. Decurion Rufius showed a great deal of humility for his part."

"He's a fine officer," I answered, "and a brave man."

Gallus narrowed his eyes. "I agree, but had it been me, I would have never admitted to such a deed, especially to you!"

I flinched. What if Gallus had been wounded on the battlefield? Would I have saved his life as I had Rufius's? After learning about his role in Kyar's death, most likely the later, I hated him all the more for his part, as if she had died by his hand. So far, I had managed to hide my rage.

"Is this why you ordered me here today, sir?" I asked, heat rushing to my face.

"Insolent as always, aren't you?" He leaned back in his chair. "But to answer your impertinent question, no. Consider yourself fortunate you and Sergeant Crispus have been selected as retainers by General Sabinus. Of course, it fits with your plans for the Equestrians, which my father will stop."

"As I said before, sir, my only intention is to serve Rome as a good soldier."

"You can dispense with the facade, Centurion. Both of us know differently. The question remains why General Sabinus did not choose loyal Romans? That's beyond me."

Because there are too many Romans like you. I held my tongue.

"I cannot prove it yet," Gallus said coolly, "but I know you and your uncle are involved with the vanishing of the Gaul. I know he was murdered."

This had been the first mention of Rix since I'd repaid Gallus's loan a few days after his death.

My mother had sent twice the amount requested, allowing me to pay the one hundred percent interest Gallus had added to the loan. Apparently, she suspected I would need more.

At the time, Gallus had been unusually silent on the matter. I had mentioned I had heard Kyar had been sold, and Rix left without a trace. I'd feigned mild anger about Rix's thievery and sale of the woman, but had quickly dropped the subject.

"That's the risk you take," Gallus had said, "when buying a whore. You're still obliged to repay my loan."

"I have the money," I answered, "including the interest." I dropped a bag containing five hundred sesterces on his table. "If you don't trust me, I'll wait until you finish the count."

Gallus lowered his eyes, opened the sack, and reached inside with a bejeweled ring hand. A muffled sound of copper coins echoed as they slipped between his fingers. "I know where to find you." He hadn't looked up. "If it isn't all here. Leave me."

Gallus pulled me from my thoughts as he continued to rant. "I will pursue this matter with or without General

Vespasian's consent." He paused and creased his thin lips into a fractured smile. "I won't be in Britannia forever. Soon, I will return to Rome and deal with you once and for all. The word of one patrician is worth more than any ten provincials, citizen or not. One day your lands will be mine. In the meantime, my father will deal with you. And he won't be as generous as I've been."

I stood clinching the hilt of my new short sword, the *gladius*.

Gallus noticed. "I see my words are disturbing you—good—at least you are wise enough not to attempt anything foolish."

"No, sir, I wouldn't."

"Good, you know your place. One other matter," he added. "My words stay within these walls. If you repeat what I have said, I will deny your accusations all the way to Mount Olympus. It that clear?"

"Perfectly, sir."

"Good. Dismissed!"

Despite my leaving for Rome, I knew that one day Gallus would return to the city. If I were still there, I would deal with him then.

* * *

During our journey to a ship waiting at Noviomagnus, Sabinus's entourage camped overnight near a meandering river. Carrying my blanket roll, I slipped away briefly to its grassy bank, my thoughts finally at ease with Kyar's memory. The ache was still there, and would be for a long time. Slowly, it began to recede, and I knew she would want me to go on with my life. I untied and opened the blanket. Out spilled the two blackened pieces of the lance split in half by lightning, a reminder of the night I saw Kyar's apparition. I picked up the charred segments, stepped to the shoreline, tossed them as far out as I could into the stream, and watched them disappear. Then taking her broach from my waist pouch, I held it just beneath the cool water's surface. I prayed to the river goddess to reunite the offering with Kyar's spirit. The broach slipped away, and I let go the part of my heart that had died with her.

PART II

ROME

CHAPTER 22

EARLY OCTOBER, 44 AD

Six weeks had passed since we departed General Vespasian's camp in Western Britannia, traveled across Gaul, and sailed the Mediterranean to Ostia, Rome's seaport. At that port, Sabinus's entourage transferred from the great merchantman to a shallow draft naval bireme for the remaining seventeen-mile journey up the River Tiber to Rome.

The general's banners fluttered as the ship glided past large villas and flourishing truck gardens on the Campanian Plain. In the distance, among gentle ridges, built upon solemn arches, snaked a gray-brown aqueduct carrying Rome's drinking water from the distant Alban Hills. The flume stretched to the horizon and melted into the golden haze of the Italian sky. Soon, we would dock in Rome.

The most pleasant part of the trip had been winning Princess Eleyne's friendship. Perhaps that word was too strong, considering she hated everything Roman. Daughter of the British King, Verica, she had been taken as hostage and was being brought to Rome, to ensure her father's continued loyalty. Now, fifteen, Eleyne's mother had died when she was only five. She was lonely, and certainly easier upon the eyes than the ugly, multi-scarred helmsman of our merchant transport ship. After saving her from drowning in a raging river, she had taken a liking to me.

My attempts to befriend Eleyne had not gone unnoticed by General Sabinus. "It is appropriate to be on good terms with the princess," he had said the afternoon our ship hurtled through the treacherous Straits of Gaul, between

Corsica and Sardinia. He watched the sea of green foam, while a screaming wind whistled in our ears, then turned to me. "Whatever else," he'd shouted to be heard, "avoid personal involvement, as you would a summer fever."

Still, I managed to speak to her at length on more than one occasion. And as the journey progressed, I sensed that Eleyne momentarily forgot I was a Roman soldier.

I recalled the evening before we landed, the long coastline of Italy loomed on the horizon, silhouetted by a rising half-moon. The night had been clear and balmy, and a sea of gentle swells lapped silently against the gliding ship's hull. Eleyne and her ever-present attendant, red-haired Karmune, leaned against the oak rail next to the carved prow, which bore the twin figures of the Goddess Isis, the ship's namesake. Tied into a single knotted braid, Eleyne's jet-black hair swung over her shoulder and rested on her light-blue mantle and yellow, tartan skirt. A golden torc ring, symbol of Celtic nobility, engraved with a little owl's head and curling leaves, encircled her delicate neck. Clasped on both arms and wrists were gold bracelets inlaid with coral and lapis lazuli.

Loudly clearing my throat, I approached the women.

They snapped their heads around. "Oh, Marcellus," Eleyne said in a shaky voice, "you startled us."

"Sorry, I didn't know you were so entranced by your new home."

Eleyne flared her nostrils and curled her lips into a frown. "Rome will never be my home, no matter how long I'm forced to stay." She turned to Karmune and said something in the lilting Celtic tongue.

"Rome no good," the freckled face Karmune grunted in broken Latin.

"At least your stay will be comfortable," I said.

The young princess sniffed. "Call it what you will, I'm still a hostage. And all because one man fears me, isn't that absurd?"

"Surely, not your father?"

"No, of course not—Togidubnus, my father's advisor. He's the dog who persuaded the Romans to take me hostage."

I studied her wind-burned features. "Why does Togidubnus fear you?"

"Because my brothers are so worthless, he's afraid I will become tribal ruler upon the death of my father. My only brother worthy of becoming king was killed in battle by Caratacus before I was born."

"So he plans to replace your father as ruler of the Atrebates and Regni."

"Of course, that's the whole point."

"But the tribal throne isn't hereditary," I said.

Eleyne paused as the muscles in her face tightened. A gentle breeze blew across the ocean's surface, swirled upwards crossing the ship's deck, and momentarily pulled at the loose strands of her ebony hair. "True, and the tribal council would have voted in my favor. Togidubnus is an ambitious, scheming creature who has ingratiated himself to the Romans. They will place him in power."

"Where did you learn all of this?"

"From some of the loyal elders."

I whistled softly. "And so he's cleared a path for his own ambitions."

"Aye, that's why I accused him in front of my father and General Sabinus of being a Roman lackey, the night I was taken hostage."

I leaned against the deadeye disk that held the sail shrouds in place, and for a few seconds focused on the mountainous coastline. I straightened and looked toward Eleyne. "Why are you telling me all this? Don't you consider me Roman?"

"In name only, but you are an outsider like me," Eleyne had said. "You saved my life, and from our conversations, I know you can be trusted." She turned her head to her stocky, brown-clad servant and back to me. "Karmune, may the Mother Goddess bless her, doesn't understand such things, but you do!"

* * *

Later, standing with Sabinus, Crispus behind us, I glanced about and spotted Eleyne and Karmune huddled near the stern. Their faces paled. Were they in awe or fear?

"There it is, Marcellus. Rome!" Sabinus said, pulling me back to the present. Standing by his side on the deck of the bireme, I followed his glance toward the teaming wharves crowded with ships tied prow to stern. Coming into view along the muddy-yellow Tiber River, the Emporium's docks hugged the foot of Aventine Hill, with hundreds of squalid tenements and factories. He gestured with a broad sweep of hands, looked at me, and laughed. "I imagine my mouth gaped the first time I saw Rome, too," he said.

Sabinus's family had been Sabine country squires and tax collectors from Reate, east of Rome. Only in the last five years had Sabinus risen from the Equestrian Order to the Senate while Vespasian was still a knight.

The high September sun boiled the humidity, and only a wisp of a breeze blew off the river's turbid waters. Sabinus, Crispus, and I roasted in our heavy ceremonial armor. A delegation from the emperor was expected to greet Sabinus upon debarkation.

I turned back to him. "Thank the gods our journey is over, sir."

"I agree," Sabinus answered, "it has been long and monotonous."

On the hortator's command, the sailors drew in the ship's single bank of oars and tied up to the tall, granite quay alongside dozens of barges at the Emporium, Rome's huge grain dock on the river front. Vessels and dockworkers lined the gangways. Roman citizens and slaves alike unloaded tons of wheat from Alexandria and Carthage. An endless stream of humanity moved to and from the ships.

"Who's that coming our way?" Crispus asked.

"By the size of the entourage," I surmised, "it must be the welcoming delegation for General Sabinus."

Opening a path through the crowd rode a mounted escort of sixty scarlet-cloaked Praetorian Guardsmen, and a century of eighty shield-bearing infantrymen. Flags and streamers waved and snapped in the slight breeze, standard bearers held the emperor's emblems and eagles forward, and trumpeters blared a warning to make way.

At the front of the guard, soldier-musicians raised their long-stemmed *tubicens* and sounded a brassy warning.

"Make way!" a centurion barked at the multitude of pedestrians. "Make way for his Excellency the Senator!"

Trailing behind, two litters followed, carried by huge, black African slaves and a retinue of other freedmen and servants. They were close enough that I saw that one sedan contained a puffy-cheeked, balding official wearing a white toga, trimmed with broad, purple, embroidered edges. This denoted his rank as a member of the Roman Senate. He munched on a large bunch of grapes, lolled indifferently upon a number of blue, gold, and scarlet silk cushions behind tied-back satin curtains. The other litter bore a slim, dark-bearded freedman, in a long multicolored tunic and mantle. He peered at the crowd with calculating eyes.

Workers and slaves alike parted and closed in the entourage's wake like water from a passing ship. The fat official viewed the mob contemptuously, ignoring their calls and waving hats that hailed his passing. The senator acknowledged one grinning dolt with a thrown stalk of bruised grapes, striking his face and staining his already dirty tunic. No doubt he considered himself *blessed* by such favoritism and the touch of purple now upon his garment.

Sabinus, who had been conversing with the ship's captain a few paces away, recognized the heavy man at once. "Why it's my old friend Lucius Vitellius! Gods, he's put on weight."

It was common knowledge that Vitellius had ruled Rome in Emperor Claudius's absence when he traveled to Britannia to claim victory over the Britons. Although known to be unpredictable, the senator was loyal and protective of the emperor. Around him, a man had to be careful what he said about the empire's First Citizen.

Sabinus raised his hand in salute. "*Ave!* Greetings, Vitellius!"

"Hail, old comrade," Vitellius replied, with a stained-teeth grin. "I see you are trim as ever. How goes the war?"

"Very well. You and the emperor shall receive a full report, of course."

* * *

Soon we disembarked. Eleyne, her waddling companion Karmune, and Sabinus's servants were escorted from the ship by marines. At that moment, a squad of eight Praetorians approached the women and servants, commanding them to halt. Eleyne, dressed in a long, green, tartan tunic, her hair coiled on top of her head, turned to

Sabinus, about ten paces away. Despite the poise of a queen, her face and lips, rouged with elderberry juice, paled. She shook her head as if not believing Sabinus would hand her over to a squad of the emperor's household troops.

"No!" Sabinus shouted. "They go to my home!" He rushed forward and pointed to one of the hills. "By Caesar's command, the princess is a guest, and is to be treated with dignity, is that clear?"

"Yes, sir," the *optio,* who commanded the detail, replied. "No offense was meant, sir. We weren't informed of her status or your intentions."

Sabinus eyed Vitellius. He shrugged. "All right, enough said. Return to your position in the century."

Eleyne sighed in relief and stepped forward. Karmune straight-armed a Praetorian out of the way and followed the servants toward Sabinus's mansion on Esquiline Hill.

Meanwhile, with the help of three struggling slaves, Vitellius stepped out of his litter. As Crispus and I stood a few feet away in the sweltering sun, Sabinus returned to our position where he and the senator saluted one another and expressed greetings. "The emperor is eager to see you and hear the latest news from Britannia," Vitellius added.

"How is he?" Sabinus inquired. "Well, I pray?"

Vitellius stepped closer. "A contrast as always," he said in a loud whisper. "At times he's brilliant, and at other longer periods he plays the idiot—though lately I wonder if it is an act. Why do you think the guardsmen behaved as they did? He forgot to give them instructions about the girl's status."

"*Good!*" Sabinus remarked cheerfully in a loud voice as if Vitellius had made a favorable comment. "I'm pleased to hear that the emperor is well and in good spirits." For a moment, he gazed at the Praetorians and the other official.

Vitellius nodded his head slowly. "Aha, I had forgotten how diplomatic you are."

The senator turned and stared after Eleyne as the retinue disappeared into the bustling dock crowd. A grin crossed his face. "By the gods, she's a most comely wench, for a barbarian."

"Yes, she is," the general answered coolly.

"Were she not a hostage, I wouldn't mind taking her for my mistress."

Sabinus gave Vitellius a scornful look.

"Can you blame me, friend?" he answered putting up his hands.

As if to change the subject, the senator gestured to the freedman who waited patiently close by. "Sabinus, you remember Narcissus, don't you?"

"Of course, and how are the affairs of state?"

"Very well, my dear General," Narcissus droned smugly, "all Rome is proud of you and your brother General Vespasian's accomplishments." A freedman from Greece, Narcissus was Claudius's secretary of state, and the real power behind the emperor.

A light breeze drifted in from the river ruffling the thinning hair of Vitellius's sweaty head and flapping the banners held by the nearby Praetorians.

"Enough chit-chat," Vitellius said, "let's be off to the Palatine."

Sabinus gestured to Crispus and to me. "Senator, they go with me."

Vitellius scrutinized us closely. He locked his eyes onto the *Corona Civica*, hanging from my new articulated armor and raised his eyebrows. "Are you the one who saved his commander's life?"

"Yes, your Excellency."

"Good man. Rome needs more like you, even if you are a Spaniard," he commented with a sneer.

Sabinus frowned at the mention of my race, but did not respond to the remark.

"Thank you, Excellency," I answered. *You pompous sack of wind.*

Vitellius invited Sabinus to join him in his litter, and we departed for the emperor's estate on Palatine Hill. Crispus and I rode horses provided by the Praetorian Guard.

As we moved out, Crispus guided his mount beside me. He leaned over and whispered in a sarcastic voice, "Welcome to Rome, friend, what next?"

I shrugged. "Probably nothing more today."

We left the riverfront and turned onto the narrow lane, *Vicus Portae*. Immediately, a horde of shaven-headed beggars, dressed in filthy rags, besieged us. "*Da! Da!*—Give! Give!" they shouted. In spite of the heavy guard, the party was swallowed by a sea of ragged caps and dirty hands thrust toward our faces.

A stinking, pocked-face woman in a greasy, long tunic, who carried a baby with an abnormally large head, slipped past the guards and ran to me. "Please, Lord, a few coppers so I can feed my baby." Wrapped in a woolen blanket riddled with holes, the baby reeked of urine and seemed barely alive.

My horse snorted. Turning to one side, the gelding used its shoulder to shove the woman away. Out of pity, and against my better judgment, I tossed her a copper *as*. She snagged it out of the air with a practiced hand. Why she hadn't exposed the pitiful creature to the elements in the hills as customary, I couldn't understand.

"Get out of here, woman!" a guard snapped.

She darted into the noisy crowd and over to another beggar. He carried a raggedy cloth picture of a storm at sea, a beggar's ploy. Supposedly, he had been a shipwrecked sailor, who had taken vows to the God Neptune to lead a life of poverty if he survived. After a lot of wild gesturing, the woman gave him the coin and ran farther up the street to beg again.

Meantime, the same scruffy charlatan snaked through the mass of humanity and approached me. He reached out with a hand missing two middle fingers. "Please, Lord, a few coins for a poor, crippled, starving sailor."

"Get out of my sight, you scummy bastard," I snarled and gave him a swift boot to the chest, knocking him to the street. He rolled to one side just as my horse was about to stomp him with a front hoof.

The cursing guardsmen regained control and sent the vagabonds crashing into nearby walls and tufa stone gutters. The rest scattered.

"Sneaky bunch of dogs, aren't they?" I said to Crispus.

"If that piece of dog meat you kicked is a sailor, then I'm governor of Baetica."

I turned my head back and forth on guard for more trouble. The Praetorians ahead of us were doing the same. "I doubt if he's stepped foot in a dinghy."

"Aye," Crispus muttered. "It's like Sabinus said during the voyage."

The beggars we encountered were professionals. Some went to such extremes as mutilating themselves rather than working for a living.

"I'd wager they get the *dole*, too," Crispus added with a snort.

"That's what Sabinus complained about. He discussed the matter with the emperor when he was in Britannia, and suggested removing them from the city relief roles."

"What did he say?"

"No."

Crispus bared his big teeth and spat, "Why?"

I scanned the onlookers watching from the narrow sidewalks as the retinue moved along the trash-filled lane. "He fears the mob, and needs their support. After all, a fat mob is a happy mob."

"He's not afraid to shed our blood so the leeches of Rome can have free bread and entertainment!"

I shook my head in disgust.

Passing through the Trigamina Gate, in the old Servian Wall, we entered the city proper. The retinue proceeded up the dismal way, surrounded by dark and ugly multistory tenements, their thin, sagging walls propped up by numerous support beams jutting into the lane. Scattered among the wooden apartments were busy shops and drab industrial buildings with barely enough room to ride at a walk through the noisy crowd. Hordes of people jostled and darted around market wares. Countless aliens mingled with the sharp-eyed Italians, who gestured incessantly as they bartered in open shops. Everyone shouted to make a point. A hawk-nosed Arab in white robes argued vehemently about the price of myrrh with a wizened, gray-haired woman. A delicate Egyptian, wearing a colorful mantle, cautiously crossed the stepping stones, at a street corner. A Nubian slave boy, his skin almost purple-black, trailed him holding an umbrella above his master's head. The stream was endless.

"I see we're not the only foreigners in Rome," I said.

"Gods, look at all of them," Crispus added, "there's more of us than Romans."

Mixed with heat and humidity, the pungent smells of the slum nearly gagged me. Yet I had glimpsed but a small area of the city squeezed on the side of one hill against the Tiber. Not until we had left that dismal area behind and encountered the giant Circus Maximus and Temple of Hercules was I overpowered by the city's enormity and magnitude. Before us spread an endless canyon of vaulting brick and concrete buildings, grandly covered by a thin veneer of marble, creeping up the sides of Rome's hills.

Thousands of citizens and aliens passed to and fro pouring in and out of enormous government buildings and temples built on a phalanx of brightly painted columns. The reflection from their gilded roofs and stately domes was blinding. Scattered in even greater numbers among them were the wooden apartments of the poor, and the blackened rubble from the city's many fires.

Dead ahead, in a tiny valley among a mountain of buildings and temples, squatted the Forum, a plaza cluttered with countless statues of Rome's heroes and those who pretended to be. The adjacent porticoes and stalls, in the Basilicas of Opimia and Sempronia, were crowded with vendors selling wares of all sorts.

"By Melkart, have you seen anything like this?" Crispus shouted above the noise of the mob. "It's incredible. I knew Rome was big but this . . ."

"Aye, Lugdunum and Messalia are squalid mud villages in comparison."

"Now I know what they mean by the old saying, 'country bumpkin.' That's how I feel, but don't tell anyone I said so." Crispus laughed.

I grinned. "I won't." I didn't volunteer that I felt the same way.

I continually twisted my head and observed the people and buildings. But it was impossible to absorb everything.

We passed between the imposing temple of the twins, Castor and Pollux, and Temple of Augustus. To the right and looming above perched our final destination, Palatine Hill, with the magnificent palaces of the Caesars.

It wouldn't be long before Crispus and I knew Rome better than ourselves—Rome, in all her glory, was filled with omens of treachery to come.

CHAPTER 23

After handing our weapons to the Praetorians at the main entrance, Sabinus, Vitellius, Crispus, and I were ushered into the Court of Tiberius, where Emperor Claudius conducted affairs of state. Sabinus had looked forward to this day since we departed Britannia. Proudly, he strode, shoulders back, through the cavernous hall as we passed among hundreds of dignitaries. Senators and knights, wealthy citizens and freedmen, decked in their finest togas or embroidered tunics of soft wool, mingled with foreign emissaries dressed in a rainbow of clothing.

Costly sheets of blue and green marble covered the stone walls lining the great audience room. Eight large niches contained as many colossal statues, wrought from Adamantine basalt, including those of Hercules and Bacchus. Around the circuit rose twenty-eight Corinthian columns of intricate workmanship. At the far end sat Emperor Claudius, as immobile as one of his statues. Dressed in a finely knit white and purple striped toga and wearing gold sandals, he sprawled upon a low dais in a silk-cushioned, ivory curule chair. Next to him, on a gilded table, sat a large black-lacquered wine amphora, and a dish of apples and rare and expensive oranges from the East. Behind the emperor stood another freedman, Pallas, his advisor and secretary of finance.

My eyes darted about as I attempted in vain to take in our surroundings. At the same time my stomach churned and muscles tightened as Crispus and I walked behind Sabinus. Sweat ran down my back beneath my uniform. In the past, I had felt uneasy when standing before generals such as Sabinus and Vespasian. Now, I was in the presence of the most powerful man on earth. I was determined not to show any fear.

Crispus and I remained at the front of the assemblage when the emperor motioned for Sabinus to step forward. All eyes turned to the general as he carefully strode to the dais, his image reflecting like a shadow in the polished, white marble floor. Upon saluting the emperor, he mounted the pedestal, bent down, and kissed the emperor's veiny cheek, a sign of homage, and stepped back.

"Welcome, n-noble Sabinus," Claudius stuttered, salivating at the side of his mouth. Spittle dripped down his cheek. He patted Sabinus's shoulder, a great sign of Imperial favor, soiling the kilted white sleeve with orange juice from his hand. "We are most pleased to receive you. The exploits of Legion Second Augusta and bravery of its soldiers have preceded you—they have served Rome well."

"My thanks, Great Caesar," Sabinus answered, "but much of the credit belongs to my brother, Vespasian."

"N-Nonsense, dear General. Our reports say otherwise, and you are not here to discuss your brother."

Pallas leaned over and whispered something in Claudius's ear.

The emperor nodded and gulped wine from a golden goblet before belching. "We wish to hear your report from Britannia."

Sabinus recited. "The campaign against the Britons . . ."

Claudius grabbed an apple from a bowl and munched loudly as Sabinus spoke. A few minutes later he twisted his bulk onto a haunch and farted. Pallas crinkled his nose, and Sabinus momentarily stopped in mid-word before continuing.

I glanced toward Crispus who arched his thick eyebrows, and then looked about the hall. Officials, including Vitellius, who stood to one side of us, shook their heads and bit their lips in a painful attempt to keep from laughing. Others barely hid their disgust. Suddenly, the emperor's head bobbed, and he fell asleep. His snoring echoed through the cavernous room.

Apparently used to the emperor's habits, Sabinus raised his voice. "Therefore, *Great Caesar* . . ."

Immediately, Claudius awoke. "Go on, we are listening," the emperor commanded.

Sabinus proceeded. "I gave a detailed written report to Narcissus for Caesar to read at his leisure," he concluded.

"Excellent. We are pleased with the report you have given us today."

Again, Pallas leaned over and whispered to Claudius.

There was a long pause, and the emperor's face began to twitch, one of his tics. "That is all, Noble Sabinus. You have Rome's gratitude and leave to go home and see your family. No doubt they are eagerly awaiting your arrival."

A gasp resounded through the chamber, as the onlookers murmured among themselves. Sabinus froze, stunned by Claudius's remarks. From our shipboard conversations, I knew he looked forward to this day. Did the emperor have a change of heart about his new position, or was this another one of his absent-minded spells?

"Well?" the emperor asked. "What are you waiting for?"

"But Caesar," Vitellius interceded, "the appointment."

"Which one?"

Vitellius gesticulated excitedly, his triple chin bouncing up and down. "Titus Flavius Sabinus's appointment to city prefect. Don't you remember, Caesar, you promised him? That's why you sent me to the docks to welcome him."

Claudius turned to Pallas and Narcissus then back to Vitellius. "We have changed our mind. Our dear friend, Senator Anicius Cestius Gallus, brought to our attention the loyal services of Senator Lucius Pedanius Secundus." Near the entourage, the emperor nodded to a short, squinty-eyed character, wearing a senatorial toga, who bowed in return.

Internally, I flinched. So this was the elder Gallus. Besides the warning, I had received from the young Gallus, Sabinus had given me further details about the old man on our journey to Rome. I had then revealed the feud between my family and his. A shrewd man of wealth, the senior Gallus made his fortune in construction, trade, and joint stock companies.

I listened again.

"We have decided his greater seniority in the Senate warrants his appointment to the post," the emperor said.

"But Caesar," Vitellius protested, "you promised!"

Claudius's face darkened. "We are not accountable to you, Senator Vitellius, for our every decision. You stand in jeopardy of losing our friendship."

Vitellius's blubbery lower lip dropped, stung by the emperor's rebuke. He glanced at Sabinus.

"Of course, the will of Caesar is mine," Sabinus interjected diplomatically, "and I shall step aside. Secundus is a good man, and I know he will serve Caesar well."

Claudius's head twitched again a couple of times. "We are pleased you understand our position, Noble Sabinus."

A slobbery smile came to the emperor's mouth as he leaned forward. "Take heart, dear friend, you shall be appointed by us to another high office shortly, we promise."

Sabinus took a short bow. "Thank you, great Caesar, for your generosity." Sabinus hid his emotions well, but no doubt he was disappointed, if not angry. Promises!

The emperor added a few more consoling remarks and departed through an almost hidden exit at the rear of the throne.

When Sabinus turned to leave, a crowd of sympathetic senators and knights surrounded him, expressing their dismay over the emperor's change of heart.

"I'm shocked," Vitellius said, "I don't understand why Caesar changed his mind. It's not like him to break a promise to a friend."

"I appreciate you speaking on my behalf, Lucius," Sabinus said, "but I'm afraid he listened to a stronger voice than yours."

"Indeed, he did, Titus Flavius Sabinus," a dour, balding senator rasped, "Secundus is the rightful candidate."

"So the emperor has deemed, Anicius Cestius Gallus," Sabinus answered facetiously. "However, both of us know differently, don't we?"

"Be specific, Flavius Sabinus," Gallus demanded.

"He is a puppet dangling by your bidding strings. Am I clear enough?"

"Secundus is his own man, and the right man."

"I noticed the *right man* has conveniently disappeared. I have never known Secundus to take charge of any office so enthusiastically. If it is like his previous endeavors, his tenure as city prefect will be a disaster."

I glanced from Sabinus to the old senator waiting his response.

"I'm sure I don't know what you mean?" The elder Gallus sniffed.

A cynical smile crossed Sabinus's lips. "His construction in bridges that collapse, his trade in horses with defaced brands, and his joint stock in repossessed tenements is an open secret to all."

The old senator glowered at Sabinus.

Crispus nudged my shoulder and motioned with his head toward Gallus, who turned in my direction. He studied me for a couple of seconds as I stood to Sabinus's side. Liver blotches covered much of his wrinkled forehead, and a large, crooked nose dominated his jowly face. He had a small mouth and natural smirk, as did his son, and the identical chilling, blue eyes, whose sharpness had not diminished with age.

As the elder man faced Sabinus, he gestured to me with a crooked finger that seemed to point towards whatever his crossed eyes followed. "Who is this young centurion?"

"My retainer," Sabinus replied.

The senator glared at me, his wrinkled mouth hardened. "You must be the one my son wrote about. Are you the son of Marcellus Reburrus the Elder, from Abdera, in Baetica?"

"Yes, your Excellency." I focused on the bridge of his nose instead of his wayward eyes.

Gallus stepped closer, "Yes . . . there is a resemblance, although you are taller. Ten years ago, your father took me, or rather my agents, to court, here in Rome."

My face grew warm. I sensed where this subject was heading and didn't like it.

Sabinus raised his eyebrows. "Oh, on what charge?"

Gallus's nostrils flared. "The thief accused me of defaulting in the payment of four black race horses I had purchased from him."

Calling my father thief, how dare he? I wanted to strike him, but held my temper. From what I had heard there was no bigger one than old Gallus.

"There must have been a reason," Sabinus said.

"Reason indeed! He sold me lame animals, and I refused to pay the balance until they were replaced. He accused my trainer of mistreating and injuring them on the voyage to Rome from Baetica."

"My father was an honest man, sir," I said, keeping my voice as even as my anger would allow.

"Unfortunately, the court agreed," Gallus growled. "Magistrates agree to anything for the right price!"

Tension raced through my body. I balled my fists tightly but kept them at my side. My father would have fallen on his sword before bribing anyone.

"I see my words have disturbed the young centurion, Flavius Sabinus. His face is red."

"Enough, Anicius Cestius Gallus," Sabinus warned. "You have insulted the memory of his dead father. Were he a senator, he would have right to seek redress, and I would be the first to advise him."

"You would," Gallus answered, a sneer crossing his lips.

"Be sensible, Gallus. Centurion Marcellus Reburrus was a boy when the dispute occurred. Why drag him into something not of his doing?"

"Because he may take up his father's cause," Gallus retorted. "Now I understand why my son was so angry when he wrote me. You are as ambitious as your father."

"I have never sought any position, sir," I answered. Had I not made a promise to Mother, I would have spoken the truth.

"The younger Gallus should consider himself fortunate," Sabinus interjected in a menacing voice. "I should have cashiered him as he rightfully deserved."

Gallus turned scarlet as he slowly faced Sabinus. Obviously, he knew about the terrible camp conditions that Sabinus had uncovered. "What are you implying?"

"You know what I mean," Sabinus answered. "My inspection of his command in February, need I say more?"

Crispus and I looked at one another, knowing exactly what Sabinus meant.

"Then it's in your report to Caesar?"

"Everything, Anicius Gallus. He received the preliminary document months ago. You know my eye for detail. I never overlook anything."

The elderly senator narrowed cold, blue eyes. "Caesar will not be pleased, Flavius Sabinus, and I am not pleased. You know it's necessary for a tribune to perform well if he is to advance through the offices to become senator, I don't appreciate your candor!"

"I won't lie for my friends, let alone my enemies, if you understand my meaning."

"Indeed, I do!"

"You must excuse me, Senator Gallus. I'm weary and eager to see my family." Sabinus turned his back on the elder Gallus, leaving him standing agape among his cronies. The old senator started to speak, but apparently decided to bide his time, and he stormed from the hall.

Crispus and I departed the Palatine with Sabinus, amid a group of his well-wishers. Although he had not received the position of city prefect, Sabinus had returned to Rome with honor, and was still considered, *Friend of Caesar.* This entitled him to an escort of twenty lantern-carrying Praetorians on his first night home. Ten marched on each side of us as we stepped from the main entrance past crimson and white ceremonial guards. Sabinus called me to his side as the last rays of sunlight disappeared below the top of Vatican Hill across the Tiber in the west.

"Beware of Gallus," Sabinus warned in a low voice as he waved to some officials passing close by. "It's unfortunate that he had to drag you into an old dispute with your father."

"His son pulled me into the feud the day I arrived in Iping, sir."

Sabinus shook his head. "Now I understand the intensity of his anger. He's a hateful old man who can't let go of grudges. The real issue is he wanted someone in the office of city prefect he could manipulate. An understanding indeed."

"Because of the tremendous power the post wields?"

Sabinus nodded. He turned his head back and forth surveying the escorting Praetorians. "It's rumored," he whispered, "although never proved, that Gallus has dealings within Rome's criminal element. The city prefect is the ideal position from which to unleash them on the city, and Secundus is weak."

I tightly gripped the hilt of my weapon, which had been returned to me upon leaving the palace. "Then Rome will be at his mercy." Should that danger arise, I wondered what plans, if any, Sabinus had to deal with such a potentially dangerous situation. More importantly, did he wield the power required to stop old Gallus and his nefarious intentions?

CHAPTER 24

Leaving the palace for Sabinus's home on Quirinal Hill, Crispus, Sabinus, and I trekked down the Sacred Way, escorted by lamp-carrying Praetorians and turned onto Pullius Street. Sabinus preferred walking to riding the litter offered by Emperor Claudius. "I have no intention of getting fat and lazy like my colleagues," he said. "My chest and neck are naturally thick enough as it is. I don't need the extra weight." As dusk covered the city like a stifling blanket, everyone scurried for shelter. Shopkeepers slammed shutters tight and locked their businesses for the night. "Why is everyone in such a rush?" I asked.

Sabinus grimaced. Three lines frowned his smooth forehead. "Unfortunately, after sunset, Rome is a land of robbers, footpads, housebreakers, and roving gangs. The people fear for their lives, and rightly so."

"What's the Watch doing about it, sir?" Crispus asked.

"It's impossible for the *Vigiles* to patrol the city adequately and scour every hiding place," Sabinus answered. "The city is enshrouded in darkness after sunset. There are no street lights except the torches carried by the populace, or those hanging outside of taverns and brothels."

"Given the circumstances, can the Watch be counted upon to perform their job?" I questioned.

In the light of a swinging lantern toted by one of the Praetorians, I noticed the guardsman's mouth turn into a derisive smirk. I glared at the soldier who stared straight ahead.

Sabinus clasped his hands behind his back. "Absolutely. They're well-trained, but their task is nearly overwhelming between fighting crime and fires. Unfortunately, like any organization, they have their share of misfits. Some of the rankers have been caught drunk, after being paid by thieves to turn the other way while they break into shops and homes. My friend, Decrius Calpurnianus, the Watch prefect, continually weeds out their kind."

"Sounds like a monumental task."

"Yes, it is," Sabinus said. "That reminds me. Since I didn't receive my appointment to city prefect, I'll see that you're transferred on parchment to Legion Second Augusta and detailed back to me on a long-term temporary basis. I have work for you and Sergeant Crispus to perform. You will stay at my home because you will be on call twenty-four hours a day." He turned to Crispus. "Sergeant, you will be billeted at the barracks of the Marines and auxiliaries, and shall report to my home each morning before we go to the Palatine."

"Yes, sir," Crispus acknowledged.

As we hiked through the darkened trash-filled lane, the odors of rotten food, offal, and urine filled ours noses. The high walls of shabby tenements along our passageway seemed to hem our group into a claustrophobic void, allowing little space for maneuvering.

After a few moments of silence, Sabinus explained the Watch consisted of seven cohorts of ex-slaves and freedmen, dressed similarly to the army's legionaries, and stationed in precincts throughout the city's fourteen regions. The position of Watch prefect, held by Calpurnianus, belonged to the Equestrian Order.

"Gallus has profited heavily from Rome's tragic fires," Sabinus further explained. "His detail of slaves are expert firefighters. Although the Watch's first duty is firefighting, Gallus's slaves invariably beat them to the scene of any major fire." Sabinus elaborated Gallus's *modus operandi*—while a building's owner stood in shock, watching his six-story apartment burn, Gallus's agents negotiated to buy the property at a ridiculously low price. The longer the fire burned, the lower the price.

"Invariably, the poor owner sells at a fraction of the price, just to recoup part of his loss," Sabinus added. "Even as the ashes smolder, Gallus's construction gang of slaves moves in and quickly builds another thin-walled firetrap. And his profits keep soaring."

I looked about the area. In the shadowy light of the Praetorian lamps, I saw numerous barred doors of the shops lining the floor levels of each building we passed. "I'm not accustomed to this sort of thing," I said. "Where I was raised, a man could leave his home and shop unlocked, and not worry about fire or thieves."

"In Rome, when shaking hands with a stranger, you'd best count your fingers to see if they are still attached. When I go to the Senate, I count mine at least a dozen times. Strange," Sabinus mused, "we have brought order to the rest of the world, but can't adequately protect our own city. Ironic, isn't it?"

"Yes, sir, it is," I said.

Crispus nodded in agreement.

As we turned onto Pomegranate Lane and approached Quirinal Hill, a woman screamed.

"Help! Robbers!"

"It's coming from the next block." Crispus pointed.

"Follow me!" Sabinus ordered, motioning his hand towards us and the guards. We ran about a half block. Our sandaled boots clattered and echoed off the tufa-stone street and slum building walls. We could barely see the street surface ahead of us, in the lurching light coming from the Praetorian's lamps, as they ran behind us.

Another scream.

We raced up an alley, and I heard a muffled voice and the sounds of a struggle. In the fetid-smelling abyss I saw the dim outline of three thugs who had wrestled a woman to the ground. One was pulling up her long tunic. At the sounds of our steps, they turned, spotted us, and ran.

"Down there!" I yelled. Crispus and I shot past Sabinus. Stumbling more than once, we charged down the dark alley. One tough managed to escape over a brick wall, but we cornered the remaining two.

Foolishly, they pulled hidden swords from beneath ragged tunics and challenged us. One lunged at Crispus, who easily parried the weapon away with his spatha. Crispus ran him through the throat, and he toppled to the ground dead. Meanwhile, I caught the other's weapon in mid-swing with my short sword, shoved it to the side, and stabbed him in the chest. He fell backwards to the grimy pathway. I knelt beside the husky youth in the lamplight provided by one of the arriving Praetorians. He still lived. Dark blood oozed from his mouth.

The young thug was no more than fifteen or sixteen years old. "Who are you?" I demanded.

"Bugger off," he answered, as he gurgled blood. Air sucked and bubbled the wound in his chest.

Crispus stooped to my left side while Sabinus stood to the right, a little to the back of me as I questioned the prostrate youth.

"Look, you're dying," I said. "You have nothing to lose by telling us your name. We can notify your family."

"Publius Lucullus, from . . . from the Subura," he answered in a voice little more than a whisper.

I had heard from Sabinus the Subura was one of Rome's worst areas. "Who are the others?"

"Don't know—met them tonight," he rasped.

"This is no time to lie," I said slowly, trying to be patient. "You don't have much longer to live. They can't get revenge where you're going. Old Charon will protect you. Answer my question."

"It's . . . the truth," he answered.

"You want to die with a lie on your breath?" I questioned. "Where did you meet them?"

The young man closed and opened his eyes, his breathing labored. "Broken Oxcart."

"I know the place," Sabinus interjected. "It's a wine shop frequented by teamsters—a den of thieves—not far from here."

I gestured close to Publius's face. "Why did you attack the woman?"

"On our . . . way to steal jewelry." He coughed some blood and continued, "At a shop on . . . the Sacred Way. One saw her, and . . . and she had a box. He wanted it."

"Why did you try to rape her?" Crispus asked.

"It weren't me. It was one . . . of them," the young tough answered, his voice fading. I looked about. The Praetorians stood about in the shadowy light of their lanterns, no doubt waiting orders from Sabinus.

Crispus leaned close to his ear. "What were you going to do with the jewelry?"

He stared blankly for a moment. "Sell it."

"To whom?" I asked.

"Sell . . . it . . ." He spat greater amounts of blood and inhaled deeply. A geyser of blood spattered from his chest wound.

"To whom? To whom?" I questioned. My muscles tightened hoping to get an answer before he died.

"Ga-Gall . . ." He vomited blood down his front, and a hollow gurgle echoed in his throat. His eyes rolled slightly and glazed. I had seen the lax, expressionless dead stare too often in Britannia and Germania to even listen for his heartbeat.

"That sounded like—" I said.

"Gallus," Sabinus answered. "That's not good enough, providing he was telling the truth. He could have meant Gaul. The half word of a dead Plebeian criminal isn't enough to bring charges against a senator. We'll need better evidence." He exhaled heavily, as if disgusted by the whole affair.

"I have come to a decision," he continued. "Tomorrow, I will visit Calpurnianus's office and offer my assistance. The organized criminal element of Rome must be rooted out. I will offer to establish a system of reliable informants out of my own pocket to assist the Watch. Marcellus, you will assist in becoming my eyes and ears in Rome."

"I'll see that it's handled, sir. My first order of business is to learn everything I can about the city." Personally, I thought Sabinus was being naive. From what I had heard, organized crime in any city, especially one as big as Rome, was impossible to stamp out.

"I'm sure you will become familiar with every alley and byway in short order," Sabinus said.

I didn't know exactly how to handle the assignment, but I would figure a way.

Sabinus commanded two Praetorians to proceed to the Watch precinct station belonging to the Second Cohort at nearby Esquilinian Gate with orders to bring back a wagon for the bodies.

Returning to the woman, we found her leaning against the wall, shaking the dirt from her clothing.

"I'm surprised she didn't run when she saw us earlier," Crispus said as we approached her.

"Probably too stunned to move," I said.

In the pulsating light of a Praetorian's lamp, I saw the woman's features. About forty, her narrow, but attractive, face bore fine lines spreading like tiny bird feet from the corners of her dark eyes and the edges of her full lips.

"Were you injured?" I inquired, as Crispus, Sabinus, and I stopped before her still-crouching form. Her eyes widened.

"Have no fear, we won't hurt you," Sabinus said in a reassuring voice.

Her body visibly relaxed, and then she picked up the small, empty box, stood, and took a couple of deep breaths. Her eyes focused on mine. I sensed terror still lurked in hers. Yet, there seemed to be determination in their dark, brown recesses to regain an earlier feeling of peace. "No, I'm not hurt," she finally answered, "but I am still a little shaky. Thank God, you arrived. Who knows what they would have done."

"What is your name, madam?" Sabinus asked.

"Pricilla, wife of Aquila."

"Where do you live?" Sabinus questioned.

"On the street of the tent cloth makers, sir."

"The Jewish quarter across the river?" Sabinus asked in an incredulous voice.

"Yes, the Trans-Tiberina," Pricilla answered.

Sabinus shook his head. "What are you doing here at this place without an escort?"

"I was visiting a sick friend."

Sabinus pinched his eyebrows together. "Does your husband always allow you out at these hours? Isn't it the custom of the Jews to shelter their women?"

She smiled and replied softly as she turned and raised her head to Sabinus. "We are poor people and cannot afford to hire escorts. So we must put our trust in God if we are to continue His work. My husband is understanding."

"You have placed enough trust in your god for one night," Sabinus said. "I'm sending a couple of guards to see you safely home."

"You are very generous, sir, but it isn't necessary."

Sabinus held up a hand. “On the contrary, we can’t have anything else happening to you, I insist.” He lowered his hand.

“As you wish.”

Before Pricilla and the guards departed, she briefly turned to us. “May the God of Moses and Christus be with you.” She and her escort of Praetorians moved away and disappeared into the blackness of Rome.

Pricilla’s remark puzzled me. I had heard about the one god of the Jews from my tutor, but he never mentioned Christus, which was Latinized Greek for *the Anointed One.* No matter, they had many so-called prophets. The Jews were especially troublesome to Rome in their homeland, Judea. Then a thought occurred to me, the witches warning. Was this the god of the East? Rubbish. I was in no mood to allow Eastern superstitions to cloud my weary mind. After the day’s excitement, I looked forward to an uneventful dinner at Sabinus’s house.

CHAPTER 25

It was the third hour after sunset before we reached Sabinus's mansion near the summit of Quirinal Hill. Only pale moonlight and dancing stars illuminated the narrow street leading to his home. In the shadowy, silver glow, the silhouette of a large plaster-covered, brick house grew nearer. Peepholes, in the form of foreboding shadows, intermittently dotted the building's lower story, painted red in the fashion of one belonging to the senatorial class. After rescuing Pricilla, I appreciated their significance.

Black, iron gates covered the large windows of the white-washed second story. The crimson flames of the torches cast ghostly images along the marble-column entrance. Two slaves armed with clubs stood sentry duty at the gate. Flares illuminated the courtyard, pooling a pleasant amber on the brick tiles, and casting flickering shadows of the guards upon the estate's inner wall. They might have been apparitions engaged in wavering combat. Melodious tones drifted from an unseen lyre.

Beneath the marble facade stood Alexias, Sabinus's tall but aging freedman and chief steward. Distorted by the wavering light, his deep-set dark eyes appeared to have in one instant a cupid's twinkling glow and in the next moment a demon's eyes. "Greetings, noble Sabinus. Welcome home."

Sabinus and Alexias clasped one another's forearm in Roman fashion and grinned like old reunited friends. "It's good to be home, Alexias. How is the Lady Aurelia?"

"Very well," he answered, motioning to the doorway. "The mistress awaits in the atrium."

"Let's not keep my wife waiting," Sabinus answered with a grin.

After dismissing the Praetorian escort, Crispus and I entered with Sabinus and his servant. Passing through the vestibule, we crossed the multicolored mosaic floor worked in the image of a chained snarling dog. Beneath the animal were inscribed the words, *Cave Canum*—beware of the dog.

A court of exquisite beauty, the atrium contained mosaics more elaborate than those in the vestibule. Carved from green Spartan marble, four elegant columns upheld the roof around the wide *compluvium.* Bronze dolphins and ornamented sea horses shot great jets of water into the moon-colored marble fountain beneath the light-well. Elaborate frescoes, broken by the heavy olivine and saffron drapes, framed the bedchamber-cubicle entries covering the walls.

Aurelia Severa, Sabinus's wife, sat on a cushioned bronze bench in front of the fountain. Quietly, she stroked the silver-gray cat lounging in her lap. She came to life once she saw us and placed the feline, who meowed indignantly, on the polished floor. She stood, beaming at Sabinus. Alexias, Crispus, and I stopped as Sabinus and Aurelia slowly approached one another. They momentarily embraced and kissed.

"Welcome, my Lord," Aurelia said in a beautiful low timbre. "I am pleased the gods have safely returned you home."

I suspected her formal welcome was more for the benefit of Crispus and me.

Sabinus smiled. "And a pleasure it is to be home."

In her late thirties, Aurelia wore a dark-blue stola girded beneath a matronly bosom. A white mantle draped from her left shoulder and twisted around her waist. Small clusters of blue sapphires, red garnets, and milky chalcedony dangled from the end of her gold strand earrings.

Although Sabinus and Aurelia had been married nearly twenty years, excitement seemed to radiate from her wide, walnut eyes. Her instant smile indicated she still loved him, and a second glance from her betrayed a desire to be alone with her husband. Aurelia Severa did not fit the image of wealthy Roman matrons, who reputedly chased after gladiators and actors in favor with the mob.

"It has been too long, more than a year, but now you are back for good." Aurelia paused for a moment, arched her head back, and looked into his eyes. "Aren't you?"

He grinned and gently pinched her full cheek. "Of course, dear lady, rest assured I am."

Turning our way, Sabinus introduced Crispus and me to his wife. We bowed slightly in respect.

"Welcome, noble guests, and especially you, Centurion," Aurelia said in a smooth and hospitable manner. Her voice revealed a dignity and grace that made us feel at home. "My husband wrote of your heroism, but failed to mention how handsome you are. If you are staying with us, I shall warn the ladies of Rome to beware." She chuckled. "Or should it be the other way around?"

"You flatter me, great lady," I answered. Her remarks caught me off guard.

"Be kind, Aurelia, he's blushing," Sabinus scolded with a gentle laugh.

"Oh, I'm sorry if I embarrassed you, I wanted to put you at ease. Really, we are country people, and not much on formality. I like treating everyone as part of the family." Aurelia smiled again. "Besides, what man doesn't like to be told he is handsome? Men are vainer than we women."

"I'll keep your words in mind." A warm glow seeped into my face.

Alexias led Crispus and me to the baths to clean up before dinner, while Sabinus and his wife spent some time alone.

* * *

"Gods, Lord Sabinus's baths are a far cry from the army's makeshift affairs," Crispus said as we stepped down into the steamy, hot pool.

Each of the three bathing areas—hot, warm, and cold rooms—were slabbed in smooth marble quarried from the pits of Tuscany. Reliefs made of Boccatello marble from Hispania adorned the walls. Elaborate paintings, ranging from hunting scenes to one depicting the tragic romance between Aeneas and Dido, covered the ceilings. Water gushed from silver faucets.

"Aye, no wooden shacks on the march for Sabinus," I answered, relaxing as the tensions of the day began flowing from my body.

Crispus exhaled and wiped the sweat from his forehead. "If this is considered a modest estate, then what's it like in a wealthy mansion?"

I shook my head. "Only the great Melkart knows."

To our surprise and gratitude, after bathing, we dressed in newly cleaned uniforms provided us by attentive slaves. Our weapons were polished to a blinding finish. Alexias guided us toward the *triclinium* to dine with Sabinus and Aurelia. As we followed the steward down the lamplit hallway, a scream, quickly followed by another more desperate shriek, echoed through the passageway.

"That's Lady Eleyne!" I barked to Alexias. "Where's her room?"

"The second floor, the guest room," he stammered.

"Where are the stairs?"

"That way," he pointed.

Crispus and I dashed up the brick stairway, with swords drawn. Another scream came from the lighted cubicle ahead. We entered, and in the dim light of the smoking oil lamp, I saw Eleyne sobbing, huddled over a crumpled and blood-spattered body. Behind her an open shutter slowly swung back and forth in the window.

I nodded to Crispus, who headed to the window.

Drawing closer to Eleyne, I recognized the pale face of Karmune, Eleyne's servant. She barely clung to life. Spitting blood, her breathing growing shallower by the second.

"Too dark—can't see anything but wagons driving by!" Crispus shouted over the noisy din of wheels slamming against the cobble-stone street below. "Sounds like hundreds out there. Could have gotten away in any of them."

"Who did this?" I demanded harshly, the soldier momentarily taking command of me.

Too shaken to say anything, Eleyne pointed to the window. She wept as she held the dying Karmune close. Running to the window, I looked into the black street beyond the wall. The moon had retreated behind fat, drifting clouds. Crispus was right. Countless produce wagons rumbled past in the darkness. Because the room was for guests and not slaves, this upper floor window was one of the few not grated.

"Why all the wagons at this hour?" Crispus asked.

"I'll explain later, right now we've got to learn who did this," I answered.

"Who was it, Eleyne?" I demanded, returning to where she had kneeled by Karmune. "We've got to find the assassin." *How did he get to the second floor?* I wondered.

"I don't know. He's big. That's all I remember . . . and . . . his hand was crooked," she added. "I never saw . . . his face . . . but she did."

I stared at Karmune.

"Karmune," I asked, going down on one knee next to her. "Can you hear me?" I lowered my face to hers, blood slowly dripping from her lips, her breathing shallow. "Who did this? Can you tell me?"

"He," she gurgled in a barely audible whisper, "he . . . a jagged . . . jagged scar on . . ." She raised a bloodied hand. A finger traced a sticky shape on my face, and then fell weakly to her side after smearing what felt like a jagged line.

"Go on, please try, Karmune. Please try," I urged.

"On his . . . face . . ." She gurgled again—the sound of death—and was gone.

"Karmune!" Eleyne cried, her eyes fixed in horror. "Karmune! Oooh . . ." On her knees, she slipped to one side of Karmune's body and wept. Her only link to Britannia lay dead in her arms.

Fury rushed through my mind and body. Why had Eleyne's good-hearted companion, Karmune, been cut down with such cold-blooded ruthlessness? She must have been an unwitting victim of an assassination attempt on Eleyne's life. Now, I understood why Uncle Budar said to beware of Rome's Imperial intrigues. Sacrificing innocent people was part of a monstrous game.

Amid the clatter of sandals echoing from the hallway, Sabinus, his wife Aurelia, Alexias, and several lamp-carrying servants rushed into the room. In the shadows of the lantern light, Sabinus motioned the slaves to stand along the nearby wall. Quickly, I related what happened.

After Eleyne regained her composure and gently laid Karmune's head on the floor, she slowly got to her feet.

Aurelia moved to her side. “You poor child.” She touched Eleyne’s shoulder.

Sabinus’s face remained sober as he looked toward the open window and back to Eleyne. “I’m very sorry about your servant,” he said in a voice etched in sorrow, “can you give us any more details?”

Eleyne sniffled, pulled a cloth from her waistband, and wiped her face. Through tear-stained eyes she looked toward Sabinus. “Karmune had finished helping me dress.” She paused.

“Please go on, Eleyne,” Aurelia said gently, “you have nothing to be afraid of.”

“It was the new gown you gave me, Lady Aurelia. Karmune saw the other new silk gown, and asked to touch it.” She glanced to Aurelia and back to Sabinus. “She’d never seen that kind of material before. I gave her permission, and I went behind a screen to look at myself in the silver mirror.” Eleyne nodded to the far corner of the room.

She related that while she was making some minor adjustments to the dress, the attacker slipped in through the window. The noise from the clattering wagons in the street below drowned the sounds of his entry.

“As I came out from behind the screen, I saw a big man in a dark tunic leap down from the sill to the floor,” she continued. “I froze and couldn’t scream.”

Eleyne explained that she had watched helplessly as the horror unfolded before her eyes. “The killer didn’t see me behind the screen,” she explained, “or in the shadows where I came out. Instead, he mistook Karmune for me. My mouth went dry. Again, I tried to scream but couldn’t. That monster silently crept up behind Karmune and took a dagger from his waistband. The blade glistened in the lamp light as he raised it.

“He grabbed poor Karmune,” Eleyne continued, “and with his free hand twisted her mouth shut to muffle any screams.” She hesitated for a second and turned her face away. “I don’t know if I can go on.”

“Please try, Eleyne,” Sabinus urged.

“It’s all right, child,” Aurelia said. “We shall see that no harm comes to you.”

Eleyne swallowed hard and licked her lips. "All right. He . . . he pulled her to his chest and stabbed her over and over! Blood spurted from Karmune's wounds, and she struggled frantically to free herself from the assassin's clutches."

The young woman paused and took a deep breath.

"Go on," I said. "What else?"

"Karmune tried shaking her head to free her mouth from his hand's grip. She managed to turn for an instant and our eyes met. They were only shadows in the poor light, but I knew my friend was dying."

She wiped more tears from her face with her cloth before continuing. "The . . . the mon . . . monster twisted his dagger from poor Karmune's limp body and dropped her like a rag. He must have sensed something, because he turned around and saw me."

"What next?" I asked.

"He slowly crept towards me. Finally, something snapped, and I screamed over and over."

Eleyne said the assassin lunged at her with a long, twisted weapon in his left hand. The poor light obscured the features of his face, but it was sinister and round. Then he tripped and crashed with her to the floor. She smelled the stench of his body, his breath reeking of garlic and fish oil-garum.

"We rolled on the floor," Eleyne said, her breathing growing heavier, "and I used both hands to grasp his wrist."

I noticed bloodstains on her hands from holding Karmune.

"I heard the sound of footsteps and screamed again," she continued. "Then he slapped me and backed away. He glanced to the door and ran to the window.

"He paused on the balcony. *I'll be back,* he boasted. He shook the raised weapon in his clinched fist and spat, *Death to your house.* He jumped and fled into the night."

"By the gods," Sabinus growled in a subdued voice, "someone will pay for this with their life!" He turned to his steward, Alexias, who had waited with the other servants near the door. "Inquire where the guards were when this happened, and bring them here."

"At once, sir." A concerned look crossed his face and settled in his eyes, as if an old fear of his patron, dredged from the days when he was a slave, had resurfaced.

"One more item before you leave," Sabinus paused for emphasis. "From now on, Lady Eleyne needs constant protection. This will never happen again—never! My wife recently purchased a new slave, a big one."

"The one from India?" Alexias interjected quickly from across the room, apparently eager to temper Sabinus's growing rage.

"The same. Send him here at once. He'll be an excellent bodyguard."

"Very good, sir." Alexias fled from the room.

"Marcellus," Sabinus said.

"Sir?" I answered.

He motioned to Crispus and me to join him.

As Sabinus was about to speak, Aurelia placed an arm around Eleyne's shoulder and attempted to console her. Eleyne buried her head into Aurelia's bosom.

"This is so dreadful," I overheard Aurelia say. "I'm so sorry, my dear."

"She was my best friend," Eleyne cried, her face streaked by tears. "Now I have no one. Is this how you treat guests in Rome?"

"There now . . . easy, dear child," Aurelia said softly, "we are your friends, and we do care about you, honestly. I promise, we'll protect you."

Sabinus lead Crispus and me to the far corner of the room. "There could have been only one person behind this," he whispered.

I looked toward Crispus and back to Sabinus. "The elder Gallus?" I asked.

He nodded.

"But there's no proof, sir," Crispus said.

"I know," Sabinus answered, "but this is something he would attempt, assassination by a hired thug."

"Whoever planned this knew which room she was staying in," I said.

Sabinus glanced to the window and grunted. "News of our arrival has been known for weeks. Unfortunately, this is the guest room, and its location is common knowledge.

We will move Eleyne to one of the slave cubicles, where the windows are barred, until security arrangements are improved."

"A wise precaution, sir," Crispus added. "Why would anyone want to murder a hostage?"

"For political reasons—Eleyne's death would have made me look very foolish in the eyes of the emperor."

"How so?" I asked cautiously.

"Had she died, her father Verica would no longer have a reason to remain loyal to Rome. He could murder Togidubnus and instigate open rebellion in Vespasian's rear. That would be extremely serious, if not devastating, to his campaign."

"Thank the twins we arrived when we did," I said. I glanced over to Eleyne as she was being consoled by Aurelia. Even in this moment of tragedy I felt a deep stirring of compassion for her and felt her hurt and grief. I knew what it was like to lose someone so close and dear and wanted to hold her. Comfort her. My heart full of care and compassion. I hadn't experienced the feeling since losing my beloved Kyar.

Even in grief, Eleyne was beautiful. The big, red mark left by the slap of the assassin, the blood, and the runny kohl lining her eyes only emphasized her waif-like face. From that moment on, I no longer considered her a barbarian princess and political hostage. For the first time, I recognized that she had touched a need within me too long dormant.

"Is there a chance Eleyne will be sent to the palace for greater protection," I asked, "especially since you aren't city prefect?"

"Had she been from one of the Eastern kingdoms, probably," Sabinus answered. "However, since she is considered a barbarian, it's doubtful. A senator's home is deemed protection enough. If she were assassinated at the palace, it would look even worse politically, weakening the emperor's position with the Senate and Praetorian Guard. Since I was involved in negotiating the surrender of the eleven British kings, the emperor has entrusted me with her well-being regardless of my political status."

Alexias returned with two staggering guards reeking of wine. A dark-brown colossus of a man held onto the arms of one sentry while Alexias along with a couple of other slaves restrained the other. "I caught these two in the wine cellar drinking your vintage Sentenian," the steward reported.

Sabinus glared at the two sentries, and a cruel, dark expression settled over his face. He addressed the slaves directly, something he rarely did. "Death visited my house this night because of your—" He checked his stern voice then continued in a controlled and calmer manner. "What I do now is with utmost reluctance, and many years have passed since I employed such punishment. You will suffer the ultimate penalty—death."

The guards immediately sobered from their drunkenness and stared wide-eyed. They begged for mercy, but Sabinus ignored their frantic pleas.

He turned to Alexias. "I leave to you the method of employment," he said in a sinister voice, "but first learn who paid them to break into the wine stores, and make it swift. Now, get them out of my sight!"

As they turned to leave, Sabinus ordered the tall slave to wait. With the other slaves' assistance, Alexias grabbed both stammering guards and dragged them away.

Later that night I heard their screams. Under the law, Sabinus had the right as master of the household to summarily execute his slaves. The attempt on Eleyne's life, a pawn in the political game of empire and war, had shaken him. Although not in character, the harsh punishment he meted out proved he was human enough to feel fear of the emperor's retribution.

Although severely scourged, the condemned guards revealed no clues to the murder. They denied having any part of the crime, but even in death were fortunate. Swift and certain, their deaths displayed at least a measure of mercy. Their heads fell before the sword, instead of suffering a lingering death by crucifixion—punishment of slaves and non-citizens.

Sabinus watched as his slaves removed Karmune's body from the room.

"I know it's little consolation," Aurelia said, comforting Eleyne, "but we will see she receives a dignified burial."

Suddenly, Eleyne composed herself and dried the tears from her eyes. "I'll prepare her myself," she announced. "It's the custom of my people to ready their own family for burial. She was like a sister to me."

The silent bodyguard appeared to watch while Eleyne's eyes stared at the dark pool of blood, then she squatted and draped a dark cloth over the stain.

Eleyne gazed at the door through which Karmune's body had been removed. "Let's go," she said with a sigh of resignation. Eleyne and Aurelia followed the slaves down the hallway to Karmune's room.

In her grief, Eleyne didn't seem to notice the giant of a man guarding her as they walked by. Garbed in the drab coarse, white tunic of a slave, his locks of curly, black hair swirled into a neat knot above his forehead. A daub of red, which I later learned represented a soldier's caste in India, stood above the bridge of a nose framed by a long face.

Left alone, Crispus and I searched the murder scene. I went to the window and examined the area. Framed by wooden shutters that opened outward, its plastered ledge was wide enough for a good handgrip. I gazed into the darkened street hearing, then seeing the shadowy outlines of freight wagons rumbling by.

I turned to Crispus and motioned him to join me.

He peered out the window, and then at me.

"Earlier you asked me why the wagons were rolling at this hour," I said.

Crispus raised an eyebrow. "I did."

"About a hundred years ago, Julius Caesar enacted a law prohibiting wagons on Rome's streets during daytime."

"Why?"

"The streets were too crowded, which not only slowed the wagons, but also resulted in many accidents, killing many people."

"I get it," Crispus said, "the wagons run at night because there ain't as much traffic. And even though there's more crime, the teamsters are a rough bunch—they don't take shit from anybody. Hell, they'd run 'em over with their rigs."

I pursed my mouth. "But sometimes an ambitious thug can take advantage of the moving wagons."

"Like how?" Crispus shook his head.

"Knowing that so many wagons pass by Sabinus's home, it was just a matter for the assassin to jump aboard one. Because it's dark and the cart wheels make so much noise, the driver probably didn't know he had an unwanted passenger."

"Which means," Crispus said, picking up the thread of my conclusion, "he made his jump, grabbed the window sill, and hauled himself up onto the ledge."

"And then he entered through the window, dropped down onto the floor, and murdered Karmune," I finished.

"Still, his timing had to be near perfect," Crispus said. He glanced to the window again. "The window ain't that wide."

"I have an idea this isn't the first time for our assassin," I said. "He's probably had plenty of practice."

Crispus's mouth tightened. "Aye, he's had the same by escaping and jumping onto another passing wagon."

"That's how I see it."

I noticed that Crispus seemed to stare long and hard at my face. "All right," I finally said, to satisfy my curiosity, "why are you looking at me like that? Do I have the pox?"

"See for yourself, old friend." Crispus stepped back a few paces, picked up the polished silver-plated mirror from the floor, came forward, and held it up before me. I stared into my reflection and upon the dried-blood scar Karmune had traced. A jagged crust of blood smeared from the center forehead, across my right eye and snaking across the cheek, hooked sharply into my mouth. A scar memory burned forever in my mind, one I would see again.

CHAPTER 26

After Karmune's murder, a deep gloom prevailed in the Sabinus mansion. No one had an appetite for dinner, and after eating, the household retired for the evening. Despite the presence of Eleyne's new bodyguard, Crispus and I took turns keeping watch outside her room the rest of the night. Sabinus sent for a detachment of the Watch to patrol the perimeter around his home and six surrounding blocks.

Rome's summer heat dictated Karmune's body be laid to rest as quickly as possible. Before dawn, Eleyne's companion was quietly buried in the cemetery for foreigners, along the tomb-clustered Appian Way.

Crispus and I and a small entourage of slaves and client freedmen accompanied Sabinus to the Palatine for an audience with the emperor. Word had reached the palace before our arrival about the rescue of the Jewish woman and the murder of Karmune. A group of officials and noblemen attempted to ask Sabinus about the details, but he waved them away, promising a briefing later.

Sabinus met with Claudius privately and gave a full account of the murder. He told me later if Eleyne had not been an imperial hostage, and the assassin's intended victim, the emperor would have ignored the matter. "Murders in Rome are like flies in a stable," Sabinus said. "No one pays attention to either, and that's what bothers me."

While Crispus and I waited outside with Sabinus's people in the Court of Tiberius, the elder Gallus lingered nearby with his contingent of clients. As soon as Sabinus had entered the Imperial apartments, Gallus sent a messenger commanding my presence.

"You wanted to see me, Lord Gallus?" I inquired after crossing the vast marble floor. He wore a scarlet mantle about his narrow shoulders. Scattered along the polished floor sat smoky, charcoal braziers on bronze tripods, futilely attempting to heat the gaping court.

Gallus motioned toward a large, empty space at the far end of the chamber beneath a huge statue of Apollo. "Come with me. We shall speak in private."

Like Sabinus, Gallus dressed in the whitest of togas, with a broad, purple stripe down the center denoting his Senatorial rank. Elaborately decorated red shoes, embossed with an ivory letter "C" on the outside of the ankle, symbol of prior magisterial service, clothed his feet.

"I'm pleased to hear the emperor's precious hostage survived," he said, as we stood in the sun god's shadow. "Senator Sabinus has been saved from an embarrassing situation."

"Yes, sir, but I suspect that isn't the reason for this meeting."

Gallus raised his eyebrows and creased his blotched forehead. "Impertinent, aren't you? I heard you weren't one for small talk."

The old senator looked about and waved away one of his approaching freedmen.

"I underestimated your worth, Centurion," he said. "You are a man to be reckoned with. Now I understand why Senator Sabinus chose you as retainer. You didn't hesitate to rescue the Jewish woman or the barbarian."

I bristled at his snide reference to Eleyne and Pricilla, because they were not Roman. "I did my duty, the proper thing to do."

"Of course, I have great use for someone with your bravery and talents."

For a moment, his bloodshot eyes studied me as he would a horse or a slave. "I am very influential," Gallus said, "and it is within my power to have you transferred to my staff, should you decide serving as a retainer to Flavius Sabinus doesn't suit you. After all . . . ," he smiled wryly, "living in Rome can be dangerous to one's health, and I'm not referring to our summers and swamp fevers. An allegiance to me can be beneficial."

"Why are you offering me a position?" I asked and eyed the area for eavesdroppers. No one. "You and my father were enemies."

"Your father is dead." He spread his hands wide. "Why should I hold you, his son, in disfavor? My grievance was with him. That's why I can help you, young Marcellus."

"In what manner?" I had an idea of what he was leading to.

"Unfortunately, your father was never admitted to the Equestrians, a fate you needn't suffer. I am very close to the emperor. It is within my power to have you admitted to the order of knighthood. Provided . . . ," he paused as if for emphasis, "you are willing to become a member of my staff, and follow orders like the good soldier you are."

"I'm not easily bought." Heat rushed through my body to my face.

He raised his hand to his sagging chest. "Come now, I don't soil my hands with such petty tactics. Think about my proposition today and give me your answer tomorrow."

I realized he had the means to carry out such a promise. This man had been my father's adversary, and my mother would sooner see me dead then serve my father's most hated enemy. "You can have it now. My loyalty is to Lord Sabinus."

He tweaked his nose. "Loyalty is a noble attribute, if not misplaced. To the emperor, definitely, otherwise it can be a terminal disease. For your sake, I pray your combat skills won't be needed to defend your loyalty. As for knighthood—forget it—you had your chance."

The elder Gallus took a step, then halted. "By the way, if anyone inquires about our conversation, say I asked about my son. Tell them anything different, and I shall deny it. The word of a senator carries far more weight than a centurion's." He stomped away, the sounds of his sandals echoing throughout the cavernous room.

"What did he want?" Crispus asked, when I rejoined him.

I explained Gallus's offer.

"Is he mad?"

"No, he's a man who possesses great power and isn't afraid to use it," I said.

"He flaunts his authority like he's above the law."

"So far, he is."

* * *

Returning from the audience, Sabinus dismissed his retinue except for Crispus and myself. I informed him of the conversation with Gallus. We strolled toward the palace exit, our boots clattering on the polished marble floor. I walked by Sabinus's left, Crispus to his right.

"Still, Marcellus, no doubt he would have persuaded the emperor," Sabinus said. "I know what that would mean for your family. I can offer you nothing."

"I have your friendship," I said, turning toward him, "and my family honor, and I'll achieve knighthood on my own worth. I can't believe how blatant he was."

"He isn't afraid to openly make offers," Sabinus said. "Old Gallus is a man who is used to getting what he wants, but clever enough to prevent any illegal activity being traced to him." He waved to a senator passing in the opposite direction.

"What about planting spies among the household slaves, sir?" Crispus asked.

"He screens his slaves too closely, Sergeant," Sabinus replied. "If they ask too many questions they are flogged and sold, if not executed."

We left the palace and proceeded to the office of Decrius Calpurnianus, the Watch prefect on the Latanian Way near the Ratumenian Gate. Headquartered in the huge colonnaded barracks of the First Cohort, outside the Servian Wall, I had learned the prefect commanded a seven-thousand-man security force used to combat crime and fight fires. Besides the First Cohort, the Watch consisted of six other cohorts, each containing one thousand men, scattered in six other billets, among the city's fourteen regions. Because part of their equipment consisted of folded, pitch-lined, rope buckets for carrying water, the Vigiles were nicknamed Bucketmen.

"The City Guards and Watch were established by Caesar Augustus about forty years ago," Sabinus explained as we jostled our way through the crowded streets.

As we pushed through the ragged ranks of a half-dozen smelly beggars, I shouted to Sabinus to be heard above the noise of the mob, "Wouldn't it be better to amalgamate their troops into one cohesive unit instead of operating two separate organizations? Common sense dictates it'd be more efficient in dealing with Rome's crime and terrible fires."

"I agree," Sabinus barked in reply. "Unfortunately, the prefects of both offices have jealously guarded their positions through the years. The city prefect is appointed from members of the Senate, whereas, the Watch prefect comes from the Equestrian Order. As you can appreciate, they vehemently oppose any change that would threaten their domains."

"Is there any chance of changing the situation, sir?" Crispus asked in a raised voice, attempting to be heard.

"That would require a massive organizational change, Sergeant." Sabinus explained the men of the Watch were recruited from ex-slaves, and promised Roman citizenship after six years of service. Whereas, troops from the City Guard are Roman citizens transferred from the army as steppingstones to the Praetorian Guard.

"After last night's tragedy," he continued, "it's imperative we make inquiries about Gallus and his criminal connections. That's why I'm meeting with Prefect Decrius Calpurnianus."

* * *

"I'm sorry you didn't receive your appointment, Senator Sabinus," Decrius Calpurnianus said. Crispus and I stood to one side, slightly to the rear, as the pasty-faced Watch prefect spoke to Sabinus. Calpurnianus slouched behind an expensive citrus wood desk in a spacious office. His pale complexion was a stark contrast to his layered, curling, black hair. "We would have worked well together in policing Rome."

"Indeed, and we still can," Sabinus said.

I looked out of the corner of my eye toward Crispus. Did he have the same doubts that I had? He kept a sober face.

Calpurnianus snapped his shoulders back and sat up straight in his chair. He wiped the perspiration running down the side of his face with a white, linen cloth. It was midmorning, but already, another humid day smothered the city. I sweltered beneath my tunic and segmented armor. I wore a light, woolen scarf around my neck to protect it from chafing from the hot metal.

"Since Gallus's man, Secundus, has been chosen," the Watch prefect continued, "it'll be well-nigh impossible."

"It's true your Bucketmen will have more work on their hands," Sabinus said, "but we can work out an arrangement."

"What sort of plan are you implying?" The prefect's watery, brown eyes surveyed Crispus and me in turn.

"I see you've brought your retainers—direct from the army, aren't they?" Calpurnianus questioned, finally acknowledging our presence.

Sabinus introduced us and explained our backgrounds. "They fought with my brother's legion in Britannia. As you can see by his decorations, Centurion Reburrus won the *Corona Civica*."

"Impressive," Calpurnianus said and pursed his lips together.

"I will develop my own sources of information about Rome's underworld, which I'm willing to share with you," Sabinus said.

"That's commendable, Senator Sabinus, but what's your price?" Calpurnianus asked. "As honorable as you are, I've never known you to give away anything without a stipulation."

"My price is your employment of Centurion Reburrus and Sergeant Crispus on any raids initiated from information we gather," Sabinus said. "They're combat veterans."

"I have my own sources and men," Calpurnianus answered in a surly voice. He picked up the wax tablet laying on his desk and briefly turned it toward Sabinus before setting it down. "I know that your first goal is to find the assassin of that hostage's servant."

Sabinus frowned, and then nodded. "True, but combined together, we may root out those involved and, in the process, much of the city's worst elements." He gestured to the Watch prefect. "You have no love for Gallus, and with Secundus in his money pouch, things will get worse."

After sparring a little longer, Sabinus and Calpurnianus came to a conditional agreement. "Give my plan three months," Sabinus said. "If it's successful, we'll continue working together. If it isn't, we go our separate ways."

"Agreed," the Watch prefect said.

Calpurnianus picked up a reed pen and dipped it into the lampblack ink of the silver-inlaid bronze inkwell. He signed one of the dozen parchment scrolls on his desk and held it up to me. "As a legionary centurion, your authority supersedes the centurions of the Watch. Therefore, consider yourself a liaison between the army, through Senator Sabinus, and the Vigiles. You'll have full authority to command a century of eighty watchmen."

Crispus and I looked at one another. I saw a problem. "There is bound to be resentment, sir, especially, since we're foreigners."

"You're soldiers of the army, they're ex-slaves, and have no choice. The tribunes, who are Roman Citizens, may have objections, but I'll see they keep their opinions to themselves."

* * *

During the next ten days, Crispus and I explored the city. Wandering along dirty, narrow streets and alleys, strewn with garbage and offal, past graffiti-tagged walls, we talked to shopkeepers, visited the majestic public baths, and the smaller private ones, and attended the public games. Our uniforms became a detriment in seeking information, making us objects of suspicion and fear, if not downright hostility. Our questions met with feigned ignorance and lies.

When asked, one shopkeeper, a Greek fuller, denied knowing the direction of Mercury Street, although we were *on* Mercury Street, and his business appeared to have been situated there for years. Five large, urine-stained earthen pots lined the trash-littered sidewalk in front of the shop. The passersby greeted the fuller, pulled up their tunics, and noisily urinated into the jars. The fuller thanked them, snapped his fingers, and two slaves came and removed the smelly receptacles inside.

Urine was used in stiffening clothing being laundered, before washing in fuller's earth to remove grease. The big jars lined every street.

"After all," the Greek explained, "I provide a free service from which I, too, benefit. The smelly public latrines charge half a copper for their use. I charge nothing and keep the street free of waste."

Crispus and I decided gathering evidence dressed as civilians might achieve better results. I suggested the idea to Sabinus, and he readily agreed. Thereafter, we roamed the streets dressed as workers, clothed in rough, red-wool, one-sleeved worker tunics, with a leather pouch wrapped about the waist. Concealed beneath the sleeve of the loose-fitting garments, we still carried army short swords. Although the weapons chafed our sides in the hot, muggy weather, both of us felt safer pushing our way through the crowded city lanes and slums.

* * *

Autumn came early to Rome, and by the end of September, the days had turned chilly. An annoying drizzle fell over the city nearly every morning, its dampness causing the scar on my left cheek to itch.

Another bleak morning dawned as I waited for Sabinus to appear before his clients at the vestibule and distribute his daily gifts and favors. Most of the hangers-on were his ex-slaves. Ancient custom demanded he cater to this dismal lot of humanity, who could not fend for themselves now they were freed. A few other parasites lurked nearby, hoping for a free handout in return for performing an unwanted service.

Shoving his way through the gathering rain-soaked rabble, a bearded and cloaked Spaniard, surrounded by four shaggy barbarians, lumbered to the gate. I recognized the Germans as belonging to the Hermundurian Tribe by the twisted, long, fuzzy knots hanging from the right side of their heads.

"I'm here to see my nephew, Marcellus. Open up!" their leader demanded.

"There's no one here by that name," the gate custodian answered in a contemptuous voice.

"Dammit, you Persian snake-eater," the Spaniard growled. "He's your master's retainer, Centurion Marcellus Reburrus. Now open this gate before I wrap it around your scrawny neck!"

Nobody but Uncle Budar would be so caustic with a senator's servant. I ordered the gatekeeper to let them pass. He obeyed grudgingly, obviously insulted by Budar's rough manner. The crusty old veteran came into the vestibule, escorted by his trusty Germans. Smelling as foul as ever, his retainers reminded me of soaked rats in their animal skins. They stayed at a distance from us, continually searching the area, waving away anyone coming into the room.

After shaking the water from his clothes, Budar gave me a bear hug.

"I said I'd come with a visit, didn't I, boy?" He laughed heartily.

Budar inspected my uniform. "Not bad, not bad at all. You look every bit a centurion. Except." He paused. "Except the hair. Why did you grow it long?" It was about a finger thickness longer than before. "These modern centurions and their long, stylish hair," he growled. "Disgusting."

I ignored his comments and explained about the attempted murder of Eleyne and death of Karmune. With the exception of several false leads, our inquiries had been fruitless, and Sabinus's spies hadn't fared any better.

Budar thought for a few minutes, glanced at his Germans. Unconsciously, he scratched an armpit and studied my face for a few seconds. "There's somebody you've got to meet. When you're through at the Palatine, come and see me at the *Sling and Onager* wine shop on Minerva Lane—you know the place?"

"If you mean the dirty hole in the wall with the ugly woman owner who's missing a left ear, I've seen it." I grinned.

"Good. It's a soldier's den, so you won't be out of sorts."

Budar motioned to his Germans and turned to leave. "I'll see you later. Have some business to take care of while I'm here." He left with his bickering Germans trotting behind.

I wondered who the person was that he wanted us to meet. Would it be someone who could assist Crispus and me in digging up evidence against the elder Gallus? Or just another waste of time?

CHAPTER 27

Crispus and I hurried through an icy downpour and met Budar at the wine shop near the Field of Mars—not far from Watch headquarters. I surveyed the cesspit, known as the *Sling and Onager,* remembering why I had avoided falling into that sewer. A small place, its masonry counter, ingrained with fragments of colored marble, faced the street. Three large earthenware jars, uncomfortably similar to urine containers, were embedded into the bar filled with steaming soup and stew. Against the wall leaned four long-stemmed *amphorae* wine jugs. Sides of bacon, dried fish, and chickens hung above the counter in various stages of decay. From one end drifted the pungent fragrance of warm spice wine, Calda, from a bronze bowl atop a hot tripod brazier.

Painted on the outside wall, a chipped picture depicted an army catapult, the *Onager*, and a Belaeric Islander hurling a keg of Syrian whiskey with his sling. In a niche next to the sign stood a small statue of Hercules, for good luck.

A goatskin covering protected the interior from the elements. Inside, strewn about the cement floor, fresh sawdust covered numerous older layers of festering compost. A snoring drunk had fallen onto the floor, leaving a partial bowl of Calda. A fat tavern maiden poured it into a fox-shaped terra-cotta drinking flask. She emptied a wooden dish of some unknown stew onto the floor with a flick of the wrist, to be covered by tomorrow's straw.

As we sat, I rubbed some heat into my frozen hands, removed my wet army cloak, and shook it before moving another step. Back in the dimly lit corner, beneath a picture of the household gods, Budar sat by himself on a brick bench. The Germans congregated over a low, cement table molded into the floor in another corner, happily swilling large earthen bowls of beer. Sitting in the opposite corner, an old craggy-faced, drunken soldier slurped from a jug.

Uncle Budar waved to us. "Ah, Crispus, this is a pleasant surprise, welcome."

"My pleasure, sir."

Budar ordered one of the wrinkled keeper's better vintages of the grape, but he warned against sampling the stew. "I'd rather lick one of them Germans' armpits than taste her swill."

We laughed. The bearded Germans, clothed in smelly tunics and breeches with wolf-skin cloaks hooked at the shoulder, looked at each other, as if trying to decide whether an insult was intended.

Budar leaned closer as he tugged on his graying beard. "There may be a way you can learn if old Gallus is behind this murder business."

"How?" I asked.

"I have a hook with the right people, the kind you'd least expect."

"Who?"

"Beggars."

I nearly dropped my cup. "Are you mad?"

His powerful hand grabbed my wrist. "Wait a minute, boy. You'd be surprised at what they hear."

"Why beggars?" Crispus asked.

Budar released my wrist. "They're all over the city—the docks, the Forum, the streets—everywhere."

"But they can't be trusted," I protested, "They'd sell their mothers for a copper."

"Aye, so they would, but they're prey to criminals, too. Like you, they want to see the streets rid of them."

"What does it have to do with us?" Crispus interjected. A boisterous roar of laughter from Budar's men delayed the reply.

"Most beggars are harmless, and want to be left in peace," Budar answered. "For a price, they're willing to give information."

"We can get that from the secret police," I said.

"The difference is these people have no political vendettas, and certainly no influence. They want the criminals to leave them alone."

"The Watch isn't about to help them either," Crispus added.

"That's why," Budar continued, "the beggars are willing to help anyone who'll protect them. All they have is one another for protection—that accounts for having their own leader."

"The idea still smells of rotten mullet," I said.

Crispus bared his big teeth and spat on the floor. "Why don't we give it a try, Marcellus, nothing else has worked."

Another outburst of laughter from the Germans gave me time to think. Crispus was right. So far, we had met with failure and frustration. A couple of days before, we'd investigated the Broken Oxcart, the place the dying young tough mentioned, and not only hadn't learned anything, but been forced to fight our way out, barely escaping with our lives.

"All right," I conceded, "we might as well. Where do we find them, Uncle?"

Budar gave me a pat on the shoulder. "You're a good man, Marcellus, but Crispus has lots of common sense. Fortunately, he's your friend. Come along, I'll show you."

The four Germans, who had been drunkenly pawing the tavern wench's ample buttocks, suddenly sobered as Budar stood. I realized their beer-swilling boisterous ruse was to cover our conversation and raised my opinion of Budar another notch.

The rain had eased, but as we got to our feet I noticed Uncle Budar smiling.

"What's so funny?" I asked.

"That," he answered, referring to the drunk on the floor. "Do you suppose if he lays there long enough they'll cover him with straw and the rest of the shit?"

We laughed and departed, trudging by the Theaters of Balbus and Pompey and down the water-swollen Cornelian Way.

We left Rome through the Capenian Gate and traveled along the Appian Way. Heading south, we passed endless private cemeteries, lining both sides of the worn volcanic-stone highway, stretching far out onto the Campanian Plain.

Travelers on foot, caught by bad weather, huddled beneath the darkened porticoes of the deserted mausoleums. Wrapped in woolen cloaks, our little party of seven traipsed onward. Periodically, rushing horseman and lumbering wagons splashed us as they passed through deep puddles.

Budar led us off the highway, between a couple of nondescript vaults, and down a ravine of heavily moisture-laden bushes. Pushing the branches aside, we entered a large cave. Water falling through cracks in the dark, eerie ceiling formed into puddles of water lining the rocky floor. In a dark corner Budar found clumps of dried faggots, and we wrapped them into torches with oily rags and twine. The amber torchlight revealed naturally hollowed-out walls of hard rock and mildewed earth.

My uncle motioned to the dark recess leading downward at the far end. "This is the way, let's go."

Cautiously, our band snaked its way through the shadowy underworld. Carefully, we avoided the bottomless chasms on each side of the path from which Budar told me no man returned—convenient places for *accidents* to occur. We bypassed dozens of caves in which one might wander forever. Mixed with scurrying rats and dark fluttering and flying things, the stench of decay and death flowed too freely.

Smelling it long before I saw it, we halted at the edge of a great, lethargic underground river reeking of sewage. The flowing sound echoed quietly through the vast cavern.

"This is the great cistern of Rome, the *Cloaca Maxima*," Budar explained.

"Smells like the world's shit has been dumped here," Crispus commented.

"It has, and a body or two now and then," Budar said.

Across the fetid river dozens of fires peaked and ebbed, and hissed and roared brightly, lighting up the other side to reveal the enormity of the sewer.

"Good gods," I said, "you could sail a trireme down this stink hole."

"Someone did," Budar replied. "Years ago, they say, under Caesar Augustus, his son-in-law, Marcus Agrippa, did. He was the victor of Antony and Cleopatra at Actium. When he was the Aedile in charge of the water supply, the old admiral drained and cleaned the sewer. Once he finished, he supposedly sailed a three-banker down to the Tiber."

"Where are those fires coming from?" I asked.

"Escaping gases from beneath the earth, the caves are full of them. Sometimes there's no fire, just the smell of sour grapes. The place reminds me of the stories of the German underworld, reigned over by their half-goddess, half-monster queen, *Hel*."

Budar stopped. He turned and cursed his bickering guards in their harsh, grating tongue. They cringed beneath his wrath. By the gods, if it were possible, I believe he actually hurt their lice-infected feelings.

"Damn, Germans are too quick with their swords under pressure," he muttered. "I don't want them chopping up the first runt of a beggar that steps out of a shadow, so I ordered them to use the flat side of their swords if threatened. Trouble is, them bastards don't know they've got flat sides to whack 'em with."

Crispus and I waited while Budar and one of the Germans walked a short distance along the bank. The smaller of the Germans stayed beside me. He grimaced and dug a dirty fingernail hard beneath an armpit. He scratched the louse and smiled a broken-tooth victory. I edged a discreet foot or so away from him.

"Over here," Budar called, his voice echoing through the vast recess. In the darkness four or five small boats huddled along the embankment. Their circular shape reminded me of the cowhided coracles used by the Britons.

"Get in." He motioned to one of them. "We're going across."

A slight commotion ensued as three of the Germans throttled the fourth until he got into the bowl-shaped boat. Budar looked at me. "The bugger can't swim."

With Budar, Crispus, and I in one tiny vessel, and the Germans huddled in the other, we deftly rowed across the scum-filled waters as more filth floated by.

The Germans began fussing again until Budar croaked, and they ceased scooping the slimy water with their hands and splashing the non-swimmer.

"Uncle, how did you find this place?"

He paused before answering simply, "A woman."

I didn't pursue the question, but tried to imagine any woman who would make it worth the effort to traverse the bowels of this Hel.

Upon landing, we hiked up the deep bank, passing the gaseous fires that conjured images of Hades, and plunged into the abyss. After what seemed an endless journey, we encountered an unusually large, torch-lit grotto. The stench of unwashed bodies engulfed the stale air. In the shadowed light, pathetic, rag-clothed creatures squatted in groups around small cooking fires. A couple of gaunt women distributed earthen bowls filled with bread and gruel.

Suddenly, nine or ten beggars jumped from the shadows, threatening us with walking sticks.

"Get out!" A toothless mendicant in a dirt-encrusted robe spat. "We don't want *your kind* here. This is our world! Go back to yours!" The echo of his voice thundered through the cavern.

As Budar's bodyguards drew their swords, he stepped ahead of us and held up his hand as a sign of friendship. "Easy man, we come in peace. We're here to see Scrofa. Tell him Budar's here, he knows we're coming."

Budar turned to his bodyguards and gestured for them to lower their weapons. They did, but their intimidating eyes threatened a sharp death if provoked too far.

The old beggar eyed them suspiciously, and then us. "Wait here." He hobbled into the darkness.

A few minutes later he returned with a shabby but familiar-looking indigent. A tattered patch covered his left eye, two fingers were missing from his right hand, and a torn skullcap partially covered his shaved head. It was the beggar I had kicked near the docks.

He turned his attention to my uncle, and the two vigorously embraced. "Budar, you old son-of-a-whore." He gestured around the cavern. "Welcome to Hel. It's been ages. How are you, old dog?"

"Good to see your throat isn't slit ear to ear, you old bastard," Budar roared. "Yet, I'm not bad, for an old trooper." They laughed heartily.

"I've been expecting you," Scrofa said.

"Knowing your chain of informants, I reckoned if I left word you'd hear soon enough," Budar answered.

"Eh, I did. What can I do for you, old comrade?" His manner changed abruptly to business.

Scrofa studied us suspiciously with his sunken, dark eye and scarred, narrow face. He looked closer at me. "I've seen you before."

Then a smirk split his jagged face. "Now I remember, you kicked me at the Emporium! A favor *for you*? By Pluto's ear, you're mad!" He fell silent for a few seconds, studying me further. "It's not often I have a boot kicker come begging," he added sarcastically.

I sensed his mock anger was to add value to granting a favor, and more importantly, a return in kind.

"What did you expect?" Budar said. "You and I soldiered together for years. We treated beggars the same way. Why I remember—"

"I don't mind giving a hungry beggar like that woman a copper now and then," I interrupted. "But I didn't appreciate it going into someone else's purse."

"We've got our reasons," Scrofa said, gesturing to the paupers by the fire. "We share what we have, so no one starves. If we resort to trickery, so what? We're no worse than the thieving senators and merchants."

"Can't you get government bread?" I asked.

He smiled and shook his head. "No. Most of these poor devils are ex-slaves. They're not eligible for Rome's generous gifts." He sneered. "We're just a simple clan of beggars and thieves—well . . . beggars, anyway."

"You have no patrons like Lord Sabinus?"

Scrofa snorted. "Few are as generous as your Sabinus, and those who are publicly humiliate their clients with insults, forcing them to cower like dogs. A man can only take so much before he'll turn to stealing or begging. I'd rather beg than crawl before one of those powder-faced pansies."

"You're still prey to thieves and highwaymen," I reminded him.

He spat. "Aye, we are. The stinking cowards rob people, many of them helpless cripples, before stealing from the strong and the rich."

"Maybe we can help," I said.

"Horseshit! What can you do?" he bellowed. "We can handle most of the thieves and robbers, it's your Bucketmen we fear."

I explained my position with Sabinus and the attempt to link Gallus to the criminal element. I proposed using the beggars to relay information they might hear.

"Why should I give information to the Imperial government? What's it to us if this Gallus steals or murders his own kind?"

"Not only do we want information on Gallus," I said, "but any bandits you hear about."

"What do I receive for my help?" As in a game of dice, the cast of Venus was thrown on the table.

"The information will be used to arrest those robbing your people," I advised, "and you'll be paid for your news."

A crooked smile wrinkled the beggar leader's stubbly face. "That's not enough. For money, I can give you a dozen witnesses who can tell such convincing lies that even Rome's most corrupt and cold-hearted judge would burst into tears. Rome hasn't done anything for us before."

He cut off my reply with a wave of the hand. "There is a way she can pay us back. Call off your dogs. Since the murder of that girl at Lord Sabinus's house . . ." He mockingly bowed with the name. "The Bucketmen have made life miserable for us. We didn't kill her! We know the killer is a Gaul, and if you meet our price, when we learn where he lives, we'll lead you to him. As for the other forms of information, we want gold."

Scrofa agreed to being paid half for any *truthful* information he gave us, and the rest when we confirmed it. He would use his chain of beggars to gather information on the Gaul, and funnel it to us. He may have cared for his people, but he didn't want the money entrusted to anyone but himself.

The question remained. Would Scrofa and his beggars follow through and send us incriminating information to be used against the elder Gallus and Rome's criminal element?

Could they?

CHAPTER 28

Within a week, the agreement with Scrofa the beggar king started bearing fruit. At dawn, early on a crisp morning, one of his weasel-faced beggars, Mico, left a message at Sabinus's home for Crispus and me. Scrofa asked us to meet him at the Probus Bridge, near the grain silos of the Emporium, a beggar's haunt.

When we arrived, we saw Scrofa lurking in the shadows beneath the rat-infested bridge crossing the polluted Tiber. Little knots of ragged mendicants hovered with thieving eyes around a dozen fires along the riverbank. Noise from the docks drifted on the frigid morning breeze as barges poled upriver from Ostia and unloaded their cargoes at the big stone docks. Scrofa ordered a group of beggars away from one fire, and motioned for us to join him.

"What do you have?" I inquired, as we rubbed our cold hands over the small fire.

"My people discovered the whereabouts of a big cache of goods," Scrofa replied. "Most of the things were stolen from shops along the Sacred Way."

"Where is it hidden?" I questioned.

"In one of the caverns."

"Near your people's home?" Crispus asked.

"No, as far as I can guess, it's at the other end of the city."

"Then you'll lead us and the Watch to the cave," I said.

The beggar king hesitated, blowing his breath into cupped hands.

I knew he would back away if he wasn't given the proper incentive. For all his boasting, he was a coward at heart.

"If you expect to be paid for your information," I said in a menacing voice, "you will lead us. Is that clear?"

"All right," the beggar leader said grudgingly. His breath steamed but instantly disappeared. "I'll guide you, but it'll cost you twice the usual price." He gestured with his remaining two fingers through mittens filled with holes. "When we made this bargain, I wasn't expecting to risk my life."

"You'll be well compensated," I answered. I didn't mention the reward for lying—the loss of his head.

* * *

In the early morning light, Scrofa and Mico led Crispus and me, and thirty hand-picked, sword-carrying watchmen, commanded by Centurion Faenus Rufus and Optio Casperius Niger, down into a cavern. As Scrofa said earlier, the cave was at the other end of the city far from the beggar king's lair.

Not only beggars, but Rome's criminal element claimed the city's vast network of caves as their home. I recalled asking Sabinus one day how long the gangs of thieves and cutthroats had lived beneath the city.

"They've festered there for countless ages," Sabinus had said. "They're considered part of the natural order of things. At night, they leave their dark recesses, surfacing to rob and plunder, and return below before sunrise."

"Has the Guard or Watch seriously attempted to rid the city of this vermin?" I asked.

Sabinus exhaled. "Occasionally, they've raided their hideouts when they got out of hand. Meaning they had robbed a senator or killed some high official."

"There must be a better reason for not making a concerted effort to wipe out the bandits."

"Two reasons," he said. "There are too many, and the Watch and City Guard fear the underworld. The risk of becoming lost and murdered in the endless labyrinth is too great. More than an entire century, eighty men, has disappeared at one time in its bowels."

As we descended into what seemed to be a pit of no return, I understood what Sabinus had meant. As uninvited guests, we had entered Pluto's empire, god of the underworld, and Roman companion to the German goddess, Hel. The light of our fluttering lanterns gave life to eerie cavern shadows. They ebbed and flowed with pulsating movement of light. I had the feeling that any moment some monster would pounce and devour us. The mind plays many tricks on those who allow their imaginations to run wild.

Carefully, the troops eased past gaping fissures, cautiously trekking through the mud and murk seething from invisible crevices. The air grew stale and heavy, and perspiration poured from our bodies. For a moment, a howling wind swirled through a crag, and cooled us. Perhaps Aeolius, the god of wind, screamed at us for foolishly invading its domain, a land of Stygian darkness. The wind laughed at our folly, sighing we might never return.

When we stopped a moment later for a breather, Crispus tapped me on the shoulder, and nodded to the men. "You see the looks in their eyes, Marcellus?"

"Aye, the sounds are playing havoc with their superstitious minds," I answered. "Can't say that I blame them. I'm struggling to keep my own imagination under control."

"That makes two of us."

"I'd rather return to the world of the living," I continued, "but we have to flush out this den of thieves and murderers. And recover the contraband."

"If it exists."

"We'll deal with Scrofa if it doesn't."

"None of these troops are cowards," Crispus added, "but it doesn't lessen their fears of this hole."

"Remind them it's like going into battle," I said, "everyone is scared." Their hands and faces glistened with sweat, and their mouths were no doubt as dry as mine.

I motioned to the troops. "Come on, let's go."

Again, we encountered the cave's perpetual fires. Escaping blue flames hissed and seethed from lignite and igneous rocks. Squealing, plague-infested rats scurried helter-skelter between our feet, and blood-sucking bats whisked by our heads. Turning a bend, Scrofa nearly tripped over a sprawled, rag-covered skeleton, a rusty dagger sticking between its ribs.

Crispus and I pushed the remains out of the pathway with the flat of our swords. At the touch of the weapons, the bones fell apart, clattering into one big pile.

Scrofa stopped from time to time, holding up his hand for silence. He cocked his head, listening for suspicious echoes. Then he waved the band cautiously forward. A brief commotion ensued as the young optio, Casperius Niger, shook his fist at a watchman for coughing after he had given the command for silence.

Once again, the detail halted. Scrofa signaled to Crispus and to me to move forward.

"We're nearly there," he whispered. "They'll have guards posted, so we must be silent."

Casperius Niger glared at the Bucketman to stifle any urge to cough.

"Do they have an escape route?" I questioned.

"Yes," Scrofa answered.

"Is there any way we can block it?"

"No. We can't circle around, but chances are they've bedded down for the day. It's the first hour of dawn. They ought to be sleeping, and won't go out again until tonight."

"They won't get the chance," Crispus interjected, "but you'd better be right. If they escape, we'll never find them, not in this black Hel."

"Which do you want?" Scrofa asked. "The men or the goods?"

"Both," I replied.

"Then get rid of the sentries if you want to surprise the rest."

"Naturally." Crispus drew a finger across the throat.

"Crispus and I will go alone. He and I fight well side by side," I said.

"Aye, that's the best," Scrofa confirmed. "Probably no more than a couple of you ought to do the trick."

"How do we approach without lanterns?" I asked. "It's too dark to move in this pit of death without them, and we'll warn them if we do."

"As you go around the bend and down to the entrance, there are scattered along the way clusters of fires flaring from the burning rocks. Stick to the shadows," Scrofa advised, "and you'll have enough light to guide you."

I waved to Faenus Rufus, the centurion in charge of the detail, to join us and explained the situation. "Your troops will stand by until we return," I explained. "Count to one thousand while you wait. If we're not back by the time you've finished, then rush the troops forward."

"You can depend on us," the broad-faced centurion answered.

I turned to Scrofa. "You'll remain behind."

"Gods," he said raising his thick eyebrows, "you think I've come this far, at the risk of my neck, not to get paid? By the goddess Hel, I'm staying here until you're done with them cutthroats." Torchlight glistened in his oily face, reflecting avarice more powerful than fear.

I nodded approval and consoled my jangling nerves with Sabinus's pledge to exterminate Scrofa's entire lot if he betrayed us.

Crispus and I stripped off our armor and swords, aware we could move with more stealth without it. Dressed in tunics and armed only with daggers, Crispus and I forged ahead into the gray-black tunnel. Despite numberless flames spewing from the dirt and rocks, visibility was no more than a few feet. We halted every four or five paces and listened for echoes of danger, but heard only the sounds of dripping water. After what seemed like an eternity, I spied a dim light ahead. Slowly, as if stalking game, we crept forward until Crispus held up his hand. He pointed to the silhouettes of two sentries sleeping next to a small campfire before a branching cave. Sneaking up behind them, we clamped our hands tightly to their mouths, pulled their heads back, and swiftly slit their throats.

We listened for any stirrings from the next cave. Silence. Melting into the darkness, we rejoined the waiting watchmen and retrieved our armor. I hadn't realized how excited I was until now. My heart seemed to pound through my chest.

"The two sentries are with the gods," I told Faenus Rufus and Scrofa. "Follow me."

The troops snaked ahead with drawn swords. Passing the dead men, one of them still twitching, we arrived at the mouth of the interior cavern they once guarded. Except for the gurgling of a small spring running near the entrance, all was quiet. Stealthily, we entered, our lanterns revealing the massive and fetid interior. Pitted into the stone wall gaping recesses spread like fingers. Dozens of leather and cloth lean-tos draped its jagged side. Entire families huddled with their men in scattered, pockmarked crags in the wall. Surrounded by ancient man-made fire pits cluttered with cauldrons and other cooking utensils, three small, natural fires provided the interior's only light. A line of drying laundry hung nearby. Scrofa hadn't lied about the community of thieves. Sprawling near the fires, about ten cutthroats peacefully slept.

Scattered in their midst rested a veritable treasure even the dim light could not hide. Countless gold and silver plates laid haphazardly beside statues inlaid with bright lapis lazuli stones. Small pieces of what appeared to be exquisite furniture sat about the dusty floor. Pearl necklaces, gold rings encased in rubies, sapphires, and other gems spilled from dozens of chests. Long-neck amphorae, no doubt containing expensive wines, squatted in neat little rows along one wall. A few broken crocks nearby indicated the essence of Bacchus did not go unappreciated. And one expensive armoire contained priceless Frankincense. Indeed, we had stumbled upon a storehouse for the black market.

Then I saw her—a little girl, not more than four, sitting alone in the dirt next to a fire at the rear of the cavern. The flickering amber light revealed her matted, sooty hair and little dirt-smudged face. She wore a coarse, linen tunic but played with an expensive ivory doll dressed in a bright stole. Quietly, she sung a toneless song to the doll as she cradled it in her arm.

We paused, but she heard us. The child stopped singing, turned her pale face toward the opening of the cave, and jumped up. She stared in our direction, her mouth dropping, her narrow, dark eyes wide. The doll fell to the earth. I put a finger to my lips in warning. Her mouth quivered. Suddenly, in a shrill voice, she cried, "Mama! Mama! Soldiers! Soldiers!" She ran to one of the wretched hearth coverings, and I waved the men forward.

To the shouts and curses of the watchmen, those slumbering around the fires rousted. Rufus ordered part of the detail to clear out the shelters. But their inhabitants came out fighting. Women screamed, and children cried, clutching to their mothers' sides as the men put up resistance. A handful of thieves attempted to escape.

A dagger shot past my head. I turned as the bearded assassin reached for another weapon in his waistband. I flung my knife, striking him in the throat. Reeling backwards, he clawed at his neck with both hands. Blood foamed from his mouth, and he fell face down into a smoldering fire ring.

On my left, Optio Casperius Niger fought one villain as a second one crept up from the rear. I ran the second through the back with my short sword as he was about to strike. Niger slew the first thief and wheeled. Seeing me standing over the would-be assailant, he nodded quickly and turned to assist another comrade.

Everything appeared flat and gray in the insane dance of torchlight and campfire shadows. I whirled and eyed Rufus as he battled two thugs and scrambled to his aid. In a split second, I warded off one blow with a parrying movement and split open his skull. A chilling scream echoed from a woman. I must have slain her man.

The skirmish ended almost as quickly as it began. Few escaped into the bowels of the earth, and a couple of watchmen were foolish enough to try and pursue them. I ordered them back before they could be lost and murdered.

After prying the wailing females from their dead men, the survivors were herded into one corner. Four blood-smeared, wounded thieves survived, along with the sobbing women and whimpering children, a sorry lot. The little girl who gave the alarm darted from her mother's side to the body of the one I had stabbed through the back. Kneeling, she tugged at the dead man's shoulder.

"Wake up, *Tata*," she pleaded, "wake up." She pulled on her father's corpse again. Another minute passed before she gave up. She ran to the woman and clung tightly to her legs. Her mother stared numbly into the fire.

"Why won't Tata wake, Mama?" the little girl whimpered to the high-cheeked woman. "Make Tata wake."

The woman bit her thick lower lip as she knelt before the little urchin. She pulled the child to her thin chest and nearly smothered her in a tattered shawl.

The child seemed to understand as she pulled her head away from the mother's wrap. Her body shook and face tightened. I thought she was going to weep—who could blame her? Then her eyes locked with mine as I supervised the shackling of the prisoners. She glared at me with the face of a wounded animal. Beast-like, her scowl turned into a vicious animalistic rage. Until then, I didn't believe a child so young was capable of such hatred. Her glare could have killed. I shall carry the image in my mind's eye to the grave.

"Marcellus," Crispus said, snapping me to my senses, "come and take a look. I found more booty."

"Where?"

He motioned with his bloodied sword to one of the caves branching from the main cavern. "There's a mountain of treasure."

The horde of riches was so vast it disappeared into the deep shadows.

"By Neptune and Hercules!" Scrofa exclaimed, as he approached the cache. "It'll take a small army just to haul off my twenty percent." He twirled around gesturing grandly with his filthy hands.

"You agreed to *ten percent*," I corrected.

"I don't recall agreeing to such a paltry figure."

"You have a convenient memory," I said as I jabbed my finger into his chest, forcing him backwards. "We just got rid of your more powerful competitor." I thumped his chest again. "Your people are free of his plundering raids. Be grateful I don't change my mind!" I dropped my hand to the hilt of my sword.

Scrofa frowned, but his mood quickly changed. "Just look at all of this."

The greedy old bastard immediately loaded up all his fingers with jewelry and pranced about like a king.

Weasel-faced Mico groped a small, gold ring, and Scrofa backhanded him. "Leave it alone, you greedy, blood-sucking dog!"

Returning to the main cavern, I felt someone's eyes upon my neck, and turned to meet the child's gaze. Her eyes flicked to the dead man and then back to me. I caught the sparkle of the doll's bejeweled figure on the ground.

Picking it up, I held the toy out slowly, and she took the plaything and began the rocking motion and monotone song she had sung when I first saw her.

We examined the dead for documents. We hoped they might lead us to the masterminds of the thefts. By the looks of our captives, I doubted if they had the intelligence to steal the quantities we found without an organization to dispose of the booty. And why did they live like beggars when there was so much wealth stored in these caves? They must have been controlled by masters, men far stronger and meaner than themselves, who kept them from stealing this treasure trove.

One of the blood-spattered bodies was a big Celt, by his tartan clothing, a Gaul. Remembering the description given to Eleyne by poor Karmune, I examined the body carefully. Carved into his ugly face, I saw a jagged scar similar to the one Karmune traced on my face with her blood-smeared finger. Spreading from the center of his broad forehead across the right, the old wound ran through the middle of his cheek and hooked into his mouth. I checked his hands. The left was ham-like and gnarled. Thousands in Rome have scarred faces. But how many were big Gauls with a similar scar and hand? He had murdered Karmune.

I searched the pocket fold inside his tunic and found an old, crumpled scrap of parchment containing an unsigned note.

My master was displeased that you killed the wrong woman. If you value

your life, you will not fail your next task. Otherwise, the idiot Claudius

shall not be the only one who dies.

I reread the note. A chill ran down my spine. "Look at this, Crispus," I said, handing him the note.

He read the message and whistled afterward. "Damn, is this what I think it means?"

"Aye, we haven't just discovered a ring of thieves, we've uncovered a conspiracy against the emperor's life. The captives must be taken at once to Latumiae Prison for questioning."

I told Centurion Rufus of the discovery. At my insistence, he left ten of his most trustworthy men, including Optio Niger, to protect the contraband, while we hauled the prisoners away. Another detail would be dispatched later to retrieve the stolen goods.

If they were still there!

CHAPTER 29

The prisoners were taken to the infamous Latumiae Prison near the edge of the city. From outside, all that was visible was a small, brick building with a vaulted roof. But inside, past fetid cells, a murky, narrow corridor led down to a subterranean world filled with torture and terror.

After sending a courier with a sealed message to Sabinus, Crispus and I, along with Centurion Faenus Rufus, waited at the prison's entrance for the senator's arrival. Because Crispus and I were his retainers and had uncovered the plot, Sabinus would take charge of the investigation and prosecute the case in court, his right as a senator.

We did not wait long. Upon Sabinus's arrival at the gates, I briefed him on the raid and discovery of the letter.

The heavy lines in his forehead tightened as he studied the note. "It's incredible to see words of this magnitude committed to paper. Only a fool would write such damning words, let alone carry them, but then again, most plots are uncovered by accident."

Sabinus scanned the list of prisoners handed to him by Faenus Rufus. "I dealt with Nonius, Fabius, and Titius a few years ago. I was an Aedile magistrate handling minor cases for the Watch. These petty thieves aren't capable of conniving a plot against the emperor. Nevertheless, I want them questioned—severely. Now this one," he said, thumping the paper with a finger for emphasis, "Decimus, is another matter. He may be our key, I've not seen his name before. I will save him last for questioning. Come with me." He jerked his head towards the inner corridor.

We entered the prison's shadowy hallway, following it a short distance, to a drafty shaft. Slowly, we stepped down a dark, slippery stairwell, wide enough for only one man to pass. Water dripped from the ceiling, a foreboding hint of what lay ahead. We hugged a curved stone wall winding its way down to the dungeon and torture chamber. About every twenty feet a torch jutted from the wall. We stalked forward until the twilight of one torch met the dawn of another. Many had fallen to their deaths here, few by accident. The air became fouler and more oppressive the farther we descended. A voice whimpered in an unseen cell. Muffled chains clanked in another cell as unseen things behind other doors slithered across straw-covered floors.

We reached the bottom level of the torch-lit dungeon and waited for the turnkey to arrive and lead us to the interrogation room.

"As you know," Sabinus began, interrupted by a desperate scream from within the bowels of the jail, "the prisoners are detained behind this wall until they are brought to trial, usually after confessing. Abroghast," he continued, pronouncing the name as if passing judgment upon all traitors, "will learn the truth as each culprit perceives it."

"Abroghast?" I asked. The very name swallowed us whole as it echoed, reverberating from the sweating stone wall beyond. "I've heard the name before. Obulco, my squadron interrogator, once said he had learned his trade from Abroghast before he transferred to Rome."

Sabinus grunted. "One and the same. There is only one Great Master in the dark art. All confess before him."

"I assume much depends on what the prisoners tell us before he applies his craft," I said.

"I prefer to see them confess without using torture," Sabinus said. "You know the Laws of Twelve Tables allow it in cases of treason?"

"Doesn't that apply only to slaves?" I asked.

"Treason is an exception. You're right about other crimes."

"In all honesty, sir, haven't many citizens been tortured for crimes other than treason?" Crispus asked.

Sabinus nodded. "Unfortunately. My predecessors never allowed the law to stop them. I find it repugnant, but I understand why they have used it. Until better methods of investigation are developed, torture will be used for treason."

"Especially since we're dealing with the emperor's well-being," I said.

"Absolutely," he agreed. "No matter what one thinks of the emperor, his position is sacrosanct. He is the empire, for better or worse, symbolic of its stability. To remove him by assassination would mean civil war. Despite his eccentricities, Rome prospers. The treasury is full and taxes are bearable."

I listened without interrupting, understanding that Sabinus uttered these words to justify his actions.

"With the exception of the British campaign," he continued, "the empire is at peace. No, this is not the time for a new emperor. I'm determined to crush this conspiracy."

The turnkey arrived and led us to the dungeon.

The torture chamber reeked of stale, humid air. Smoke drifted along the low ceiling toward an invisible vent lost in the upper shadows. The coppery smell of blood wafted about the room. To the right of the entry two large cartwheels squatted where two hapless prisoners lay shackled and stretched. Beyond stood a large, glowing brazier on four iron dog legs.

A potbellied torturer, not Abroghast, dressed in a scorched, blacksmith leather apron and tunic, tested one of the hot irons by searing a piece of scarred leather. It hissed, and bluish smoke rose to the ceiling. With a look of satisfaction, the questioner hummed a crude soldier's ditty in a husky voice. He walked to the cartwheel where a dirty loin-clothed prisoner, feet lashed to the spokes, was being interrogated by a centurion of the Praetorian Guard. When he refused to answer to the officer's satisfaction, the inquisitor applied the iron to his thigh adding to a long line of oozing blisters. The captive howled, and the stench of burnt flesh wafted through the room. The torturer grinned and spun the wheel for good measure.

On either side of the condemned man, amber torchlights illuminated the mildewed stone pillars and exposed the source of the smell. The dungeon's porous, cobblestoned floor had absorbed ages of spattered blood and feces.

Across from the wheels rested a wooden rack with pulleys and levers for stretching a victim's arms and legs, until the bones popped from their sockets. Prisoners confessed, truth or lie—any tale as long as the pain stopped. A barrel of brackish scum-covered water stood nearby.

After saluting Senator Sabinus, a brawny interrogator, speaking through his nose, brought in the prisoners, their hands bound behind them, one at a time from a holding cell.

Sabinus recognized the sorry lot that stood before us dressed in filthy rags. "Well, well, Nonius, Fabius, and Titius, we meet again—you never learn, do you?"

The prisoners hung their heads in silence.

"I will question them separately," Sabinus said. "Starting with Fabius."

The prisoner, Fabius, paled.

Sabinus motioned to the torturer who stood behind the prisoners. The interrogator grabbed Fabius and shoved him down on the bench in front of Sabinus.

"Use the cord," Sabinus said in a flat voice.

The inquisitor pulled a small coiled, leather strap from his waistband. Unrolling it with his calloused, dirty hands, he wrapped it around Fabius's forehead to the back of his head. He gave it two twists before inserting a hardwood stick through the two strands and tied it into a knot. Slowly, he twisted and tightened the cord around the prisoner's head.

Fabius's face flushed, his eyes bulged. He screamed, the echo resounding through the chamber.

Sabinus nodded again, and the torturer pulled the strap tighter.

Another scream.

Fabius's agony did not move me. Unfortunately, over the years I had seen this method of interrogation applied so many times, that I had become jaded to its use. Still, it didn't mean it was the right thing to do. I looked about—the faces of Crispus, Sabinus, and the watchmen remained blank.

Sabinus raised his hand. The torturer released the tension but held the prisoner's head firmly.

Fabius exhaled and lowered his eyes.

Sabinus took a seat in front of Fabius and studied him. "Look at me, Fabius."

The prisoner raised his eyes and stared blankly at the senator.

"Now, will you answer my questions?" Sabinus asked in a quiet voice.

Fabius gasped. "Yes, my Lord, anything."

"Only the truth," Sabinus said.

He confessed without hesitation to stealing the goods from shops along the Sacred Way. Fabius claimed that Decimus, the fourth prisoner, had instigated the robberies.

The other two, Nonius and Titius, needed no *persuasion* by the interrogator to confess to the same crimes.

Sabinus turned and motioned me closer to him. I stepped over and bent down where he whispered, "In my experience when dealing with these three characters in the past, you need only question one and the other two will readily confess."

Sabinus motioned to Fabius and continued his interrogation. "What else is Decimus involved in?"

"He's the go-between, your Lordship, for a middleman, a freedman who represents what he calls *special interests*," gaunt-faced Fabius answered. He seemed to be the brightest of the three thieves. He also told of a fifth member of the band, whom they feared: the Gaul.

"Decimus said the Gaul specialized in collecting high-interest loans," added the matted-hair Nonius, who stood next to Fabius, "whatever that is. If somebody don't pay back the loan, he breaks their bones. And if you want a body killed, he's your man."

"I heard the Gaul say that he killed a woman a while ago," confessed squat-legged Titius, "but he wouldn't say who or where he did it. But something went wrong, because he hid with us."

Titius confirmed my conclusion that the Gaul was our assassin. A gang of thieves, filling a list of wanted items for waiting clients, and dealing in murder for hire. The group offered everything in one, with a minimum of names involved, and none at their level knew the real powers in charge.

"Too bad the Gaul died," I said to Sabinus. "He was probably a quarry of information."

Fabius told Sabinus that neither he nor Nonius nor Titius knew the freedman. They had turned to burglary after being approached by Decimus.

"Decimus offered us a higher price for stealing goods than we got before," Fabius said. "He gave us a list of what he wanted for the freedman's clients."

Sabinus jabbed his hand toward Fabius. "What about the contraband in the caves?"

"We stored it there until the freedman arranged to move it to his customers' homes," Fabius said. "They're all rich."

"What do you know about the conspiracy against the emperor's life?" Sabinus asked.

Fabius turned his head in the direction of Nonius and Titus. "Nothing, sir. We're thieves, not traitors."

"Place them on the rack," Sabinus ordered.

"I swear it's true," Fabius pleaded, "we know nothing!" Fabius bawled as the torturer placed him on the pallet and strapped him in. He shrieked denial again as the pulleys tightened on his limbs. The two others did the same when they, too, were put on the rack.

Despite the excruciating pain, the three thieves denied any knowledge of the conspiracy.

"I'm doing this for the edification of Decimus," Sabinus said to me, nodding to the nearby cell where Decimus had been watching from the beginning. "I suspect he knows the answers, and I want him to appreciate the agonies awaiting him if he doesn't confess."

Only a fool or a madman would refuse to confess after such a horrendous experience, I thought.

Once again Sabinus turned his head in the direction of the cell where Decimus waited, his eyes gazing at the iron door. "Everything depends on the answers I get," Sabinus said.

CHAPTER 30

When the three thieves had suffered enough, Sabinus halted the torture. Each had screamed so loudly and harshly they spat blood from ragged and torn throats. Although I had fought in many battles and seen horrors no one should witness, it was still unnerving. Had they slit my mother's throat, I might have plead mercy even for this slimy lot. Surely, Decimus would beg to confess now.

"They have told the truth as they know it," Sabinus said. "Release them from the rack. Prefect Calpurnianus will try them in his court for theft and burglary but not treason." Sabinus motioned to the torturer and his two assistants.

He turned to the pitiful trio as they were being shackled for transport to the jail at the *statione* of the First Cohort to await trial. "You have graduated to *three lettered men*."

Nonius, Fabius, and Titius glanced to one another and knew what the senator meant. When convicted, their foreheads would be branded with letters, *FVR*, indicating they were habitual thieves. Sabinus ordered the thieves' removal from the torture chamber.

The centurion, who had earlier been interrogating a prisoner on the wheel, quietly stepped over to where Sabinus, Crispus, and I were standing as we waited for the prisoner, Decimus. The soldier gave the senator a respectful nod.

Decimus had to be yanked out of the holding cell by two turnkeys. I judged him to be about nineteen or twenty. Calling obscenities, he spat in their faces, and in turn was kicked in the groin. Doubling over, he fell to the floor and was dragged to the rack. After being tied to the pallet, he let more spittle fly at anyone coming near him. Beneath his beetling brows and eyes carved into a missile-shaped head, his high-bridged nose flared.

"Go to Hades, you bastards, I ain't telling you nothing!"

A turnkey slapped him with the back of his hand and ripped away his loincloth, leaving him naked.

"He's a professional," Sabinus said, gesturing to the nasal-speaking inquisitor. "You'll save yourself a lot of grief by answering my questions. I promise you a swift death—or one that will last an eternity."

Decimus spat in Sabinus's face. "Go fuck your mother!"

Sabinus calmly wiped the filth from his face with a towel quickly handed to him by one of the torturer's assistants. Another man would have half-beaten the tough to death.

"How unfortunate," Sabinus said. "You had your chance. I have summoned an especially gifted torturer for you."

Like a spirit, Abroghast, the master torturer, slipped into the chamber past the original interrogator. I felt his presence before seeing him. Perhaps it was his reputation or Obulco's stories. A sudden chill raised the hairs on my arms and neck. He stood in the shadows and seemed to be a part of the darkness near the cavern walls. When he stepped forward at Sabinus's beckoning, he carried darkness with him.

The grand interrogator stealthily approached his victim, his face partially masked in the gloom of a black cloak. Torchlights flamed brilliantly nearby, moving his shadow from the curved wall across the damp floor until it fell upon the victim. A distant dripping sound echoed from a dark, unlighted chamber. Decimus prostrate upon the rack must have felt the shadow or smelled its source, for he twisted about to see. The silent figure stood at his head and walked slowly around the strapped-down naked form, Decimus no longer crying out defiantly.

"I am—Abroghast," he rasped as if knowing his very name would strike terror. No doubt his assistant had prepared the victim in his cell with tales of his torture.

The prisoner held his breath at the spoken name, but a sharp gasp escaped his throat, like a whimper, as his rebellious curses melted away. Abroghast stood behind the man's head, forcing his victim's eyes to tilt up to see him.

"I am Rack Master," he said, his voice barely above a whisper. Abroghast ran his fingers gently through the man's dark hair, twirling a curl about his index finger, and then massaged his temples softly. "Pain . . . and pleasure . . . are closely related."

Although mustached, I saw his jagged upper lip through the graying hairs, as if torn and healed, which revealed stained teeth. I detected a lisp as he continued.

"In distant lands," he said, "both are considered an art. I am master of both."

The grand torturer's right hand stopped the tender massaging of Decimus's temple and glided across the man's pronounced cheekbones. His middle finger touched the skin as if trying to calm a nervous tick, and his other fingers floated, casting a shadow plague of dappled light and darkness like an eclipse of life and death. His finger continued down a strong jawline and paused, exploring a dimpled double chin. Abroghast brushed his calloused palm tenderly against the grain of the stubbly beard, its resisting hairs bristling audibly. His index finger made little circle motions about the chin and slowly drifted down the neck, pausing in a threatening hover as if his intent was to strangle.

"Your skin is fair, and white," he muttered. "Free of scars from pox and diseases—yes, fair indeed."

Delicately, Abroghast's hand moved downward onto the prostrate man's smooth chest, his fingers rustling the tops of light chest hairs and circling the nipples until they became taut. He smirked with pleasure as his fingers drifted down the torso like a shadow without touching the skin, yet close enough for the warmth of his hand to be felt as it aroused invisible hairs along the way. The man's stomach muscles quivered and danced involuntarily at the passing hand.

The master torturer's fingers eased down the thug's right leg, skipping a thick, leather restraining strap, and then with a firm, smooth touch moved back up along the inside of his thigh. He paused at the groin, stroking the dark pubic hairs with his palm, combing them with fingertips, circling and caressing gently. There was a slight stirring in Decimus's manhood as it began to fill.

"Yes, pleasure and pain are both beautiful, much like a bitter herb prepares one to appreciate the sweet taste of honey."

Decimus remained silent, breathing uneasily, the green irises of his eyes fully ringed in white, and then whimpered slightly as his member stirred.

Abroghast ignored those of us watching. "And to *appreciate*, one must first taste honey, and know beyond all doubt that whatever comes next will be worse."

As the master moved around the rack to the other side, his fingers trailed in his wake across the body, again pausing at the groin with raking and stroking fingers. Abroghast's cloak hood fell away, but the long, black hair kept much of his face masked in shadow.

"I once killed a man, accidentally, by misjudging what he could stand. I killed him by merely *talking* to him, and telling him what would soon happen. It was more than his weak and aging heart could stand. But you are young and strong." His eyes fell to the gorged stiffness. "It was while I was explaining a device I created especially for him. This one." Abroghast held forth a small, dagger-like instrument in front of the wild-eyed man.

"You see? When I squeeze the handle, the dull-prong point opens, forming a triangle up to two finger widths at the tips. A simple device really," he hissed. "Three slightly curved pieces of metal that, when closed, appear to be a crude rod of a single-blade dagger."

Abroghast grinned at Decimus, who no doubt wondered what would befall him by the device, as did we all. He squeezed the handle several times, demonstrating how the spike-like blades moved apart, into three spikes, and clicked back together again when released. Abroghast's other hand by now had slowly grasped and was gently milking the man's erect member.

"You see," he said in a melodious and deep hypnotic voice, "the point is inserted into a small hole, and when the handle is squeezed, the blades expand the hole to a width great enough to insert something—*vile*—or worse.

"Look at the handle of this dagger," Abroghast commanded. "It's hollow. In fact, it is a very small cage." He pointed the tip at the man's eyes. "You see? When the handle is gripped hard and the blades expand, a little trap door to the cage opens at the hilt and frees my hungry pet to enter whatever hole the tips are in."

I glanced about the area. All eyes were focused on the head interrogator and his fiendish device. The centurion, whom had earlier questioned a prisoner on the wheel, appeared wide-eyed, seemingly appalled by what was to take place.

Sabinus's face hardened as he looked on through narrowed eyes.

The other torturers, who had stretched the three thieves on the rack, smiled through jagged and missing teeth, no doubt having watched Abroghast on many occasions plying his terrifying art.

Crispus shook his head and for a split second turned away.

Even though I was a veteran of five campaigns in Britannia and Germania, seeing more than my share of bloodshed and gore, it was all I could do to hold down the bile raising in my throat and keep an impassive face.

Abroghast smiled crookedly and rasped, "I forgot to tell you about my pet, an earth monster of a sort. Not quite mole-like, or beetle-like, yet it tunnels and is even cannibal. I've seen it eat its young. Closer to being a worm, it consumes the earth, or flesh before it, and excretes it on its journey, ever deeper, into the bowels like needles of fire and brimstone."

He held the handle so close that Decimus could clearly see the thing confined in its hollowed-out enclosure. A sudden gasp of terror and an involuntary shudder overcame Decimus.

"Pincer-jaws to grab its prey, and jagged-bone teeth to rip and tear, and a ferocious appetite," Abroghast said with a grin.

The rack master then rested the tip of the dagger on the man's cheek bone below his twitching left eye, moving it slowly to a nostril, down the chin's dimple, then the neck, across the chest, inserting it gently into the navel, pausing briefly with a slight clicking. He then brought the instrument quickly to the swollen but flaccid member, and quickly inserted the tip deeply into the foreskin pulling it onto the blade like a sock.

Decimus fainted.

Abroghast waited patiently for Decimus to regain consciousness. Such tender compassion graced his face that I could not, but for my eyes, believe the deed he awaited to consummate.

Decimus groaned, then remembered and bellowed for mercy.

Abroghast squeezed the dagger handle several times, sharply stretching the foreskin open and closed, but not freeing the thing from its cage. Decimus's cries of anguish split the air, along with laughter from Abroghast, and murmurs calling upon the gods from several spectators present, including me.

"But this . . . is . . . is for later," Abroghast croaked, quickly withdrawing the device and placing it gently on a tool table where the prisoner could see the moving creature inside. "Now, I have some questions." Abroghast motioned to the assistant torturer who began slowly cranking the pulleys.

As Decimus's face tightened and flushed from the pain, he screamed in renewed defiance, "Do your worst!"

"Ohhh—but I will," Abroghast said, his grin widening.

* * *

After the torturers finished, Decimus confessed to all but the name of his master. He told of a conversation with the dead Gaul that confirmed our suspicions, but refused to name the middleman who might lead to the real conspirators. The Gaul had gotten drunk one night and bragged about killing a British woman in the house of Sabinus. In turn, Senator Sabinus asked the prisoner what he knew about him.

"He's sent lots of my friends to the gladiator schools," Decimus answered bitterly, "I won't forget it."

"They should consider themselves fortunate," Sabinus retorted, "I could have easily had them thrown to the wild beasts of the arena!"

Decimus rolled his eyes and groaned.

When Sabinus asked Decimus about the Gaul's name, he replied with a quivering lie. He had only been with the band two years. When he again refused to name the middleman, Abroghast was asked to persuade him.

"It is time to feed my pet!" Abroghast said.

Shaken, I moved away, closer to the air shaft. I closed my eyes and enjoyed its refreshing breath of sour bile, where decades of those with queasy guts had no doubt retreated.

And then I heard him.

At first, a moaning plea for mercy, then a shrill pleading with the guards to kill him, and a rambling cursing prayer to the gods. A sudden quietness filled the chamber, then a piercing animal shriek burst forth as torment stung and seared its agony through Decimus's being and past human words or abilities to convey.

Never had I heard such sounds of pure terror and horror, though they yet echo in my mind and ears. A guard vomited. I turned and saw Abroghast silhouetted by torchlight, the prisoner's foreskin stretched by the dagger blades to near transparency, and watched—horrified—as the monster-worm *thing* bulged its way slowly down the inside of Decimus's swollen member, like a rat swallowed by a snake. Through it all, Abroghast's heinous laughter was beyond description and filled the dungeon with a song of grotesqueness.

Before the insanely raging Decimus was allowed to die, he named and cursed the freedman, Calenus, an Egyptian living along the Tiber waterfront. Calenus had conscripted Decimus as go-between with the other three prisoners to watch out for his interests.

* * *

In the early gloom of the following morning, Calenus, the Egyptian, was arrested in a tiny, vermin-ridden, sixth-floor tenement apartment in the area inhabited by the poorest people. Two watchmen kicked in the door, surprising Calenus, who sat on the edge of a cot. He was dragged away and shackled as the rest of us searched the premises.

Pieces of broken furniture and dirty crockery were scattered on the floor of the cramped flat. On a pockmarked, cheap, marble slab sat a small drinking cup, and five cracked food jars lay reeking of stale, pickled fish. On the floor sat an old chest of Greek books gnawed by unlettered mice. Nearby, a rusty brazier perched on a table missing one leg. If Calenus was a middleman, why did he live in squalor? I discovered the answer. In one of the room's dark corners rested a number of empty wine jars. Heavy drinking had claimed his fortune.

The Bucketmen and I searched the apartment for the written documents, needed for conviction. The thieves were small eels. We were after those in higher positions—nobility. Against a senator, the word of a freedman, foreigner, or slave was worthless without outside corroboration. Although Roman courts purported to deal with evidence given under oath, in reality the reputation of the accused had greater influence on the final verdict. The Senate tried its own, and unfortunately, bribery was all too common. As I soon learned, an honest senator and prosecutor like Sabinus was the exception rather than the rule. However, written documentation was another matter, and a charge of forgery was not enough to discount it.

We did not find any documentation, but when Calenus confessed, and he did when *counseled* by Abroghast, he revealed the location of incriminating papers. Documents leading to the heart of the Senate were concealed in a nondescript urn in the family mausoleum of Gallus the Elder.

Would it be enough to put old Gallus on trial and lead to a conviction?

CHAPTER 31

NOVEMBER, 44 AD

On a freezing, clear November night, Crispus and I cautiously forced open the iron gate to the elder Gallus's family tomb. A light frost marked our footprints as we crossed the mausoleum grounds bordering on the Appian Way. Acting on Sabinus's advice, we worked alone, keeping our intrusion a secret. Tomb breaking was a sacrilege. Discovery meant condemnation to the mines for life. What irony that among the ashes of the dead, evidence of a death list might be found.

The approaching winter had changed the vault's park-like setting of well-manicured pines and cypresses into a desert of withered limbs and weeds. The pretentious square building towered to about fifty feet, peaked with an arched, tile roof. White Dorian pillars and weathered, life-sized statues of the family's greatest ancestors stood atop the vault's four corners.

Inside the musty *columbarium,* dozens of niches containing funeral urns lined the wall like a great honeycomb. Depending on family status, they differed in shape and size, ornamented or simple, and included favorite freedmen and loyal slaves.

Although the Egyptian, Calenus, said the evidence was hidden in a plain urn, we searched them all. Painstakingly, we probed the ashes and little bone fragments with our daggers by the shadowy light of our bronze and oiled canvas lanterns. I hated tampering with the dead, and earlier Crispus had said as much.

"When we're through," he said, "I'm making a votive offering to Melkart to protect us from paying for our sacrilege."

"In the meantime, pray we don't get caught," I answered.

About an hour passed when a now-sooty Crispus exclaimed in a loud whisper, "Marcellus, come here! Take a look!"

He pulled a series of folded parchments from a pitted clay urn. "Calenus was right," he whispered excitedly, "the urn is poorly made, and that's what caught my eye." His voice carried like shouts in the crisp air. And when I moved, the steps sounded as if I had toppled a tombstone.

"By the GODS! QUIET!" Crispus hissed.

I examined the reused, old, yellowed parchment scrolls, written in Greek. My blood ran cold as I read the newly scribbled words.

"Gods, your face is white," Crispus said, "that's the one, isn't it?"

"Aye, the death list, the emperor's name is right on top."

"Great Melkart, who else is on there?"

"Sabinus has the dubious honor of being second in line."

"How many are on the list?"

I scanned rapidly. "Twenty senators, including Sabinus's friend, Vitellius, the two consuls of Rome, Decrius Calpurnianus, and the freedmen Narcissus and Pallas."

A low whistle shot from Crispus's mouth. "By the gods of my people, the Egyptian told the truth."

"There's a list of conspirators as well, with instructions for the murders, signed by old Gallus. See this." I pointed to the red-waxed seal. It bore the imprint of a rooster clutching a snake in its claws. "Gallus's seal. It's his ring, I . . . remember it from court . . . but how could he be so stupid?"

"Stupid? Or so confident of success? And successful he would've been, except for our stumbling over the Gaul in the caverns."

"The important thing is now we have him!"

I was partially right.

* * *

"W-we are shocked by the documents th-that you have discovered," a bleary-eyed Claudius said to Sabinus,

Crispus, and me as we stood alongside his bed. "If they are authentic, then Gallus the Elder must die." The emperor looked past us to the rest of the late-evening audience who hovered behind us, his freedmen secretaries Narcissus and Pallas, the Praetorian prefect, and a couple dozen senators, including Vitellius. All of them had been named on the death list.

Silence. For a split second, I turned and noticed several disheveled senators still wearing crumpled night tunics after being rousted from their beds. Fidgeting, they stepped from one foot to the other, or wrung their hands.

The emperor perused the papers, hands trembling as he sat up in bed. Heavy purple-trimmed, silk blankets, embroidered with gold stitching covered him to the waist. Surrounded by fluffy, silk pillows, his red and gold nightgown seemed comical given the situation. Again, he squinted at part of the damning evidence. He raised his head with its unkempt, thin, white hair and looked about the smoky, oil-lit room. Claudius paused and studied the ashen face of each senator, as if allowing them time to absorb the gravity of the plot. No doubt he realized the noblemen had suffered two major shocks within the last hour. To be summoned to Caesar's Palace under armed escort usually meant the direst of consequences. Then to be told they were marked men on a list with Caesar, for assassination, must have come almost as a relief to the senators. The emperor's eyes fell on Sabinus.

Sabinus glanced to the senators and back to Claudius. "Unfortunately, Caesar, it is all too true. And Gallus may now have been forewarned of our discovery and try to carry out the death list tonight. Otherwise, I would not have awakened you at this late hour."

"The hour is of no consequence, Sabinus," the emperor said. "I seldom sleep past midnight. For years I have had problems sleeping for any length of time." He sighed. "Besides, there is so much work that must be done. The duties of an emperor are staggering," he said with a clarity that I had seldom heard from him on the previous occasions when Sabinus and I had visited. And then, as if to himself, mumbled, "That might account as to why I occasionally fall asleep while holding audience." He focused his eyes on me then on Sabinus and snapped, "But we say to you—Gallus has slept his last peaceful night."

Before the senators had arrived, Sabinus had explained to the old ruler the developments leading to the discovery of the documents, starting with the night that we saved the woman Pricilla from robbery.

"Do you not have spies?" Claudius asked.

"Yes, Caesar, but Senator Gallus is very clever and devious."

"That should not have stopped you."

Sabinus shook his head. "It didn't, but the information gathered by Centurion Reburrus and Sergeant Crispus up to that point was circumstantial. It came from slaves and freedmen. As Dominus realizes, that kind of evidence is worthless against any senator, even in cases of treason. But this information is such . . ." He pointed to the yellowed parchments in Claudius's venous hands. "I have never seen more treasonous evidence in my life."

"We fear that you are right," the emperor said in a tone of resignation, again viewing at the documents. "We commend you for the honesty and frankness in explaining the situation." Claudius scowled at Vitellius, the freedmen, and the senators. "We regret that cannot be said for the others."

Claudius had explained the situation to the senators, including Vitellius, after they had arrived. He passed around the documents for their examination.

"He is right," the ruddy-faced Vitellius said as he approached the emperor's bedside. Until that moment, he had been standing with the rest of the senators. He gestured with a flabby hand to one of the sheets. "I would know Gallus's pig-scrawl handwriting anywhere, and that is his seal."

Vitellius's foul breath wreaked of rancid wine. "But by the gods, why?" he asked. "Why would any man sign such a thing as this?"

The emperor's jaw tightened exposing the blue veins in his neck, and his cheeks turned crimson as he frowned. Fresh spittle ran down dried spittle-tracks on the sides of his mouth. Ignoring the question, he handed the sheets to Narcissus.

The freedman examined the documents, and in his cold, monotone voice said, "I am of the opinion, and of course with Caesar's permission, that we must bring Senator Gallus to trial before the Senate on charges of treason. There is no doubt that he is a traitor. The same goes for the other conspirators on the list."

"I agree," Vitellius said. "Look at the names on the death list." His hands gesticulated wildly. "Not only are you at the top of the list, great Caesar, but so are your most trusted advisors, including myself." As an apparent afterthought, he said, "Of course, there is also my friend, the noble Sabinus."

How good of you to name my patron, you overstuffed baboon.

The emperor fixed his gaze on Sabinus. "Then we shall deal with the traitors at once."

* * *

After Claudius gave orders to the Praetorian prefect to arrest the treasonous senators, he dismissed the rest of us with an admonishment for secrecy until the conspirators were imprisoned. He provided contingents of twenty Praetorians to escort each senator on the death list home, including Sabinus.

"It is nearly an hour after midnight," Sabinus said as we left the emperor's bedchamber. He turned to Crispus. "Sergeant, instead of returning to your billet, come along with us. You can stay at my home tonight."

"Yes, sir," Crispus answered.

"We have a lot to do in the morning, and we'll be up very early," Sabinus said. "You'd have to get up all the earlier and travel half way across the city to join us."

I turned to Crispus and nodded, and he shrugged.

After our weapons had been returned to us, we left the palace with an escort of twenty fully armed guardsmen. Sabinus, Crispus, and I wore tunics and cloaks, and each of us carried a sword and dagger hidden beneath our clothing.

We stepped out into the chilly night air. Stars shimmered in the clear sky. Directly overhead, a full moon illuminated the Forum, Circus Maximus, and the heart of Rome in silvery light. But it failed to penetrate the perilous darkness of the city's crowded slums, narrow streets, and alleys.

A light breeze drifting from the direction of the cattle pens, and slaughter houses along the Tiber reeked of dung, the acrid smell of dead animals, and raw sewage.

With the exception of the guards' clattering armor, all was quiet as we marched down the Palatine. We passed the marketplace, temples, and basilicas and climbed the narrow, winding streets en route to Sabinus's home on Quirinal Hill. His home was in the wealthier part of the region, a cluster of spacious homes and mansions, bordered by wide lanes.

As we approached Sabinus's home, we heard a scream.

"Halt!" Sabinus ordered.

I nodded towards the house bathed in moonlight. "Assassins. Four of them are climbing the wall."

"We've made too much noise, they see us," Crispus said.

Like spiders, the dark figures scurried up ropes held in place by grappling hooks and disappeared over the side.

A chill ran down my back. *They'll kill Eleyne!*

I glanced to the grate-covered window of her room on the second story. The dim light from the olive lamp was still burning.

Sabinus turned to the men. "After them, before they kill my wife and my ward!"

Swords hissed as the guardsmen drew them in unison from their sheaths.

Crispus, the Praetorians, and I followed Sabinus at a dead run as he led the way.

I ripped off my cloak and pulled my sword. My first instinct was to race ahead, throwing caution to the wind to rescue Eleyne. But why did I think of her and not the rest of the household? Was I developing feelings for her that I hadn't thought about since Kyar's death? Now wasn't the time to think about it—my training and discipline came into play. We didn't know how many assassins were inside the home. We had to work together as a team.

Sabinus motioned us to halt a few paces from the front gate. Pulsating light from torches ensconced in two bordering pillars spilled across the bloodied body of a slave guard sprawled by the entrance.

The senator turned to us. "Stay alert, those butchers may have set a trap." He motioned to me. "Marcellus, take ten men and go to Eleyne's room. Sergeant Crispus, you and the rest of the men follow me. We must find my wife!"

We entered through the narrow vestibule leading to the atrium and beyond. Oil lamps set into wall niches gave off a murky light. We stepped over the figure of the dead gatekeeper. Blood from his corpse flowed between the small tile pieces of the mosaic floor. Beyond the remains of the other slave guard was face down in the compluvium, the basin's water turning a crimson shade. I prayed we weren't too late to save Eleyne and Lady Aurelia.

I rushed to the brick stairway at the far end of the atrium that led up to the second floor.

"This way," I said to the men, "Lord Sabinus's ward, the Princess Eleyne's room, is the second door on the right." I dashed up the stairs.

For the space of a few heartbeats, I stopped at the top and looked in the direction of the poorly lit hallway. Candra stood in front of Eleyne's door warding off the attacks of three assassins. He slammed one against the opposite wall with a loud grunt. The bandit dropped to the floor like a rag doll, dead. The second one came after the big Indian, knife in hand. Candra grabbed and twisted his arm until it snapped. The thug screamed as Candra threw him into the path of the other villain.

At the same time, another assassin snuck past Candra into Eleyne's room. My heart jumped in my throat. *No!*

Before I could react, an assassin leaped out of the shadows, swinging his sword at my head. I blocked the blade with my weapon, metal banging on metal. He nearly pushed me off the stairs. I started to fall, but the guardsmen behind me caught and pushed me forward. I gained my balance and parried the bandit's weapon down to the right. Instantly, I raised my sword, whisked it down, and sliced off his hand. A blood-curdling scream shot from his mouth. He grabbed the stump and went down on his knees. I slammed my blade again, decapitating him, blood spurting onto my tunic. The body fell to the floor with a thump next to the head and hand.

At the same time, the Praetorians had slipped past me and confronted three more assassins. The troops made easy work of them. I spotted Candra lifting another assassin off the floor and throwing him down the end of the hallway followed by a crack and gurgle.

I stepped passed him but paused for a heartbeat before entering Eleyne's room. Running into a trap was the last thing I needed. I kicked open the door. In the low light, Eleyne stood in the far corner holding a bloody dagger. A dead man lay at her feet. She saw me and screamed.

From behind Eleyne's clothing screen sprang an assassin. A dagger sailed past my face, missing by a finger's width. Pulling an army short sword from his waistband, he jabbed it toward my side. I parried it, but my blade slipped off his. Quickly, he raised his weapon, the edge of the blade grazed my left side as it slipped by. Pain shot through my body. I swung my sword upward, the blade slicing through his crotch, into his intestines. He howled, dropped his weapon, and doubled over, the foul odor of filth filling my nose. I grabbed his hair, pulled back his head, and ran the edge of my sword across his throat. Blood gushed from the wound. He slumped to the floor, dead.

Eleyne dropped her knife, stepped over the body, and ran to me. Tears welled within her eyes as she placed her hands around my waist and head upon my chest. "Oh, Marcellus, I was so scared. They . . . they were going to kill me!" She dropped her hands, stepped back, and gasped. "Marcellus, you're bleeding."

"Most of the blood isn't mine," I said.

Eleyne looked at her hands, stained with blood from my wound. "But what about your side?"

"It's just a graze. What about you, that blood on your skirt?"

Eleyne glanced back to the corpse. "It's his blood. I killed him. He must have been surprised a woman could defend herself. Then that other animal came in just before you killed him. He must have sneaked past Candra like the other one I . . . ," she hesitated, "I killed." Her voice trailed away. "All women of my tribe are taught to defend themselves, but I've never done that before."

Three Praetorians stepped into the room. "We've killed them all, sir," the tallest of the three said. "On this floor and below. Altogether, there were fifteen of them."

"Is Lady Aurelia all right?" I asked. Blood slipped through my fingers as I held my side.

"Yes, sir. Lord Sabinus saw to that. He, the sergeant, and the other men killed every last one of the bastards." He saw Eleyne. "Sorry."

She shrugged.

"How many did we lose?" I asked.

"Four, sir. The butchers were professionals, they put up one hell of a fight."

Eleyne nodded to me. "He needs a doctor."

"The same goes for her slave, the Indian," I said. "He saved her life."

"So did you," she said.

Sabinus entered the room, tunic spattered with blood. "I'll send for my personal physician." He nodded to the shortest of the three guardsmen and gave him directions to the doctor's home. The soldier raced downstairs.

Sabinus stepped to Eleyne. "Are you unharmed, my dear?"

"Yes, my Lord. I'm just a little shaken, that's all. What about Lady Aurelia?"

He grinned. "She is unharmed. She had the presence of mind to bar the door to the room before the assassins could enter. We arrived just as they were breaking through it."

"Thank Mother Goddess for that," Eleyne said.

"I thank all the gods," Sabinus said. "Unfortunately, my cook died trying to block their way. Alexias was wounded and left for dead, but he will live. Gods only know what they would have done to her and you."

"Don't forget Candra. He saved my life." She looked to me. "So did Marcellus."

"I won't," Sabinus said. He frowned and shook his head. "The butchers murdered half my household. They may have been slaves, but they were good people, loyal to me and my wife. Gallus will pay for his treachery."

Sabinus ordered the Praetorians to assist me downstairs and left the room.

I told them I didn't need any help and managed to go down on my own. The guards followed me into the atrium. The floor was riddled with the corpses—assassins, soldiers, Sabinus's slaves. Bloody footprints crisscrossed the area. The place reeked of body fluids and the coppery smell of blood. I sat on a couch and waited for the physician to arrive.

Eleyne fetched Candra, his tunic ripped and bloodstained, and led him behind us. He bled from both sides of his torso, lacerations to both arms. Despite the blood, the wounds appeared to be minor. Eleyne told him to sit on the floor next to my couch.

She came to my side, kneeled, and touched my shoulder. "Oh, Marcellus, you're still bleeding. I'll get clean cloths for you and Candra."

Minutes later she returned with several clean, white cloths. She called for one of the surviving slaves and gave him dressings to clean Candra's injuries. She approached and pressed a cloth to my wound and held it in place. Tears came to her eyes. "I couldn't bear it if anything had happened to you, Marcellus."

I sucked in my breath. I had no idea she felt this way about me. I had long tried to deny it, but I felt the same. All I could do was smile. I was about to say more, but Sabinus returned.

Sabinus scowled. "No physician?"

"No, sir, not yet," I answered.

"If he isn't here in the next few minutes, I'll have him flogged." Changing the subject, he said, "We're in luck. One assassin survived long enough to confess."

"What did he say?" I asked, feeling groggy, shock setting in from the wound.

"He said an Egyptian hired them."

"It has to be the same one we arrested, the one who confessed," I said.

Sabinus's nostrils flared for the length of three or four heartbeats. "It is. The thug said they were mercenaries hired by an Egyptian who bragged about working for someone high above him. No expense was to be spared in hiring the best. He and the other vermin were to kill my entire household, including you and Eleyne. That's all he knew."

I shuddered, pain from the cut piercing my side.

Sabinus exhaled. "He said they received five hundred pieces of gold in advance and would receive another five hundred once they had murdered everyone."

"Then old Gallus is behind it," I said.

Sabinus turned and glared at the physician as he arrived. "It's about time." He nodded to me and then Candra. "You are to see to the wounds of these two brave men first. If either dies, so will you."

CHAPTER 32

NOVEMBER. 44 AD

The same night, when Sabinus's home was being attacked, the Praetorian Guard arrested the fourteen senators named on the conspiracy list. Carted off to Tullianum Prison and questioned by the Supreme Rack Master, Abroghast, he forced each member to confess their part to the sordid plot. Later, they were sent home under house arrest. One had died during Abroghast's questioning.

The traitors were given a choice of standing trial and placing themselves at the mercy of the court in hopes of acquittal. Or, do the honorable thing and commit suicide, thereby leaving all properties, titles, and goods intact for loved ones. Before dawn, four had opened their veins in hot baths at their luxurious mansions. Within three days, the other nine were tried in a closed proceeding presided over by the praetor, the chief civil magistrate, and a special panel of judges appointed by the emperor. Seven were found guilty, and chose death by suicide. The judges exonerated the remaining two.

In the meantime, news of the arrests and trials became public. Fearing a riot, the entire City Guard and Watch were placed on patrol. The Praetorian Guard protected the palace, the Senate, and other public buildings. Rumors spread about demands for a return to a republican form of government, a time long passed. Many, who had spread the false tales, were arrested for treason and dispatched in the deep bowels of Tullianum Prison.

Senator Gallus was kept under house arrest while awaiting trial. Neither he nor his family were allowed to leave their residence. Sabinus told me about Gallus's outrage of being accused of treason and murder, and his anger upon learning that the information had been found in the family mausoleum.

* * *

"It has begun as I had expected it would," Sabinus said. He didn't look up from his office desk while reading the dispatch from a palace clerk. He motioned for me and Crispus to sit across from him. We waited for him to elaborate. Light from the cold mid-morning sun filtered through the opaque windows built into one side of the room. A smoky brazier sat in one corner giving off little heat. I stifled a cough as its acrid fumes penetrated my mouth and nose. Crispus snorted.

"Has Gallus started lining up votes in Senate?" I asked. Five days had passed since Gallus had been confined to his home.

Sabinus nodded. "He may be under house arrest, but servants are allowed to come and go, supposedly, for shopping purposes. Obviously, they are passing verbal messages to his cronies."

"What now, sir?" Crispus asked.

Sabinus glanced to Crispus and back to me. "I am calling in all favors from my friends in the Senate. It was easy for the special judges to try the other conspirators without the consent of the Senate, they had no influence, but Gallus is another matter."

"Definitely," I said. "He has power, influence, and wealth."

"He does, but it will be to the emperor's advantage to have him tried publicly."

I pulled my cloak tighter about my shoulders against the cold. "I wish I could believe that."

Crispus nodded in agreement.

Sabinus tossed the scroll on his desk. "Both of you should. Narcissus correctly pointed out to Claudius that such a trial would show his, 'magnificent benevolence.'"

"But the emperor has shown benevolence in the past," I said.

Sabinus leaned back in his chair. "Nevertheless, he will be seen as a just ruler who abides by the decisions of the Senate, strengthening his considerable credibility. And he also attends all their meetings taking a seat as an ordinary senator, and gives his opinion only if asked. But there is another point in his favor."

"Which is . . . ?" I asked without interrupting his lawyer's dissertation.

Crispus arched an eyebrow.

Sabinus held up a hand as if obvious. "Claudius has restored the provinces of Macedonia and Achaea in Greece to Senate control."

I turned my head to one side, puzzled by his words.

"Don't you see?" Sabinus said in a manner as if tutoring a pupil, "They owe him a debt."

"But would they dare find Gallus not guilty?" I asked.

Sabinus leaned forward again and seemed to consider the possibility. "Perhaps, incredible as it would seem. A few senators have been eliminated during the last three years since he came to power, but not enough to make them fear him as they did Tiberius and Caligula, who killed dozens. They still view him," Sabinus looked around the office and peered at the door and whispered, "as an idiot. And at times he is, but other times he borders on the brilliant."

Crispus looked at me and then Sabinus. "He is taking a great risk, sir."

Sabinus sighed. "That is why I'm taking action that may compromise my values, but safeguard the empire. It will insure that the Senate brings in the *correct* verdict."

"Must it always be that way?" I asked. "Political intrigue and backbiting even when the life of the emperor is at stake."

"Especially when the life of the emperor is at stake," Sabinus said in a rueful voice. He leaned forward. "This is not the army. Roman noblemen are past-masters of palace intrigue. Army plotting by comparison pales to the wolves of the Senate. Generals don't have the patience to bide their time like the Senate. They are more open and more inclined to use force of arms, as did the Praetorians when they killed Caligula and raised Claudius to the purple."

A chill ran up my back. My body shuddered. "Then what are we going to do?"

"Counteract with persuasion, whenever I can. The Senate is not completely corrupt—yet. If I have to do a favor here and there, I will. It is part of the political game." He straightened his back. "However, I hope my prosecution speech at the trial will be enough to command the votes needed for conviction. We will present the documents, which I have safely hidden, and the confessions of the convicted. It is all very damning evidence—as Gallus well knows."

* * *

The intrigues continued. We received rumors that the consul, Titus Statilius Taurus, a pinched-face nobleman, who would be the presiding judge at Gallus's trial, was presented with a young slave girl noted for her sexual dexterity by one of Gallus's supporters. We had heard other senators had also received presents of not only money, but young slave girls and boys. No wonder Sabinus had to resort to doing favors for his colleagues.

If this weren't enough, we noticed with concern during our daily visits to Claudius's chambers that he had reverted to his usual lackluster personality and absentmindedness. He started keeping company with a young almond-colored Parthian slave girl while holding morning audience. Sabinus was informed by Posides, the court-chamberlain, that Claudius was occupied with her a great part of the time. Apparently, his wife, Messalina, known as *the whore of Rome* because her amorous exploits, didn't seem too concerned. Rumors said she had slept with half of the Senate. I prayed that she was doing so on the emperor's behalf.

CHAPTER 33

EARLY DECEMBER, 44 AD

Within a week after the trial of the surviving nine senators, and two weeks after the assault on Sabinus's home, the day for Gallus's trial had arrived. The emperor, at the suggestion of Sabinus and Vitellius, dared not wait any longer. The Senate and the people grew restless. A few minor riots had erupted and ruthlessly smashed by the Praetorians.

Consisting of more than six hundred, most members of the Senate came from Rome's greatest families. Recently, Emperor Claudius had admitted Gallic and Spanish noblemen to that esteemed group. As a lifetime position, membership was passed from one generation to the next. The so-called noble fathers ranged from the minimum age of entry, thirty, to doddering old fools, in their seventies and eighties, too senile to understand what was happening around them.

Senators, who currently or in the past had held the elected or appointed high offices of consul, ceremonial head of state, praetor, chief civil magistrate, and legate–army general, sat on the lower two levels of benches. The rest who held power to lesser varying degrees took up the remaining upper levels.

In the chilly, early morning darkness, Sabinus and his entourage arrived at the senate building, the Curia. Winter came early, and soon the city would be white with its first snow. Flurries swirled around us, melting with the touch of earth. We pushed our way through the large crowd, who shivered in their cloaks and mantles, as they gathered around the outside of the building. There had been no official announcement of the early December trial date, but that had not prevented rumors from spreading like a tenement fire throughout the city.

A trial of such magnitude with the emperor presiding would turn out the entire Senate. No bailiffs or consul's tipstaffs had been necessary to round up the needed quorum of fifty for the court case.

Located at the north end of the Forum, the Curia sat next to the smaller less important Forum of Julius Caesar. The tall, imposing building had been rebuilt after a fire, four years before the assassination of Julius Caesar, more than one hundred years earlier.

Sabinus, including Crispus and I, and his chief steward, Alexias, climbed the high marble porch in front of the Senate. Alexias carried the urn that Crispus and I had taken from the Gallus family tomb, still holding the incriminating documents, concealed in a heavy cloth inside his cloak.

Bracing ourselves against the piercing wind, we continued trudging up the steps, togas and tunics whipping sharply about our bodies. The biting cold taunted the battle scar on my cheek until I could feel its welt standing boldly in protest. We passed between delicately chiseled, perforated pillars, through tall, bronze doors into the great hearing room. A galaxy of statues encircled and bordered the dimly lit interior. Inside, tightly packed tiers of comfortable and beautifully carved benches climbed up and aligned in a curving semicircle where the senators sat in a sea of white togas and woolen cloaks, directly in front of the dais.

The Praetorian Guard stood shield to shield along the Sacred Way, through the Forum and up to the Curia, surrounding the outside and inside of its chambers, in full battle dress armed with javelins at the ready. Their menacing presence sent a message that any riot would be crushed.

At the entrance the consul's lictors, minor magistrates checked for our names on the list of those allowed access. Then we were searched by the Praetorians for weapons. All others, including the mob, stayed outside. Wind permitting, the people could listen to the trial proceedings. Since the Curia's numerous doors had been flung open, the echoing sounds from within carried a long distance. Those of us inside suffered almost as much from the cold as those outside.

Several more braziers had been placed about the cold chambers, and along with many lanterns gave the dark and shadowy hall a gray-yellow smoking pattern of illumination.

In spite of the piercing cold, thousands more swelled the Forum, packed to overflowing. Late arrivals, who entered the Curia, murmured of fighting their way through massive crowds. However, the shield- and javelin-bearing Praetorians kept the rabble at bay. Two-thousand combat-ready City Guardsmen and Watchmen stood in reserve close by, should a riot erupt. Since many of the populace were expected to be at the Forum, a cohort of one thousand Bucketmen patrolled the market places and residential areas of the city. Events like a major trial or holiday afforded thieves a great opportunity to commit burglary while their occupants were away.

All the senators had arrived, including many known to be ill. By deference to rank and seniority, the first row went to ex-consuls and praetors. They huddled together in an apparent attempt to warm themselves from the icy breeze that penetrated the building.

Last to enter was a haggard-faced Gallus. The Praetorians escorted him and his family to benches opposite Sabinus. Attended by several friends and distinguished senators, he wore a gray mourning toga symbolizing his distress. His weeping wife's deeply wrinkled face matched her mourning clothes. Other relatives, similarly attired, followed her wailing lead. Gallus glared at Sabinus with cruel little eyes, which seemed to say that he would have his revenge.

His advocate, the lawyer Ulpius, wore a shiny, solid-white toga, a sign of the wealth he had accumulated in defending the rich. On his plump fingers large, jeweled, gold rings, befitting a successful lawyer, encased his puffy fingers.

As the old senator entered the chamber, a number of ex-praetors and consuls shifted to the other side of the hall in a show of contempt. That didn't go unnoticed by Gallus, as he whispered something in his lawyer's ear.

On the center of the dais stood an impressive gilded statue of Victory stretching her wings. The beautiful face looked blankly down upon us from the top of a globe. Her flowing and revealing robes caressed her breasts as a delicate, outstretched hand held forth a laurel crown. A small, ornamented altar containing smoking coals stood near the image.

The murmuring within the walls came to a halt. Everyone rose as the court chamberlain announced the arrival of the emperor and magistrates.

Two cornu trumpet players chimed a ceremonial entrance hymn while Claudius strode in behind an army of minor magistrates. The haughty lictors, dressed in flowing, white togas, swaggered forth carrying the *Fasces,* double-bitted axes encased in a mat of five hardwood sticks, the symbol of justice and religion. The presiding consul, Titus Statilius Taurus, who wore the white and purple toga praetexa of his office, followed behind. The praetor and several other judges trailed the consul and proceeded to the backless cushioned chairs where they turned and faced the Senate.

A cheer rang out through the Senate, "*Ave Caesar!* Hail Caesar!"

The emperor stopped at a brazier. From a pouch handed to him by the augur-priest, he took a pinch of incense and sprinkled it on the burner as custom dictated. The augur signaled two acolytes to bring forth a small wooden cage holding two of the sacred chickens. Opening the cage, an acolyte fed them grain, which they ravenously ate. As grains dropped from the side of their beaks, the augur studied the birds. He turned to the dais. "I see no evil sight, nor do I hear any evil sound."

A sigh of relief raced through the Senate as servants quickly swept up spilled grain and scooped up the squawking fowl. Stuffed into the cage, they were carted away. The augur ordered the acolytes to place the allotted hour glasses on the tables of the prosecution and defense. As prescribed by law, the accusers were allowed six and defendant nine. However, as much as the emperor liked to conduct court, he was known for his impatience. No one expected Gallus's trial to last more than one day.

The augur took his place beside the magistrates.

Claudius shook out his voluminous, finely woven toga and announced the ritual words, "Affairs divine have been attended to, affairs human now can begin." He nodded to Sabinus. "Let the accusers of Senator Anicius Pedius Gallus the Elder stand forth." Claudius sat down.

I glanced toward one of the opened doors. Word had already spread of what was happening to the masses outside. The level of an already noisy mob increased.

Alexias, Crispus, and I sat behind Sabinus. He stood and bowed to the emperor and the other magistrates. Sabinus turned and addressed the Senate who appeared to be waiting in silent anticipation. Sabinus took two deliberate steps past the prosecutor's bench, upon which lay his documents, and stopped. He turned and pointed his right hand at Gallus, exclaiming in a deep but resonant voice, "You stand accused," he paused, "before this illustrious tribunal and peers of the Senate." He gestured to the crowded benches and bellowed, "High crimes against these great and noble fathers whom you would have so willfully murdered. Infamous crimes of high treason, conspiracy to murder our beloved Emperor Claudius, and twenty of his greatest and most honored senators—your peers. And conspiracy to commit murder against Princess Eleyne, daughter of our ally, the British King Verica—an honored guest of the emperor—and murder of her lady-in-waiting the metic woman, Karmune. And conspiracy to commit burglary and other heinous felonies against the people and the gods of the state.

"If that were not enough, he sent twenty assassins to murder my wife and myself. Fortunately, they were stopped by my brave retainers," He nodded to Crispus and I, "and loyal members of the Praetorian Guard who were escorting me back to my home on orders by the emperor."

Gasps and shouts of "No," erupted among members of the Senate.

"Yes, it is true. The surviving assassin confessed before he was put to death."

Sabinus turned his back and walked to the prosecutor's table and scooped up a small bundle of papers in his left hand. Sabinus proceeded to where the senators sat and scanned their attentive faces, ignoring Gallus's trailing glare. He lifted the documents and tapped them neatly with his right hand. "We have before us the confessions of fourteen senators—Gallus's fellow conspirators." He read their names slowly, and those of the thieves, and the Egyptian, and the charges.

"If that evidence is not enough," Sabinus continued, "I have the written documents found in Gallus's family tomb." He turned to Alexias and nodded.

Alexias stepped to the table and pulled from beneath his cloak the plain urn that Crispus and I had discovered. Sabinus removed the lid and took out the parchments containing the damning information as Alexias returned to his seat.

A shocked murmur and a rippling gasp erupted from the senators, Gallus's sympathizers. Some cried, "Sacrilege! Sacrilege!"

Sabinus cut the cronies off. "SACRILEGE? There is no SACRILEGE concerning conspiracies to MURDER the emperor!" He turned his head slowly meeting the eyes of those who'd cried out, silencing them as if daring each to contradict him.

Continuing, he waved the documents towards Gallus. "These are in his handwriting . . . stamped with his seal, as discovered by Centurion Reburrus and Sergeant Crispus, loyal soldiers of the army."

I felt heat rushing to my face as I glanced about wondering what these men thought of Crispus and I. Didn't we do the right thing?

My patron glared at Gallus. "It is because of your lengthy and distinguished ancestry, and your past services to Rome, that you have been offered the privilege of an open and public trial by your peers. Under the laws governing treason and conspiracy to murder the emperor, you could have suffered an ignominious death."

Gallus gnashed his teeth and scowled. By custom, neither he nor his advocate were allowed to make objections during the prosecution's presentation.

Sabinus took a deep breath. "The charges against you are very grave, and the evidence that I submit to this esteemed body," he bowed slightly to the senators, "and the esteemed tribunal," bowing a little deeper to Claudius and the magistrates, "will show beyond a reasonable doubt that you are guilty . . . guilty of crimes that could have shaken the Roman Empire to its very foundations, and laid waste the gains made by our emperor. Not even mighty Jupiter and all the gods in heaven could have stopped the consequences had you succeeded."

Returning to his table, the sounds of murmuring trailed in Sabinus's wake, as he gently dropped the parchments. He turned to Gallus. "It is by the emperor's divine justice that you are afforded this open and impartial public trial . . . which by reading of these documents you do not deserve. We know that this plot was not planned in haste, but you . . . !" He shot an accusing finger towards the old man, "Yes, you, began conspiring three years ago—as soon as our August Caesar was proclaimed emperor by the Praetorian Guard and confirmed by the Senate! You wasted no time in showing contempt for the government of Rome and its duly acclaimed ruler—confirmed by the Senate."

Grandly sweeping his hand palm up, Sabinus gestured to the white- and purple-trimmed, toga-clad audience. I thought to myself, as he said those words, how the Senate was intimidated by the Praetorians into proclaiming Claudius emperor. Yet, he had to play on the Senate's vanity, the hypocrisy of it all.

"We know that this felonious scheming reached beyond the Senate," he said as his voice echoed through the Curia and outside into the cold morning air. "For the assassination of Caesar's sacred person could not have taken place without help from inside the palace—by those charged with his safety. At this moment, as I am addressing this illustrious body, six junior officers, centurions and cohort commanders of the Praetorian Guard, are being arrested by Praetorian Prefect Rufrius Crispinus for their parts in this plot."

A gasp and stirring went through the Senate. Looks of surprise crossed their faces and several of the Praetorians stationed around the Curia nervously glanced at one another.

Crispus and I looked about and to each other and shrugged. Neither of us had been privy to this information.

"The discovery of the conspiracy came none too soon, for the date of the emperor's murder was to take place on the first day of the holiday, Saturnalia, in December. We know how everything, including security, becomes lax during those festivities.

"The plot was to be executed by the cohort commander on duty with the guard. As you know, it is customary to exchange one's place with a servant or slave during Saturnalia—this was the idea of the commander. He would dress as a slave in a tunic and while serving dinner, slay the emperor with a hidden dagger. You, Gallus," he shot a forefinger at him, "paid a hefty sum to commit that piece of treachery, one million sesterces, more than enough to qualify a villain for the illustrious position of senator!"

Nearly every senator raised eyebrows, exchanged glances, and shook their heads.

"Was that the commander's price?" Sabinus questioned. "The prostitution of his position for this broad sacred purple trim on a toga?" he pointed to his garb.

My patron moved in a small circle and an arm extended at shoulder level pointed a finger at the silent senators. "I see a great number of togas in our midst, each trimmed in widths of Imperial purple, by the grace of the one raised to the purple itself, Emperor Claudius. A valued purple band granted to us in recognition of having been found worthy to the Senate of Rome, and the greatest empire in the world."

Many eyes were drawn to the purple trim on their own garments.

"A purple band," he continued, "as trim upon—not a black toga, nor a brown toga, but trim upon a pure, near-divine, white toga."

He raised his voice and raged directly in front of Gallus. "And you would dare permit such a murdering beast to defile these pure-symbols we wear? DARE you permit, no, pay that imposter to come within our midst with the blood of our beloved emperor stained upon his hands and robes?"

Gallus appeared to be stunned silent, as was the Senate at large.

"This . . . ," Sabinus wavered as if near fainting, then recovered, " . . . sickens me," he said in a voice clearly audible within the chambers. "To grant a title, which he rightfully did not earn in an honorable fashion? Is . . . barbaric." He turned to the senators. "Are those the kinds of men we want to inherit Rome? To inherit our morals and institutions? Inherit the peace we enjoy because of our gracious emperor? NO! I say they should not."

Another cry sounded through the hall from supporters of Sabinus, "No! No! Death to the traitor! Death to the traitor!"

The praetor raised his hand, and silence returned to the chamber. Sabinus used the distraction to rub his hands together for warmth. A cold wind soughed briefly through the chambers, the breath of snow heavy in its wake.

Dropping his hands to the side of his toga, Sabinus scanned the faces of his fellow senators. "The emperor's sacred life is worth more than all the gold in the empire, the world. What was to be the outcome had the emperor died?" He paused, turned, and pointed a finger at Gallus. "You promised to restore the Republic. The Republic is dead and it can never be restored."

Gallus shook his head and muttered, "Preposterous."

Sabinus ignored the remark and eyed certain senators known to still harbor republican sentiments. "The Republic was brought down by the greed, corruption, and indecisiveness of the Senate. Rome suffered from decades of civil war as its members played off one general against another. Great men, like the noble Julius Caesar, who sought to restore order and dignity to the Senate, were assassinated by a few treacherous members of this great body, thus prolonging the destruction."

I caught myself nodding in agreement.

"It took the leadership of the divine Augustus, great uncle of our beloved emperor, to finally restore order and stability and bring back sensible government," Sabinus said. "The Senate insisted on giving him more and more authority. And why? They knew that by themselves they could no longer govern the empire. But, through the guidance of the emperor, the Senate ably performs a great many duties that would otherwise be burdensome to the emperor. Need I remind you that he has made very important concessions to you. Among them he has returned the provinces of Achaea and Macedonia to your control. They had been under Imperial rule since the time of Augustus."

Sabinus stopped to drink a cup of water on the prosecutor's table. Placing the cup back on the table, he turned in Gallus's direction and back to the senators. "But Gallus would destroy all of that with an unworkable institution. He would lead the empire back down a dark path of anarchy and destruction—may the gods forbid! And for what purpose? To serve the people? No, not hardly. He serves no one's needs but his own. It was to his own glory and bloated vanity that he would destroy Rome. Only he would have benefitted from the emperor's death."

He hesitated and then shot a finger to the fidgeting audience and cried, "And yours!"

"No! No! Liar! Liar!" shouted Gallus's supporters.

"Am I?" Sabinus questioned. "Gallus would have directly benefitted from his death. He would have become city prefect. He never forgave the emperor for not appointing him that position, one of great responsibility. Not only is the city prefect responsible for public safety, but controls the prices of all goods and commodities coming into Rome. Gallus would have extracted personal payments on all goods coming in under the threat of revoking business licenses and state monopolies of those merchants who refused to comply. Is that what you want? Then he would have subjected them to the abuse of the City Guard and attacks by criminal elements in his pay."

Sabinus paced back and forth along the marble floor for the length of about thirty heartbeats. He halted, faced Gallus, and back to the senators. They waited for him to speak.

"Again, personal greed, not patriotism, was the motive for his treachery," he said. "Therefore, I say to you noble fathers, there can only be one verdict—*guilty*, and to you, great Caesar," Sabinus bowed slightly to Claudius, "only one sentence that you can pronounce—death! We are a government and a people whose heritage is based on traditions and the law. Without our great legacy, which calls for respect of the gods, our families, leaders, and the law, Rome cannot exist and would not have endured for these many generations. Therefore, I call upon you great fathers to reflect carefully upon the words I have spoken, and search your souls before making your decisions."

Sabinus dropped into his chair apparently exhausted and stared at the tiled floor.

In unison, the Senate stood and applauded and cheered Sabinus. "Bravo! Bravo! *Euge!*—well done! *Sophos!*—wisely said!"

Claudius shakily arose and joined the clapping, slobbering as he did. Even those known to favor Gallus politely applauded.

The trial was not over, yet.

CHAPTER 34

There was a brief recess for lunch as the sixth hour, noon, had arrived. No one left the hall, as each official brought his own meal prepared by slave attendants.

Although still overcast and cold, the snow flurries had stopped. Many well-wishers congratulated Sabinus. Vitellius gestured with a flabby hand. "My friend, you must rewrite your speech for posterity. All the famous orators have done as much. After all, Cicero rewrote his famous *Murder Trials*, adding what he wished he had said, and the better rumors attributed to him."

Sabinus shrugged and shook his head. "I don't care if my words survive. What I said stands on its own merit. If not, so be it."

"Don't be so modest, Sabinus. Really, it was wonderful, but any speech can be improved," the fat senator insisted.

Sabinus smiled. "I appreciate the thought, my friend, but it will have to suffice. I know I am a windbag, and my enemies will be sure that aspect of my personality is duly recorded."

I smirked. Sabinus was as honest as one could be and still survive the Imperial court.

* * *

Now was the defense's turn to rebut the accusations brought by Sabinus. Gallus's advocate, the bloated Gaius Ulpius, stood to defend the accused. He was about to speak when the glowering, scarlet-faced Gallus smashed his fist on the marble table and immediately stood. His wife, a white-haired woman cried, "No don't . . ."

An irate Ulpius turned to Gallus. "What are you doing? Don't be a fool. You are playing into his hands."

"No, Ulpius," Gallus snarled. "The indignations that man has heaped upon me are more than I can bear. I won't tolerate it any longer."

Ulpius tugged at Gallus's shoulder sleeve. "Don't you see? That is what he wants. Now if you allow me to do my job, defending you, acquittal will be ours."

Gallus yanked away from Ulpius, who gave up in disgust.

Sabinus looked his way, eyebrows arched, and back toward the magistrates.

The old senator stood. After the usual bowing, Gallus addressed the Senate. "The charges of which I have been maliciously accused are based on forgeries planted in the tomb of my forefathers—an abominable sacrilege. Trumped up confessions of fellow patricians and colleagues." His eyes narrowing into crooked slits as he glanced in the direction of Sabinus.

"I have served Rome long and faithfully, both in the Senate and the army. As a young officer I served General Tiberius, who later became emperor, on the German expedition to punish the renegade Arminius. This was after he had ambushed and destroyed the three legions of Verus in the Tutaborg Forest. Is that not loyal service to Rome?"

His voice grew conciliatory. "Like you . . . fellow senators, I am from a very old and distinguished family that dates back nearly to the founding of Rome. My family has served Rome faithfully and loyally and has given the state many praetors and consuls." His voice shook. "Never, I repeat . . . never . . . could I commit evil against our beloved nation, and I never shall. These charges are vicious and utterly false." He glared at Sabinus. "The idea of betraying Rome, and may the gods forbid, assassinating the emperor is unthinkable—absurd.

"Why is Sabinus accusing me of these unthinkable acts, I ask? I will tell you why," his voice rising. "ENVY! That is what it is. Lust for power! It is he who is determined to become city prefect, not I! Next to the emperor, he yearns to be the most powerful man in Rome. But that is not enough. No. He wants more, but he knows he will never obtain it. Why? Because he is not from a noble and distinguished patrician family like yours and mine, fellow colleagues," he rasped. "He is the son of a publican, a tax collector."

He spat and turned toward Sabinus with a look of contempt upon his sinister face. "His father bought his way into the Senate by extorting the poor, by bleeding hard-working farmers and prosperous merchants dry. That is how his father made his fortune. This is how his family gained access to this august body. I say it was a mistake, and you bear witness to the result—a man who condones the robbing of graves, especially in the middle of the night.

"I still can't believe the sacrilege, yet there before our beloved emperor sits proof—the desecrated urn of my father's faithful servant; I cannot say his name as it pains me so. He is arbitrarily accusing innocent men like our colleagues and I of the most trumped-up, despicable crimes. By putting us to death, he replaces us with his own kind, tax collectors, merchants, grave robbers, and foreigners." He spat again. "Do you know that he would allow Gauls in the Senate and Spaniards to the Equestrian Order?"

"No! No!" shouts rang out in the hall. He failed to mention that admitting Gauls and Spaniards was Claudius's idea.

Gallus nodded to his supporters. He then renewed his attack glaring at Crispus and I. He stabbed a finger at us and screamed. "These are the officers, Sabinus's officers, who should be put to the rack! It was these barbaric Spaniards that broke into my family vault and planted those scurrilous documents."

My muscles tightened and my heart seemed to run into my throat. Again, heat rushed to my face. I turned to Crispus, his mouth tightened into a pair of thin lips.

"Are these the kind of men we are to admit to the Knighthood?" Gallus continued his rant. "Foreign barbarians that have no respect for honor, or the dead?"

"No! No!" Gallus's sympathizers shouted.

Gallus turned and pointed to Sabinus. "Yet those are the kind that he would have serve in this great house. Their presence within this sacred chamber is an affront to Rome, and a stench to my senses."

It was all I could do to control my rising anger.

Gallus lowered his hand. "My accuser has made much of the color and purity of the white togas of the Senate. As you can plainly see, I wear a gray toga of mourning, for I can assure you that it is a sad day indeed to stand accused, falsely, by the son of a corrupt and greedy tax collector. A man who's toga of white, bought with the blood money of honest men, defiles us all, and in truth should be colored black for the shame he brings upon this house of Rome. Black stands for the true color of his heart."

Sabinus sat stoically keeping a sober face. I admired him for keeping so calm.

Gallus exhaled. "Again, I appeal to your conscience when you consider the charges against me: confessions made under duress. Forged documents. Accusations and confessions by foreign barbarians, and metics against the word of a patrician, a pure Roman—unthinkable."

Gallus continued his diatribe for another three hours. I had learned long ago that unlike military tribunals, relevant evidence had no meaning in a civilian court, especially when dealing with a senator or other high official. One's ancestry, status, and pocketbook was all that mattered. He flaunted all of them before the Senate.

Gallus concluded his defense in a rasping voice. "Remember, what has happened during the past few weeks can happen to you, to anyone of this venerable group. You, too, can suffer public humiliation as I have, and private ones too painful, too shameful to voice. You, too, can feel the breath of lies of such infamous charges that opening your veins seems the only way to save your precious family and all that is cherished by you."

He paused, covering his eyes for the space of ten heartbeats. "You may ask why I have not followed those innocents before me who chose death rather than risk all in trial, knowing I could bring down my great house?"

The chamber remained silent, awaiting his answer. He shuffled his sandals pacing before the defense table. "Well, I will tell you . . . it's too simple, really, and the words seem so trite. I love my dear family more than anything and risk everything that you should know these simple words in your heart . . . *I, am innocent*."

I looked in Sabinus's direction, his face remained sober.

"Consider this when you make your decision," Gallus continued, "and you will know the truth of my innocence. If you choose otherwise, not only will it be a disservice to

Rome, but it will set a dangerous precedent that in the will have grave consequences on this great and noble body."

Gallus glared at Sabinus as if gloating before taking his seat next to Ulpius, who nodded as if approving his defense.

The Senate stood and clapped loud and long. It was hard to tell whom they believed the most, or who had been paid off the most. Many of the same shouted their congratulations to Gallus as they had Sabinus.

Claudius raised his hand for silence, then addressed Gallus. "Senator Gallus, you have made an issue on the matter of foreigners and their admission to the Senate. We do not see its relevance to the case."

Gallus stood, slightly bowed. "It is most relevant, Caesar. What Roman, what Italian, in his right mind, would dare to act against your eminent person? But a provincial, that is different. They are neither bound by tradition nor loyalty."

"Have you forgotten that we were born in Gaul, in Lugdunum?"

"No, great Caesar, but that is different. You were born of Roman parents. Your father was Drusus, brother of the Emperor Tiberius, and a great hero."

The emperor's nose flared, his eyes growing cold. "Nonetheless, by your definition we are still alien, as we're not born on Italian soil. Need we remind you that many provincials are loyal Roman citizens. They constitute fully one half of the army, and that doesn't include our loyal auxiliaries. Your accusations are not substantiated by evidence. It was a loyal Roman citizen," the emperor paused and looked in my direction, "a Spaniard, that discovered the conspiracy against our life. We are grateful to him and any others who would save our life."

Gallus's gray-shadowed face flushed, his jaws clenched. He glared at Claudius and blurted, "You are a stupid old idiot!"

As gasps arose from the audience, he reached for a wax writing tablet on the table, stood, and hurled it at the aging ruler, striking his left cheek. It glanced away and struck a bowl of apples on the small table next to Claudius's chair, scattering them on the floor.

"Down with the traitor! Down with the traitor!" echoed through the chamber from friend and foe alike. The clanging of armor added to the din as sword-drawn Praetorians rushed towards Gallus. But the stunned Claudius quickly recovered his wits. "Leave him be!" he commanded. The troops halted and stepped back to their positions.

A physician who had rushed to the emperor's side, assisted by a number of slaves and a concerned Pallas, placed a moist towel to the lacerated wound and gently attempted to wipe the oozing blood from his face. Claudius squirmed so that the doctor succeed in little more than smearing his face with blood.

Because Claudius's health was frail at best, a doctor was never far away. The shaken ruler ordered the attendants away, growling that he was all right. Gallus had signed his own death warrant. There could be no other verdict by the Senate. I couldn't believe anyone would have the nerve to assault the world's most powerful ruler, in the presence of so many, and survive.

A furious Ulpius yanked Gallus to his chair by the shoulder and chastised him, the words lost in the Senate's uproar. His wife became hysterical and attending relatives attempted to calm her. The advocate jumped to his feet and begged the mercy of the emperor, who raised his hand in silence. Ulpius attempted to minimize Gallus's outrage by pleading his client had been under a great deal of strain and asked for his divine clemency. He explained Gallus hadn't known what he was doing.

Gallus was about to say something further, when his corpulent lawyer loudly ordered him to shut up, spouting that he had caused enough damage without making it worse. Gallus replied that he could forget about receiving the Galatian slave boy promised as payment. Several within earshot laughed. Ulpius threw up his hands in disgust and sat. He gathered his wax tablets and pretended to study them.

Then something puzzling occurred. Claudius looked about as if in a daze. His bloodshot eyes seemed to have lost all signs of intelligence. He turned to the consul, Titus Statilius Taurus and inquired, "Grapes? Has anyone seen my grapes?"

The beady-eyed consul stared at him in dismay and seemed to be at a loss for words. But the quick-witted Pallas, who stood near the physician, stepped to the emperor's side. "You ate them, Caesar, remember?"

Claudius cupped his slobbering mouth with a shaky hand. "I did?" He lowered his hand and looked down to the spilled basket of fruit and glanced about again. He turned back to Pallas. "Oh, but of course, how could I have forgotten. Nevertheless, I want my grapes. Be a good fellow and bring me more."

"Of course, Great Caesar." The freedman turned to the court chamberlain and snapped his fingers. The chamberlain in turn sent a slave scurrying for the grapes. All the while a low murmur pervaded the Senate.

"Now, where were we?" Claudius asked. "Oh, yes." He slowly got to his feet. His injured head twitched, and he seemed to have difficulty bringing it under control. In a slow but steady voice, he spoke the ceremonial words of instruction to the Senate as if nothing unusual had occurred. "We do now take the opinions of the Conscript Fathers, concerning that which it befits should be done in the case of Senator Anicius Pedius Gallus, this day arraigned and tried. You have heard his accusers and his defense. I shall call the album of the Senate."

The consul, Taurus, stood and received a list of tablets from a lictor, listing the senators in order of official rank and precedence. He turned to the emperor and under the rule of *right to speak first* asked if there was any he would like to say. Claudius declined.

Taurus then addressed the Senate after giving Gallus a disdainful look with his little dark eyes. In a solemn but gritty voice said, "Venerable Fathers, we hold true that Senator Anicius Pedius Gallus is a man of great patrician birth; the more the disgrace, if he has dishonored the name of *Clarissimus*, Most Illustrious Citizen, of the Senate. It is true that his intended victims were the emperor and men of the Senate, your brethren, and freedmen serving the noble Caesar. But the law is impartial, the Roman Empire was consecrate upon the inflexible rule of 'piety,' giving alike to the gods and men that which is lawfully their due. If he has plotted to take the emperor's life, then the case is clear. The emperor can be compared to the master of a ship. Its crew is like the people, and together they run the ship, which is the State. An emperor killed by the people is the same as mutineers murdering the ship's captain. Without the guidance of either, both flounder and sink. If Gallus has planned the same for your colleagues, then does not that, like the crimes against the emperor, demand lawful vengeance at our own hands? Were not his fellow conspirators found guilty, and have they not paid the penalty?"

Silence

"Therefore," Taurus continued, "it is my opinion that the defendant is guilty of all crimes with which he is charged. And since Titus Flavius Sabinus has plead the cause of the state with diligence and fearlessness, let him receive thanks from the Senate. This is my opinion."

There was strong applause, but also shouts of "hangman" and "butcher" from the, until now, sedate relatives of Gallus. Their tongues seemed as loose as those already condemned.

One by one, the magistrates, ex-consuls, and praetors were summoned and in turn gave their opinions. They unanimously concurred with the consul. It was growing late and the outside gray light faded into darkness, leaving the chamber cast in a dimly smoking-lamp light and state of tension. A cry came from the assembly chambers as hundreds had yet to vote. "Divide! Divide!"

Claudius gestured to the magistrates. "Conscript Fathers, you have heard the opinions of these noble men. There are two propositions before you. Those who favor the verdict of guilty for Senator Anicius Pedius Gallus as proposed by the Consul, let them move to the right! Those who believe that he is innocent, move to the left."

The more than six hundred rose as one solid toga. After a moment of hesitation, when many waited to see who and how many would move left or right, about thirty moved quickly to the left. This included a few Sabinus counted upon for a guilty verdict. Sabinus turned in my direction, and I saw the disappointment in his eyes. But the tide turned. First, it was a trickle and then like a flood they flocked to the right, overwhelmingly unanimous, guilty as charged.

Apparently, anticipating the worst, Gallus and his family had quietly slipped away as was the custom in a trial of that magnitude and returned home. Upon order of the consul, the senators returned to their seats. "Senator Gallus," the consul bellowed, "is hereby allowed twenty-four hours to arrange his affairs. If he has not at the end of that period, the Senate will reconvene the following morning, and Caesar will pass sentence."

It was common knowledge what that meant. Gallus would be allowed the honorable choice of committing suicide and thereby keeping the family's titles and properties from confiscation. It also meant the younger Gallus, my former commanding officer, would not lose his position of command or rank in the army. If the elder Gallus procrastinated, he would surely be sentenced to death by strangling or beheading. He could also be exiled. But a sentence of exile could be dangerous, as he might plan another coup, death was the only alternative. Either way, his family would lose all.

I went to bed that night believing it was all over.

CHAPTER 35

Early the next morning I was rousted from bed. Someone tugged my shoulder vigorously.

I turned over in the snug goose-down bed.

"Sir, wake up!" he persisted. It was Alexias. He had recovered quickly; his wounds by the assassins had not been serious. "The emperor has pardoned Senator Gallus!"

"What?" I answered groggily. "Is this some sort of bad dream?"

The firm hand on my shoulder said otherwise. "No, sir, Gallus is free."

His words pierced my clouded brain, as I struggled to believe my ears. Opening my eyes, I looked into those of Sabinus's Greek freedman. He usually left waking me up to one of his underlings.

I pulled back the blanket and got out of bed. "There must be some mistake." I quickly dressed.

"No mistake, sir. A messenger came from the palace early this morning."

"What was your master's reaction?" I asked as I finished buckling a dagger to my belt.

"He hasn't said a word, but seemed disturbed."

I snorted. "That's an understatement. Old Gallus must be laughing."

"Perhaps."

A young slave stuck his head through the doorway and informed Alexias a messenger from the palace was at the door.

"Don't stand there like a fool," he snapped, "let him in." The slave made a quick retreat, and Alexias excused himself, mumbling something about the inefficient help they were getting these days. "Don't they realize the master will eventually free them?" he added.

As I staggered to the kitchen for breakfast, I found Sabinus questioning a Praetorian Guard centurion in the atrium. "Are you positive?" the senator asked.

"Yes, sir."

"Very well, you may leave."

Sabinus motioned to me. Dark circles surrounded the bloodshot eyes in his unshaven face. "This has been a strange—" he remarked in a musing tone. "No, perhaps an ironic morning is more like it."

"Sir?"

"I should be pleased, but I feel nothing, absolutely nothing."

Pleased? At a pardon?

"After a sleepless night, I was awakened to the news the emperor had pardoned Senator Gallus. Given Claudius's erratic behavior, I wasn't too surprised," he said in a sardonic voice. "I wonder what old Gallus will scheme next."

He hesitated. "And now, I receive this." Sabinus held up a piece of perfumed parchment, with the emperor's seal. "The gods tricked them both," he said. "Gallus the Elder took his own life before the proclamation of pardon reached his home."

"No one deserved it more than he," I said, relieved the old man had died after all. "How did he do it?"

Sabinus snorted, "Gallus knew all was lost. He proceeded to his bath and undressed. Afterwards, he stepped into a hot tub of water, opened his wrists, and died."

By committing suicide, an honorable death, Gallus saved his estates and titles from being confiscated by the state and his family from disgrace. That also meant the younger Gallus would one day return to Rome and claim his father's seat in the Senate.

"Nonetheless, I am sad," Sabinus said. "Not for Gallus, but for the Senate. With every conspiracy, they lose more power to the emperor. Soon, they will be no more effective than the people's tribune in court. Gods pray I won't be of this world when it happens."

He closed his eyes, shook his head, and exhaled heavily, and for a few seconds seemed lost in thought. "Have you seen her this morning?" he whispered softly.

"Her?" I asked, taken aback by the sudden change in conversation.

"Rome is so beautiful and innocent cloaked in a light dusting of snow," he replied as if thinking aloud. After all the turmoil, he still considered her beautiful. I realized then how much he loved the only mistress he would ever know.

He opened his eyes and asked quietly, "Have you eaten breakfast?"

"No, sir, not yet."

"Once you have, come and join me for a stiff drink of Syrian whiskey. I can't face my clients or the emperor this morning without something to numb my senses."

"If you don't mind, I'll join you now."

He clasped my shoulders and smiled for the first time in days. "Fair enough."

Again, Rome had triumphed in her moment of peril, drama greater than any seen in any amphitheater. But there were other traitors and murders and would-be emperors awaiting their hour of glory and death. Only later did I learn that the elder Gallus had planned his revenge from the grave.

More To Follow

CPSIA information can be obtained
at www.ICGtesting.com
Printed in the USA
FSOW03n0722150318
45745FS

9 781620 067192